Coil of Boughs

By Penny Moss
penny-moss.com

Copyright © Penny Moss 2024
Published 2024 by Penny Moss

All rights reserved. No part of this publication may be reproduced, stored in a retrieval system, or transmitted, in any form or by any means (electronic, mechanical, photocopying, recording or otherwise) without prior written permission from the author.

Cover Art by: Penny Moss

Print ISBN: 9798324873530
First Edition

This is a work of fiction. Names, characters, businesses, places, events and incidents are either the products of the author's imagination or used in a fictitious manner. Any resemblance to actual persons, living or dead, or actual events is purely coincidental.

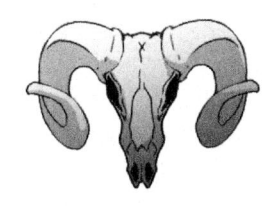

THE UNDERFOREST DUOLOGY

COIL OF BOUGHS
THORNS OF VALE

Warnings/Triggers

Descriptive violence, body horror, descriptive gore, attempted (and failed, not between couple) SA, strong sexual content, excessive swearing, death.

Ryurikov: Ru-ree-koff

Awimak: Aw-ee-mack

Jezibaba: Ye-she-bah-bah

Table of Contents

Chapter 1..1
Chapter 2..4
Chapter 3..9
Chapter 4..14
Chapter 5..21
Chapter 6..27
Chapter 7..33
Chapter 8..41
Chapter 9..47
Chapter 10..55
Chapter 11..62
Chapter 12..71
Chapter 13..81
Chapter 14..90
Chapter 15..98
Chapter 16..106
Chapter 17..118
Chapter 18..129
Chapter 19..139
Chapter 20..155
Chapter 21..167
Chapter 22..178
Chapter 23..190
Chapter 24..200
Chapter 25..214
Chapter 26..227
Chapter 27..238
Chapter 28..244
Chapter 29..256
Chapter 30..267
Chapter 31..275
Chapter 32..283
Chapter 33..292

ONE

Deep in the forest, the creak of walking trees broke through persistent silence. Leaves whispered in a rush of movement, branches cracked, and roots thrashed the earth with each heavy step. The trees soared high, the hut nestled within the crowns quaint, its occupant far out of reach and nowhere in sight.

Ryurikov sucked in an excited breath, hiding behind an ancient oak, his leather boots scuffing leaf-wilt and twigs as he moved to peer past it. Three enormous trunks tromped past, roots and boughs swaying. He broke into a run after them.

A swish, the noise peeling his eyes wide open. An arrow, narrowly missing his head to penetrate the bark of a tree-leg ahead of him. Ryurikov jumped, arms extended, and grabbed hold of a branch. He spluttered against sprinklings of grime as he climbed, his cloak fluttering and legs kicking with each of the trunk's forward steps, robbing him of his support.

Another swish, followed by a sharp pain in his calf.

"FUCK!"

He hoisted himself further up, ignoring the arrow now in his leg as best he could, grasping roots and branches until he reached the canopy, vibrant green shrouding the hut's underbelly. Fierce winds whipped his hood off his head, copper locks flitting about while he balanced on a bough and glanced down.

The gang of enforcers who had chased him into the forest were now at the hut's heel, their gaudy yellow and crimson attire visible even from such a height.

Ryurikov grumbled in annoyance. He thought he'd lost them hours ago. He reached over his shoulder, groping for arrows he no longer had. Well, *fuck*.

He continued the ascent, eventually reaching the tree's crown, where outgrowth wove into crooked steps. He held on tight to a branch, lichen crumbling under his leather gloves. Swaying back and forth as the three trees continued their stride, Ryurikov waited until the odds were a little more in his favour, then leapt.

His chest collided hard with the bottom of the stairs, hands slapping across the worn wood before he grabbed hold of a spindle and pulled himself up. Heavily, he leaned on the wooden balustrade and inspected the damage to his right leg. The arrow was still there, tip firmly lodged into flesh. That hurt. A lot.

With clenched teeth, he grasped the shaft in both hands and snapped it off.

His pained yowl sent birds skyward, the rapid strike of wings echoing. He watched them, briefly, then pulled the dark green hood back over his head and adjusted his scarf to hide.

It wouldn't do for the witch to know his face.

From the scabbard at his hip, Ryurikov eased free a borrowed short sword, old and ornate, when an otherworldly roar sent more birds aflutter.

The canopy of the tree-legs below him blocked the ground from sight. Not that he needed to see to know what was down there, likely tearing the enforcers apart.

Past the treetops in the distance, the sun melted into the horizon, remnants of blue still streaked across. He better get this over with and escape before nightfall.

Ryurikov climbed the steps—limped, mostly. That arrow *really* hurt. Blade at the ready, he brought his fist down on the door's gnarled surface, banging with such force the glass of the circular window rattled.

"Come out, witch," Ryurikov bellowed over the loud gales and wood-groan of moving trees. "You have something I want."

"You and everyone else."

He stilled, eyes widening. The voice hadn't come from inside the woodsy dwelling. His mind galloped with frantic thoughts. Would he have time to turn, to swing his sword? Or would she curse him the second he moved?

Something prodded him in the back.

"Well, fuck," Ryurikov said. "Mind if I look at you? Least you can do, if you're going to kill me."

"You can turn," croaked the witch.

He didn't trust she would just let him see her when no one else had, but he didn't fancy being stabbed in the back either. Steeling himself, Ryurikov turned, blade lowered, and found himself staring at…

No one.

Just more leaves flittering, until he heard a creak on the steps behind him. He spun back 'round and came face to face with an aged fist slamming right into his nose, shattering it.

Ryurikov staggered back, dropping the sword as he flailed before catching himself on the balustrade near the bottom of the steps.

Eyes watering and face throbbing, he barely saw the diminutive woman standing before him, but he saw that broom in her hand. A broom she swung, and it connected with the top of his head hard enough to make his teeth clack together. Straw swept his feet out from under him and he fell the rest of the way.

Branches broke under him, snagged his cloak, tore at his skin. His world spun endlessly—until there were no more tree-limbs to catch him. Wind lashed Ryurikov's head, and the last thing he felt was the bone-crunching end to the fall that broke his back.

Two

The shout he awoke with vanished into the dark. Ryurikov gazed up at a starry night sky, heard the trees whisper in a zephyr, the owls hoot in the distance, and the wolves howl for his flesh.

Oh good, he was still in the forest, still on his back, pain barbing every inch of him.

Ryurikov groaned, aware that the only thing he could do was lie there until something came to put him out of his misery. Based on the faint footfalls, the crunching of twigs and leaves that pricked his ears, he wouldn't have to wait long.

"Can you go for my neck first?" he croaked at the sky, voice claggy with blood. The trees overhead waved, stars twinkling beyond them, and he narrowed his eyes. They were mocking him. "I'd rather not be eaten alive."

There came chanting whispers then, so soft he couldn't make out what they said. Not that he needed to concern himself with that when his vision was obstructed by a silhouette, and it was *massive*. Tall, powerful shoulders and large, thick horns that could very well be considered boughs on their own, curling around a head veiled by shadows. Ryurikov knew what this was all the same, he'd heard its terrifying roar earlier, and smelled the stench of enforcer blood on it. It stank the same as all other blood, but it seemed a plausible suspicion.

Awimak, the Demon of the Unbroken Wilds, stood over him, as tall as a sorcerer's tower, staring down at his broken body with blazing eyes. And the only thing Ryurikov's pain-addled mind could come up with was to wonder why he had to wake long enough to meet what would devour him. He tried to move, but succeeded only in twitching his fingers.

Moonlight illuminated Awimak's outline as it turned its head when the volume of susurrant chants increased. Then there were branch-like white horns, and dark faces belonging to bulbous, translucent shapes, and eyes twinkling like the stars above. They too peered down, encircling him, drawing ever closer until all he saw was their shadowy faces, the bright glints of their eyes.

"Stealing is immoral," one of them whispered, right into his ear. Ryurikov tried to jerk his head away. He still couldn't move.

"I don't steal," he rasped.

"Lying, too, is immoral," another whispered.

"Al-Alright, guilty. Guilty on both counts."

"So is murder."

Ryurikov tensed his jaw. "Guilty on three counts, then."

"Adultery."

"Good grief," Ryurikov ground out, "are you in a position to judge when you're going to eat me alive? Just get on with it!"

An overlapping chorus of whispered anger met his impatience. Awimak moved, vanishing from sight just as a string of clouds obscured the moon. The pallid spirits paid Awimak no mind as they extended slender arms and scattered sticks over Ryurikov with long, thin fingers. He feared it might be kindling.

They didn't stop, haphazardly piling more atop him, burying him with dead leaves and shrubbery. So much, it weighed on him.

Ryurikov gagged on blood swamping his throat, his vision blurry as his mind drifted in and out of consciousness. There were no gods he believed in, but he prayed for sleep, regardless.

Ryurikov squinted against the light filtering through the canopy of trees. He swore under his breath and sat upright, twigs and leaf-litter tumbling down around him. It looked like he was in a grounded nest, a giant human bird with tattered clothing and... Healed bones.

"Well, fuck."

So the little bastard spirits healed him. They had even tended to his leg, now free of the arrow. Awimak hadn't killed him, either. Ryurikov wondered *why*. They sure seemed adamant about throwing judgements about. With a scoff, he wiped forest dross off himself and stumbled to his feet. He was stiff, but that was a hell of a lot better than a broken back.

A glance up at the sky told him it was afternoon. A more thorough look at his surroundings declared he was lost. Ryurikov moved over brush and old, broken trees laden with moss, hoping to find tracks of the witch's hut. Birds above were chipper, he heard the distant burbling of a brook, but there were no traces of Jezibaba. And it had taken him months to uncover her. Fuck.

He did find what was left of the enforcers, their remains scattered across the forest a short distance from where he walked.

With a grimace, Ryurikov toed the mangled bodies, but they were stripped of their weapons. Unfortunate, when he was out of arrows, had lost his bow and sword, was now down to a dagger and miles away from settlements. Worse situations to be in, he supposed. He could be someone's meal right now, for a start.

He made his way to the brook, where he dropped to his knees and guzzled, the cool water rinsing tarrying drowsiness from his mind. Lush green encircled his gently rippling reflection.

Ryurikov rarely looked at himself, and it wasn't the scarred half of his face that bothered him. Rather, it was the ghostly spheres for eyes that irked. A parting gift from a disgruntled lover, who told him that if he was going to be soulless and unfeeling, his eyes ought to reflect that.

Ironic, coming from a prince of darkness.

He slapped the water and replaced his dark scarf and hood to hide. It was then he caught sight of the white silhouettes some distance away, watching him. In daylight, they looked more like concentrated flurries of snow, their faces and wide eyes owl-like.

"What now?" he demanded, pushing to his feet.

"Immoral," they whispered. There were five of them, all peeking from behind trees. *"Owe us a favour, now."*

"I didn't ask you to heal me."

All the same, Ryurikov hopped over the brook and approached them. Many considered him uncouth, but he liked to think he wasn't entirely without manners. He stopped nearby and glared down at them. These peculiar spirits were short, reaching up to his thighs. His abdomen, if he counted the horns.

"We can return your bones to the way we found them," they whispered in unison. Ryurikov tried, and failed, to suppress the shudder that jerked down his spine.

"I'd rather you didn't," he said, moving as they did to keep a comfortable distance between them.

"Then owe us."

"What do you want?"

"Redemption."

"I'm all out of prayers and forgiveness, but I'm sure there's a chapel in the nearest town if—"

"For you," they hissed, clearly annoyed.

"I don't need redemption."

"We beg to differ. Liar, thief, murderer, adulterer."

Ryurikov glowered at their glinting eyes. "I'll have you know I wasn't aware she was married."

"Liar."

He sighed. "Fine, so I had a vague idea." He wouldn't justify himself to these beings, even if they spared him from a potentially slow and painful death. "What is it I can do for you?"

"Take," one hissed.

"Give," another whispered.

Ryurikov held out his hands in confusion.

"Take from the undeserving." That whisper came from behind him, and he spun to glare at the one that had snuck 'round.

"Give to the worthy."

He flattened his lips. "And if I don't?"

"Crack, snap," sibilated the one in front of him, their spindly fingers mimicking the breaking of what he presumed would be his leg.

Ryurikov sighed in frustration. "This is a terrible way to do business, you know, but fine." He spun on his heel and stalked back to cross the brook. "Fine!"

"Wrong way."

When he turned, all five spirits pointed west. He shook his head once, and continued to walk in the same direction he had been, just until he was out of sight, at which point he veered to the left.

Three

By the time Ryurikov reached a road, indigo suffused the sky. Only a vivid ribbon of sunlight peered through the trees, effectively blinding him. The sound of horses clopping along packed dirt had him skittering behind a tree, grateful for the green cloak allowing him to blend in, although it was tattered now. He peered past the trunk, bark and moss crumbling under his touch as a carriage came into view. A garish orange wood with citrine trims, the driver dressed in a red uniform, surrounded by tassels.

Good grief, it was hideously perfect.

Ryurikov waited for the thoroughbreds to trot past before spinning out from behind the tree. He launched at the back of the carriage and grasped its cargo rail, hoisting himself up to the roof. He slipped free the dagger from his belt and jumped onto the driver's back, blade at the man's throat.

"Stop," Ryurikov commanded.

With a pathetic whimper, the driver pulled the reins, slowing the horses to a standstill. Inquiring voices called out from the carriage while Ryurikov patted the man's shoulder.

"No need to be brave, they aren't worth dying for." He swung his long legs over the seat's side and hopped down, cloak flapping behind him.

With one swift tug, he opened the carriage door. Another pull, and a male occupant came tumbling out, swiftly held at knifepoint, back pressed against Ryurikov's chest. He smelled of citrus and flowers, of *wealth*.

"Your valuables, if you please," Ryurikov said to the woman now screeching. Because manners were everything in these situations.

Manners the driver clearly didn't have.

Ryurikov caught movement from his peripheral and swayed to the side. The sharp whistle echoed beyond the nearest trees. Horses whinnied in fright and jerked the carriage a few steps forward. He sneered as the body of his hostage collapsed to bleed through fine, periwinkle silk, a bolt firmly wedged in his chest. The silence was swiftly shattered, the woman's screeching an encore accompanied by sobs.

An undignified sound left the driver when Ryurikov's glare flicked to him. The man hurried to reload his crossbow with trembling hands. Ryurikov's steadier touch flung the dagger, blade glinting in the tarrying sunlight before lancing the driver's neck, sending him sideways off the seat and to the ground with a thud.

A rush of blood pooled the earth when Ryurikov yanked free the blade. The man gurgled, throat clicking in his failure to swallow. Mood now soured, Ryurikov marched back to the carriage, the woman within still screaming loud enough for it to score his ears. Fuck. This was not how he wanted it to go.

"Valuables," he barked.

The woman's racket didn't stop, her face twisted with horror, but she pulled the pearls from her neck and dug around the large pink dress for a pouch. She tossed both his way. Ryurikov almost felt bad for leaving her with two bodies in the middle of nowhere, but he had no time to squander on pity. This was not his fault.

Well. It wasn't *all* his fault.

Ryurikov put it out of his mind and fled.

Hours of walking without food wore him down. It made him tetchy. He didn't especially fancy stopping so near a skimble-skamble he still wasn't going to take the blame for, but a pitiful village of log homes greeted him at the forest's edge. Hearth smoke drifted along a cool breeze, distant merriment bringing an odd comfort Ryurikov couldn't find a home for in his heart.

Down a narrow dirt road shrouded by night, he approached a tavern and invited himself in, the door already open—only to discover that it was not, in fact, a tavern. Rather, a home of an intensely large family.

They all froze, looking up from where they sat on rickety benches surrounding a firepit, mouths agape and eyes wide. Ryurikov shuddered.

Children. So many children.

"Pardon me, I thought this was a tavern." He spun back 'round to leave.

"We can put you up, sir," said the eldest. He looked twenty, barely. Honey-coloured eyes bright and short auburn curls a mess.

A more thorough scour told Ryurikov that there were no parents, only twelve children. He pressed his lips together. "And you've a bed to spare, have you?"

"Yes, sir." The lad jumped up from the bench to bring him the bowl he'd been cradling. "You can have my stew if you're hungry."

Ryurikov peered down into the bowl. "That's not stew—"

"It is sir. It's basic, is all. It'll only cost you an ore."

"For the half-eaten porridge?"

"The stew sir, and the stay for the night."

"Don't suppose this pathetic excuse for a hamlet has a bordello?"

The lad considered this for a moment. "No, sir. Please, stay. The tax collectors have been, and we haven't enough food for the month."

Ryurikov sighed. "Fine, but I'm not taking your *stew*." No matter how hungry he was.

He brushed past a frail shoulder, his gaze journeying along the curious faces before he discovered the beds in the back. Wood planks slapped together with string, covered in spare leather and pelts.

It wasn't that Ryurikov was picky about where he slept. Years of being a wanted man had taught him not to be a chooser, but he drew the line at sleeping directly next to *children*. He shuddered again, then made to move a bed. The moment he tried, it threatened to collapse, propped up on stones.

Fuck.

When he turned, they were all still staring at him, with only the youngest licking their bowls clean. They couldn't be any older than a year. Ryurikov closed his eyes, counted to ten.

"Lad," he said.

"Andrew, sir."

Ryurikov motioned for him to approach, which he did in a scramble, still holding the bowl of pretend-stew. Gritting his teeth, Ryurikov procured a crone from the stolen pouch and tossed it with a flick of his thumb. The coin fell, nose-first, to the dirty planks with a *plink*, its hag-like contours glinting in the low light. Andrew was too perplexed to even pick it up.

"Take it," said Ryurikov.

With that he laid down, the bed creaking and wobbling under his weight. He turned so he wouldn't have to look at their stupid little faces, while Andrew picked up the coin, gasped, and did a poor job of stifling a sob.

"This is too much, sir."

"Shut up, I'm trying to sleep."

In a faintly choked whisper, "Thank you."

Ryurikov settled his head on an arm and shut his eyes against the sound of excited chatter, of parentless children eating their shitty, watery porridge, who were persistently being shushed by Andrew, and still failed to be quiet. He listened to them crawl into their beds, planks creaking. None tried to touch him, to pickpocket him. Once everything fell silent, Ryurikov allowed himself to relax.

His eyes flew open to darkness once again. He must have rolled onto his back at some point, and now lay with his arm around one of the toddlers, who had nestled against his side and was using his arm as a pillow, cloak as a blanket. Crafty little shit.

That wasn't what woke him, though. It was the nimble fingers working to undo his belts and lower his breeches that had stirred him.

"What do you think you're doing?" Ryurikov demanded in a whisper, using his knee to knock away the hands.

He could barely make out the honey-coloured eyes in the dark, but guessed who it was. Andrew shifted. A flinder of moonlight drifting in through a narrow window touched his face, delicate features glowing silver. So young, and determined, apparently. Ryurikov smacked his hands away this time.

"You've given us too much, sir. I know–I know what they do in the city for that kind of coin. I can do it. I won't let my sister do it, she's too young."

"If you keep going, I'm throwing this child at you." Ryurikov jerked his head at the sleeping form on his numbed arm.

Andrew's gaze flicked to the toddler, then back to him. "You don't want...?"

"What I want is to sleep."

A nod, then the lad slipped off him. Ryurikov would have breathed a sigh of relief, if he didn't see Andrew walk to lie on the floor by the pit, the fire within long since dwindled to embers. He gnashed his teeth, forced himself to lay back down, and go to sleep.

FOUR

Ryurikov sat upright and watched in detachment as two children rolled off him and crashed to the ground. Three of the shits had successfully joined him, and he hadn't even noticed. Children, ugh. This was exactly why he didn't trust them, they were too damned sneaky.

He tugged his cloak out from under the one still snoozing, swung his legs off the bed, stepped over the two now crying, and walked out of the hut.

It was dawn, the crow of the rooster betraying his departure.

"Sir?"

His foot barely lifted to take the first step away. "What is it?"

"Where are you headed?" asked Andrew behind him.

"To find me a witch." Foot still raised, Ryurikov pivoted to face him. "Don't suppose you've seen the Jezibaba?"

Those eyes widened. "She steals children and eats them."

"I know. Any of yours gone missing?"

"No, sir. We see treetops moving and we run to hide."

So, Jezibaba could be spotted even from here. He lowered his foot.

"How often?"

"Once every fortnight." Andrew stepped closer, his look admiring.

"Are you going to hunt her down?"

Ryurikov backed away. He didn't have the patience to deal with fawning. "When's the last time you saw her?"

"A little over a week ago, sir."

"Good to know." That meant he wouldn't have time to head for the nearest town to liberate a few fine folks of their weapons. *Fuck.* "Good-day."

In a whirl of his cloak, Ryurikov walked off, back to the forest. He moved through the trees, his footfalls silent, passed by the gaudy carriage now abandoned, the horses gone and two bodies still there.

Not a frequented road, then.

It had taken him a long time to learn the signs of Jezibaba's whereabouts. Subtle dustings of dirt and concentrations of worms and glittering beetles, sprinkled down from uprooted trees serving as the hut's foundation. The tree-legs left no other traces, somehow broke nothing in their path, and it could only be heard when a coin-toss away. If what Andrew said was true, then it would be another few days until she showed herself.

Ryurikov made do with berries and edible mushrooms found along the way, drank from brooks and stopped only to catch his breath. He'd put too much into finding Jezibaba the first time to let up now.

The sun passed him overhead. Dipped low again, and nightfall came. He didn't bother with a fire, slept in the hollow of a tree while ignoring the odd sense of being watched. He got up before daybreak and carried on. Three days passed in quick succession without so much as a trace of the hag.

Ryurikov took refuge in a deep gully, back resting against cool stone overgrown by moss and tiny white flowers attracting glowants. He lowered his hood to wipe damp hair from his forehead, taking a moment to breathe. With the dawn of summer, the days grew ever warmer.

His eyes closed, and his mind drifted to long flowy hair. Coppery like his own, a smile much like his own, and eyes hazel the way his used to be. He reached out to hold a pale hand, looked into a hazy field of freckles—so much like his own.

The smile was sweet. It blossomed into pure happiness, then kept curling up. Until it twisted into a massive grin, stretching past the blurred face. Fiery hair churned, morphing with the grin into a monstrous, featherless bird, opening its elongated, bone-like beak to reveal long, blood-stained teeth.

Ryurikov awoke with a start.

He was still in the gully, the sun had barely shifted, light dappling the otherwise shaded earth. A frown worked itself across his brows. His sleep was rarely troubled. In fact, he couldn't remember the last time he had a nightmare. With a grunt, he pushed upright to dust off the green glowants wandering across his arm, and froze.

Down the gully's other end stood Awimak.

Gigantic. Incredible coiled horns reaching well past the height of the earthy walls on either side, sunlight grazing the rough, bark-like texture. If Awimak had a face, a skull hid it. Deer, he thought, although it looked more sinister than that.

The demon was watching him.

Skin prickling with fear, Ryurikov took a step back. Awimak remained where he stood, yet there was a sound—an arrhythmic skreigh and crunch. A colossal shadow slipped over the demon, hiding him in full. Tree-legs trudged along the top edges of the gully, passed him over, and Ryurikov spun on his heel to catch up.

He scaled the walls, kicked up and latched onto a rough tree-leg, digging his fingers into the bark with enough force to hurt. Branches lashed him, a sharp pain along his cheek had him jerking away. His heart dropped out every time his boots slipped. He grabbed hold of yet more offshoots to climb. Back up the colossal trees, he jumped to reach the first of the steps, no more graceful than before.

Ryurikov stood facing Jezibaba's hut. Slender trees made up its framework, walls of wattle and ancient daub, overgrown by leaves and ivy. It had at least four floors, stacked haphazardly atop the main structure, none of the windows alike.

Staring at the arched front door tucked under the porch, Ryurikov gave himself a moment to consider how he would approach the hag. A sword hadn't saved him the first time, his dagger—an even shorter blade

—would do nothing.

With a click of his tongue, he lifted the hood back over his head and knocked, gently.

"You again?" asked the witch, her voice stentorian, all around him.

"Me again," he confirmed.

"Adamant about that mirror."

Ryurikov cocked his head. "Indeed."

Astonishingly, the front door swung open with a drawn-out squeak, but there was no hag to greet him.

This was obviously a trap, but he hadn't gotten this far by shying from danger.

He stepped inside.

His boots scuffed across old woven rugs, the hut's interior cramped with bookcases, shelves riddled with dirty bottles, and bundles of herbs hung from beams. Ryurikov ducked around bone chimes and empty bird cages, sidestepped plants, making his way to the large hearth. Its fire roared hot, flames licking at a cauldron of what smelled like stew. Real stew.

"Hungry?"

His gaze flicked to the old woman whom he was fairly sure hadn't been standing in the back of an untidy kitchenette before now. Sunlight pouring in through the paned window turned her silver hair yellow, stacked haphazardly atop her head with various braids, a thin, patterned scarf holding it all together. She hobbled closer. The red tunic wasn't long enough to cover knobbly knees, let alone the grim feet with long blackened nails. Ryurikov stepped away, ankle knocking into the rocking chair nearby. *Ouch*.

"My name is Andrey." Manners. They were everything, even if he was lying. They had gotten him inside, they might keep him alive, too.

"That wasn't my question." Jezibaba looked up at him with odd, inhuman eyes.

"I am hungry, but that's not why I'm here."

"Yes, yes, the mirror. Upstairs."

Ryurikov squinted at her. "First you try to kill me because I want it, now you're inviting me to take it?"

"I didn't try." She held out an old, gnarly hand and wiggled her fingers.

Brown smoke wafted from the tips, swirling around her palm, growing ever more dense until it formed a solid, wooden bowl. "I *did* kill you."

He shimmied his hips for emphasis.

Jezibaba's lizard eyes flicked back up to him. She hummed, filling the bowl with rich-smelling stew before holding it out to him. "You can look. That's all you want, isn't it? So look, if it'll help sate your curiosity and get you out of my hair."

Ryurikov would have pointed out that he was the least of her worries, when the hag had beetles crawling around the silvery pile, but chose not to. He took the bowl and failed not to jump when a wooden spoon materialised inside it. "Upstairs, you said?"

"Door to the left."

He barely kept from running up the rickety staircase, taking the steps two at a time with ease. Past the bedimmed landing, he pushed into a room choked with lit candles, a cluttered desk and even more plants. A large, stained glass window featured an intricate image of three birds and trees, but it was the round mirror floating midair in the back that got all his attention. He set the bowl down on the desk among books and papers, and approached.

It was a simple enough mirror, its frame silver, repetitive details grimy. He supposed he didn't have to steal it, when he could get his answer in this place as well as any other. Hesitantly, Ryurikov lowered his hood and pushed down the scarf. Ghostly eyes stared back, scouring his scarred image, waiting for the mirror to show him what he needed it to.

All Ryurikov saw, however, was himself, becoming visibly angry.

"Not who you were expecting?"

He swiftly concealed his face again before regarding the hag. "This is the wrong mirror."

Jezibaba hobbled further into the room, grabbed the bowl of stew and held it out to him. "So you weren't after the Mirror of the Lost?"

He frowned. "If this is it, then it's not working. All I see is myself."

The hag hummed again, wrinkles fanning her eyes while she peered up at him. "What could that possibly mean?"

Framed like a question, but it wasn't.

He narrowed his eyes. "I'm not lost."

"Eat."

Ryurikov took the bowl and sat down in the chair by the desk with a frustrated sigh. He glanced down at the chunky pieces of vegetables swimming in a thick broth, but all hunger had vanished, replaced by a deep-seated resentment. It hadn't occurred to him that the one thing he'd believed in would fail.

Jezibaba drew toward the mirror and stood on her toes to look into it. Then she tutted and turned, the teeth and bones strung around her neck rattling. She dug around an old chest on the floor nearby, filled with twill, rusty tools, and tiny cauldrons, and produced a pair of scissors along with a spool of blue thread.

"You...use the mirror to find things," Ryurikov said flatly.

"My organised chaos is less organised than I'd prefer." Jezibaba idly snipped the scissors. "What was it you were hoping to see?"

Ryurikov busied himself eating in response. Polishing off the stew took little time, the earthy flavours a welcome change from the tart berries he'd been surviving on. He didn't let Jezibaba watching him eat bother him and set the bowl back down, a singular mushroom slice stuck against its side.

Another glance at the mirror.

"It'll only show you the same thing."

"It might not."

Ryurikov stood, intending to look again, but his stomach cramping had him doubling over. He steadied himself with a hand on the desk, eyes widening in horror. Fuck.

Fuck.

Fuck.

The unsteady thumps of his footfalls became hollow echoes as he staggered out of the room, cold sweat dampening his clothes. His foot caught on something. He hurtled face first down the stairs, knocked his elbow and head along the way, before reaching the bottom to roll across the floor and ending in a pathetic heap.

A stream of pink drool slipped from his mouth in his struggle to push back upright. His stomach twisted and clenched, the pain pulling an agonised moan out of him. In the distance, he heard the creak of stairs, the sound of bare feet walking past him, of Jezibaba opening the front door.

Ryurikov didn't know why he was trying to escape, when he was dead either way. On his hands and knees he crawled outside, grabbed hold of the balustrade and hoisted himself up with pained grunts.

Swaying leaves became an unbearable racket, each crunch and crack of walking trees like a thunderclap. Over it all, the croak of Jezibaba's voice.

Too loud, too clear, "Let this be the last time we meet, Ryurikov of the fallen Thuidal Kingdom."

A foot connected with his back, sent him flying forward, and down to the forest floor.

FIVE

Detritus muffled Ryurikov's harsh moan. He slapped his hands down to the ground, pushed himself up, and every bone and muscle in his body throbbed with excruciating pain. Twigs and leaves and more forest-wilt tumbled around and off him. He knelt, turned to the dark sky obstructed by shadowy green and heaved a tired sigh.

"Owe us twice."

Ryurikov closed his eyes. Those aggravating bastards.

"I didn't ask for this," he growled. Getting to his feet took several attempts. He wrapped an arm around his still cramping stomach and squared against the five, likely self-appointed enforcers of morality. "What the hell do you want from me?"

One spirit drifted closer. It held up a stick in its long spindly fingers and he narrowed his eyes. This was starting to feel like a threat.

"Take, give," it whispered.

"I did!"

"Not enough."

"I took plenty, I'll thank you!"

The moment pallid fingers applied pressure to the stick, Ryurikov felt an ache in his shin. And as the stick splintered, the ache twisted into an agony that had him crying out. He fell to his ass and clutched his shin —not quite broken, but it had to be fractured.

"You fucking shits!"

"Take, give," they sibilated in unison, then floated away, their shadowy faces visible through the backs of their heads.

"At least fix what you broke!"

No acknowledgements were forthcoming.

Ryurikov swore. First under his breath, then loud enough to startle birds. Wings slapping nearly disguised heavy footfalls approaching. Ryurikov stilled. The hair on his neck stood up, his skin prickling. The temperature dropped as an unearthly shadow slid over him. He grit his teeth and hunched his shoulders against the inevitable attack.

Nothing.

He knew the demon was there, Awimak's rasps heavy, his scent woodsy, and there was the unmistakable shift of a thick hoof through deadened leaves.

Ryurikov released a quivering breath. Slowly, he slid his hand down to reach for the dagger at his belt. It wasn't there. He squeezed his eyes shut in fury, then abruptly stood up.

"Fuck!"

He'd forgotten about his leg. So much for escaping.

Using the nearest tree to steady himself, Ryurikov hopped on one foot to turn around, sucking in a startled breath as his gaze settled on the gigantic demon.

DREAM.

A single word, the demon's voice a deep rasp, like the snarled curse of a wraith that launched Ryurikov's heart up into his throat. Trying to run was pointless. When he did nothing, Awimak took a step toward him, hooves like those of a draft horse.

DREAM FOR ME, HUMAN.

Ryurikov's hand clenched around the branch he used for support. "I don't take well to commands, demon."

"Sir?"

The colossal, shadowy form vanished without a trace right in front of him. When Ryurikov glanced over his shoulder, Andrew lingered there, eyes wide, holding an old basket

"Are you well?"

He cleared his throat, still tight with the panic that had just been strangling him. "What are you doing here?"

"I'm foraging, sir."

"At this hour?"

"It's dawn." Andrew stepped closer, revealing a child hiding behind him. She too carried a basket nearly as large as her, one of her braids in her mouth. "Do you need help?"

"Aren't you worried the Jezibaba will get you?"

"No sir, she never turns back."

Ryurikov motioned for Andrew to stay where he was. "You really shouldn't be here, there are demons in this forest." Not that he was worried about him.

"I know sir, but I've no choice. Please, let me help."

"There's only one thing I need you to do." Ryurikov lowered to sit on the ground with a tired sigh, more mindful of his fractured shin this time. "I need you to take this."

From the pocket of his breeches he pulled free the leather coin pouch and tossed it toward Andrew, who didn't catch it. It dropped with a dull *plunk*.

Dumbfounded, the lad only stared.

"It's all yours." Ryurikov would have added a 'please' to that, but he didn't want to seem too desperate. Even though he was.

Despite shadows veiling Andrew's face, those honey-coloured eyes never left Ryurikov as Andrew bent low to gather the pouch. He pried it open, and gasped.

"I can't take this!"

"Fucking hell, just take the damned money and get out of here." Ryurikov's tone was harsh, but his words seemed to fall on deaf ears. He worked his jaw. "You'd be doing me a favour by taking it."

"Sir, I *can't*, not without—let me help you." Andrew lowered his basket, but again Ryurikov frantically gestured for him to stop.

"Consider it a payment to leave me alone, then!"

The lad's chin wobbled and terror clapped Ryurikov across the heart. "Don't—"

Too late. The tears spilt, and he found himself cinched by a surprisingly powerful embrace. He winced at the accidental nudge to his injured leg, but couldn't stop the reflex of holding Andrew with an arm to support him. Something unintelligible got sobbed into the side of his hood, along with a smear of snot, no doubt. Awkwardly, Ryurikov patted a bony back, his eyes flicking to the young girl still standing there, chewing her braid.

"Just promise me you'll buy that girl something to eat besides her hair."

"Sophia," Andrew blubbered, leaning back to wipe his eyes.

The sight of him contorted Ryurikov's insides. In a way he didn't appreciate. He crawled backward to put distance between them, ignoring the woodland debris digging into his palms and ass cheeks.

"Now go. It's not safe here." Now that had come out all wrong. "Not that I care."

A wavering smile blossomed across Andrew's lips. "I will never forget your kindness."

He stood, tucked the pouch into his pocket, collected the worn basket off the ground, and took Sophia's tiny hand in his. Before leaving, he turned back around. Ryurikov tensed.

Andrew asked, "May I get your name?"

"...Ruri. Now go."

Andrew's mouth moved as if tasting the name. Ryurikov refused to meet the lingering gaze, finding lichen-festooned branches nearby to be much more interesting. Only when the two were out of sight and the girl's excited babbling no longer reached him did Ryurikov flop down to stare at the vibrant green above him, the beginnings of morning blue peering through.

His whole body ached, a bit like he'd fallen to his death. His stomach still hurt.

When he heard footfalls again, Ryurikov sighed in aggravation.

"You better fix my leg now."

"I'd rather they didn't."

He froze.

For the first time in a long while, Ryurikov felt a chill run down his spine that had everything to do with fear. Orange eyes peered down at him.

"Fuck you, witch."

Awimak was terrifying, sure, but hadn't killed him yet. Jezibaba had done so twice now. *Twice.*

A mass of wrinkles twisted with amusement, though her attention was caught by something else. Ryurikov raised his head to see a spirit gliding past a cluster of young trees, carrying an armful of mossy twigs.

"Stop that," Jezibaba snapped.

The spirit razzed at her, a snake-like tongue flapping out of its inscrutable mouth. Ryurikov snorted, his own lips twitching with a smirk when it dropped everything onto his leg and wriggled its spindly fingers. The pain in his fractured limb eased, tingling coursed from ankle to knee, and bone audibly snapped back into place.

Ryurikov swung his legs, sending forest dross raining around him, sweeping to knock Jezibaba off her feet—she'd already moved. He snatched up the closest thing to a weapon and whirled to block the incoming lunge of a familiar broom with a thick branch. He shoved away, circled the annoyingly agile hag, grip tight on his makeshift wooden sword.

"You're a nuisance," Jezibaba uttered in her scratchy voice. She still wasn't wearing any shoes, although now had fabric tied around her feet and ankles.

"I would've left you alone after looking into the mirror a few times." Ryurikov lunged to close the distance with a downward swing. Jezibaba blocked, the dull clack of branch on broom barely echoing. He hopped back, out of reach. "*If* you hadn't killed me a second time. Once I can forgive." He stepped sideways, steadied himself. "Twice is personal."

"What if it is?"

Ryurikov hesitated, enough for the hag to whip out of his sight. He pivoted to impede her downward thrust—she'd come from above, pushing him to a knee with the force. Jezibaba landed further away, leaves crunching underfoot.

The trees sibilated in a cool breeze.

"I see." Ryurikov straightened up. Stepped back again. "Was it something I did, or my parents?"

Jezibaba lowered her broom. By now, he knew better than to trust her and spun away from a swarm of *something* coming out of nowhere.

His cloak swished. Before it settled back around him, the bats fluttered off with screeches. The hag was nowhere in sight.

"Since the King and Queen are no more—I don't see how it matters if it was them." Her voice soared fieldwide, making it impossible to tell where she loitered.

Ryurikov edged forward, keeping his eyes on the canopies above as much as the ground. The spirits were nowhere to be seen. All that surrounded him were moss-laden trees and thick, twisting roots.

"I can't answer for the sins of my parents," he said. "But for mine, I can try to make amends."

Not that he would.

A rustle behind him, barely audible. He turned, dodged another lunge of that accursed broom, swung his branch up and watched in satisfaction as it snagged the necklace, tearing it from Jezibaba's creased neck. Teeth and tiny bones scattered to the leaves between them as the hag bounced backward. She straightened up—and was rammed into her side by a giant beast.

The broom swivelled midair before it dropped. The hag flew into a tree with a sickening crack. And where she had been standing now loomed Awimak, a goliath even among ancient trees.

"Fuck me," breathed Ryurikov.

Six

The demon remained while Ryurikov inspected the limp form lying by large roots. Her tunic, now tied down by sashes and other fabric, was hiked over her knobbly knees, the silver pile of hair strewn across her face, hiding the wrinkles and enormous nose. An unflattering position to have died in, to be sure.

DREAM FOR ME, Awimak snarled behind him, sending shivers down Ryurikov's spine.

All the same, he faced the demon. "I will dream as much as you want for killing her."

SHE IS NOT DEAD.

Ryurikov raised his eyebrows. "No? I know a remedy for that."

He collected the broom off the ground and spun it in his hands, trying to decide which end to use on her, then heard faint whispering off to his left. "Good fucking grief."

The five spirits flanked him. *"Immoral."*

"You're joking, right? She killed me. Twice!" And it really hurt the second time. He jabbed her flabby belly with the end of the broom handle. "She'll be lucky if all I do is ram this down her throat. I ought to cut her head off, parade it around the cities!"

"Murder is immoral." They peered up at him with those

umbrageous, owl-like faces.

Ryurikov growled, then regarded Awimak. He'd not yet moved. "You're the one who got her. What say you, demon? Let her live, or—"

THE HUT WILL DIE WITH HER. Awimak's distorted voice wasn't loud, but it was encompassing in the worst way.

Ryurikov suppressed a shudder. He slung his focus back to the unconscious form. "Fuck." He lowered the hood to run fingers through jaw-length hair, raking it out of his face. "Fuck! Okay, fine! She gets to live to try and kill me a third time."

Crouching, he tugged free the sash around her head, rolled her lumpy form over and tied gnarly hands together at her back. The fingertips were stained green. "But I swear, if she does try, you can break every bone in my body and I'll *still* kill her."

The spirits exchanged looks with one another, then whispered, *"Fair."*

With a grunt, Ryurikov hoisted Jezibaba's diminutive body up and over his shoulder, grateful that despite all the fabric and beetles weighing her down, she wasn't particularly heavy.

"Suppose I should thank you for resurrecting me." He looked at the spirits, watched their odd, shapeless bodies shift like concentrated blizzards. "Anyway, I'll see you around."

He ignored their hissed anger, approaching Awimak and craning his neck to look up into his eyes. They burned like fire. "Don't suppose you'll show me to her hut?"

ONLY THE WITCH CAN.

Ryurikov flattened his lips. "Unfortunate. Well, you didn't kill her, but I suppose I owe you a...dream?"

GOOD.

With the broom, he motioned for... Well, for Awimak to show him what he wanted, exactly. "After you?"

Awimak's hooves were heavier than tree trunks as he stomped through the forest, leading him to goodness knew where. Ryurikov didn't think it would be to his demise, although whether the demon would release him again was still up in the air.

They walked deeper into the forest, the silence broken by bird songs and the morning breeze combing through leaves. The number of young trees slowly dwindled, large, ancient ones with thick roots curling around mossy boulders casting all in darkness.

Hopping over a stream, Ryurikov faltered as his surroundings leapt upside down like an onslaught of vertigo. They were still in the forest, but *beneath* it, he thought.

Roots resembled bare trees, the underside of rockery trickling with dirt and crawling with insects. Looking up, it startled him to see the stream flowing above him. Through its ripples he made out the canopy of green and hints of a bright morning sky. The air here was damp, the scent of earth heavy, and the light peculiar. It had a yellow tinge to it, even though the dirt and network of roots—the ceiling—blocked most light.

COME.

Ryurikov snapped his attention back to the demon. "I'm coming."

Since they stopped in an area that essentially looked the same as everywhere else in this place, he wasn't sure why they had bothered to go further. With a tired sigh, he dropped Jezibaba as hard as possible to the ground and stretched his aching body. His stomach still troubled him, and he rubbed an open palm across it.

Awimak was watching, something that didn't bother him. Not at first. But he kept watching, and Ryurikov quickly ran out of things to do, so he dropped the broom and cleared his throat.

DREAM.

"You understand, to do that I need to sleep."

Awimak nodded. There was an eagerness to it that Ryurikov wasn't fond of.

"Right, well I don't—where?" He gestured around him. "And anyway, I'm not taking my eyes off that witch." Or the demon, for that matter.

I WILL WATCH HER. Awimak lowered to his haunches. He held out a giant claw just above the damp ground, fingers flexing as roots slithered out from the soil, snaking around Jezibaba's limp form.

"Right." Ryurikov paused, then lowered to sit. "So, I'll just...lie here and fall asleep long enough to dream?" At the demon's nod, he laid down and covered himself with his ragged cloak. "Dare I ask why?" When Awimak said nothing, he sighed. "If you're going to kill me, do me the courtesy of not waking me beforehand."

He closed his eyes, trying not to let the chilled earth get to him, and folded an arm under his head. When he heard heavy hooves shift, Ryurikov adjusted the hood over his face, enough to peer out from under it undetected. Awimak had merely moved further away.

This was very unsettling.

Ryurikov focused on getting to sleep, regardless.

His mind wandered to the Mirror of the Lost, how all he'd seen was himself. Inwardly, he scoffed. He wasn't lost, but his sister *was*.

He hadn't seen Valka in so long, having parted ways thirteen years ago. That day was as fresh on his mind as a crisp winter night. Ryurikov remembered the cerulean light filtering in through the dense forest, how it had graced his sister's face, illuminating the expanse of rusty freckles.

Valka's smile was the happiest he'd seen in ages, yet her hazel eyes were bright with unshed tears. The knowledge that they might never see each other again hurt, but she would be free.

He would make sure of that.

She wrapped her arms around his neck to pull him close. Ryurikov knew she would tease him about being shorter than her, that he should stop feeding his vegetables to the dogs.

"You're going to fail us all."

A frown pulled his brows together. He opened his mouth to respond, but couldn't.

"Our entire kingdom will burn, the lands will be ravaged, and it'll be your fault."

He leaned away, a scream lodging itself in his throat as Valka's smiling face split itself across the centre, skin stretching, tearing. Top parting from bottom to give way to a protruding skull, elongated like a beak. Bone white streaked with blood, large teeth set in a grin, the two halves of his sister's face now serving as scalp and chin.

Hollow eyes stared, rivulets of red trickling down the pallid neck and chest, forming a script he couldn't read. Fingers long and knobbly extended toward him. They jabbed him in the chest, pierced skin, and twisted. Ryurikov stumbled backward, his foot slipped past an edge.

He fell.

His startled cry echoed. Wild-eyed, he took in his surroundings, blinking against the strange amber light, almost certain he was now awake. He lifted a gloved hand to his face and did a double-take.

He was trembling and sweating.

Ryurikov's gaze shifted to the demon, standing in the same place as before, the last of glittering white smoke journeying into the nostrils of the deer skull.

"What the fuck?"

Awimak released a long, rattling breath. A sigh of relief. *THANK YOU.*

"You're a fool. Even the village idiot would know better than to follow a demon into his domain."

Jezibaba sat upright, legs crossed, looking decidedly more haggard than when they first met. Her arms were strapped to her sides by entwining roots.

Ryurikov smirked at her. "Alas, we can't ask him, since he drowned in a well. You're just pissed we beat you."

He got up and strode over to Awimak, positioning himself next to the monumental being. Ryurikov often had the good fortune of being at least a head taller than others, but Awimak absolutely dwarfed him. He came up to the demon's elbow.

He reached to rap his knuckles against an exceptionally muscular arm, prompting the spheres of Awimak's burning eyes to flick down to him. Earth-chill clung to the demon's skin, storm grey and soft under his touch, becoming increasingly more bark-like toward his forearms. The tattered cloth covering his hips resembled delicately woven wood with the drape of dupion, hiding whatever he might have for a cock.

"And what do you plan on doing with me?" Jezibaba jostled him out of his admiration.

He grabbed the broom from where it rested against dirt-trickling roots and gave it a spin. "First, you're going to let me revisit that mirror."

Jezibaba tutted. "I know a lost soul when I see one. Don't need a mirror to show me that."

"Get fucked, *crone*," Ryurikov snarled. He pointed with the broom, less than an inch away from her prominent nose. "You're going to take me back to the mirror."

"What if you still only see yourself?" Jezibaba's lizard eyes narrowed. "What will you do then?"

Ryurikov ran his hand across the straw of the broom, and snapped one of the stems. The hag's left eye twitched.

"I sort of had all my hopes pinned on that mirror." He faced Awimak. "Don't suppose you're any good at finding lost people?"

The hag cackled, which made him whirl back on her.

"What's funny?"

"Humans can't be found if they don't consider themselves lost, you saphead."

Ryurikov stilled. Valka, if even alive, might not think herself lost. He'd not considered that possibility. "Wait, does that mean...she's alright?"

Jezibaba scoffed. "Of course, it's a woman."

"No, you ancient prune," he snapped. "I'm after my sister."

At that, Jezibaba frowned. "Valka?"

And Ryurikov gaped.

Seven

Ryurikov paced, each step scuffing dirt, mind steeplechasing. Suddenly, he stopped, spun around, and snapped his fingers at Awimak with a realisation. "You steal dreams!"

I DO NOT STEAL THEM. It was hard to tell, but he thought Awimak sounded offended. *I REPLACE ONE WITH THE OTHER.*

"Hm. So how do you know Valka?" He regarded the hag, still trapped by roots and sitting in damp soil.

"We met every once in a while in the woodlands."

A simple enough answer, but Ryurikov knew what this meant. "So, the Thuidal forests are your home."

"Well done."

He hummed. "And of course, you think it's my fault some of the land was destroyed."

"Some?" Jezibaba seethed, sinewy arms flexing against the restraints. "*All* of the woodlands were burned to the ground!"

Ryurikov jerked his focus elsewhere, refusing to let her see his shock. There were rumours, but he hadn't known the extent of the damage and in truth, had not been inclined to find out. He certainly wasn't going to take Jezibaba's word for it, either.

"Do you know where she is now?"

Jezibaba grumbled, "It's been years since I've last seen her."

"Fuck." Ryurikov lowered his hood and combed fingers through his messy hair.

So, his only other option was to return to his kingdom and sift through the ashes for traces of her.

There *had* to be another way.

"You'll take me where I need to go," he said at length.

"Why would I?"

"Oh, I don't know." Ryurikov ran the broom handle across his thigh, holding it with both hands. "You seem attached to this broom. Would be a damned shame if something happened to it."

That earned him a nasty glare and he grinned. "Awimak," he held the broom out, "would you be so kind as to accompany me and hold on to this broom, ensuring this hag can't get to it? In exchange, I'll suffer all the nightmares you want."

YES. Awimak readily grabbed the broom.

Ryurikov clapped his hands together. "Perfect!"

He trudged alongside Awimak, allowing Jezibaba to lead the way. Since he would rather stick his cock in a nest of glowants than trust her, the hag's arms remained roped to her sides by roots.

Reappearing from the strange Awimak-dwelling into the forest was as simple as crossing the threshold of a doorway, yet it left Ryurikov disorientated. Like waking from an intense dream and not quite knowing his ass from his face.

"Are you allowed to leave the woods?" he asked the demon. He trailed his gaze along Awimak's lengthy body. Goodness, the demon was something to behold, and surprisingly benign. Even if he stole pleasant dreams.

I AM NOT TETHERED TO THIS FOREST, ONLY HAPPEN TO ENJOY IT.

"That's fair." It *was* a pleasant forest, murderous hags aside.

Finding the hut was irritatingly simple when all Jezibaba had to do was tap her foot three times for it to come running like an eager pup. Except it was a burl of soaring trees that could easily stomp things to death.

Coming to a gentle stop just before the hag, it lowered, trunks bending like knees and tree crowns parting to create a path directly to the steps. A look up at Awimak, and Ryurikov followed, temporarily walled in by branches and greenery until he, for the third time, marched up to the arched front door.

His stomach turned in protest, and he hesitated going much further than the entrance. Jezibaba came to stand in the middle of the room by a clunky table, only a tree trunk sawed in half. She glowered, arms still strapped.

"Are you just going to stand around like the idiot you are?"

Repeated *thuds* behind him wrenched Ryurikov's attention to the door. He paused, staring, while Awimak attempted to get his large horns in through the doorway. He burst into laughter. It sounded nervous to his own ears.

"Allow me to assist," he said.

Awimak breathily grunted as he placed both hands on the large coils. He pushed the demon back out, then helped manoeuvre the horns past the frame with minimal damage. Broad shoulders and the rest of Awimak followed. What they ended up with was a squatting demon whose deer-skull looked disgruntled despite a lack of facial features.

"Maybe we should keep you outside," Ryurikov mused, earning himself an unhappy snort.

With a faint smile, he strode past Jezibaba, headed upstairs for the mirror. He tried to ignore the painful, queasy clench in his stomach, rolling his shoulders against the lingering pain of death.

The stained glass window momentarily caught his scrutiny upon entry. The birds in its design—Mourning Doves, he realised—flapped their wings, movements staggered. They took flight into a mixture of sky coloured glass, gradually transforming into smaller and smaller flecks until vanishing.

He took a minute to look over the desk, the many books piled atop it. Several bore a script he couldn't decipher, others appeared to be journals on herbs and medicine, even studies of the human body. If he didn't know any better, he would have thought Jezibaba to be a practising doctor.

Running his finger down the leather spine of a particularly large tome, Ryurikov realised he was stalling, hating the possibility of looking into the mirror only to see himself again. He didn't like being nervous, it was a nuisance.

He sucked in a breath, then closed the distance to the mirror in three quick strides. It was still plain and tarnished, and still only reflected him. Even when he lowered the hood and scarf, all that stared back at him were empty eyes and a scarred face.

"I told you."

He didn't bother to cover himself back up. "You certainly did."

It interested Ryurikov to discover Jezibaba's reflection wasn't visible in the mirror. In fact, it showed very little, his surroundings an inscrutable blur.

"Now what?"

Ryurikov faced the ancient woman. She had righted herself, more or less, binding roots gone. A beetle crawling around her stacked hair glinted green in the light sifting through stained glass. The birds returned, coming to settle at the forefront on branch-like shapes.

"Did Valka tell you where she was going at all?"

Jezibaba glowered up at him. "She didn't tell you?"

Ryurikov scoffed. "Don't make me ask Awimak to break your broom." He stalked away from the mirror, back to the door. "You know damned well I couldn't know where she was headed."

"Because the King would've tortured it out of you?"

Words that jabbed him like hot iron right in the back. He didn't whirl, barely resisting the need to lash out. "I'm fucking tired of those rumours. My parents weren't anything like that before—"

"Before the Skin Crawlers infested them? There's a reason they were infested in the first place, Prince."

Ryurikov gnashed his teeth, glaring without seeing down the dim hallway. "I should've just ignored those stupid spirits and rammed your broom down your throat, crone."

Said crone huffed in amusement. "Too late now."

"Never too late to kill me a witch," he said coolly, then walked off.

Jezibaba's voice chased after him, "It's still two-to-zero, about time you tried!"

Angry as he was, he couldn't help the snort as his gaze landed on Awimak upon reaching the bottom of the stairs. Long legs covered in glossy, undulating black fur drawn up to his chest, he sat cramped in a corner, still holding the broom, only a twig in his oversized claws. Cages and bundles of dried herbs had caught on his horns, some now littering the already messy floor.

IS THIS WHAT HUMANS MEAN BY COSY?

Ryurikov's eyebrows furrowed with amusement. "More or less."

He shifted things away from the demon to give him some room, including what turned out to be a large sack of grains. Dragging it to a different corner left him panting.

"What's your deal, anyway?" he asked, grunting with the effort it took to move an entire cauldron of something away from those giant hooves. Certainly not stew. The indigo contents were pungent and sharp in his nostrils, sloshing over the rim in thick glops. "With the whole dream thing."

I DEVOUR NIGHTMARES.

Ryurikov glanced at him in confusion, kicking an empty bucket into another corner of the room. "Don't you mean 'feed people nightmares'?"

NO. I PROTECT.

Awimak was either lying, or unaware of the difference between protecting and harming. He *was* a demon, after all.

"Are you related to those other spirits?"

Awimak shook his head, knocking down a bird cage. It clanked to the floor, the cage door falling open. The sound of frantic wingbeats carried through the hut.

YOU REFER TO THE QUINARY.

"Sure?" Ryurikov looked around for the source of the noise, but saw nothing.

NOT RELATED.

"Good." Ryurikov let his eyes journey over thick hooves, the muscular legs and dark grey skin. All the way up to those burning eyes. "You...protect people from nightmares?"

Again, Awimak tried to shake his head. Dried herbs fluttered down. *IT IS A BURDEN I WAS CHARGED WITH. BUT I AM TIRED.*

Ryurikov opened the front door, walked back to the broken cage, and kicked it hard. It clanked and rolled out, down the stoop, disappearing into rustling leaves. He hadn't realised the hut was on the move already.

The wild flapping of what had to be an invisible bird zipped past him, and out. He shut the door after it. Jezibaba needn't find out.

"I can relate to that, my friend."

So, Awimak had decided he wanted to feast on good dreams instead. Ryurikov now understood why the demon was after him, specifically. With a slight shake of his head, he meandered to the log table and dropped onto a low stool. Leaning back, he kept his eyes skinned for the hag. What in the hell was she doing up there?

WHAT IS YOUR DEAL? Awimak asked.

Ryurikov's lips twitched up. "What do you mean, friend?"

YOUR EYES.

"Ah." He leaned his forearms across his thighs. "They're—"

LIKE THE MOON.

Ryurikov raised his brows. He hadn't thought of them like that before. "I suppose they are. I'm not overly fond of them, truth be told."

WHY?

"They're..." He shrugged.

Awimak's eyes flickered in the sockets of the deer-like skull. *THEY ARE TRANQUIL.*

"That's one way of looking at it." Ryurikov's smile returned, he couldn't help it.

A scoff, paired with the slap of bare feet on wood, announced Jezibaba's return at last.

"And what have you been up to?" Ryurikov demanded, certain she was devising plans to regain her broom, or another way to kill him. "We need to stop for food." He didn't think he could stomach anything yet, but he hoped to eat eventually.

Jezibaba passed him with a scowl, hobbling to the hearth. "I have food here."

It was Ryurikov's turn to scoff. "I am not eating anything from here. Stop the hut."

"Go out in the garden if you want something to eat!" Jezibaba lowered into the rocking chair. "I don't know what you think this is, but I'm not looking after you, *child*."

"Garden?" asked Ryurikov, flatly.

The witch jerked her head to the kitchenette behind her. Ryurikov made his way to the paned windows, the glass dusty and rippled. Through it, a sizable vegetable patch was visible, and what he presumed to be fruit trees. That made sense. The hag had to survive somehow.

Crashes behind him told Ryurikov the demon was on the move. He didn't even bother to look, Jezibaba's angry screeching said plenty.

"Where is Panellus?" she cried.

"What's that?" Ryurikov asked, now admiring the beautiful skies, dotted with birds and flocked clouds.

"Her cage is *gone*!"

"Oh, the invisible bird? Yeah. It escaped."

"You useless nitwit!" Jezibaba wheezed. "That was a mushroom and it took me months to capture!"

Ryurikov moved down the short hallway to reach the backdoor. He suppressed a chuckle, watching the demon struggle between narrow walls with those broad shoulders, hooves relentlessly sliding across wood boards as he scooted forward.

A warm zephyr greeted Ryurikov when he emerged onto a porch overlooking the garden, an islet held aloft by the boughs of the trees below. If he didn't know any better, he would have thought it to be a pleasant summer morning. Despite the distant creaks of large trees on the move, it was peaceful, bright green birds twittering in a berry thicket just to the right. They didn't seem bothered when he plucked a raspberry from it. He held it up for inspection.

Could Jezibaba spell poison into food, or did she have to touch it?

He would have asked, but something heavy and hard rammed into his back.

Ryurikov flew forward, sent sprawling on stepping stones and scuffing his cheek.

MY APOLOGIES. I WAS STUCK.

Ryurikov groaned. "It's fine."

This was going to be a long and painful trip.

EIGHT

Crunchy, juicy, sweet.

"This is the best damn carrot I've had in ages," said Ryurikov. Awimak looked a touch ominous, lurking in the shade of trees fencing in the garden. The demon had assured him that any food plucked from its soil was safe to consume. Since he had no reason to doubt him, Ryurikov ate as much as his unsettled stomach would allow, which wasn't much.

There was plenty of fresh food, from an assortment of long, violet mulberries to vegetables he didn't even recognise. In the shadiest corners among turquoise and honey-scented flowers, there was a stone hollow housing mushrooms. All edible, according to Awimak. Somewhere around the corner of the hut and out of sight, he thought he heard clucking.

Ryurikov bent low to pluck another carrot from rich soil, giving it a wipe across his thigh before holding it out. "Do you eat?"

YES. I CONSUME DREAMS.

"Right."

"When you're done stealing my vegetables," Jezibaba snapped, standing in the doorway, "mind telling me where it is you expect to go?"

"Wouldn't that have been a question to ask before we started moving?" At the hag's glower, he sighed. "To the nearest town. I need to..."

What, exactly?

Ryurikov couldn't face going home. He could glean news from other places, surely. Besides, hadn't the Quinary told him he needed to take from the wealthy and give to the deserving? Now was as good a time as any to start that nonsense. He might even learn something along the way.

"Care to finish that thought, or has that feeble head of yours purged itself of coherency already?"

There was a moment, only a brief one, where Ryurikov debated asking Awimak to kill her. He had a feeling the demon would do his bidding, within reason. But that wouldn't do. If the hut died with her and they were at least a hundred feet above ground, that would lead to another unpleasant descent.

He had enough of those to last him a lifetime—however long this one might be.

"Listen, you pungent old trout," Ryurikov growled. "I need to go to the nearest town that isn't the log village. Can't have you stealing more children."

Especially if those children were Andrew and his siblings.

"For someone who's tired of slander against the late King and Queen Maksim, you're certainly eager to believe other rumours." Jezibaba padded to the rocking chair in the corner of the back porch and eased herself into it with a tired grunt. "I do not steal *or* eat children."

Ryurikov's lips quirked up in victory. So he'd hit a sore spot. Good. "Tell your hut to head for the nearest town, if you please. I need to stock up on supplies."

Eastcairn.

Its sign had seen better days, and the town itself was worse. What might have once been fine structures of white wood and blue shingled rooftops was now decrepit, in parts burned to nothing but embers still glowing hot.

The heat of smouldering structures and the stench of smoke spiked fear through Ryurikov's chest. He had half a mind to turn back 'round and leave.

ARE YOU WELL?

"Quite well," uttered Ryurikov, casually stepping over the blue stone of what might have been a beautiful arch once.

Bringing Awimak along hadn't felt like a brilliant idea at first. Now, Ryurikov was glad of it. The town remained inhabited, its people going about their day as though nothing was remiss. But he saw the fear in their eyes, and it had nothing to do with the massive demon walking alongside him, he was sure. Ryurikov's lips thinned into a line, apprehension eking its way into his heart. He suspected he knew what lurked behind the damage—the leather of his gloves creaked as he clenched his fists, wishing he had some sort of weapon on him.

He scoured the streets, his gaze skipping from one fretful face to the next as townsfolk rushed by, until he spotted a sign creaking in the dull wind. *Hammer and Hand.* A quaint name for a blacksmith, truly.

Sweltering temperatures stifled the inside, dark and smoky. The door creaked shut behind Ryurikov—Awimak remained outside. He hoped the demon wouldn't run off with Jezibaba's broom.

An impressive array of hand-drawn designs cluttered the walls, pinned by knives and nails. Aside from some chainmail however, there wasn't much else on display. The blacksmith, a barrel chested man with thick leather gloves and apron, sat on a stool in the back, eating what Ryurikov presumed was his lunch. It smelled of fish and—Ryurikov sniffed the air intently—herbs and rice.

"What do you want?" groused the man, barely above fifty years of age, if Ryurikov had to wager. Sunlight filtering in through grimy windows behind him outlined his bald head and wide shoulders.

"Daggers," Ryurikov replied, lazily.

The blacksmith looked at him for a long moment, bushy moustache hiding the scorn that became blatant in his voice. "Smithing weapons for anyone but the Jarl is no longer allowed."

"Shame."

Ryurikov snaked his hand into the pocket of his breeches and fingered the necklace before pulling up. In the forge's low light, the pearls shimmered in invitation, their purple radiant despite the surrounding murk. Heavy eyebrows rose, and so did the burly man. He set his bowl down and approached, the thud of large boots heavy. Dark eyes peered at the pearls, and a broad hand reached for them. Ryurikov snatched the necklace back.

"I'm willing to bet you have a stash somewhere," he said, his voice faintly muffled by the scarf. "Let me take my pick, and the pearls are yours."

The blacksmith straightened up and folded his arms over his chest, thick biceps threatening to rip the rolled-up shirt that revealed a series of intricate tattoos. "Hmph, you seem sure of yourself."

"I see the expert craftsmanship on that chainmail," said Ryurikov. "A man of your talent won't let himself be kept from smithing what he wants."

The bushy moustache moved to reveal a smile. "It *is* fine craftsmanship, isn't it?" He waved his enormous arms, beckoning Ryurikov to follow him. "The Jarl once thought so, too."

The blacksmith stomped the floor behind the counter, and a trap door sprang up, sliding away with a nudge of a foot to reveal a staircase. Ryurikov followed down the creaky steps, into a basement lit by flickering lanterns. The orange flames gleamed against a bounty of blades, proudly displayed along the walls.

"Delightful." Ryurikov made his way to a long dagger, its blade curved, the hilt a masterful design of a skull and ram horns. A bit like Awimak. What harm would it do to flatter a demon? Ryurikov lifted it off the wall, flicked it up and caught it in quick succession. Well balanced, an utter delight to hold.

"A man of refined taste," said the blacksmith.

Ryurikov hummed, and helped himself to another dagger. Shorter, and serrated. For good measure, he reached for a third, a hunting knife, small enough to conceal inside a boot. He tossed the pearls at the blacksmith, who caught the necklace with ease and inspected it with a keen eye.

"Fair?" Ryurikov asked.

The blacksmith shuffled his moustache. "Fair."

If it weren't for smouldering fires and smoke tarring the air, Ryurikov would have been glad to be back outside. Awimak lurked by the door as if standing guard, looking entirely out of place and still, no one paid him any mind.

"Can others see you?" Ryurikov craned his neck to look into burning eyes.

Even though Awimak didn't have a visible mouth, even though there were no signs to indicate it at all, Ryurikov *knew* the demon was smiling, and that it was a sly smile.

THEY CANNOT.

"So, I'm talking to myself as far as others are concerned?" Awimak's chuff was confirmation enough. Ryurikov raked his eyes across the townsfolk again, and sighed. "I don't want to stay here much longer."

THE SKIN CRAWLERS, said Awimak.

Ryurikov rolled his shoulders. "Yes, them."

His gaze snagged on a woman in a simple brown dress and dirty apron, standing by the entrance to a narrow, sunlit alleyway. Her eyes wide, heart-shaped lips parted. She stood eerily motionless, aside from her head, jerking and twitching as though manipulated by strings tied to her head. Ryurikov pursed his lips in disdain.

Fucking Skin Crawlers and their companions.

Lingering would only invite trouble, and so Ryurikov hastened down the road, once more crossing over blue stone to get the blazes out of there.

WE WILL NOT BE GIVING AND TAKING?

"Taking and giving." Ryurikov darted alongside the demon, who barely needed to pick up his pace. "Although I might prefer it the other way around."

He hopped off the road and sprinted into a boscage, somewhat pleasantly surprised to find Jezibaba's hut waiting for them. Rapping his knuckles on one of the colossal trees, he stepped aside as they bowed low and branches again parted.

Jezibaba was where he left her, sitting on the rocking chair by the hearth. Gnarly hands held a pair of needles that Ryurikov was certain were of bone. Whatever she was knitting, it looked like a pile of moss.

"Back so soon?" Lizard eyes briefly flicked up. "And without food, I notice."

"No shops open, couldn't believe it." Ryurikov perched himself on a stool by the table. Awimak had, perhaps wisely, chosen to go around the hut. His gigantic frame shifted past the kitchen windows.

"May have something to do with the Skin Crawlers plaguing the town."

Ryurikov glared at the hag, who wasn't looking at him. "I don't know what you mean."

Jezibaba sneered at her knitting. "You won't even face them? Cowardice runs in the family, clearly."

He looked elsewhere. "Nice try." But he would not be goaded into fixing that problem.

Mostly because it couldn't be fixed. The demons were out, there was no putting them back. He suppressed a sigh and rose to his feet, out the back door before he knew it.

Awimak had returned to his corner in the shade below a tree bearing the first signs of fruit. Apples, possibly. Ryurikov could have pondered why the demon's presence suddenly soothed him, but that meant *thinking*. In particular, about his state of mind, which he preferred to avoid. With a cock of his head in greeting, Ryurikov lowered himself to a patch of grass and leaned back against the tree nearest Awimak.

Faint clucking emerged from between beanstalks supported by bare branches. Ryurikov quirked an eyebrow at a very plump chicken, scratching around the dirt. It had a dizzying pattern of black and white.

"Well, I know what to kill if I get too hungry."

DREAM FOR ME?

"Speaking of food, yes," Ryurikov sighed and waved a dismissive hand. "I suppose I will nap. Nothing too horrific this time, if you please."

Awimak made a most eager sound that Ryurikov didn't especially like.

NINE

Ryurikov convulsed with a startled outcry.

Panting, he stared wide-eyed at beanstalks, the clucks of the chicken—*chickens* nearby. There were two now, the second a deep black, slivers of sunlight highlighting its emerald shimmer.

A sideways glance, and he saw Awimak inhaling the last of whatever pleasant dream he *should* have had. A spine-chilling exhale from the demon, and Ryurikov leaned back against the tree with a trembling breath.

THANK YOU, said Awimak.

"Do you have control over the dreams you give me?" Ryurikov asked, although didn't especially care about the answer when it wouldn't make a difference either way.

NO. YOUR MIND DOES THE WORK FOR ME. Awimak shifted, one hoof sliding out to stretch a massive, muscular leg. *I SHOULD SAY, YOUR CONSCIENCE DOES.*

Ryurikov narrowed his eyes at the bright sky. "I don't like what you're implying."

THE SKIN CRAWLERS.

Burning eyes held a meaningful look. Ryurikov wasn't sure how he knew the look was meaningful. Awimak's eyes were riveting, but emotionless.

He sighed. "Yes, *them*." Then he turned a baleful look at the demon. "I'm not sure how long I can keep this up if..." If his past was going to chase him through his mind like this. "I don't exactly need to be reminded of..." Not *his* sins, per se, but...

Ryurikov released a puff of air, lips vibrating. "You're turning me into a mess." And he didn't *like* admitting that, either. He didn't know why he did admit it. Something about Awimak's lack of judgement made it easier—

WE CAN CONSIDER THE DEAL VOID, IF YOU PREFER.

Awimak's wraith-like snarl was a touch more wraith-like. He shifted to stand, casting a cold shadow as he loomed over Ryurikov, holding out the broom. Ryurikov stared, then the meaning slid into place.

"You *fucke*r," he said in a snarl of his own. He stood and brushed nonexistent dirt off his ass. "Yeah, that figures. You're a demon, after all. The deal is still on. Keep hold of the broom, snap it if Jezibaba steps out of line, and I'll feed you dreams in exchange."

He stomped past the chickens—three now, the third a fox red—and up the porch's steps.

SO ANGRY, HUMAN, ABOUT A DEAL YOU MADE WITH GREAT EAGERNESS.

"Fuck you."

Ryurikov slammed the door shut behind him.

"Lover's quarrel already, *toad spawn*?" Jezibaba's sneer followed him as he stalked through the cluttered hut to the front door, which he kicked open.

"Stop the hut, I've got things to kill!"

"We haven't started moving," said Jezibaba.

"And fuck you too, *beldam*!"

For the third time that day, Ryurikov stepped over the collapsed arch of Eastcairn. The twitching woman was gone as he passed that same alley, moving through the streets, making his way to the largest—and unscathed—building up a slope. The Jarl would likely await him there. Or rather, what was using his skin as a suit. Up a grey bricked path flanked by odd, swirling trees with pink blossoms, the knell of a church bell accompanied his steps. The ocean lined the horizon, smoke dwindling it to a briny haze in the distance.

As Ryurikov approached the lavish edifice, it was less intact than he first thought, its east-wing burnt down to blackened struts, stark against the blue skies above.

Fucking Skin Crawlers.

The large blue door was heavy, its groan loud through an empty foyer. Dark, and warm. He stepped inside, ash kicking up, his footsteps hollow echoes. Sooty windows barely allowed light to pass, still enough to illuminate an abundance of deer antlers adorning the walls and chandelier.

At the top of a long, winding staircase stood a maidservant, motionless but for the jerking of her head.

So there were at least two Clutchers hiding somewhere in this town.

Ryurikov slipped out his long dagger and scowled at its demonic cross-guard before moving to ascend the stairs.

The door slammed shut. Shuffling behind him had Ryurikov spinning 'round. He arched back, dodging a swipe of someone's arm—the woman in the brown dress, movements like a clumsy marionette with loose strings. And she was slow.

He drifted behind her, clapped his hand around the side of her head and rammed the blade into the base of her neck. There was no blood, only the crunch of a severed spine. Dispassionately, he watched the body fall face first to the stone floor. A halo of ash bridled up in curls of grey, the large hole in the back of her skull, through which the Clutchers had liberated her organs, gaping at him.

The maidservant moved down the staircase, the wet crunch of broken ankles grating Ryurikov's ears. He darted up to meet her, footfalls near silent on the chalky blue runner. Within an arm's reach, he jumped up onto the balustrade, back down behind her. His blade punctured the maidservant's spine, and her body crumpled down the stairs in a series of thuds and cracks.

With a sharp flick of his wrist, blood flung off his blade. The maidservant must have been a more recent capture.

Ryurikov proceeded further up. Blue carpets and white walls led him down several hallways into a manifold of rooms, most of them empty. Those that weren't were occupied by more victims of the Clutchers, heads twitching. Some tried to attack, others took no notice. The nest of Clutchers had to be within this very house.

Entering a sizable kitchen, the air pungent with blood, he discovered his suspicions correct. The dark, cloaked forms of Clutchers weren't easy to see behind all the floating viscera. Organs, arranged with anatomical care, held up by pulsating cords protruding from beneath their soaked robes. Steady clicking noises became restless, excited even, at Ryurikov's arrival.

He slipped free the serrated dagger, a blade now in a hand each. He jumped over a bloodied counter, the blades slicing sinew and blood vessels and gore to make way. Guttural clicking and wet slaps of mashing organs followed, the Clutchers moving away from him as a collective.

Stone painted incarnadine was slick underfoot—Ryurikov lunged forward, swiped the blades into the pulsating cords, emancipating the stolen remains. They slopped to the floor. The Clutcher angrily clicked at him, its face hidden in shadow, its raggedy robes dragging through blood as it shuffled forward, fleshy tendrils regrowing, whipping toward him. Ryurikov ducked, narrowly missing one reaching for his forehead.

No thanks. He liked his brain where it was.

A swing upward, but he missed. More tendrils shot toward him. He leaned to the right. To the left. Cut the one making for his guts and hurtled himself forward. The long dagger found its way into the side of the Clutcher's hooded skull.

It dropped with a damp smack. Ryurikov decided not to rid the others of their bounty of organs, instead lunged and sidestepped until he could plunge his blade into their veiled heads. The serrated dagger pulled free damp cloth and soggy hair, human remains slapping to the ground with each Clutcher that died.

The nest of nine were done away with quickly, the floor more slippery still, and Ryurikov's saunter became an awkward dance of flailing limbs. He trod on something bursting under his boot, squirting fluid from either side, nearly sending him down to his ass had he not caught himself on a bloodied countertop.

He emerged from the kitchen drenched in viscera, took a moment to deliberate, then wiped the blades on his breeches before resheathing them. His clothes were beyond saving now, anyway.

Walking along a dark hallway, portraits leered down at him. They all looked related—and unattractive, he didn't fail to notice.

The Jarl had yet to show themselves. Nudging into what turned out to be a storage room of some kind, Ryurikov's ears pricked with a crash. Loud, like a vase meeting its end. It wouldn't be more Clutchers, they only ever gathered in one place as far as he knew.

It had to be the Skin Crawler.

Ryurikov huffed, nerves setting root in his stomach. He'd never actually gone *looking* for one before, they just tended to show up. And he tended to run away from them.

Following blue runners up the main flight of stairs, he took a moment to ponder his reason for being here. To prove some kind of point, probably. Assuage whatever plagued his subconscious, perhaps. Lessen the burden of his deal with Awimak, *possibly*.

His brows furrowed. He stopped halfway to glance at the state of his boots again. Burgundy with blood, strings of gore clinging to the leather.

Killing the Clutchers had been surprisingly fun, but he didn't need to face the Skin Crawler. There was no point in risking himself for... For these people, who were slowly being consumed, their lives ruined as their town turned into another wasteland.

He owed them nothing. This wasn't his fault. Not really.

Well, maybe a *little*.

A long line of black snaked through the runner, down each step toward his feet. Blue flames sprang up around him with a sizzling hiss. Ryurikov's focus snapped to the top of the staircase. His heart flipped backward in terror, then propelled straight out of his ass.

What was left of the Jarl stood there. The four-legged demon had long since outgrown the body. From the middle of the Jarl's face, a bird-like skull protruded. Elongated tibia and femurs had ripped through wrists and ankles, broken human feet and hands outstretched at the sides, eerily, like they waved at him.

"No, thank you." Ryurikov took a cautious step back, then another.

The harrowing demon cocked its head, not unlike a bird, empty sockets watching. Blood dripping from the stretched Jarl turned to embers, raining down with hisses and fluttering smoke, setting all ablaze. Even the stone caught fire, flames burning a deadly blue, flaring as the Skin Crawler screeched, tearing a chill through Ryurikov's spine.

He darted down several steps at a time. Sizzling and rapid snaps of elongated limbs gave chase. Ryurikov vaulted onto the balustrade, narrowly dodged a swing of a scythe-like arm overhead, and jumped.

His fingers closed around the antlers of the chandelier. Its chains rattled as he swung forward—his grip slipped, leather gloves too blood-slick. His feet met the dusty stone flooring with a crack, wrenching free a startled cry. Ryurikov fell back, sibilating in pain.

"*Fuck!*"

The Skin Crawler scrambled down the rest of the stairs, fire trailing, fore and hindlimbs akin to blades of bone. It halted, cocked its head again, and scrabbled forward while Ryurikov crawled away.

He rolled over, narrowly avoiding the lunge of a stalked leg, and hopped up to face the demon with a swing of his arm. The blade of his long dagger plunged deep into a bony elbow. He twisted it, heard a hollow *crack*, and yanked it free to dodge another lunge.

Ryurikov limped, ducking around a slew of embers flung his way. He rounded a corner and hid behind a thick stone archway. Smoke wafted up, and he sucked in a breath, realising his cloak had caught fire. Swift pats to the already ruined fabric sorted that out. Unfortunately, his situation would not be resolved as easily. He should've left when he had the chance. He shouldn't even have come here in the first place. He should've—

Another piercing screech made him clench so hard, he feared the squeak of his ass cheeks would give him away. The Skin Crawler was directly behind the arch where he hid. There were no breaths, only palpitant fire and the clack of bone hitting stone flooring with each slow and deliberate step.

"*Prince Ryurikov,*" it rasped, the sound sharp and oddly distant. Too human. "*Let us in. It won't hurt.*"

He doubted that.

Ryurikov glanced down the hallway. Dark, and there were no exits. He made to edge away, ignoring the throb in his ankle. Sharper hisses were his only warning before a scythe-limb swung in through the archway, catching him in the biceps of his right arm. He cried out as it dug deep, through flesh and bone, jerking him forward. He planted his feet firmly on the ground to resist, to pull free.

His arm split down to the elbow.

The Skin Crawler poked its elongated skull in through the archway, pulsating with pleasure at his ululating cry. Ryurikov ran his dagger into the thin layer of stretched skin across the scythe. Ripped the blade out. Drove it back in. Feverish in his attempt to get free.

It drew him in no matter how wildly he knifed it. Until Ryurikov was tugged forward in full, released, and fell to the floor with a wet smack, the stone freezing under his cheek.

The Skin Crawler shuffled to position itself behind him. The ridged edges of its limbs nudged his back, pushing into the skin as if ready to burrow. Ryurikov's mind flicked to the fact he wouldn't be a much better fit than the Jarl.

His vision swam, the tide of his own blood drenching his face, spattering with each desperate breath whipping past his lips. A sudden gust of wind eased the pressure on his back, its chill biting, followed by a distinct pattering. Chunks of ice pelted him, the wind kicking up a storm of dust, carrying shrill shrieks and clacking of bony limbs.

Ryurikov grunted, fighting to push himself up on the elbow of his good arm. A pair of bare feet slapped down in front of him, toes wiggling with long, blackened nails.

"How you're still alive is anyone's guess, *dimwit*."

He cast Jezibaba a resentful look even as she extended a hand to help him up. Ryurikov accepted, only because he wanted to get the hell out of there. He got as far as to his knees before he swayed. Jezibaba tutted and untied one of the many sashes around her waist.

Thick hooves clopped across stone, followed by the unmistakable sound of horns ramming into the Skin Crawler. Its thin, four-limbed form flew sideways and crashed into the white wall. Ryurikov gasped in pain when Jezibaba jerked his arm, the sash tight and secured around it. He used her bony shoulder to push himself to his feet, turning in full to see Awimak standing among a whirl of ash and hail, broom slotted within the coils of his horns.

Red splatters coated the white wood where the Skin Crawler now twitched on the floor, its limbs flailing as it fought to rise again. Woozy and limping, Ryurikov fled to the large door.

Fuck them all. He was out.

A mere few dashes away from the exit, and another screak echoed through the foyer. Different, *deeper*. Another Skin Crawler skidded to a scraping halt in front of the door, blocking his path. What might have been the Frue stretched over its bony body, long dark hair matted with blood clinging to the curved skull.

Ryurikov swung the serrated blade to stop a lengthy tibia from connecting with his face. He pushed away from it just as a powerful, icy whirl smashed a bottle against its ribbed chest. A plume of orange smoke encased it, gossamer-thin skin bubbling and sizzling and bone corroding.

"Don't get too close," Jezibaba called over the gales, no longer visible in the miasma of smoke and fire.

Ryurikov didn't need telling twice, hobbling to the bottom of the stairs, where he collapsed, too light-headed to remain upright. Awimak fought the other Crawler nearby, his enormous claws around the bony scythes of its forelimbs. He yanked it forward, slammed a hoof against the arced stomach, and *pulled*. Cracks and blood-logged snaps—the forelimbs tore from its body, slung aside with casual ease. The Crawler collapsed to the ground, all its blood spreading like burning oil slick fanned by the hailstorm.

Roaring blue fires surrounded, undulating across the floor and ceiling, whirling up the door where the other Crawler gradually regained itself. Ryurikov's heart hammered, vision spinning, the heat smothering his lungs, scalding his throat. Scars throbbing with the memory of being caught in a similar firestorm, thirteen years ago.

His breaths, already too rapid, turned desperate. The last thing Ryurikov saw were the rolling flames consuming a once white ceiling.

Ten

Lyrical notes of flowing water accompanied the steady trill of a bird. When Ryurikov opened his eyes, it was to a sky of gold and rouge, in part shrouded by dark clouds. The stench of smoke still curled inside his nostrils and with a groan, he sat upright. Blearily, he glanced across the shallow river, a young forest just beyond it, then looked down at his right arm.

Someone had tended to it, and robbed him of his outerwear, bracers, and tunic in the process, leaving him exposed. The patterned sash covering his upper right arm hid the damage, but the pain made him want to weep. He tried moving the limb, and sucked in a sharp breath.

Fucking *ouch*.

"You won't be able to use it for a spell. Might even be a lost cause."

Ryurikov grunted at Jezibaba's grating voice, reaching with his good arm to pull the hood up out of habit. He grunted again when his fingers closed around nothing.

"What did you do with my clothes?" At least she hadn't freed him of his breeches. He almost wished she had, claggy as they were with gore.

There was no answer. She sat on a large rock with her legs crossed, knobbly knees stained with soot, much like the rest of her. Jezibaba jerked her head in the opposite direction, silvery hair shaking loose a beetle, its sheen catching golden sunlight.

Awimak sat on his haunches nearby, and Ryurikov weakly scoffed at the sight. His cloak was wrapped around the demon's horns like a shabby headdress, scarf around the thick neck, and the rest of his clothes rolled in a ball beside furry legs.

THEY DO NOT FIT. Awimak sounded disappointed.

"I'll have that back."

He ignored the pain barbing his body as he limped across river rock to snatch his clothes off the ground. Unfurling them, he examined the fabric in dismay. Even in the waning light, it was clear the linen was ruined. He didn't really want to put any of it back on. Neither did he wish to stand around half naked while the temperature dropped.

A sudden touch to his ribcage made Ryurikov flinch. His hand twitched with the instinct to stop him when Awimak reached out a second time, but he resisted. Strong fingers glided across the scars mantling the entirety of his right side, stretching across his stomach.

Burning eyes flicked up to his chest, and fingers shortly followed, tracing the uneven pattern of further scarring with startling gentleness. Ryurikov flicked his tongue across his lower lip, unsure of the meaning. Compared to him, Awimak was immaculate. No scars, no blemishes. Nothing but smooth grey skin and dark glossy hair reflecting the setting sun. Even his touch was unflawed.

Clawed fingers reached Ryurikov's face, partially marred like the rest of him, and he jerked back in full.

That was enough of *that*.

Swiftly, he pulled the blood-soaked tunic over his head, grimacing at the way it stuck to his skin, cold and damp, and shrugged back into his green surcoat. He unwrapped his scarf from the demon's neck, replaced his belt and bracers, then snapped his fingers at Awimak for his cloak.

The demon abruptly pulled himself up to his full height and hulked over him.

Ryurikov fought the urge to duck away. There was no need for Awimak to speak. They both knew his princely entitlement had taken an inopportune moment to show itself. Rather than shrink, or apologise, he squared himself against the demon, now a beastly shadow against the pink sky.

"My cloak, if you please," he said, holding out his hand.

TAKE IT.

Ryurikov narrowed his eyes, recognising the words for a dare. He glared at the skull. The stench of smoke intensified, and the silence between them stretched. Tense, brimming with challenge.

"It's drenched in blood," he ground out.

YES, said Awimak.

Fucker.

Ryurikov bared his teeth, but did not reach for the cloak. Instead, he stalked back to the river. He was parched.

"What the hell happened?" he grumbled, loud enough for Jezibaba to hear.

"What do you *think* happened, you fool?"

"I don't know, you lumpy salamander, I lost consciousness."

"Fat load of good you were, for something *you* started," Jezibaba quipped behind him. "Why don't you go and see what your imprudent behaviour has accomplished?"

He glared across the river, wiping his mouth with the back of his hand. The cold water did little to ease the burn of what felt a startling amount like shame. Without another word, he hobbled away, to the east. The sky had darkened to a band of glowing orange along the horizon, while the air stung with every inhale, the smoke thick. Pushing branches out of the way, Ryurikov stepped out from a cluster of trees and froze.

Eastcairn was no more.

Every building reduced to ash, charred protrusions of broken pillars still ablaze. There was no sign of life but for the distant screeches of Skin Crawlers.

Twigs crunched under hooves behind him. The cold air drifting off the demon was a sharp counterpoint to the heat that radiated from the demolished town. Ryurikov couldn't bring himself to move yet. He swallowed against the lump in his throat.

"How long was I out for?"

A FEW HOURS.

They had laid waste to an entire town. There was *nothing*. Nothing but glowing earth.

YOUR VISIT AGITATED THEM. Awimak's hot breath ghosted across the back of Ryurikov's neck.

His jaw tensed at the implication. "Are you saying this is my fault?"

THEIR ENTIRE PRESENCE ON THIS PLANE IS YOUR FAULT, IS IT NOT?

Ryurikov whirled to glare at Awimak's chest, then craned his neck. His cloak was still up there, around large horns.

Ignoring the searing pain in his mangled arm, he pounced, scaling the demon and delighting in the way he'd caught him off guard. With a firm grip around a horn and his legs entwining the wide ribcage, he swung his head forward to tug the cloak off using his teeth.

Awimak stepped back with a snort, branches beating Ryurikov across the head, then swung 'round to fling him off. His hold on the demon tightened, teeth clenching around blood-soaked fabric, the metallic tang vulgar on his tongue. Claws bored into his thighs, and he cried out in shock, easing the lock of his legs.

The demon reared back. Ryurikov collapsed across the deer-like skull with a grunt and grit his teeth against the pain in his arm. Then, Awimak thrust forward with such force, Ryurikov lost his grip and hurtled off, flying backward to collide with a trunk.

He crumpled to the ground and wheezed, back throbbing from the impact. The sound of thick hooves trudging through grass disappeared, and he glared up, although could scarcely see any longer. The only light came from the orange glow of what used to be Eastcairn, casting harsh shadows through the forest.

With a wet cough that had spittle clinging to his lips, Ryurikov struggled up to his knees. He grimaced at the taste of metal in his mouth and spat.

"Fucker! We're not done yet. Come back here!"

"Such language."

Ryurikov tilted his head back in defeat. "Go away."

The Quinary didn't go away. They encircled him, looking particularly ghostly as they twitched their spindly fingers with eagerness.

"I fucking tried, alright?" Ryurikov ground out. "I *tried*."

"*You did,*" they agreed in unison.

One of them bent low, gathering handfuls of forest dross.

"*You failed,*" it said.

"*Did your best regardless,*" added another.

Twigs and dried leaves were tossed like confetti at his arm and ankle.

"*Yay for you!*"

Ryurikov glowered. "Well, fuck you very much."

As he lowered his gaze to his ruined arm, now hidden by the tunic, the pain eased. He flexed the limb and tested his leg. They'd healed him in full. It shouldn't surprise him, when they'd brought him back from the grave, *twice*. He still owed Jezibaba for that.

"Why do you keep helping me?" There was a distinct—*suspicious*—shift of their glinting eyes at the question. "Out with it!"

They exchanged another glance, saying nothing, and irritation whisked his chest. Ryurikov opened his mouth to demand answers, but they razzed at him then quickly took off into the darkness.

He sighed. For the first time in so many years, he couldn't evade a sense of defeat. Leaning back against the birch that had broken his fall, he angrily booted dried leaves. For a long while, he sat there, darkness interrupted by smouldering fires creeping ever closer. Another few hours, and they would devour this forest, too.

"Are you going to sit here and simmer until you turn crispy?"

Ryurikov chewed on the foul taste in his mouth. He really ought to drink more, or eat something. Jezibaba's joints popped as she toed his side. Sharp nails dug into him, and he clicked his tongue in annoyance.

"Get up. I'd like to sleep at some point tonight."

He didn't move. Instead, he asked, "What were you to Valka?"

"If she didn't tell you, she didn't want you to know."

Ryurikov shook his head. "If she's even still alive, I doubt she'd care whether you told me a childhood secret."

Jezibaba huffed. "That was exactly the problem with you." When he looked up at her, he could scarcely make out the lumpy silhouette. "You always treated her like a child, never told her the truth, always trying to protect her by lying. What? You didn't think she knew you were keeping things from her?"

He frowned. Valka had always readily accepted anything he told her. "She *was* only a kid."

"Nineteen is young, but she wasn't a child. You should have told her what the consequences would be if she left you to your own devices."

"You assume I knew." Ryurikov looked hard at a forest floor no longer visible.

"You knew what would happen." The acidity returned to Jezibaba's quavering voice.

She wasn't wrong, but Ryurikov wouldn't give her the satisfaction of admitting it. He got to his feet, beginning his stride out of the trees.

"Either way, she didn't have to marry that ponce." At Jezibaba's inquiring hum, he added, "I fucked him fifteen different ways that night. Let me assure you, he was *decidedly* happier that way than he would have been marrying Valka."

And Valka got to adventure like she wanted to, instead of enduring the role of queen.

Awimak had returned to the river, an ominous silhouette against the glimmers of orange. The cloak remained wrapped around his horns, like a symbol of a battle won. Ryurikov said nothing, indignation adding to his sour mood, and simply bent low to drink more. Three slaps on stone nearby, followed by the laborious creaking of trees, suggested Jezibaba had summoned the hut.

As he reentered the dimly lit hut and spotted Awimak's shadow slipping past the paned windows of the kitchen, Ryurikov quelled the need to go out into the garden and continue their tiff.

"Do what you will, I'm going for a bath and then sleep."

"You bathe?" Ryurikov asked. "How?"

She said nothing else, disappearing up the stairs. Trying not to let the state of his clothes get to him, Ryurikov removed the surcoat, leaving him in his bloodied white tunic, and tossed it across a stool before making his way up the stairs. He beelined for the room with the mirror, the door creaking as he shouldered it open. Candles were still lit, yellowed wax dripping off the desk and windowsill. The doves in the stained glass window dozed, heads buried in their wings, and the mirror remained where he'd left it.

He approached, gut churning with the knowledge of what he would see and yet, as Ryurikov gazed at his reflection, it startled him regardless. Streaks of black and splotches of red stained his face, clumped his hair. His eyes were aglow, as they always were at night.

Like the moon.

Eleven

Ryurikov slept entirely without nightmares. The way his sleep ought to be. He woke to a piece of parchment stuck to his cheek. Grimacing, he peeled it off, letting it flutter to the floor as he slumped back in the chair.

Cursing a fair amount at his own reflection the night before, he had eventually given up and settled down by the desk. The clutter held his attention for a while, piles of notes and books, and various sketched portraits. All of children, and Valka.

Her face continued to stare up at him from parchment. Light sifting in through the window splotched it in various shades of emerald and azure. If this was Jezibaba's work, then she had captured his sister's likeness well. It was only a sketch, but the shrewd look in her eyes and freckles were there, the strong set of her jaw and sleek cascade of hair, too.

Ryurikov had known Valka met with someone in the forest back home. He always assumed it was a secret lover. As if *he* of all people would reprimand her for practising sexual freedom while spoken for by a prince she disliked.

With one last glance at the useless mirror, he invited himself to snoop further. Three doors beckoned him to explore by the short

Coil of Boughs

landing, and one led into what was clearly Jezibaba's bedroom.

Since it was currently vacant, he dared to inspect. More plants, and a simple but messy bed in the corner with a troll's hoard of blankets. That was surprising. He expected her to sleep in a nest of children's bones.

He strolled to peer out of the circular window, so large it stretched from floor to ceiling, its framework of branches. It oversaw the garden and had a marvellous view over the forest through which they strode.

Far away from Eastcairn, hopefully.

Movement in his peripheral snagged his attention. Atop a ramshackle wardrobe sat a giant, fat toad, mottled with browns and greens. He grimaced. It wasn't a joyful looking toad.

"You're going to tell her I was in here, aren't you?"

To his horror, the toad sat up on its back legs. It blinked, slowly, making direct eye contact with him as it stroked itself across the rotund belly. *Sensually*.

"Delightful." Ryurikov grabbed one of the many blankets from the bed and hastened out.

Next he opened a door that led up a staircase, which he left alone for now, while the third brought him to a bathing tub. The room was... humble, but it had a hearth nearby, its fire cosy. Fresh cloth lined the wooden tub, filled with clean, steaming water, the scent of mint and rosemary teasing his nose.

An invitation, if ever he saw one.

He stripped in a rush and sank into the tub with an obnoxious groan, the heat easing stiff muscles within moments. Rubbing a wet palm across his aching neck, he couldn't remember the last time he bathed like this.

Well, he could. A few weeks ago, after he'd robbed someone's home blind and helped himself, but that seemed like aeons ago now. So much had occurred between then and now, not least of which, nearly being caught by the enforcers and that hound of a reeve.

Thank goodness for Awimak, or they would still be after him.

Ryurikov extended his legs as far as he could while squatting, and scrubbed himself clean, using a familiar wooden bowl to rinse his hair. He took his time, despite the water turning pink and staining the white lining.

Once he finally emerged, it was with the burgundy blanket wrapped around his shoulders and feeling decidedly more relaxed. Clattering below drew him downstairs. He adjusted the blanket slightly when Jezibaba glared up from where she sat eating at the table. Beside her bowl of porridge there lay his bow and short sword.

"Ah! You shouldn't have," Ryurikov said, gliding over.

As he reached for his trusted bow, a bony claw slammed down on his hand. Their eyes locked in silent challenge. Then, he relaxed his hold on the blanket, and it fluttered to the floor.

Jezibaba released his hand with a look of disgust. Triumphantly, he pulled the bow toward himself and gathered the blanket to wrap around his shoulders once more.

"My clothes are soaking, currently." Not that he had much hope for them. "I'll need to visit the next town once they're dry."

"Pray it doesn't have more Skin Crawlers." Jezibaba turned her attention back to the porridge.

"I'm all out of prayers," he said on his way to the back door.

Awimak was out in the garden, still wearing his cloak around those gigantic horns. The absolute fucker. Ryurikov spent some time gathering raspberries from the bush just by the door with the use of one hand, the other keeping a firm hold on the blanket. Verdant birds fluttered about on the branches, twittering at him as if in protest.

GOOD MORNING.

He rolled his head in the demon's direction. "Fuck you."

Awimak huffed. In amusement, Ryurikov was sure. *STILL ANGRY.*

"Not in the slightest." With a handful of berries, he claimed a spot in the dewy grass by the tree near Awimak and leant against its trunk, blanket now pooling around his hips. He pointedly eyed his cloak, the broom still slotted in the horns, now mostly hidden. "I just didn't peg you for a petty thief."

That earned him a chuckle. At least, he thought it might be a chuckle. It was raspy and honestly, rather terrifying.

COMING FROM A PETTY THIEF.

Ryurikov tossed a berry into his mouth. "I've stolen great and valuable things. Nothing petty about my thievery."

Awimak shifted his head slightly. *HENCE, THE ENFORCERS WERE AFTER YOU.*

A statement that had Ryurikov smirking. "Yes. Thank you for nudging them out of this existence."

I WILL KEEP THE CLOAK, said Awimak, sounding smug, *AS PAYMENT.*

He sighed. "I repeat, fuck you."

IF YOU WOULD LIKE.

Ryurikov's gaze swung toward the demon, seated so casually, a muscular leg outstretched and claws folded across the toned stomach. Awimak still seemed smug, but it was impossible to tell if he was being sincere.

In the end, all Ryurikov could do was puff out a breath. "Later, perhaps."

Enlumine's Wish.

An unusual name for an unusual town, lurking in the oldest part of the Bryum Woods, with trees as wide as they were tall, the canopy so thick daylight had no hope of penetrating. Were it not for the abundance of townsfolk bathing all in a golden glow, the place would have been darker than the devil's asshole.

Circular doors and charming lattice windows affixed the wide trunks, casting patterned light across Ryurikov's path. Shop signs swung in the cool breeze pulling through, sending leaves above aflutter, their whispers ethereal. Its people weren't often seen outside of these woods, in that their light depended on the darkness. Whether they were looking at him or the colossal demon walking beside him, Ryurikov couldn't be sure, but their lantern heads turned with faint squeaks as they passed by.

"Can no one see you, still?" he asked, just loud enough for Awimak to hear.

NONE.

"Being able to see you, does that make me exceptional, or insane?"

PERHAPS A BIT OF BOTH, replied Awimak in amusement.

Ryurikov raised his hand to smack the demon's arm but stopped. There was no need to look mad in front of others. Pausing by a wide, round red door, he fiddled with the scarf hiding the lower part of his face. His clothes were far from tidy, washing them had done very little good and without his cloak, he felt exposed.

"I don't have coin on me," muttered Ryurikov. "Once I've picked something I like, will you cause a distraction so I can get away?"

WHAT WILL YOU PROVIDE IN RETURN?

He struggled for an idea when a broadside caught his gaze, hanging from a branch nearby. With an interested hum, Ryurikov searched the elegant lettering.

"An archery contest," he murmured. "That's right, the Candescent enjoy sharpshooting." Ryurikov rapped his knuckles against the parchment. "How would you like to be entertained in exchange?"

Awimak glanced from broadside to him and back. *I WOULD LIKE.*

"Excellent!" Such good fortune he'd just been given his bow back. Suspiciously convenient, even. "The prize is a lantern and forty crones."

A pittance, truly.

Burrowed into the trunk of a tree, the tailor's shop was surprisingly spacious. If not a touch too dim, the only light source the shopkeeper's head. The Candescent were particular about the quality of their goods, and it showed. Running his fingers along a displayed overcoat, it was clear to Ryurikov that their wool was of the finest quality.

"Good afternoon," trilled the tailor, approaching him with clanking footsteps, feet but blocks of metal.

Ryurikov wasn't sure how he might describe their voice, when it sounded more like a fly buzzing against glass. Since they only had a lantern for a head, the flame within flickering mildly, it wasn't easy to tell where they were looking, either.

"In need of some new attire, are we?" Words brimming with judgement.

He would have responded, but his rebuttal fell away at the sight of a cloak near the counter. Ryurikov beelined for the crossed logs holding the garment up, running his touch down the fabric. Its navy a deep midnight, embellished with walnut brown leather at the front, embossed with a pattern of leaves and branches, the fine details painted gold.

It was perfect *and* came with a surcoat and breeches of armure fabric. A blend of silk and cashmere, he was certain of it. A gasp escaped Ryurikov at a matching pair of boots and equally detailed belt.

"I haven't seen anything this fine since…a long time ago."

"The very finest is all I offer," buzzed the tailor, lingering behind him, "*and* the price reflects it."

Ryurikov gnashed his teeth. Stealing from this asshole would bring him much joy. Awimak crouched just outside. Watching, perhaps, for a signal. Ryurikov collected a tunic of fine white linen and a pair of leather gloves to match with the boots, the tailor but a foot away from him at all times. Then, Ryurikov turned to the demon, and winked.

The solid slab of wood rumbled beneath his feet. The tailor uttered something unintelligible as thick branches swiftly grew upward to ensnare, their squawks of shock drowned out by loud, crackling wood that gradually turned into a solid casing. Ryurikov stepped away and helped himself to the cloak and black breeches, making do with what little light poured past Awimak's massive shoulders.

"Make sure no one comes near," he hissed, stripping and discarding his old clothes to the floor, hastening to dress.

For good measure, he snagged three more tunics before rushing out, past the now imprisoned tailor. His stunning new leather boots were silent as he ran. He eased the hood over his head, his heart pounding in exhilaration. Awimak's heavy footfalls caught up to him, both running to escape down a road enclosed by the wide trees. Not until they took their sixth turn did Ryurikov stop to catch his breath.

He collapsed against a trunk, his chest heaving with strained laughter. Lowering the hood again, he ran fingers through his hair. Awimak stood before him, burning eyes trained on him in askance. Ryurikov cleared his throat and waved a dismissive hand.

"I'm usually alone doing these things."

He couldn't say he hated having an accomplice.

Awimak made an agreeable sound, causing something in Ryurikov's stomach to stir. His gaze flicked back to the deer-like skull, heart still trouncing his ribs.

If his eyes were like the moon, Awimak's were as the sun, burning hot and fulgent with sinister beauty. The demon took a step closer, the air turned ravening. Ryurikov's inhale caught in his chest, hand twitching with a sudden need to reach out, glide his palm across that muscular stomach, rising and falling with breaths as heavy as his own.

A group of Candescent walked by, their chattering an odd buzz, metal feet clacking on pebbles, and Ryurikov straightened up. He raised the hood back over his head and adjusted the scarf around his face. With a muttered pardon, he sauntered past the demon and quietly drifted behind the group.

Their fine overcoats were of silk, gold embroidered embellishments shimmering in their light. Deftly, he flicked out his hand, liberating one of their coin pouches from a thick leather belt, and snaked it under his cloak to hide. He let his eyes roll into the back of his head, the beautiful fabric of his breeches a fantastical glide against the skin of his wrist.

FROM GRAND TO PETTY, said Awimak.

Ryurikov shot him a slick smile. "I need to pay for arrows and the entry fee to the contest, don't I?" He was at the demon's side again, strolling down a narrower street, lined by yet more overspreading trees. "The contest won't be for another few hours. Care to have a drink?"

He didn't wait for an answer, stopping by a wide circular door, this one a vibrant yellow, and extended a hand, bowing to let the demon enter before him into a lively tavern. Brightly lit, what with the many lantern heads inside. There were several other species, including two humans at a table furthest in the back, their heads bowed together.

Feeling far better than he had in ages, Ryurikov held up two gloved fingers at the barkeep upon nearing the counter and perched on a stool. Awimak lowered to his haunches in the nearby corner.

The barkeep was an unusual one, in that they had two beady black eyes bobbing among the red flame inside the lantern. "You can hold your fingers up all day, but unless I know what you want, I can't serve you."

"Ah, right. Two of whatever you recommend," Ryurikov said, swiftly recovering from his embarrassment—Awimak's bemused snort didn't help. Quietly, he muttered, "Fuck you."

"Pardon?" The barkeep's tiny eyes turned within the flame to look at him, their metal frame coming to a squeaky stop.

Ryurikov repressed a cough. "I said, thank you."

"Mm."

Three-fingered metal hands scooted tankards of a glowing drink across the counter toward him. It looked like liquid steel, spills singeing the worn wood.

"And for my next trick," Ryurikov raised his tankard, "my piss will light up a wall after I drink these."

NOT FOR HUMAN CONSUMPTION, Awimak warned and Ryurikov clicked his tongue in annoyance.

"Why the fuck serve me something I can't drink?"

"You asked for my recommendation. I recommend you perish."

Ryurikov jerked his head back in affront. "I beg your pardon?"

"You're here for the contest, aren't you?" asked the beady-eyed fucker, looking bold in their dashing leather vest. "Got to eliminate the competition so my kin stands a good chance."

"This asshole," Ryurikov grumbled in disbelief, glancing at Awimak and jerking his thumb at the barkeep. "Not much of a competition if you eliminate all other competitors."

The barkeep seemed to consider this. "True. Drink up."

"Don't mind Theo," said another droning voice, "they're just like that."

Ryurikov's gaze settled on the approaching Candescent, this one with a much brighter flame and in a dazzling periwinkle dress, glittering like frost in moonlight. A snow-white sash hung loosely around exposed metal bars, the joints to the shoulders silver, complimenting their dark framework.

"And what's your name?" Ryurikov spun in his stool to face them.

They tilted their head back slightly, the eyes within the flame two white dots. "Theo."

"Theo and Theo." Ryurikov pushed the tankard in Nice-Theo's direction. "These are on Mean Theo. Enjoy."

"Thank you, but I prefer to keep a clear head," said Nice Theo. "My kin might not think I'm good enough to compete against *living* competitors, but I am."

"I've no doubt," said Ryurikov. White dots flicked up and down, scrutinising him, and he resisted the need to fiddle with his scarf. "I look forward to competing against you, then."

"Thank you." Those white dots flicked to the side. "I'm told there will be a prodigious audience today."

He followed where Nice Theo had glanced, but saw nothing out of the ordinary. Aside from the two men still in the back, still with their heads bowed together. Were they jerking each other off under that table?

"I do love an audience," he murmured. When he regarded Nice Theo again, they bowed their head, then left. "Huh."

YOU SHOULD BE WARY.

He would not say this out loud, but Ryurikov thought Awimak was right. Something foul was afoot, and he couldn't wait to find out what.

Twelve

Flickering shadows dominated the shooting range, the light of the audience near blinding as they gathered to watch, forming a sea of encased fires. The canopy high above appeared denser still, trunks so wide and tall they resembled towers. What would happen should the Candescent lose their heads? Everything would surely light up like a witch burning gone afoul.

Ryurikov adjusted the straps to his new quiver, gaze fixed on the wide array of targets several yards down the range and, more importantly, the prize. It stood atop a tree-shaped pedestal off to the left, a pouch of coin resting below a floating lantern, its design intricate even from such a distance.

Six other contestants stood in line with him, each keeping to their own hay bales—why was everything highly flammable here? It did not escape Ryurikov's notice that the two men he'd seen at the tavern were taking part. Nice Theo stood to his left, and he gave them a courteous nod.

"That's a lovely bow," said Theo, flexing the string to theirs. "Yew?"

"Of course." He fidgeted with his bracers and tried not to let Awimak's heavy breathing behind him perturb. He was no longer accustomed to being around this many people, and this was not a good time to feel flits of nervousness. "We've been friends for many years, this bow and I."

Theo's own appeared to be made of silver, its shine elegant in the washes of orange and yellow. An interesting choice for a competition, to be certain. He wouldn't have thought it to offer much flexibility.

The overseeing Candescent's flame flickered indigo nearby, and the first contestant on the far right steadied themselves. Ryurikov couldn't recognise the wood of their bow, but it was dark, beautiful.

"One chance, one arrow!" buzzed the overseer loudly.

The archer hit the sack target without hitting gold.

The other three were better. In particular, one of the men, whose face remained hidden beneath a black cowl. Taking his turn, Ryurikov aimed up to a shrouded sky and flexed his bowstring thrice, then took his stance. A quick inhale, and he let his arrow fly.

Dead-centre, and delight jolted his heart.

IMPRESSIVE, said Awimak in the brief pause it took for the audience to start a racket of clanking metal.

Theo's turn, and they were on target too, dead-on. At least there was *some* competition. It would have been painfully dull, otherwise. The audience settled down, and the overseer's flame changed to purple.

"One chance!"

The furthest contestant to the right took aim again and the sack target hopped back several paces on its own accord. The man's arrow grazed the edges of the target face, hitting the wall beyond. Ryurikov refrained from laughing, *barely*.

The targets became unpredictable. One sack sidestepped, the other back flipped. Ryurikov's mind raced as he watched the mysterious man's target pivot on the spot. His arrow hit the face, but only just.

Slowly, Ryurikov drew two arrows, held one in reserve, and fired the first. The moment his target lunged forward, he let the second arrow fly, and hit gold. He tried, and failed, not to let smugness blanket him. They'd said only one chance and one arrow the first time, but omitted the mention of arrows this time.

CLEVER, rasped Awimak behind him.

"Yes," Ryurikov murmured, sparing little thought to the blossoming sense of satisfaction Awimak's approval brought. He didn't disagree, of course, knowing damned well he was clever. It had been such a long time since he partook in anything of this sort, however, and it was a relief to find he hadn't gotten rusty.

Unfortunately, he'd now given Theo an advantage, and they took it. His heart lurched in a beat when Theo missed gold by a coin's width as their target flailed about.

The targets dismissed themselves, hurtling backward and over the short wood wall into the audience. In their stead, small flames erupted from the canopy overhead. They lowered to float, disembodied, some feet above the range, closely pursued by moths. Ryurikov squinted to better see.

The flames had eyes. They danced about in the air, and he was certain he could hear squeals of delight.

"Are those Candescent babes?" he asked no one in particular.

"They are." Theo waved at them with their three-fingered hand.

"Never thought I'd use children as target practice."

Theo's chuckle was reminiscent of someone rapping a knuckle on glass. "Assuming you'll be able to hit them."

Ryurikov couldn't resist casting a glance over his shoulder at Awimak, a goliath among everything else. The demon inclined his head. Ryurikov cocked his in turn, the smile tugging at the corner of his mouth confident.

"Two chances, three arrows!"

The overseer's flame had turned violet, and the first contestant made an attempt, then another—the flamelets spun in mad whirls of unpredictability with cheery squeaks, both arrows missing entirely. They were *fast*, flitting from one spot to the next. None of the other contestants had much success, either.

Ryurikov aimed his bow up, pulled at the bowstring thrice. Within a split second he drew and fired one arrow, instantly followed with two at once. The first arrow missed. The others hit the wispy tail ends of two speeding flamelets. There came an uproar, deafening in its intensity, and Ryurikov didn't know whether it was anger or amazement.

Theo regarded him, bright flame flickering. "You've made yourself unpopular."

He extended his arms on either side in confusion, but couldn't utter a rebuttal when Theo took their turn, and hit one by miming his technique. Ryurikov smirked as another uproar followed, sounding equally unhappy. When he turned to look at Awimak again, the demon simply shrugged. A big, one-shouldered shrug. He still had the stolen tunics tucked into the cloth around his hips. Hopefully, Awimak wouldn't keep them.

"One arrow!"

The overseer's flame turned blue, as did the many flamelets. They picked up speed, moved as one, swivelling in a large circle until it became a ring of fire, singeing moths now struggling to stay afloat, turning to embers. Ryurikov side-eyed the furthest contestant, curious to see what the meaning of it was, and froze.

All contestants—including Theo, he was sure—had their aim on him. The man in the black cowl sneered, visible beyond the shadow cast across his bearded face.

Ryurikov's heart gave a great thud with recognition of his long-time Keeper.

"Well, fuck," he breathed, raising both hands as the reeve drew near. "What an unfortunate delight to see you again, Vasili."

Vasili yanked Ryurikov's bow out of his grasp.

"What, not even a 'good afternoon'?"

"Shut,"—Vasili snatched his wrists in a tense grip—"the *fuck*,"—twisted Ryurikov's arms behind him, wrenching free a pained grunt—"up."

As suspected, Theo too had their bow and arrow trained on him. Ryurikov's gaze momentarily snapped to Awimak, who only watched in stolid silence. He was unlikely to bail him out of this unless he traded for something else, and Ryurikov was all out of things to trade.

Fuck.

Vasili tied his wrists in swift movements. Ryurikov grunted again, the rope digging into his skin, his folded arms fastened painfully against his back.

"You were supposed to be the nice one," he slung at Theo as Vasili shoved him forward, away from the range and down a darkened alleyway.

Fuck, *fuck*.

They entered a tree, its round blue door shutting behind them with a bang. Ryurikov glowered at his murky surroundings, fully aware he and Vasili were the only two inside. An office of sorts, with only one narrow lantern suspended from the ceiling and no windows. In the back, the cold steel bars of a jail cell glinted with the threat of immurement.

A hand came down hard between his shoulder blades, pushing him further inside. His boots scuffed across growth-rings, and soon he was spun back 'round to face Vasili and the full brunt of his bitter anger.

The man slung Ryurikov's bow across the room onto the desk nearby, before rough fingers jerked the hood off and shoved the scarf down to reveal his face. Instinctively, Ryurikov moved to get his head out of the grasp trapping his chin, but it was firm and tilted his head from side to side.

Vasili scoffed in disdain. "Look at you. Scarred. Soulless eyes. Can't even grow a proper beard." Words that dripped with a venom cultivated by years of jealousy. "Dead King and Queen. Princess lost to the dragon. *You've* turned to theft and murder. How the majestic have crumpled. *Pitiful*."

Those same rough fingers clamped around his face, squeezing hard enough to pucker Ryurikov's lips, and shoved him away. He stumbled back, ass colliding with the corner of a desk. *Ouch*.

"Says the guy who's still not over being denied," Ryurikov ground out. "Wait—lost to the dragon? What the fuck are you on about?"

He whirled on Vasili, now rounding the desk and lowering the hood of his cowl. A once lean face had squared out, as had the shoulders, his tawny hair dusted with grey. Vasili was the image of strength, the sword he pointedly sheathed at his side suggesting years of practice with it had helped turn his frame into the robust shape it now presented. Ryurikov was toned himself, but he was lean. While his shoulders too were broad, Vasili held a certain power in his that was... *Well*. Had things not ended so poorly between them, he might have considered taking him up on his proposal made so long ago.

"Get over yourself, *Ruri*," Vasili spat.

"I would, but it occurs to me that you've been chasing me for months." Ryurikov laughed, loud and mockingly, even threw his head back for effect. "It took some elaborate ruse of a contest to get anywhere near me."

Vasili slammed his fist down on the desk, sending ink bottles rattling. "You butchered thirteen of my men in the Unbroken Wilds!"

Ryurikov paused. He'd killed a few of them, sure, but not in the forest and 'butcher' was a strong word. Sliced their throats while asleep in a barn would have been more accurate.

"Oh. Yes, those. Wish I could take credit, but that wasn't my handiwork."

"Whose, then?"

"Those woods are full of demons, you know. As it happens," Ryurikov continued, taking a step to the side, *hoping*, "I'm friends with one. Awimak ring a bell?"

The colour in Vasili's face turned ghostly.

"That's right. I excel at summoning demons, as you might recall," said Ryurikov.

"That wasn't you."

He forced his smile into something more menacing. "Wasn't it? What, you think they knew how to find their way into the castle all on their own?"

Vasili growled low in his throat, then lunged. Across the desk, knocking parchment and bottles to the floor. Gloved hands grappled for Ryurikov, who jerked to the side, and Vasili fell. A long leg swept across the ground, the boot-clad foot hooking around Ryurikov's ankle and pulling his feet out from under him. He fell to his back with a cry, pain hurtling along his arms where they remained tied behind his back. He planted his feet on the ground, intent on swinging himself up. Vasili clambered atop him, straddling his stomach and pressing a hand down on his throat, clenching hard.

"I'm the one who saved you!" Vasili snarled, spittle flying from his mouth and face an ugly twist of hatred. Ryurikov stared into brown eyes, bright with rage, as he gagged against the clenching grip. "I'm the one who pulled you out of that consuming fire. You're alive because of me! All I ever did was save you!"

He opened his mouth to retort, only to make an unattractive noise. The hold eased, *slightly*. Ryurikov rasped around a quivering inhale. He scraped his gaze over Vasili's face, down his neck, where hints of scarring peered from above the silver embellished collar of his crimson overcoat.

They were burn scars.

He swallowed hard. "Should've left me to burn."

"I should have," Vasili agreed. "I should have left you to the demons instead of caring for you. You wept like an infant day in and day out, refusing to eat. You've been the bane of my existence since the day I was sworn to you!" Then his hold slackened entirely, becoming tender. A thumb stroked along Ryurikov's scarred cheek, the rage in those eyes morphing into sorrow. "But I couldn't leave you. I've *loved* you for so long."

Ryurikov winced. His arms throbbed under him, he wanted to move. Unfortunately, Vasili had become enamoured with his mouth, that thumb pushing past his lips. He resisted the urge to bite down, even as Vasili leaned in, hot breath swiping his face.

"We've come full circle," Ryurikov said, his tongue curling around the taste of leather. "Angry I never fucked you, even after you saved my hide. Well, *part* of it."

The fist that connected with his cheekbone was expected, but it hurt all the same.

Ryurikov shook his head, clearing his vision of black dots as Vasili hoisted off him. Fucking hell, that brute packed a wallop. Said brute moved to the desk, straightened things out, and pulled a piece of long parchment up to his face, taking a moment to scan it. Ryurikov sat up with a groan, swaying slightly.

"Prince Leonid Ryurikov Maksim, I'm placing you under arrest for the crimes of theft, adultery, and murder." Vasili's tone had an icy bite, his expression equally chilly. "The latter two are punishable by *death*."

Ryurikov's lips flapped as he pushed a breath past them. "If you want to scare me, try threatening me with something I haven't done twice already."

"Then maybe the third time will stick."

Vasili descended upon him and snatched him up by the cloak, hoisting him to his feet.

"Watch the cloak!" Ryurikov snarled. He'd *just* stolen it, damn it.

Vasili pushed him toward the holding cell and Ryurikov's mind leapt to Awimak, wondering why the demon wasn't here yet. Were his dreams no longer valuable?

Rather than force him into the cell however, Vasili spun him back around and thrust Ryurikov up against the bars. A hand clamped down on his throat again, thumb pressing hard against his pulse.

"Tell me you were lying." A snarled hiss so close to his face, smoke stormed Ryurikov's nostrils. "Tell me you didn't summon those demons. Tell me I didn't save the man responsible for what will be the very ruin of Vale!"

He jerked his head out of the firm grip and glared into umber eyes, mouth twisting around a riposte. Memories of an angry king's face flickered like a flame in his mind. Ryurikov heard his own laughter, and jeering. He swallowed, unable to respond, and that hand around his throat slackened.

Lips crashed against his mouth, so hard it hurt. Vasili must have taken his silence as denial, and Ryurikov's mind spun when a thigh wedged itself between both of his. He grunted in protest as the thigh snapped up against his groin, refusing to open his mouth to a tongue lashing his lips. Cold steel bars dug into his arms, Vasili's broad frame pinning him against them. Fingers twisted into his hair and yanked hard.

"*Fuck off*," Ryurikov ground out, wrenching his head free and wincing at the throb in his scalp. "I'm *not* into power imbalances."

The man scoffed. "You've always been a liar."

Ryurikov squared against him—as best he could, anyway, tied up with a thigh still rammed against his cock. "Think about it. Take a fucking moment and *think* about who I took to bed." He left the 'you brutish dumbass' out of it, for now. Once realisation flitted across Vasili's face, he had to refrain from smirking, in addition.

"My knighthood—"

"Would've been taken from you." Ryurikov wished that thigh crushing his balls would move already. "More than anything, you were my friend, and I didn't want to hurt you."

That was a lie. He had never appreciated Vasili's devotion to him, it had always bordered on *too much*.

The hold on him eased somewhat, and the thigh moved out from between his legs. For a moment, Vasili looked to be questioning everything he knew.

"For all those years," he croaked. "I've wanted you. More than that though, I *hated* you." Those umber eyes turned back to him, so bright Ryurikov feared the brute might weep.

"It's fine, we all move on at our own pace—"

A fist slammed into his temple. He crashed to the floor, given no time to recover as hands unfastened his belt, yanked open his coat and grabbed the waistband of his breeches. Ryurikov kicked, a cry of outrage pelting dully against the tree's interior. His knee connected with Vasili's hips, but did little to stop the man from tugging at his clothes, tearing fabric.

"*I'm not into it!*" Ryurikov bellowed.

A loud bang, followed by crashes, and the looming silhouette of a demon descended upon them within the tight space. Awimak's eyes were a firestorm, scorching red, his curled horns scraping the ceiling, leaving grooves. His great claw muffled Vasili's scream, coming down around the whole of his face, yanking him up. Slinging him around like dirty laundry in the wind. Vasili's body slammed into the ceiling, the floor, the sound of bones breaking unmistakable.

"Awimak, NO!" Ryurikov cried when the demon raised a giant hoof over Vasili's head, readying to crush it. He forced himself to sit upright, chest heaving with breaths that didn't reach his lungs. "Don't kill him."

Awimak's eyes blazed still, turning to him. *WHY?*

"Because he saved my life, more than once. I owe him."

HE WILL NOT STOP COMING FOR YOU.

Ryurikov faltered. "You could have…phrased that better." Awimak had a point though. Vasili would not forget this, now he'd witnessed that he was in cahoots with demons. "I'll kill him if he comes after me again. Right now though, it's a life for a life."

Awimak snorted out his displeasure, but lowered his leg and crouched low by Ryurikov. With one quick swipe of his claws, Ryurikov's arms fell loose at his sides. He flexed the pain out of them and glanced at Vasili. Motionless, but the rise and fall of his chest was there.

"Let's get the fuck out of here." He didn't complain as Awimak helped him to his feet. He steadied himself with a hand on a smooth shoulder, adjusting his clothes to right himself. "That fucker ripped something." He heaved a sigh. "What do I owe you for saving me?"

NOTHING.

Ryurikov cast the demon a look. His eyes were no longer conflagrations. He squeezed the firm shoulder, then stepped over the unconscious body to collect his bow.

THEY ARE OUTSIDE, WAITING.

"They?" Ryurikov checked the bow for damage and frowned at an ink spill slathered across its honey-coloured wood.

THE ONES WHO TRICKED YOU.

Wiping the ink on Vasili's coat, he turned back to the crouching Awimak. "See, I don't think I was tricked by them."

NO?

"This was a set-up alright, and I bet you can guess who the conceiver of this plan was."

Thirteen

Ryurikov's anger smouldered deep in the pits of his chest as he watched Awimak vanish through the door without opening it. He cast Vasili a final look, certain the demon was right, that he was making a mistake. Unfortunately, he owed the brute. For more than just saving his life, and nursing him back to health, apparently. Ryurikov frowned. He scarcely remembered any of that.

Rolling his shoulders against any lingering feelings, he nocked an arrow and waited for the signal.

Screams of terror bounced against the door from the other side. He yanked it open and ran out to witness Awimak ram a claw into the chest of an enforcer. He slung them aside, a wide arc of blood raining down around his great form.

It was dark, most of the Candescent must have fled, save for two wearing that same gaudy yellow and crimson distinctive to the enforcers. With their attention on the demon, Ryurikov sent his arrows at the remaining humans further down the shadowy road, hitting one in the temple, the other between the eyes, and the third in the throat.

He darted to Awimak, shooting another arrow to thwart one incoming—from one of the Candescent. It splintered and dropped limply to the ground.

THANK YOU. Awimak dashed forward and snatched the nearest lantern head up to slam them into a tree. Glass shattered, the metal crushed, and they collapsed into a lifeless heap.

"My pleasure." Ryurikov aimed at the remaining Candescent, who wisely hesitated with nowhere to run or hide. "The competition, is it still going?"

"Ye–Yes." They lowered their bow and took a step back, pebbles crunching under metal clogs.

"Excellent."

Ryurikov's arrow cut through the air, piercing glass and the deep orange flame within. It sputtered, then went out, the Candescent's body falling to the ground with a loud *thunk*. He approached the scrap metal, helping himself to the rest of their arrows, slipping them into his quiver.

Whistling behind him. Ryurikov spun in a whirl of his midnight cloak. Narrowly avoided being hit, an arrow piercing ground just by his foot. Awimak appeared beside him and placed a large claw on Ryurikov's shoulder.

In a wink they were somewhere else—or maybe still in Enlumine's Wish. The trees were there and their quaint houses within. Yet everything appeared more ghostly, shadows tinged with yellow, as if they were back beneath the forest. Sounds became clearer, even distant ones. He heard conversations, hundreds of them at once, yet none overlapped, every word as clear as the twitter of a robin.

"Where are we?" he queried while Awimak moved him out of the way of another incoming arrow. It seemed to be moving more slowly, as though pulled back by the drag of a heavy wind.

And then with equal swiftness, they were back in the real Enlumine's Wish, the slowed arrow speeding up and missing them by several paces.

"Fascinating." Ryurikov took aim at the archer who had been hiding behind a thick tree.

They ducked away with a startled yelp, everything else gone silent. Ryurikov waited. When a glimmer of their sweaty forehead appeared, he shot them down, steel effortlessly boring into bone. The thud of the archer's body followed.

"Dear Awimak," said Ryurikov, "would you mind if we crashed the competition? I feel I would have won that, and I'd like my prize."

FURTHER ENTERTAINMENT, YES.

With a running start, Ryurikov scaled the goliath's side. He secured his left leg around the front of one horn and steadied the right knee on a powerful shoulder, his thighs astride Awimak's head. A massive claw wrapped around his shin in response. He thought Awimak might fling him off and braced himself, but there came only a gentle, nigh comforting squeeze before Awimak sprinted forward.

Ryurikov had ridden many horses as a sport, even untamed stallions. This was *nothing* like riding a horse. It was smooth and eerie as they slipped in and out of the bizarre, shadowy version of the town.

They emerged onto the range, and he left nothing to chance, shooting anything that moved. His arrows lingered in the air as if frozen, until he and Awimak winked back out of the shadows, the arrows downing unsuspecting contestants, the overseer, stray enforcers. Ryurikov took a second to relish in Theo's shock at the sudden appearance of such a colossal demon galloping at them.

"Fuck you, Shitty Theo!" he shouted over the heavy thuds across packed earth.

He hit Theo in the top of their head, the *twhack* audible even over the clangour of the audience scrambling fleeing the grandstands.

Ryurikov scanned the seats for Worse Theo, spotting them vaulting over the short wall to reach Shitty Theo, now down on their metal ass—alive still. His focus shifted to Awimak, who grabbed the floating lantern off its tree-like stand, along with the pouch of coin. He tossed it up. Ryurikov snatched it out of the air, just as more yellow and crimson flooded the range, chain mail rattling, swords glinting in the ever dwindling light.

"Let's get out of here," he said, patting Awimak's skull. "But I want that silver bow!"

Hissed whistles from every direction forced Awimak to weave. Ryurikov grabbed hold of his horn and tipped himself sideways, twisting out of the swing of blood-starved blades. He reached far enough to hurt, snatching the bow right out of Shitty Theo's hands. He slung it over Awimak's horn and put a turn in his hips to dispatch two enforcers firing longbows behind them. There was something exceptionally satisfying about the clang of his arrows hitting their lanterns, about watching their fires extinguish in a glittery puff of smoke.

Trees flitted by, only umbrageous blurs. They had to be journeying between worlds when running past others didn't alert them. All the same, Ryurikov ducked when they reached boughs trained to form an arch, its welcome sign grazing the top of his hood.

The canopy above gradually opened, revealing lilac skies. Awimak slowed, muscular chest heaving and breath more sepulchral than a midnight wind.

Ryurikov glanced behind them. They weren't being chased, and were far enough for him to walk on his own. Readying to dismount, his hand connected with something below Awimak's horn.

He did a double take, fondling the small, soft protrusion. Pushing away glossy strands of the dark mane, two furry ears revealed themselves to him. Ram's ears. He grinned in utter delight.

"You have ears!"

WHAT OF IT? Awimak sounded a touch defensive.

Ryurikov chuckled, swinging his leg over the horn to dismount, his landing nigh soundless. He rapped his knuckles against the demon's bark-armoured forearm. "They're precious."

A snort was the response. As tempting as it was to tease, he focused on their prize, bobbing in the air between them as they walked side by side. In the bedimmed sky and the lantern's ghostly glow, its metal showcased iridescence-like mist catching sunlight in a gamut of colours.

"Mind handing me the bow?" Ryurikov asked, a rumbling noise of satisfaction vibrating his chest when Awimak silently unhooked it from his horn and handed it over. He closed his fingers around the silver bow, giving the silk string a few tugs. "I've never wielded a silver bow. It's surprisingly flexible. Reckon we can kill a dragon with this?"

He knew little about dragons.

YOU REFER TO WHAT THE REEVE CLAIMED.

"Yes, that," Ryurikov said. "Knowing Valka, she probably made it her pet, but...just in case. Don't suppose you know anything about it?"

A strange noise left Awimak. It took Ryurikov a moment to realise it was a contemplative hum.

I KNOW OF THE DRAGONS THAT EXIST. THERE ARE MANY. His deer-like skull turned toward him, and Ryurikov allowed himself to appreciate the intricate carvings within the bone. *IT MAY BE A WILD GOOSE CHASE.*

"Well then, it's a good thing I'm hungry enough to catch fowl." Famished, in fact. "I should eat something before we kill Jezibaba."

ARE YOU CERTAIN?

"Can't murder on an empty stomach."

Awimak huffed. *ARE YOU CERTAIN YOU WISH TO KILL THE WITCH? THE CONSEQUENCES MAY NOT BE WHAT YOU EXPECT.*

Ryurikov rolled his head to flex his stiff neck. "They never are, my friend."

As if in answer to a prayer he hadn't considered, a man dragging a tumbrel emerged from the shadows that had befallen the forest path. He looked worse for wear, the hems of his white robes stained, sandal-clad feet slipping over pebbles and dirt. The man looked up, and since there was no scream of terror, Ryurikov assumed he couldn't see Awimak.

"Evening," he said, rounding the tumbrel to peer at its contents. "By chance, is that food you're peddling?"

"Ah, yes," panted the balding man, easing his hold on the cart to wipe a sleeve over his damp forehead. "I am spreading the word of Miathos with food and drink."

"The snowmoth girl," Ryurikov murmured, edging closer to the tumbrel and slinging both his bows onto his back.

"*Saint!*"

Ryurikov quirked an eyebrow. "Sure, but seeing as moths ate her alive at the tender age of nine, I rather think she was an unfortunate *girl* above anything else."

The monk spluttered, face practically glowing red, while Ryurikov snaked a hand toward the goods. Then he stopped himself. He cast a quick look around, expecting to see the Quinary lurking behind trees, ready to scold him or break his fingers. There was no sign of them, but he was sure they were watching, regardless.

"Can I offer you some coin for food and drink?"

That appeared to mollify. "Ah, no thank you. I'm not supposed to accept—but I can't *afford* to do all these things without—but, I cannot —"

"Just take some coin." Ryurikov flicked two crones, aiming for the monk's shiny head and somewhat disappointed he caught them. "I'll help myself. Fair?"

"Yes–fa-fair."

He rummaged through sacks, pulling out a sizeable chunk of smoked meat, a loaf of bread, and wrapped an arm around a rundlet. At Awimak's inquisitive gaze, he shrugged. "I'm thirsty."

Still gaping at the two gold, profile-shaped coins in his open palm, the monk spluttered, "I–Take more! All that you want!"

"This'll do," said Ryurikov. "If I were you, I wouldn't go into Enlumine's Wish right now. I hear there's a demon running around."

The man's expression became horrified. "Then I must go there, at once! Save those poor souls!"

And he was off, hoisting the tumbrel back up with strained grunts.

Ryurikov absentmindedly released the rundlet when Awimak pulled it out from under his arm. "He puts a lot of faith in a dead kid."

A FAITH WELL PLACED IF IT ALLOWS HIM TO BE BRAVE.

The look Ryurikov gave him was one of incredulity. "Or he could find his spine on his own."

Veering off path into the forest closely followed by the lantern, he ignored the way Awimak watched him while he devoured half the bread and motioned for the drink. He pried out the stopper and tipped it to his lips, taking large gulps of what turned out to be wine. An odd, savoury wine. Not especially refreshing, but it would have to do.

Ryurikov gulped several mouthfuls and released a bellowing burp, handing the rundlet back. "Help yourself."

YOU ARE MOST ENCHANTING, said Awimak.

The jibe made him smirk. "My apologies, did that offend your adorable little ears?"

Once far enough into the forest, Ryurikov lowered behind the thick roots of an old tree and leaned back against its mossy trunk. Using his teeth, he nipped off the gloves, laid them across a thigh, and picked at the smoked beef.

ARE YOU WELL?

He straightened up his slouching shoulders, but didn't raise his eyes. "I'm fine. Vasili has always been a bit much."

I WOULD CONSIDER THAT MORE THAN A BIT MUCH.

Ryurikov's gaze flicked up. Awimak stood before him and if he didn't know any better, he would have thought him to be standing guard.

"At age seven, he was sworn to be my Keeper the day I was born. It was his duty to be by my side at every turn, to protect me no matter the cost. I guess he took the title too literally." When Awimak said nothing, Ryurikov shrugged. "I always took him for granted, even ridiculed him behind his back, and I'm sure he knew about it." He toyed with the smoked meat, hunger waning. "Still, no matter what my dad did to me, Vasili was always there to help me up." Ryurikov scoffed with a roll of his eyes. "Once, he even put everything on the line for me by standing up to my father—his *king*—when Dad's *lessons* went too far."

He grimaced at the foul taste in his mouth, little to do with the mix of savoury drink and smoky beef. The sick, wet sounds of a whip tearing skin from bone echoed in the outskirts of his mind.

Awimak's hooves kicked up tree-wilt as he stepped closer. *THAT DOES NOT ENTITLE HIM TO YOU.*

"You don't have to tell me. I told him several times I wasn't interested. Thought he'd get over it, eventually." He shrugged again. "Suppose he never did."

With a sigh, Ryurikov kicked out a leg. "In any case, Vasili doesn't concern me. Jezibaba has tried to kill me for the last time."

WHAT WILL YOU DO?

He nodded at Awimak. "The broom. What will happen if I break it?"

Awimak moved closer, lowering to sit right beside him. The roots curled around them were like a crescent, there was plenty of space, yet that powerful leg was so close to Ryurikov's, its terrene chill drifted through his breeches. That strange something was back in his stomach, stirring restlessly.

HER POWER IS TIED TO IT IN SOME FORM, said Awimak eventually.

Yes, he'd gathered that. "Will we kill her if I break it?"

I DO NOT KNOW. Awimak's leg shifted, and their thighs touched. *THE ENCHANTRESS IS POWERFUL. IT MAY BE WISER TO LEAVE IT ALONE, PRETEND YOU SUSPECT NOTHING.*

It was becoming increasingly difficult to concentrate when Ryurikov's heart decided now was a great time to misbehave, flailing worse than a disobedient broodmare. He tensed his jaw and dug his fingers into the slab of meat.

"I'm not afraid of the hag."

Awimak chuffed. *YOUR SPINE IS TIED DIRECTLY TO YOUR OBSTINACY.*

"There are worse traits to have."

Obstinate and courageous, at least one of those he considered true. Gritting his teeth against the peculiar flitting in his stomach, Ryurikov discarded the food to the ground. When he faced Awimak, those sun-like eyes were already set on him. A claw moved forward, large enough to crush his head, nails sharp enough to drive into a man's chest and kill him. As the demon reached for his face, pushed the hood down, and fingers ghosted across his cheek, it was gentle. Considerate of his bruising, *tender*.

I CANNOT HEAL. The wraith-like snarl seemed softer.

Ryurikov dragged his tongue over his lower lip, and those burning eyes flared, tracking the movement with precision. It spiked his heart rate into chaos. "It's–It's fine."

His own fingers touched something soft. It occurred to Ryurikov he'd just settled his hand on Awimak's knee. The dark fur so silky, he couldn't help but run his touch through it. His throat clicked with a sharp swallow.

"Awimak."

YES, RYURIKOV?

Whatever he had wanted to say fled his mind so abruptly it left him speechless. He floundered for far too long, and he shook his head, away from Awimak's tender claw. Ryurikov got to his feet, replacing his gloves without looking at the demon.

"I'm going to kill me a witch now."

Fourteen

The hut was as they left it, the quiet creaking of trees and wind ominous as Awimak's snarled warning echoed in his head.

Wiser to pretend he suspected nothing.

It probably was, but Ryurikov did *not* shy from danger. The trees bent low, the verdant crown parting to make way. He strolled in, Awimak close behind, and paused by the door. He closed his eyes, counted to ten, then pushed inside the hut.

A few candles lit up the interior, now accompanied by the spectral glow of the lantern floating in after him. A spot of light outside swung in through the paned windows of the kitchenette, Jezibaba's outline hunkered over it.

"Meet you in the garden," Ryurikov murmured as blazing exhales whisked the back of him. Only when he heard Awimak shift around the hut did he move further inside to open the back door.

Green birds were silent, the scent of honey particularly strong. Awimak had rounded the corner, his breath misting before him, orange in the glow of his eyes. Jezibaba held up a lantern in a knobbly hand, the other rummaging around the vegetable patch. All else was silent, the air rippling with the threat of embroilment. Ryurikov's glove creaked, hand clenching around the broom handle.

"I should have predicted your return." Jezibaba's voice held its usual aged tremor, but it was calm, bordering on cold.

A sneer pulled Ryurikov's lips back, the anger boiling inside his chest rising into his throat. He raised the broom. Brought it down across the width of his thigh. Its *snap* echoed against the trees.

He lunged off the porch, feet barely touching ground before the splintered, sharp end of the broom handle speared Jezibaba's stomach.

Her lantern clattered to the ground, and patterned sashes turned dark. Ryurikov hoisted her up, ramming the handle deeper into her belly. Green-tinged blood oozed over his arms. Staining his clothes. Splattering across his face as he swung her impaled form in an arc. Slammed her down with a *crack*.

He straightened up with a tired exhale and scrutinised her limp form. Grey hair strewn about, thick blood draining into the soil. Eyes wide open. Cloudy, and lifeless.

Ryurikov regarded Awimak nearby and deliberated on what to say. Huzzah, the infernal lizard's dead? Care for a celebratory fuck?

He opened his mouth and squawked in surprise as the ground trembled, gave a lurch, and tilted. Like an exhausted beast, the tree-legs groaned, and Ryurikov went tumbling sideways into the fruit trees. His chest collided with a trunk. He held on, wrapping his legs around.

"Fuck, I forgot about that!"

Awimak lowered to dig his claws into the soil, up to the forearms. The earth churned like a rolling boil around him. Roots sprang up, serpentining across the garden, spreading into every crevice, over the hut and beyond. The tree-legs below staggered, then eased back up, until Ryurikov no longer had to hold on for his life. Carefully, as if expecting everything to cave under him a second time, he sidled toward Awimak.

"Awimak," he began, faltering at the way the demon's body trembled, muscles flexing with effort. Multifarious roots protruded from his body, leading into the soil. Was he holding the entire hut up on his own with those? "Do I need to cut you free?"

IF I RELEASE, IT WILL ALL COLLAPSE, Awimak rasped. *YOU SHOULD LEAVE.*

Ryurikov's lips curled. He'd be glad to get away from this place, travel alone, or maybe with Awimak. "You'll be fine, I presume?"

YES. He sounded a little stressed.

Ryurikov spun on his heel and darted for the hut. "I'm going to raid the place, hold on a little longer!" He turned back to flash the demon a grin. "If this whole thing comes down, I'll know I took too long."

Awimak's snort sounded desperate now.

"Okay, hurrying!"

Darting past Jezibaba's corpse, Ryurikov closed his hand around the broom handle. A trophy, for his troubles.

A *crack* and a *squelch*, and as he pulled it free, her body vanished in a great plume of dark smoke, wafting up in a circle overhead before dissipating. Ryurikov swore, the crone's cackling disturbing the air, scratching at his neck and ears.

FLEE! Awimak snarled.

Ryurikov knew he ought to heed the suggestion, but the hag-smoke curled around Awimak, and he could see it in those sunset eyes, hear it in the way he grunted with distress that this would not end well for him.

With a growl, Ryurikov swung the silver bow forward. He released an arrow into the churning smoke, transforming to resemble some kind of giant, rippling beast. It dispersed, then reappeared right in front of him.

A smoking fist swung up. It connected with his chin hard, clacking his teeth together, flipping him onto his back. Reeling and chin pulsating with pain, he shook his head, swivelled on the ground, jumped to his feet and swiped the bow through the cloud. It split, then returned to Awimak with a gleeful laugh, enveloping him. The wind picked up, the scent of honey sickly, burning Ryurikov's throat.

He nocked another arrow, intent on freeing Awimak, the crunch of vegetables beneath his feet lost within the gales and dry creaking of the hut. The trees enclosing them shifted, their movement unnatural, branches curling forward to wrap around Awimak, his large body shrouded by the witch's smoke.

Ryurikov hesitated, unsure of where to fire his arrows. Branches imprisoned the demon entirely, and he cast around for something, panicking. His sights landed on the black chicken clucking and flapping its wings in distress beneath the porch.

"Let him go or the chicken gets it!" Ryurikov shouted, arrow trained on the bird. He could do with some poultry for dinner, anyway.

Awimak howled, agonised. The ground beneath Ryurikov's feet lurched again. The smoke came out of nowhere. Hurtled at him harder than a wild horse. Sent him into a tree. Pain speared his shoulder as he collapsed to the ground, groaned, and pushed back up.

The fumes vaguely took on the witch's shape, settling near the beanstalks. White eyes stared at him from writhing curls of shadow, and Ryurikov made a face at her.

"Fuck you, you antediluvian sprout."

He steadied his own bow, the silver one glinting uselessly in the distance near the carrots, and made to shoot the chicken. A long swathe swiped at him. He ducked to avoid a blow to the face, yet it hooked around the back of his neck and yanked him forward.

Ryurikov spat out dirt, now in the vegetable patch, and staggered upright. A beastly force connected with his stomach, the intensity of it lifting him off the ground before he crashed back down. He coughed, then retched, spittle clinging to his lips as he grabbed at carrot bushels to help hoist himself up again. He wrenched the vegetables out in the process, and weakly tossed them at the witch, swaying where he stood.

"Don't hold back now," he wheezed.

His blurry gaze landed on Awimak behind the dark cloud, now completely lost within thick roots and boughs, likely crushing him. There was a reason she hadn't killed him yet, but he couldn't be so sure she had a reason to spare Awimak.

"Let him go. Your issue is with me."

"*This is your doing!*" The discomfited warble of Jezibaba's voice raised his hair.

Unsteadily, he lifted the bow off the ground, nocked another arrow, and pointed it at Jezibaba's form, more turbulent than the surrounding winds. She cackled again, luminous white eyes slitting with mirth.

"I know," Ryurikov murmured. "You're smoke, can't hit you."

But he could hit the prized lantern, bobbing and swaying in the gales by the porch, its pallid flame fluttering madly.

The arrow hit the glass, shattering it, and the lantern dropped with a *clunk*. Fire pooled like a liquid set ablaze, festooning all within its reach and spreading. As the flames journeyed up the hut, a shriek pierced the air—and his eardrums. It came from the hut itself.

Boughs whipped away from Awimak. He was curled in on himself, but still alive, his wide shoulders dropping with every heavy breath.

"*No!*" Jezibaba uselessly spilled herself at the white flames to stop their spread.

Ryurikov laughed even as he darted to Awimak and unsheathed the long dagger. "I'm cutting you loose!" And he hoped it wouldn't hurt.

"*Put the broom back together!*"

He ignored Jezibaba's demand, slicing the finer roots first. He winced as Awimak grunted in pain, thick, lava-like blood spilling from the wounds.

"Fuck's sake," Ryurikov snapped. "Why did you attach yourself?"

FOR ENTERTAINMENT. Burning eyes raised to bore into him.

"Not the ideal time for a jest," Ryurikov breathed, "but I like your spirit."

"*I'll stop killing you if you fix it!*" Jezibaba wailed.

The ghostly fire had engulfed most of the hut, its shrieking relentless. Her smoky form flitted back and forth in panic and Ryurikov realised there was nothing she could do to save her home. Nothing at all.

He laughed again. "Serves you right!"

"*I swear it!*" The disembodied voice echoed all around him. "*I will spare you and help you find Valka. Fix the broom!*"

Ryurikov glanced at Awimak. Pallid flames snaking toward the demon snapped him into motion. His grip curled around the broom handle he'd dropped by cabbages. His boots scuffed through dirt as he came to a stop by the straw end, having found its way into the thicket of the garden's edge.

An agonised, raspy groan jerked his focus back to Awimak. The blaze had set on him and sent Ryurikov's heart hurtling through his ribcage. He jammed the splintered ends back together with trembling hands. Jezibaba's blood was sticky enough to act as glue, but he tugged off his scarf and tightened it around the fracture for good measure.

No sooner had he tied the knot than the black smoke swarmed him, ruffling his hair as it sucked back into the broom with a great *whoosh*.

The winds died and Ryurikov relaxed his shoulders. Still clutching the broom, he watched as Jezibaba's solid form darted past him, muttering things in a foreign tongue and raising her bony hands up at the hut as if praying to it.

He staggered back to the demon, dark smoke wafting off singed hair and skin. Awimak didn't move.

"Fuck, are you dead?" Had he been less concerned for Awimak's well-being, Ryurikov would have taken slight at his own voice, the way it quavered.

NO. Awimak grunted. The root-like protrusions gradually snaked back into his skin, leaving behind raw pocks oozing with orange glowing blood.

Ryurikov kept his hold on the broom, cradling it against his chest, and knelt in front of the demon to peer up at the skull. The spectral light of the lantern's fire became muted. Then, they were cast in darkness but for Awimak's eyes, thankfully on him again.

"Why the fuck did you do that? You know the Quinary would have just saved me again."

Probably.

Awimak huffed, breath misting between them even in the dark, but he didn't answer. With a slight shake of his head, Ryurikov stood and faced the hag. She grumbled and sulked over the damage to her hut. Admittedly, it was extensive, the wood scorched and bubbling with sap. Shame.

"So, control of the hut is tied to the broom?" He glanced at the object in question. Even in the darkness, its wood resembled that of the hut, and he realised himself an idiot. Of course the hut was tied to it.

Jezibaba glared at him. "My *home*."

Ryurikov hummed. "It's a real pity. Deal's a deal, witch. You better stop trying to kill me now. *And* take me to Valka."

"Assuming she even wants to see you!"

"She's not getting a choice."

Although he might need to slay a dragon on the way.

The garden was a slew of ruined vegetables, flowers, and agitated chickens angrily clucking about, but gold lights reminiscent of moths illuminated it. It was strangely enchanting. Jezibaba had retreated inside, and Ryurikov kept a stubborn hold on the broom while guiding Awimak to his favourite tree. Its fruit had grown. A few more days and the apples would be edible.

Instead of moving away once Awimak sat, Ryurikov squatted between the powerful legs. He laid the broom down in grass, and shifted closer to peer at the singed skin and the many open wounds. He really wanted to touch them.

"Does it hurt?"

Awimak leaned back, the sigh a wraith's death rattle. *I WILL BE FINE.*

"Not exactly what I asked." Ryurikov's lips quirked up. "You said you can't heal me, but can you heal yourself?"

IN TIME, YES.

His fingers twitched where he had them on his own knees. An odd feeling snaked its way into his stomach, plenty to do with the dawning realisation that had he not been so imprudent, Awimak wouldn't have gotten hurt. His jaw tensed, Jezibaba's words after Eastcairn returning to him like an annoying fly buzzing around his head.

"You could have just left me."

BUT I DID NOT.

"Why?"

Burning eyes regarded him. *OUR DEAL.*

"Doesn't extend as far as you've been reaching."

A TREE ONLY KNOWS TO GROW.

Ryurikov's lips vibrated with a puff. "You're being very evasive—"

A furry and heavily toned leg curled around him, eased him forward, careful enough that should he put up any resistance, it would stop.

Ryurikov's heart did a thing, a thing he didn't like. It lurched and stuttered at the same time. His hands connected with Awimak's torso, fingers splayed against the muscular chest to catch himself. The scent of earth and stone greeted him, drifting into his very soul with a deep, nervous inhale.

Slowly, carefully, like he might run off in fright, Awimak's virile arms coiled around him. Before he knew it, Ryurikov was in an embrace. Not trapped, but he was unquestionably encased and left blinking at the rough bark of the apple tree, chin resting on the soft skin of a wide shoulder.

The last hold he'd been in was Valka's, thirteen years ago on the day they said goodbye to each other. He never hung around long enough to be held by anyone, yet he'd somehow stumbled into this hold and was... disinclined to move.

It didn't matter that his ribs hurt, that his chin throbbed and his stomach was likely forming a cluster of bruises. Being with Awimak like this, surrounded by the rustling of trees, while great claws capable of maiming held him in the gentlest of ways was...nice. For once, he could think of little to say.

Well, there were plenty of things he could say, jibes he could make, and actions he could take, but he didn't want to.

Awimak had put his life on the line, Ryurikov wasn't unaware of that, and he'd done so specifically for him. Because trees grew, apparently. It still made no fucking sense.

YOU ARE WARM, Awimak said, the snarl but a gravelly murmur.

"And you're cold."

Cold in the way the grounds outside his castle were on a summer's morning, where he found solace in the dew and mist clinging to the grassy expanse on the rare occasion he'd been allowed out.

Ryurikov shifted to free his tingling legs, knees nudging the inside of Awimak's thighs. Admittedly, being held put him on edge. When Awimak's solid chest rumbled with what had to be a hum, Ryurikov jerked—not in fright, exactly. But close.

"You must be famished," he murmured. The arms dropped away from him the moment he moved back.

STARVING, said Awimak.

Fifteen

Soft snaps of a fire filled the narrow room. Ryurikov sat in the tub, wine-red rose petals clinging to his knees, one to the centre of his chest. Their scent curled up to tangle into his hair, seep into his skin.

This would not have been his first choice, but like before, the tub had been there, filled and waiting for him. Steam made his face feel hot and clammy, but after the cursed nightmares—*several* of them—he'd endured, he needed to relax. A moment away from Awimak. The demon hadn't jested, saying he was starved.

Good fucking grief.

Ryurikov peeled a petal off his leg and rubbed it between thumb and pointer finger. Waking drenched in cold sweat by the other tree had been about as enjoyable as a fuck on a bed made of briar. A startling contrast to how he'd felt coming away from being held by Awimak, and that on its own was unsettling. Ryurikov did not embrace others. That was for lovers, or siblings.

With equal inattention, he flicked the furled petal away, then hoisted himself out of the tub. When he strolled down the stairs, it was in only one of the stolen tunics Awimak had graciously returned to him. Scarlet, of the finest linen, and it covered his cock just enough not to be offensive around Jezibaba.

The aroma of cooked mushrooms and freshly baked bread greeted him at the bottom of the stairs, and his eyebrows rose at the two plates set out on the table. Jezibaba pushed a wooden tankard across to the second plate and glowered.

"Expecting guests?" Ryurikov asked, eyeing the mushrooms and boiled eggs.

Jezibaba's look soured so much he thought her face might turn inward. "It's for you."

"Hah! Not falling for that again."

He made to walk past, but she growled at him. An actual, animalistic *growl*. Ryurikov's look turned incredulous.

"I meant it." She said it like it was physically harming her. "I won't kill you again."

"And you'll help me find Valka," Ryurikov added, gleefully.

Jezibaba looked more agonised still, and ground out each word, "And that. Consider this meal a peace offering."

Ryurikov hummed. "Alright, but I'll be taking this outside."

To Awimak, specifically.

GOOD MORNING.

"Fuck you," said Ryurikov walking down the steps. His lips twitched up just enough to let the demon know he wasn't being serious.

YOU HAVE ADEQUATELY RECOVERED, THEN?

He sat across from Awimak, folding his legs and setting the tankard down into the grass. "I have. No thanks to *you*. Now tell me, is this poisoned?"

Awimak leaned forward from where he rested against his favourite apple tree. *NO.*

"Alright, if it is and I die again, I'll be cross with you."

YOU ALREADY ARE.

Ryurikov tilted his head from side to side. "I'm not cross. A deal is a deal. You didn't have to hit me so hard, though."

I APOLOGISE. I WAS... HUNGRY.

"You don't say?" He softened his expression. "Given that you spared me a painful descent, however, I'm inclined to forgive you."

Seeing as he had no knife on him, Ryurikov ate using his fingers. The mushrooms were large, earthy and spiced with something he couldn't place—not poison, he hoped—and the drink was a surprisingly refreshing ale. Where the fuck did Jezibaba get her hands on these things?

ARE YOU WELL?

"Yes," Ryurikov murmured around a mouthful of bread. "Why?"

YOU SMELL DIFFERENT TODAY. Awimak inhaled, deeply. ROSES AND CEDARWOOD.

Ryurikov crammed the last egg into his mouth and tossed the wooden bowl away from him before he stretched out his legs, dragging his hand over fine grass to wipe it. "I had no control over that."

Another one of Awimak's hums, yet this one sounded more approving. Ryurikov flicked his gaze up at the demon, whose eyes were most certainly not meeting his, trained on another part of him. He buried his face into the tankard and drained the sweet ale in several gulps. He tossed that into the bushes too, and now woefully lacked things to occupy himself with.

"Do you fuck, Awimak?"

Sunset eyes became a firestorm at the words, and Ryurikov's heart saltated in ways that became uncomfortable. His mouth went dry. He licked his lower lip.

YES, said Awimak, and he thought his heart might give out.

Ryurikov wanted to ask, "Who?" and, "When?" and, "Why haven't we, yet?" but discovered himself speechless, paralysed in a way he didn't want to fight. Not when the demon moved forward, not when his extraordinary form inclined over him, and not when Ryurikov was eased onto his back by the careful press of claws, bit by tantalising bit.

The breath he released trembled, it seemed to rattle from his chest when Awimak's claw cupped his face. So tenderly again, it was almost annoying. He met those burning eyes as the other hand trailed down his chest, the nails digging in just enough for his breath to hitch. His cock twitched and hardened, hidden beneath his tunic—until it wasn't. Awimak pushed the fabric up, exposing more of him, more of his scars, yet didn't look at anything other than into his eyes.

Ryurikov belatedly remembered he too had hands, jerking out of his paralysis to run fingers down the smooth, soft skin covering the wide expanse of Awimak's chest. And it *was* so smooth, and so soft, the injuries still there, still raw. He avoided them no matter how tempting it was to stick his finger in, just to see if the blood was as scalding as it looked.

Awimak's nails skirted his bruised stomach, toying with the coppery hairs beginning at his navel and leading down. Ryurikov bodily twisted with some impatience, longing for more, but Awimak didn't move further. He appeared to hesitate.

"Awimak," Ryurikov ground out. "Please, feel free to proceed."

Seemed that was what he'd been after, for the next thing Ryurikov knew, that enormous claw enveloped his cock in a firm grip. Rough, textured, fucking *fantastic*. He groaned, allowing himself to buck his hips up a few times to fuck that grip before he turned his attention on the fabric around Awimak's waist. It took some fumbling, seemingly attached to the skin. And once he pushed it aside, exposed the demon's throbbing erection, his breath had every right to catch the way it did.

"Fuck me," Ryurikov breathed.

A rumble in Awimak's chest. *I WILL.*

He could barely muster a smirk, reaching between them to wrap his fingers around the girthed length, dark grey like the rest of him, cabled with thick veins leading to a narrow tip, blushing mauve. He shifted his hand up to the leaking slit, teased it by circling it with his fingertips, and when Awimak groaned, he found the willpower to smirk in full.

Until Awimak let go of his cock, gathered Ryurikov's ankles in great claws, then hoisted him up, ass to the clear sky. The tunic slipped past his chest to cover his face. There was no room for indignation, something *hot* and wet slithering against his hole.

"What the fuck?"

His neck was at an awkward angle, his top half pressed into the ground and straining the injured shoulder, but Awimak had his face buried between his thighs and that *had* to be a tongue. Exceptionally long and slick and exploring in all the right ways. So that's how it was. Keeping secrets from him until the last minute.

"First the ears, now *this*," Ryurikov griped, but the effect was lost entirely when he let slip a moan the second that tongue—*pointed tongue*—pushed into him.

He lost all desire to complain, hands useless at the side of his head, fingers flirting with blades of grass while Awimak fucked him using his mouth, salacious lapping audible over the birds in the raspberry bush. That slick, hot muscle slipped out, slithering around his balls instead. Ryurikov squinted up, sunrays streaming in through the trees particularly vivid, casting spots of light on the intricate carvings of the skull. Awimak's eyes remained on him, long grey tongue protruding from a jutting chin. Ryurikov caught a flash of teeth, sharp and deadly, and his cock twitched with unexpected thrill.

When that tongue snaked up the shaft of his erection, pointed tip tasting the head, he tensed up, the tide of his orgasm drawing in far too quickly. He wanted to warn Awimak off, but he was *good* at sex, and coming too quickly was not a thing that happened to him. Ryurikov twisted out of the demon's grasp. His bare feet connected with the grass again and he swiftly moved to straddle those massive thighs, eyes practically rolling into the back of his head at how marvellously soft the fur was against his bare skin.

Deftly, he pressed a few fingers against the nasal tip of the skull and nudged it up. That too appeared to be attached, but he wanted to take a peek at what was under there. Awimak didn't seem to mind, elongated jaw parting to lash his face with that tongue. Ryurikov didn't jerk back. He wasn't one for kissing, but opening his mouth to let it dance along his own tongue could hardly be considered kissing. Could it?

Awimak's mouth tasted piquant, of all things earthy. He sucked on the tongue, shimmying further up those muscular thighs to press his erection against Awimak's decidedly larger cock. Warmer than the rest of him, but his terrene chill prickled Ryurikov's skin. He thrust his hips forward to gain friction.

Then those claws edged to the cleft of his cheeks, and a saliva-slickened fingertip toyed with his opening.

"Hey, now, I've seen what those claws can do," Ryurikov said, not at all eager to have his innards shredded. Besides, he preferred to be on top.

Awimak too leaned back, a chuckle quaking his abdomen when he released his ass cheeks to hold up a hand. Ryurikov watched in fascination. Those sharp, deadly nails shrunk away.

"Handy," he lilted.

The finger returned to press into him, and he was all out of complaints again. The digit was long, tormentingly slow, *gentle*. Ryurikov pushed himself downward, hoping to get the message across. His hands fisted against Awimak's chest, the message received, that finger landing a direct hit against his prostate with startling competence. He uttered a swear, and then another once a second finger slipped into him, followed by a third. Ryurikov's hands found the silky mane cascading down Awimak's neck as pain made itself known, and he ran his fingers through the strands to distract himself. The side of his face pressed against the skull, head trapped between it and the large, coiled horn. He still had his old cloak wrapped around them.

Fucker.

Awimak's fingers pulled out and wiggled back in, flicking away the lingering resentment. Ryurikov fisted his own cock, ensuring the tip connected with Awimak's while rugged fingers stretched him. The demon's breaths went heavier and, pressing their chests together, Ryurikov realised there was a heartbeat. It pulsated more than thumped, intense and overwhelming, like the very life of Vale undulated inside him.

Sturdy digits slipped out, that same claw coming up between them. Awimak ran his tongue all over it. Ryurikov's back connected with the grass again, damp and chilly beneath him. His mouth watered at the sight of Awimak running the slicked claw along his own cock, the other pushing Ryurikov's legs apart.

His heart continued its frantic dance while Awimak got to his knees and positioned himself, looming as an ancient tree, casting him in shadow. The tip of his cock slid against the whorl of Ryurikov's asshole, yet didn't push in.

YES? Awimak asked.

Ryurikov grunted with impatience. "*Yes*, Awimak, I'm into it."

And he was. By gods he was, previous disinclination gone entirely.

He clenched his eyes shut and tensed his jaw as Awimak's cock eased in, slowly. So fucking achingly, torturously slow, Ryurikov shoved his hips down to get it over with.

Much to his own chagrin, it hurt. Worse still, his gasp was one of shock. He grit his teeth in affront.

Awimak smoothed a claw down the scarred side of his face. Those fiery eyes held a look of concern. Ryurikov still didn't know how he could tell.

"Just fuck me." Something told him that this was a command Awimak wouldn't take offence to.

Strong, thick arms hooked his legs over them, and Awimak thrust his hips forward, pushing the entire length into Ryurikov's body in one swift movement, wrenching free a jagged cry. No time to recover when that cock pulled out again, nearly to the tip, the cabled veins ticking past his opening as if in a countdown, then thrust in again.

The momentum built into something hungry, gluttonous even, coaxing noises out of him that Ryurikov hadn't thought himself capable of. Awimak took to slamming into him with rasped groans of delight, the slap of skin meeting skin richly vulgar, promptly shoving him to the precipice of utter bliss.

Ryurikov hugged the demon's torso with both legs, driving his hips downward to meet every frantic drive straight into the nub of nerves within. He fisted the grass, pulling it up in chunks, stars dancing before his eyes and mind spinning. Awimak fell on him, heated bursts of breath crowding, turning his skin near incandescent.

Awimak was the first to drop off the edge, his final thrust brutal, his howl loud, sending birds out into the sky. Sweltering climax filled, and Ryurikov happily launched himself off that cliff into delirium after the demon. He went rigid, his cock gave an avid twitch and toes curled. He came with a guttural groan and startling force, draping his own stomach with pleasure.

Panting hard, he collapsed. Awimak gently slipped out to give him breathing room. Heat decanted from his opening as Ryurikov lay there, legs parted wide, whole body limp and refusing to cooperate as he shuddered with aftershock. He remained that way for a while, unable to muster even the smallest quip.

Awimak settled down beside him and, had Ryurikov not been so useless, would have had something to say about the way he stroked his face. It was very gentle. He couldn't even be bothered to fix his tunic, bunched up around his ribcage.

"So, you fuck," Ryurikov breathed at length.

YES. Awimak sounded amused.

He turned to look at the demon, tongue pressed up against the inside of his cheek. He was trying to hide the smile taking control of his mouth, but damn it, he couldn't.

YOU SEEM SATISFIED.

Ryurikov snorted. "Something to that effect."

"When you two are done," warbled Jezibaba, voice shrill with something akin to panic. A *thunk* nearby followed. "It's time you do your part!"

He glared at the bucket rolling across the ground toward him and Awimak. "What do you mean?"

"Chores!"

Ryurikov sat up, wincing at the throb in his ass. "I beg your pardon?" But Jezibaba wasn't anywhere in sight.

Probably a good thing. He wasn't sure he wanted to know how much of that she saw.

Sixteen

"Where do you come from?"

Gathering ruined vegetables from his dustup with the witch was a menial task, so far beneath him, Ryurikov should have gone into that hut and mounted Jezibaba's head on a pike. Fortunately for her, his mood soared higher than the trees, feeling satiated enough to humour her.

It helped that the giant, terrifying demon of the Unbroken Wilds was there alongside him, obediently returning vegetables to the soil.

FROM THE UNDERFOREST. I BROUGHT YOU THERE.

"I *meant* how did you come to exist, and you know it."

Awimak replanted a carrot, patting the dirt around it with great care. *I DID NOT REALISE I NEEDED TO EXPLAIN PROCREATION TO YOU.*

"You're fucking hilarious." Ryurikov hurtled a piece of cabbage at Awimak's arm, breaking it against the bark-like forearms. The chickens flocked to it with eager clucks. "Don't answer me, then."

Awimak rose to his full, glorious height and regarded him. *I WAS FORGED FROM THE EARTH.*

"By *who*?"

Jezibaba's shuffling footsteps irked Ryurikov's ears. "Will you put

Coil of Boughs

the rest of your clothes on?" She came up beside him, glower firmly fixed in place.

"No," said Ryurikov, and bent over with his ass facing her to collect more of the ruined produce. He ignored the painful twinge that bolted up his backside. "I happen to like the breeze around my balls."

Not to mention his clothes were currently drying out, flapping in said breeze from where they hung along branches. He'd done what he could to get the hag's foul blood out, although feared the stains would forever be there.

"I don't see how fixing your mess is going to help find Valka, either," he added, tossing the bucket away with careless ease. It tipped and spilled most of what he'd collected. Fuck. "Vasili said a dragon got her, but I don't believe for a second she got herself turned into anything's roast dinner."

Jezibaba squatted to stroke the fox-red chicken over its head. It had taken a keen interest in Ryurikov for the past few minutes, pecking around his boot-clad feet.

"Who?" she asked.

Ryurikov sneered. The very memory of Vasili putting his hands on him pushed bile up into his throat. Even Awimak's attention snapped to the hag, a certain angered intensity in the flare of his eyes.

"The *reeve*, you roughdried prune."

Lizard eyes glanced at him and grey brows furrowed. He glared at her, daring her to confess to it. To tell him she'd set Vasili on him deliberately.

"It's a misconception that dragons spit fire."

Ryurikov heaved a weary sigh. "They shit it, I *know*." It was like being back at home where the governor tried to beat useless facts into him. "Does it even matter what end it comes out of?"

IT DOES NOT.

"Exactly. Thank you, Awimak." He flashed his demon a smile. "Either way, she wouldn't have gotten herself cooked. *Which* dragon would it have been?"

"There are too many, I couldn't tell you," Jezibaba grumbled, now stroking the patterned chicken.

"Oh, fuck me." Ryurikov ran fingers through his hair. "I'm going to have to hunt dragons until I find the right one?"

The old trout straightened up and pursed her lips. "The last thing she told me before we parted ways was that she would head for Stoutburn."

Ryurikov groaned in exasperation. "The guild town."

"She wanted adventure."

"Sounds about right. Wait," Ryurikov darted after the hag as she walked away from him, "does that mean she's been here, in this hut? In this garden?"

"Of course she was!" The old woman hobbled back inside and Ryurikov pursued.

"Why?"

"I had things to teach her. Then she became bored."

Was that a hint of bitterness? Ryurikov smirked. "Yes, Valka. What were you teaching her? Has she developed a taste for children?" He snapped his fingers. "I knew I should've worried more when she showed an interest in caring for our cousins."

Jezibaba halted in the kitchenette so abruptly he nearly bumped into her. "I do not eat children!"

"Whatever you do," Ryurikov said, taking cruel delight in this newfound ability to crawl under her skin, "sketching your victims is *wild*. I've seen the portraits."

Finally, there was some colour in that wrinkled face, blotchy and red and hideous. When Jezibaba spoke, it was in a barely restrained bellow, "If you don't want me to spell your limp mole rat off and feed it to my chickens, then I suggest you get back in that garden *right now*."

For a solid moment, Ryurikov considered his chances. Spelling off his cock wasn't murdering him, she could and likely would do it. He decided against taunting her further.

"Fine, but get that hut moving for Stoutburn."

"We're already headed there," Jezibaba called after him.

Ryurikov glanced at the surrounding trees. It was impossible to tell they were on the move, the sky too clear to hint at anything. When his gaze settled on Awimak, down on one knee and petting the chickens, he leaned his elbows on the rickety porch railing to watch.

Aside from Angelus, Ryurikov never stuck around long enough to discover any feelings for anyone. *Because* of Angelus, he'd been reminded of why. His soulless eyes bothered him slightly less these days, but the anger at the prince of darkness for permanently altering his features still burned hot in his chest.

Yet here he was, after a good lay, still inclined to stick around. Awimak wouldn't betray his trust like that, he was almost certain of it.

ARE YOU WELL?

Ryurikov horse-kicked his focus back to the present. "Yes."

Stoutburn.

Built around a ravine—and Ryurikov had no hope of understanding the logic behind *that* decision—the city's streets reached across the wide gap as bridges, crooked and towering structures of raven black lining either side. He and Awimak had walked several hours to reach it, the forest line barely visible along the hazy horizon.

With the sun beating down on black stone, Ryurikov wished he'd stolen a cloak of more breathable fabric. It was *suffocating*. Trudging past colossal ebony pillars standing sentry on either side, he made it a point of avoiding eye contact with guildspersons waiting to lure him inside with empty promises.

"Hey, you! Fellow in the cloak!" A stocky woman in a handsome vest waved him over, sleeves of her tunic rolled up to reveal powerful biceps. "Are you looking for adventure, fame, *riches*? Only the best quests here! Come, sign up!"

Awimak took a step in her direction. *MORE ENTERTAINMENT, YES?*

"No. Ignore them," Ryurikov murmured as discreetly as he could. "They'll only trap you and charge you a fortune for collecting a thousand sticks or something. And anyway," he glanced at the guild's sign with distaste, "I'm not signing up to a place called Gallant *Steelers*."

"That *is* a terrible name!" bellowed a heavyset man a few paces down, clad in a leather loincloth and harness that did nothing to hide his bulging muscles, or the tiny bulge between massive thighs. "You'd be better off with us, Wood Shields!"

Ryurikov grimaced again, moved away, and the next guildsperson frantically waved them over, long, thin arms wobbling like wet rawhide.

"Come in here for the most glorious of tasks!" An odd creature, ashy face void of any features but two round eyes with peach-coloured irises that were, quite frankly, ghastly. "We might not kill you."

Ryurikov placed a hand on Awimak's forearm to stop him approaching the Seeper. "We are not joining a guild called Capering Corpse either."

IF WE WILL NOT JOIN ANY, WHY ARE WE HERE?

"Don't pout." Ryurikov's lips twitched with a smile. "I'm looking for someone specific. I promise I'll entertain you later."

He let his hand drift down, grazing the bark-armoured forearm, until his gloved fingers traversed pronounced knuckles. Awimak's claw twitched forward, the backs of their hands connected, and fingers threaded. Ryurikov swallowed.

He'd come to a standstill, as had the beating of his heart. Too many thoughts kicked up in his mind. An absolute whirl of chaos, it was impossible to grasp at one thought and focus on it. Awimak's fingers squeezed his, then let go. He carried on walking, leaving Ryurikov to stare after him until he gathered his wits.

It took a long time.

Once the storm in his head settled, he dashed past Awimak, walking a few paces ahead. He reached up to fiddle with his scarf, belatedly realising he no longer had it, still tied around the broom, again slotted in Awimak's great big beautiful horns.

A section of the bridge stood clear of the narrow structures, granting them a full view of the ravine and the city that occupied it. Grasslands stretched on either side of them. Yonder to the south lurked the mountains shielding dragons from the rest of the world.

Awimak looked out across the expanse with him. WHY HAVE YOU CHOSEN TO SEARCH FOR YOUR SISTER?

Ryurikov tapped his fingers along the heated stone of the parapet. He relished in Awimak's closeness, in particular because he cast a welcome chill into his immediate surroundings.

"Honestly? I'm not sure," he admitted, quietly. "I doubt she'll even want to see me. If she's alive, she'll have heard the rumours."

RUMOURS THAT ARE MORE THAN HEARSAY?

He sighed. "Yes, Awimak." He turned, resting his back against the stone to look out across the other side, and the floating lily pads, tethered by thin, russet stalks, reaching as high as the bridge they occupied. "It occurred to me when I was caught by the enforcers." He rubbed his thumb over the length of his pointer finger, idly. "I was only hunting for some deer, they didn't appreciate my doing so on Monarch Mulgar's land. Between you and me, I don't even know how to cook."

WHY HUNT FOR DEER?

Ryurikov's smile was wry. "There was a maiden I hoped to seduce into doing it for me. Bread and fruit are easy enough to steal, but meat? Most towns still standing have broadsides with my face on it."

YOU WEREN'T SUCCESSFUL.

A glance at Awimak suggested he remained judgement free. "They spooked the deer, clubbed me over the head with something. A mistake I'll never make again. Anyway, you could say that facing the threat of being made into a meal myself had me reconsider a few things."

HOW DID YOU LEARN THE JEZIBABA POSSESSED THE MIRROR OF THE LOST?

At that, Ryurikov chuckled, not at all surprised that this too was something Awimak was aware of. "I found it through this place."

He pushed away from the parapet and proceeded beyond the bridge's crest. The floating lily pads provided shade to the bridges further below in the ravine, but didn't reach this far up. The sun hammered their reflective surfaces, the vividness of it forcing him to squint. By the time they reached the shade the other side of the rocky wall provided, he had green spots dancing in his vision.

Fewer structures occupied the vast quantity of irregular stairs descending to the next bridge, although alleyways dissevered the dark rock, where peddlers and lone guildspersons gathered. Most of them were beggars desperate for coin, and other things. Deciding it couldn't hurt, Ryurikov flicked ores and even a few crones at some. The youngest, in particular, and they were all disgustingly grateful.

The deeper they went, the more darkness overwhelmed. A pink glow emanated from the underside of the lily pads to light the way and, perhaps unsurprisingly, a few Candescent occupied the lower levels.

Ryurikov kept a close eye on the ropey humanoids lurking in the shadows. They were all members of the Capering Corpse, he knew, and was glad to have his bow at his side again. Especially when those creatures were capable of flight, their long ashen bodies flapping like loose undergarments in a windstorm.

He veered through the wide doorway of a library, its facade carved out of the ravine walls, twisted pillars on either side. Awimak waited by them, the library wouldn't house someone his height.

Ryurikov's footfalls were silent as he strode across rugged floor tiles, keeping his eyes skinned for the Lyke. His gaze drifted around the displays of weaponry and armour, attention soon caught by the massive sword resting on several stands. The sword of a goliath. Idly, he wondered if Awimak could wield the weapon, before a giant tome in the back caught his attention. It glowed with an ominous blue on its lecterns, and pouring over them was the Lyke.

"Apatura," he murmured, quiet enough not to disturb the few other occupants carefully inspecting weapons to borrow.

The Lyke's head jerked up, and she whirled, ghostly face hidden within the shadow of her ochre hood. "I had a feeling you'd be back."

"I'm sure you did."

"It's funny," she continued, her voice an unsettling cross between a croak and a hiss, "because I'm certain you swore to me I'd never have to look at those barren eyes again."

Ryurikov rolled his shoulders against the insult. "I'm after information."

"I take it the mirror didn't pan out." Apatura slammed the glowing tome shut. She needn't have bothered, when its script was illegible to him, although it looked faintly familiar.

"It did, in a roundabout way."

"I warned that you'd only see yourself."

"Yes, but I would've been a fool to take you at your word," Ryurikov snapped.

"True." Apatura smiled, sharp teeth grimy with green algae. "Whatever you want, it will cost you, as always."

He waved a dismissive hand. "I've been told Valka has tangled with a dragon. I don't suppose you know which one?"

Apatura took a long moment to respond, during which she stared at him with two pebble-sized dots, glowing pallid. "You assume she's alive."

"I assume nothing." Ryurikov patted himself across the chest. "I can feel it deep in my heart, she's alive. We're connected in spirit—*I don't fucking know* if she's alive! I'm only hoping, for fuck's sake."

"Shhh!"

He glared at the short fellow standing on an antiquated table, toying with a frayed noose, then returned his withering look to the Lyke. "Why does everyone have to be so fucking difficult? Just tell me what I need to know."

"Great Dragons spank me, you've turned into an even bigger ass," Apatura snarled. "Ten crones, and I'll tell you what I know."

"*Steep.*" All the same, he flicked each crone at her, some landing on the ground to twirl on their noses.

Apatura didn't move, yet the still spinning coins vanished in a faint puff of silvery smoke, reappearing in her open palm. Thin fingers closed, and Ryurikov caught sight of rotting skin on the back of her hand. So, she'd been rejected by her own magic. Fortunate then, that he'd caught her before the decay consumed her in full.

"It wasn't the dragon who took her, it was the drakes." Apatura turned back to the blue glowing tome to stroke its rigid leather spine. "Studious types, those. You may have some luck approaching them in peace."

"How? They shit on anything that comes anywhere near the foot of their mountain."

"That sounds like a problem."

"Dare I ask how you know it was a drake?"

"Drakes are meticulous. They write everything down." Apatura's thin blue lips twisted. "At least, they try."

"Right, right. Of *course*." Ryurikov waved his hand again, and it wasn't in farewell. He paused when a realisation hit him. Indignation burned his insides and he palmed the hilt of his long dagger. "You couldn't have told me this *before* I went hunting for Jezibaba?"

Apatura didn't look at him this time. "You get the answers you pay for."

He grit his teeth, calculating the risk of attacking her right there and then. She was a powerful mage, and dabbled in things that disconcerted even Ryurikov. But was she faster than his blade?

"Your companion."

Ryurikov wrenched his focus back to the rotting Lyke. "Pardon?"

"An interesting choice," she said. "You may want to get back out there."

He took that as a warning, maybe even a threat, and scoffed at Apatura in farewell. Passing the imp on the table, he said, "Try putting it around your neck and jump from a height."

Ryurikov dipped out of the library and froze.

"Awimak, what the—"

IT IS LOOKING AT ME.

Ryurikov stared at the sinewy Seepers clustering around his demon, indeed staring at Awimak as though they were aware of his presence.

He shook his head. "It?"

THEY ARE WITHOUT SOUL.

"Ah." They were just standing there, flapping in the wind, pale orange eyes fixated on the horns. "You're invisible, yes?"

YES.

Ryurikov hesitated. "Let's go."

The moment he grabbed hold of Awimak's forearm, the Seepers snapped up straight, elongated limbs reaching for the bridge-obscured sky, heads frozen-still, and eyes bulging.

Fuck, that was unsettling.

Ryurikov slowly reached for his bow. An infestation of eerie breaths rattled down the length of the ravine, spiking fear into the puckered crevices of his asshole. Before he had an arrow ready, they sprang up, twisted themselves around Awimak's limbs and horns, and collectively pulled him to the ground.

Awimak reared, tore at them with his claws, sending tattered pieces flying. There was no blood, no viscera. They ripped like empty sacks of skin.

Arrows did nothing to stop the Seepers from spinning around muscular limbs. Ryurikov swore, grabbed his serrated dagger and cut at the ones around Awimak's legs. He swept his blade upward, slashing one trying to wrap itself around his own face, its two halves fluttering past either side as he swiftly scaled Awimak and held on.

"Awimak, dash!"

His demon galloped up a set of stairs, massive hooves striking stone echoing. He didn't shift like in Enlumine's Wish. Ryurikov made a note of asking him why later, gracelessly waving his dagger in an attempt to counter the unpredictable inpour of boneless flesh-sacks. They were surrounded, whipping bodies and rattling breaths blocking out surprised outcries from those they passed.

The ghoulish creatures were trying to tie Awimak down again as he crossed the first bridge, but most aimed for Ryurikov in particular. He held onto the horns tight, leg hooked around one coil while he fought the Seepers off as best he could—they had taken to slapping him in the face, at his hands, prying loose his hold on Awimak by unravelling the old green cloak. Ryurikov ran his blade in between the eyes of one entwining his leg, only to release an undignified yelp when it peered up at him with those peachy eyes and—

"It has a mouth!"

And *so* many teeth, more than there was room for.

Awimak took a sharp turn, headed across another bridge, his limbs still wrapped in ghoulish layers. Ryurikov steadied his hold and made a noise of repugnance, pushing his blade into a Seeper's soft skull as it sank its teeth into the green cloak, suckling on it.

Those that had tied themselves around Awimak slithered up, their ashen skin glistening silver in the sunlight as they ran out from the other side of the ravine onto yet another bridge. More mouths opened, more teeth snagged his cloak, slurping. Sucking the old, dried viscera off it.

Ryurikov moaned in utter dismay, then sawed the stained fabric away from the horns. He ignored Awimak's growled protest, the old cloak ripping and shredding under his blade, under teeth and hungry sucks.

More rattling was his only warning before a Seeper wrapped itself around his face. Ryurikov inhaled with shock, drawing part of its loose skin into the back of his throat. He gagged, flailed, and lost his grip. His back collided with hot stone. He clawed at gelatinous skin to peel it off, his shouts muffled, panicked, his dagger dropped somewhere.

With ever-increasing desperation, Ryurikov groped for his long dagger, of no mind to calculate the risk by slashing it so near his face when the Seeper abruptly unlatched itself. He inhaled and coughed so hard it hurt. In his faded vision, he caught sight of his old cloak fluttering past, in the mouths and floppy fingers of Seepers, each fighting for its share.

Lying flat on his back and gasping for air, Ryurikov stared up at the bright sky. A large shadow slipped over him and he closed his eyes for a moment before rolling onto his stomach to see the ghouls feasting on what remained of his cloak further down the bridge.

Awimak helped him up, pressed his serrated dagger back into his hand, then bowed to let him straddle his neck again. All without saying a single word.

The Seepers fussed noisily behind them while Awimak walked back out of town. Ryurikov ignored the baffled stares by guildsmen. With a strained cough, he slung himself over his demon's head.

In the heat, Awimak's breath wasn't visible, despite his harsh panting.

The silence that stretched between them was filled with unspoken inference. Awimak's breathing eventually evened out and, walking past the two crooked pillars, they were back out in the open, an expanse of yellowing grass surrounding them.

"So." Ryurikov tapped his fingers along the skull's forehead. "The cloak you wouldn't give up—*my cloak*—ended up attracting a bunch of ghouls."

Awimak said nothing.

"I nearly *died*."

His demon snorted in displeasure.

"Awimak."

FINE. I AM SORRY I TOOK YOUR CLOAK.

"Thank you. That's all I wanted."

SEVENTEEN

$\mathbf{I}$T MAY BE A BAD IDEA.

Ryurikov kept his focus on the forest just ahead, the shadows within ever growing. Awimak referred to braving the mountains, of course, and if history taught Ryurikov anything, it was that his demon had a good sense of when something was a shitty idea.

"I should probably listen to you." Fiery eyes were on him, but he didn't meet them, the corners of his mouth twitching upward. "So, I suppose we're headed for Od Peming Rise."

Awimak's chuff was one of amusement.

"You're not obligated to come along." Ryurikov ghosted over bushes and ferns, while Awimak simply ploughed through it all, causing a racket, large hooves crashing into logs and tearing past shrubbery. "I realise trees must grow and all that, but they're also flammable." He cast a deliberate look at the tree in question.

Mirth flickered in those sun-like eyes.

YOU SEEM CONCERNED FOR MY WELL BEING.

Ryurikov scoffed. "I'm not."

NO?

"You're a demon, most likely somewhat older than I am. I'm confident you can take care of yourself. That reminds me," he continued, cloak flying behind him as he spun to face Awimak. "Why didn't you move between worlds like you did in Enlumine's Wish?"

Awimak halted in his tracks, skull turned downwards. In the advancing darkness, his eyes were a reprieve. I CANNOT WITHOUT THE LIFE OF A FOREST.

Ryurikov's brows furrowed. "In that case, you shouldn't come if there's nowhere for you to hide."

YOU ARE CONCERNED. Said with smugness.

His lips flapped with a dismissive noise and he waved up at the broom in Awimak's horns. "Just because the hag said she won't try to kill me doesn't mean I believe her."

Awimak's footsteps followed as Ryurikov carried on through the dense forest, weaving between the trees until the familiar thick trunks leading up to the hut came into view.

YOU ARE WRONG.

"About what? That you're flammable?"

NO, WE ARE ALL IGNITABLE. I AM MORE THAN SOMEWHAT OLDER.

Ryurikov absent-mindedly glanced up. His stomach growled low with hunger. "How old?"

OLDER THAN YOU.

Tree crowns parted to give way, and old steps creaked under his boots. "You're hilarious." *And* evasive.

Before disappearing inside, he faced Awimak and... Struggled. With what exactly, Ryurikov didn't know, but there was a sense of unease taking root in the pits of his stomach, and it had nothing to do with the gnawing hunger.

He hesitated, fidgeted with the sleeves of the pilfered tunic. His gaze lifted to Awimak's, he opened his mouth. Then, he swiftly turned back 'round and opened the door. It slammed shut behind him with a backward kick. He leaned against it, scanning the room for Jezibaba while listening to heavy footfalls circling the hut. She was nowhere in sight.

With a curious hum, Ryurikov climbed the stairs. He peered into the mirror room, and after praying to gods he didn't believe in, checked inside the bathing room. Empty save for the tub, once more filled with fresh steaming water. That left the bedroom and whatever lurked upstairs.

The staircase up was longer than it had any right to be, winding to a landing that led to a door and yet more stairs. Ryurikov shouldered open the door. Bewilderment stilled him in his tracks.

A child's bedroom. Or rather, the bedroom for a dozen children, going by the number of beds crammed into the space. Crudely fashioned wooden toys lined shelves, splotchy ink drawings by young hands hung from the walls. The beds were small, some stacked atop in threes.

Floorboards creaked as he walked further inside and ducked around chimes. These were made of snail shells, twigs, pinecones. Decidedly less grim than those downstairs. The window overlooked thickets and wild berry bushes. Treetops passed in lurches, suggesting they were again on the move.

Ryurikov tapped the window's rippled glass, his mind working around what facts he'd garnered. The rumour that Jezibaba stole and ate children was well known, but would she go so far as to make them a *home*?

The air clinging to the space did not feel like a prison, nor did it look like anyone had been held captive here. No signs of distress, of scratches in the wood made from desperate attempts to escape, and no blood.

The click of his tongue fell dully into the dusty room. Ryurikov pushed away from the window and went back down, where he invited himself into Jezibaba's bedroom without knocking. He started at the sight of her in a rocking chair by the large window, eyes peeled wide open and staring at him, lifelessly.

"Oh fuck, did you finally kick it?" Ryurikov drew near, ignoring the lusty croak from the toad atop the wardrobe.

Jezibaba didn't so much as twitch when he poked the tip of her big nose, although there was a subtle rise and fall to her chest and fat belly. Asleep, then. With her eyes open. Just when he thought she couldn't get any worse.

A moment's deliberation, then he kicked the chair hard enough to send it rolling back.

The hag flailed with a squawk, but Ryurikov had no opportunity to gloat. A citrine powder exploded in his face, flared up into his nostrils and down the back of his throat.

He sneezed, *violently*. It sent him stumbling. His back connected with the wardrobe, hood falling off his head as he furiously scrubbed his itching face with both hands. Another sneeze, this one nearly causing him to piss himself. His lungs squeezed tight, and he struggled to breathe when yet another sneeze fulminated from him, sending him crashing to his ass.

"You absolute—"

Ryurikov couldn't hear whatever insult the hag hurled at him, once again overpowered by a billowing sneeze. The back of his head knocked into the wardrobe so hard it rattled. Something fell into his lap, he thought he heard a low-pitched croak. Eyes and face burning, Ryurikov crawled out of the bedroom, padding around the floor to find his way, seizing up with every brutal sneeze. By the time he reached the tub, he feared he might shit himself with the next onslaught.

He dunked his head right into the water. Mint and heat soothed his face, the severe itching in his nostrils. He swung back out with a loud gasp. A fan of water pelted the floor behind him. Peeling off the leather gloves, he splashed his face, dug yellow gunk from his nose, and spat out the rest.

"What the fuck!" he rasped, turning to glare at the hag entering the room. It wasn't the hag, but the toad, round belly swaying side to side as it waddled on its back legs toward him. "What the fuck?"

"Mauvella!" Jezibaba hobbled in and snatched the fat toad up. It released an indignant croak, now trapped by sinewy arms.

Ryurikov settled down near the tub, panting, the need to sneeze still burning the back of his nose. "Mauvella? As in *Princess* Mauvella?"

Jezibaba glared. "What of it?"

He wanted to snort, but a pathetic groan left him instead at the ache in his throat. Unable to think clearly, Ryurikov waved the subject away.

"Now what, pray tell, was so important that you had to wake me?"

"*Hngh*—I'm hungry." His voice was muddy with snot.

Jezibaba's lips thinned into an angry line. "And? I told you, I'm not taking care of you. If you're hungry you can cook something."

"I don't know how to cook." He wiped tracks of moisture away from his face, rising to his feet. "And I'm tired of living off berries and raw carrots."

Jezibaba's lizard eyes looked him up and down with scalding contempt. "You're pathetic. All these years and you haven't once bothered to learn how to fend for yourself. Only ever took advantage of others."

The words stung more fiercely than Ryurikov would have preferred. "Fuck off, you gristly slab of mutton."

"I don't know what Awimak sees in you."

The crone left Ryurikov to stand there, a riposte stuck in his mouth, ready to burst with an intense rage he didn't know what to do with because she had already gone. He snapped his gaze around the room, looking for anything to kick. There was nothing.

Ryurikov thundered down the stairs, through the kitchenette and out into the garden before he could think about it. Awimak had resumed his task of tidying the vegetable patch, stilling once catching sight of his angry approach. With a swift tug, Ryurikov undid the clasp of his cloak and let it drift to the grass. He parted his surcoat with equal deftness.

His demon caught on quick, claws clutching his ass to support him the moment he jumped up and wrapped his legs around the sturdy waist. Awimak brought them over to a tree, ripening apples and branches knocking against Ryurikov's head, but he didn't care when that pointed tongue slithered into his mouth for him to suck on. He grunted as his back slammed into bark, his boots and breeches yanked off with relative ease, leaving him in his surcoat and tunic and a slicked finger delving mercilessly into his hole.

There was nothing tentative about the way Awimak took him. Ryurikov fisted his own erection, the other hand grasping at the silky mane as that thick, long cock thrust into him with reckless abandon. Raspy grunts accompanied Ryurikov's moans, raw with an aching need that had replaced his anger. He buried his face into the crook of

Awimak's neck, burning throat soothed by the coolness clinging to grey, earthy skin.

Each unforgiving buck of Awimak's powerful hips drew him closer to his climax. Each nudge against his prostate sent fire from his feet up into his legs, to his belly, drew his balls up tight. Ryurikov eased his bite around flawless skin to gasp for air, to lean back, to watch himself spill his release over Awimak's broad chest.

He glanced back up through half-lidded eyes, and fulgent ones locked with his. A final, brutal thrust into him wrenched free a yelp, and Awimak spilled deep inside, his demon's moan an eerie melody that would surely haunt Ryurikov's dreams.

They settled down by that same tree. He allowed himself a moment of lax resistance as Awimak tucked him into an embrace in his lap, muscular arms encasing him. Like his cloak. Safe, hidden away.

He pressed the side of his face against that heaving chest. It glistened with a fine layer of sweat, like dew caught in a spider's web turned golden by the fluttering moth-lights that had sparked to life around them.

Awimak's heart roared like a distant river, a powerful strum against his ear. Ryurikov took comfort in it, although Jezibaba's words came clangouring back inside his skull, and he grunted with irritation.

WHAT IS YOUR DEAL?

Ryurikov stiffened in the hold. "Don't know what you mean."

YOU ARE ANGRY.

With a fingertip he chased a droplet down Awimak's chest, catching it before it could slide past the curve of the lower pectoral muscle that featured no nipples. He didn't especially feel like talking, content to sit here with his ass throbbing while he stewed in his anger. Unfortunately, his stomach complained with an audible growl.

PERHAPS YOU SHOULD EAT. YOU WILL FEEL BETTER.

"I'm not in the mood for more berries, or carrots, and I'm *fairly* certain cabbage isn't any good raw." Ryurikov shifted, fidgeting with his surcoat to better block out his demon's earthy chill. "And before you say it, I told you I can't cook. That's... That's what I'm pissed about."

YOUR INADEQUACIES ANGER YOU.

Ryurikov glared up in affront. He opened his mouth to retort, but a sturdy finger pressed against his lips. The very *gall* of Awimak shushing him—

THERE IS NO SHAME IN HAVING LIMITATIONS, RYURIKOV. ONLY IN ACKNOWLEDGING YOUR LIMITATIONS CAN YOU GROW.

"I'm not a fucking tree."

TREES, HUMANS. THERE IS LITTLE DIFFERENCE. YOU COME FROM THE EARTH. YOU BLEED. YOU DO WHAT YOUR NATURE TELLS YOU TO. Awimak cupped Ryurikov's face and gently stroked his cheek with a thumb. A REFUSAL TO GROW IS ALL THAT WARRANTS SHAME.

Ryurikov met those enchanting eyes with scrutiny. "What are you saying?"

I AM SAYING YOU SHOULD CONSIDER BURYING YOUR EGO LONG ENOUGH TO ASK IF SHE WOULD BE WILLING TO TEACH YOU SOMETHING. PERHAPS TO COOK?

The very thought made Ryurikov want to shrivel up.

OR YOU CAN STARVE.

"When you put it that way..." Ryurikov sighed, exhausted. "I suppose I should."

YES. Awimak's smugness made a comeback. PERHAPS YOU CAN ALSO ASK HER HOW TO REMOVE THE YELLOW FROM YOUR FACE.

Ryurikov staggered upright and vigorously wiped his forehead, bringing his palms back stained. Swearing, he rushed to dress without looking at Awimak, hoping that the yellow would at least cover his burning embarrassment.

He reentered the hut in a storm, mouth full of insults to be spewed at the witch now stoking a fire in the hearth. Then he stopped, and hesitated, and as Awimak's words swirled around him, Ryurikov deflated.

"What do you want?" the hag snapped without looking.

"Teach me how to cook."

Jezibaba scowled.

"I *mean*," Ryurikov continued before she could refuse him, "I would—" Ugh, his insides squirmed so hard it hurt. "I would *appreciate* it—" Fuck. He didn't want to do this, but neither did he want to return to Awimak and confess he'd not even tried. Ryurikov grit his teeth against the sheer agony, each spoken word a tortured hiss, "If you could teach me how to cook, I would be grateful."

The witch's look turned suspicious. "Why?"

Ryurikov wanted nothing more than to ram his blade down her throat. Instead, he uttered a most strained, "*Please.*"

Silver brows rose, but Jezibaba didn't say anything. It seemed to have done the trick, since she jerked her head at a cauldron perched on the log table. Ryurikov carefully draped his cloak over a stool, then grabbed hold of the cauldron. He brought it over and awaited further instructions.

Jezibaba tossed a log into the fire, now burning hot, and groaned as she got off her knees. She caught sight of him and sighed in exasperation. "Don't just stand there, you weed, fill it with water!"

Ryurikov gnashed his teeth against the insult. "*Where*?"

"You've been out in that garden how often now?"

By some miracle he left through the back door without hag blood on his hands. Awimak was where he'd left him under the tree, one knee raised and looking quite pleased with himself.

"I hope you're happy," Ryurikov grumbled. "I'm fetching *water*."

A TASK YOU WILL COMPLETE WITH RESOUNDING SUCCESS.

"Oh, fuck you."

YOU ARE READY TO TAKE MORE?

Ryurikov smiled before he could help it, then resolutely bit down hard on his lower lip. "Where is the water?"

Awimak pointed past the vegetable patch to the side of the hut. When he rounded the corner, Ryurikov crooned in surprise at the sight of a chicken coop. Beside it stood a decapitated tree that, upon closer inspection, was hollow but for the gurgling water running up its centre, like a fountain. He held the cauldron under a branch more akin to a spout, and watched in amazement as water poured from it. Once full,

Ryurikov took a moment to better wash his face, the water crisp against his skin.

His demon's eyes burned him as he walked back into the hut, feeling pleased with himself. Resounding success indeed, and he only spilt some of it by plonking the container down by the hearth.

Jezibaba sighed with the weariness of someone too old to be teaching, much like his governor who would regularly take a stick to his hands for not paying attention.

"Are you planning on just consuming water? That's too much," said Jezibaba. "Tip some of it out into the ewer there, then."

Ryurikov tilted his head back, already bored. He did as told with a disgruntled mutter, regardless.

If he'd hoped learning how to cook would somehow become more interesting, he was regrettably mistaken. He sliced carrots and cabbage, diced potatoes, *and* chopped onions, a task he *hated*, along with several other things. Then, he noticed an unfortunate lack of meat and voiced his concerns while watching the hag toss everything he'd cut into the cauldron, now hanging over the fire.

"I don't eat meat," she said.

"I'm...sorry?"

"You should be."

Ryurikov shook his head, the better alternative to slapping Jezibaba's. "What do you mean, you don't eat meat? I can hunt. Stop the hut, I'll go down there right now and—"

"Not for a lack of, you idiot. I choose not to."

He stared at her, utterly baffled. "You're mad. Absolutely and unequivocally unhinged."

"You enjoyed the stew before, didn't you?"

His lips flattened in a line. "That killed me."

"This one won't." Jezibaba gathered jars of dried things to add to the cauldron, but Ryurikov snatched her by the wrist before she could. She glared. "It's *seasoning*. I told you, I won't kill you again."

All the same, he tracked her every move and kept a watchful eye on the stew itself. Easily done, when she made him stir it on occasion as it simmered, while she rocked back and forth in the chair, knitting. The thing that had resembled a pile of moss before now looked like a peculiar coat, too small to fit any of them.

"I've been upstairs," Ryurikov said, peering into the cauldron for the hundredth time. When was this going to be ready? He courted malnourishment at this point. "How many children did you take over the years?"

Tales of the child-devouring witch were several times older than Ryurikov, who had hit his mid thirties a few months ago. There must have been hundreds of them, if indeed rumours were to be believed. Rumours, he knew, often sprang from a seed of truth. Always embellished, needing a discerning edge to cut down to the roots of verity, but deep down that seed could always be found.

Jezibaba did not answer him, but the rhythmic click of bone needles halted. Ryurikov stopped scalding his face over the fire long enough to peer at her, and was met with a scowl.

"Make no mistake, *beldam*," he said, straightening up, "there are lines I draw, and I draw them at murdering children. The only reason you're currently sitting here, inhabiting that wrinkly body of yours, is because I happened to care about Awimak more than burning your hut down."

"You should keep your nose out of things you know nothing of," Jezibaba hissed through her yellowed teeth. "Now get your stew, and leave me be."

He kept his eyes on her, long enough for the sprigs of silence to twist into thorny stems. The hag's expression was guarded, mouth a wrathful line. She wouldn't entertain him for much longer, even Ryurikov recognised that.

With the rich scent of vegetable stew wafting up his nose, he eagerly filled a wooden bowl to the brim and, cloak slung over his shoulder, sauntered outside while ignoring the stinging pain in his hand when some of his dinner spilled. Awimak had moved to the other tree, and Ryurikov joined him in the grass, holding out the bowl for him to see.

YOU COOKED.

"I did." He blew across it thrice. "It has no meat, but it'll have to do, I suppose."

Awimak appeared amused. *I AM CERTAIN IT IS MORE THAN ADEQUATE.*

Ryurikov ate in companionable silence, sitting so close their thighs touched. The stew warmed him enough for Awimak's chill not to bother. He soon banished the empty bowl into the bushes and wrapped himself snug in his cloak.

"Right then," he said, noting with some delight how eagerly Awimak opened his arms to invite him into an embrace, "I'm falling asleep on you this time." It had to be better than huddled up alone in bedewed grass.

Once settled comfortably against that mighty torso, Ryurikov closed his eyes with a quiet sigh. In a mutter, he added, "Hope you're less starved this time."

IT WON'T BE BAD, Awimak said in something akin to a murmur. The statement was followed by a tender stroke down his bruised cheek.

EIGHTEEN

The ass crack of dawn was terribly early to be up, the sky still an eminence of indigo. All was quiet, aside from his panting breaths and the obscene slurping around his cock. As promised, the nightmares hadn't been too bad, but Awimak saw the need to make it up to him, anyway. Ryurikov wasn't about to complain.

He twisted his fingers into soft dark hair, let his bare palms journey across the coils of bough-like horns, rough against his skin. His hold on them tightened and Awimak stilled his movements, permitting him to thrust into the long, consumingly hot mouth to his heart's content. When Ryurikov climaxed, it was with an arch of his back, and a low, drawn-out groan. Awimak swallowed his offering with an audible gulp, and released him with a final long, hard suck. He licked around his own mouth with languid delectation.

A lazy smirk draped Ryurikov's lips. "Thank you."

Leaning on an elbow, he reached up to wipe saliva from the jut of Awimak's chin, barely visible underneath the skull. Still hazy with sleep and lust, he gave in to temptation and stroked his knuckles over the side of his demon's face. In the rising sun, the labyrinthine carvings on Awimak's skull glowed gold, reflecting pinks and oranges, filling Ryurikov with fascination and a warmth that quickly overwhelmed.

The sudden, desperate need to kiss his demon slammed into him like a fist to the chest.

Fortunately, he recognised *that* for what it was, and just as quickly, Ryurikov was awake and on his feet, hoisting his breeches back up, walking away. He grit his teeth against the surge of emotion, forcing it all the way back down into his guts and hopefully, right out of his ass.

YOU CANNOT ESCAPE FOREVER, Awimak called after him and *damn* him for sounding so fucking pleased.

He entered the hut—*not* escaped into—to find the hag in the rocking chair by the hearth. With his lips pressed in a line, he manoeuvred around cauldrons and cages to perch on the raised edge of the stone hearth. He waited for Jezibaba to say something, but she only kept knitting, now working on something maroon.

"I'm told Valka was taken by a drake, so I'll need the hut to head for Od Peming Rise."

A brief pause of the clicking needles. "We're already headed there."

Ryurikov raised his brows. "How does it know?"

The sigh that left Jezibaba was long, broken by phlegm, and told of the suffering of someone ancient. "The broom, weedling. It knows."

"Right." He paused, unsure of what to do. Going back outside was out of the question. Ryurikov didn't do feelings, and the onslaught of them needed to be felled and burned. Something he couldn't do if he was around Awimak. So he lingered, fidgeted, helped himself to some cold stew, then watched Jezibaba's gnarly hands work uneven wool.

If the hag had anything to say, it fell away at a slight jolt vibrating the hut. Jezibaba glanced up, grey brows knotting with a frown.

"We've stopped," she said.

"This is unusual, how?"

Jezibaba grumbled incomprehensibly, adding, "We're out of forest to walk through. Guess you're going on foot from here."

Ryurikov grunted and stood to grab his things, but hesitated. "In Eastcairn. What...was the risk to Awimak?"

The hag's gaze darted to him. "What do you mean?"

"He's basically a tree, isn't he?"

At that, those lizard eyes rolled so far Ryurikov thought they might pop out the back of her skull.

"He is not a tree, he is of the *earth*."

"Last I checked, trees were very much rooted in the earth. Well," Ryurikov motioned around him, "aside from the hut's legs. Just tell me if there's a risk of him getting hurt. I'd ask Awimak, but the fucker is evasive."

"Said fucker can hear everything you say, you know." Jezibaba jerked her head in the direction of the kitchenette window. "He's listening in as we speak."

"Awimak!" Ryurikov pivoted to glare out the paned glass. The demon's goliath shape ducked away.

"If there had been no risk," Jezibaba continued when Ryurikov made to walk out, "Awimak would have been able to vanquish the Skin Crawlers himself. They pose a threat to his livelihood as much as the rest of Vale, in case that detail escaped your sapless head."

Ryurikov's mind hurtled faster than a spooked horse. Fuck. She was right, he'd never given it a thought. He excelled at not deliberating matters, it was his best and most useful skill.

"I'll deal with it later," he muttered, grabbing his bow and quiver from the table. "Stay here, Awimak. I don't want you with me."

With that, he exited the hut, left through the parted trees and hopped down into a hazy forest. Blue-tinged smoke curled up off the ground. He wrinkled his nose, his footfalls silent as he made for the edge. He couldn't hear a bird or the chitter of an insect, the atmosphere churning with an eerie frisson that had Ryurikov wrap his cloak more firmly around himself despite the invasive warmth.

He knew where that warmth came from, and by fuck, he hated it, somehow still surprised when he emerged from the last of the trees into nothing but ravaged lands.

Whatever once stood here was gone, burned entirely to the ground. Like Eastcairn, like his home. The air thick with dark smoke, blocking daylight. Fat droplets of rain dragged swirls of dusty blue with them, sizzling and turning to steam.

The puppets of Clutchers walked through ash-laden ground, what remained of their clothes scorched into blistered skin. There were no

Skin Crawlers *yet*, although Ryurikov thought he heard their screeches echo far in the distance. Od Peming Rise was difficult to make out through the smoke, but if the hut had been on its way to it, then the path to the mountains would lay ahead.

He grasped his long dagger tight and snuck, although there was little to hide behind. Charcoal crunched under his boots, the heat threatening to melt the leather. Ryurikov cursed under his breath when a smouldering protrusion singed his cloak, and gathered the fabric around himself a second time.

Squatting behind a half wall of molten stone, he peered around for a way forward. The surrounding ruin sloped upward and, assuming it would lead him to the foot of the mountain, he continued to walk in a crouch.

A chorus of dry crunching bones forced him to a stop. He hid behind another structure, mostly broken, and peered around its corner. Ryurikov started at the group of mobile corpses, heads twitching and jerking, stumbling about in a specific direction, like a unit of marching soldiers. There were at least twenty of them—the nest of Clutchers here had to be impossibly large.

Ryurikov lowered to sit in ash, pliant like snow, to wipe his sweat-damp forehead. The heat was unbearable, entirely different to that of the sun. Smoke hitting his lungs made it difficult not to cough and alert nearby creatures. His thoughts flicked back to Awimak, and his gaze to the forest, now but a shadow behind brumous blue, glad he'd told the demon to stay put. Awimak might have survived the disaster in Eastcairn, but this was on an entirely different level.

Everywhere he looked, there was naught but desolation. Skin Crawlers would have laid waste to this place years ago and most of the everlasting fire had moved on. Ryurikov rubbed his index finger over his thumb in thought. Was this what the Thuidal Kingdom looked like, with nothing left but corpses sucked dry and reanimated?

A shake of his head cleared the thought. From where he sat staining his beautiful clothes, the smoke curled away from rain enough to reveal the foot of the mountain. Once the dry crunching faded, he pushed up and darted toward it, hopping over debris in a rush to get the hell away from there.

Hours of walking but the sky didn't clear, although its hue changed from azure-tinged to obsidian. Scree awaited him at the bottom, the stones jagged and darkened with soot. They clattered down with each precarious inch he climbed, the noise echoing through the haunting stillness clinging to the air. He hoisted himself up a crag and sat on its edge to rest, throat sore and breathing laboured.

There was little to see from here, the smoke shrouding all in a blanket of death. Ryurikov lowered his hood with a tired sigh, glancing over his shoulder. There was much to climb, still. And once he got on top, what then? Dragons and drakes and whatever else lived there would burn him to nothing, most likely.

Was this even worth it, for someone who was in all likelihood dead?

Ryurikov got back to his feet before his cowardice caught up with him. If nothing else, he could confirm Valka was gone. He would no longer have to wonder, to yearn for what could have been.

Od Peming Rise wasn't steep so much as it was a precarious climb. He was thankful for his gloves, the stone rough and painful even through the leather. The higher he climbed, the harsher the winds became, and the more rain lashed him. Scaling a particularly steep drop, among the patter and gales, Ryurikov realised there was another sound.

A tune.

The tune of a flute, its melody sweet, like a lullaby.

A thrill of excitement darted down his back, prompting him to climb faster. Once he reached the top at last, he took a moment to catch his breath, then to appreciate the beauty of his accomplishment.

Lush verdancy, a manifold of waterfalls, and brightly coloured flowers lay ahead of him, sunlight transforming mist into luminous rainbows. That was nice too, he supposed, but that *climb*. Glancing down, the ashen wasteland was no longer visible, thank *fuck*, and he hadn't yet been burned to a crisp by defecating dragons, either.

He waved his hands, encouraging the fresh air up into his nostrils, and inhaled deeply. That melodious flute was louder now blustery winds and rain were no longer beating him over the head.

This place was what one might consider a paradise. Flowers of impossible hues in full bloom, clover carpeting the entire stretch of ground as far as he could see. Ryurikov realised he could have brought Awimak with him, after all. His big demon would have loved this, there were trees everywhere, too.

Od Peming Rise appeared to be as harmless as it was beautiful. Most astonishingly, the first sign of life were lizards. Brightly coloured ones, easily lost among the vibrant flowers as they ran to and fro, standing on their hind-legs and taking... Notes.

They were taking notes, parchment and quill in claws.

Drakes, Ryurikov realised, no taller than the height of his boots. One skittered past him, entirely unbothered by his presence, pink scales radiating like abalone shells. It stopped by a large plant with a long stalk and flame-like flowers, balanced itself on its thick tail, and began scratching away, the ink a shimmer of blue.

Ryurikov burst into laughter. A full on, loud guffaw that had him clutching his stomach and gasping for air.

All this time, Od Peming Rise was believed to be a fearsome place, where dragons and wyverns and drakes, even the odd lindworm, tore anything to pieces, burned all to blackened crisps. No one who valued their life went venturing into these mountains, they had learned to leave these creatures alone centuries ago. Yet here he was, standing doubled over in waterfall-softened grass, in one of the most picturesque places he'd ever travelled to.

The little pink drake glanced at him, its cold grey eyes measuring, maybe a little judgy.

Ryurikov finally controlled himself enough to wheeze, "You crafty fuckers."

His lungs seized with lingering chuckles as he straightened up and carried on. This didn't seem like a place Valka would spend all of her time, but it was worth looking around, at least. There had to be someone willing to pay handsomely for this sort of information.

He followed the sound of the flute, rounding a tall cliff awash with several narrow cascades. He jumped over brooks, hopped across large boulders. The drakes were everywhere, and they were all equally studious. Ryurikov stopped to observe one as bright as a sunflower, studying what appeared to be two blue insects, mating midair.

He opened his mouth before he could even think of something uncouth to say—something hit him between the shoulders, *hard*, sending him off the boulder he'd ascended and to the grass below.

"What the *fuck*—"

What felt a suspicious amount like a *boot* slammed into his back next. Unfortunately, he had no chance to recover when another blow hit him in the side. He rolled over, caught the foot trying to stomp his stomach with both hands and twisted it. The sharp yelp that bounced off the cragged cliffs was feminine, and even before he saw the bright flash of copper hair, Ryurikov *knew* who it was.

His heart skipped a beat as he jumped back up while Valka retreated a few paces. He tried to lower his hood, but she raised a flute, long and bone-white, and played a tune.

Not a sweet lullaby this time, but something sharp, *vicious*, and it prompted every drake nearby to turn its head toward him. Within a flash they descended upon him, a swarm of vivid scales. Teeth sank into his limbs, tearing through clothes, his skin.

Ryurikov cried out. Attempted to pry them off as they piled on. They were heavy, he struggled to remain upright as they climbed, jumped, *gnawed*. He punched one leaping at his face and sent it flying sideways while Valka retreating further to keep playing that fucking flute.

"Valka!" Ryurikov shouted over the drake's wet snarls. "Stop, it's me!"

He cried in agony at the shrill series of notes. All drakes collectively chomped down, tearing into him. His hands found his daggers, ran the blades into the skulls of those latched onto his feet and arms. They were easy enough to kill, to kick off, but *fuck* it hurt, each bite worse than the next.

The tune stopped, and so did the oversized lizards, slithering away through grass like possessed snakes. Ryurikov staggered to his feet and the tip of a gleaming sabre greeted him. It slashed upward.

He saw the blood whip from his face, heard the blade cut through the fabric of his hood, then the pain set in. He stumbled back, clutching at the right side of his face with a trembling hand.

Valka stood before him, unwavering, her face twisted with rage.

"Valka," he said again, pleadingly. He took a few more steps back, soon realising he was at the edge of a cliff, that the fall down would be exceptionally unpleasant. "For fuck's sake, it's *me*, Ruri!"

"I know."

That was all she said. Yet his heart frosted at the chill in her tone, the cruel iciness in her gaze. In the way she licked her lips, then set them back down on the flute.

Oh, *fuck*.

A sharp trill, and a kaleidoscope of scales and sharp teeth came upon him. Ryurikov's foot slipped off the edge. He flailed his arms to regain his balance—would have too, if it weren't for Valka booting him in the centre of his chest.

When Ryurikov fell, his mind jumped from, "what the fuck," to, "if only I'd brought Awimak along." His ruined cloak flapped around him. He kept his gaze fixed on Valka, who watched him descend to his demise.

He met with something hard, the grunt tearing from him loud and startled. Ryurikov's head spun, the fact he was within powerful arms, hardened by bark and muscle, slow to set in.

Awimak had his face turned upward, eyes streaking a fiery glow, thick hooves making simple work of scaling the mountainside. The sound that left Ryurikov would have been embarrassing on a normal day, but seeing as he'd just evaded death a third time, saved by none other than a demon, *his* demon, the mewl seemed appropriate.

He wrapped his arms tight around Awimak's neck, cradle-carried as they ascended, quick to reach the very cliff from whence he'd fallen. When Awimak came to a standstill among vibrant greenery, Ryurikov murmured his thanks, then hopped down to face his sister again.

"Valka," he said, more sternly this time. She did not offer a response, merely sheathed her sabre and brought the flute out again.

Ryurikov drew his bow before he even knew what he was doing, arrow pointed directly at her head. Her lips were but a breath away from the flute, the stony look replaced by something darker, while a knowing, mirthless smile tugged at the corners of her mouth.

"Kill me, and you'll have finished all of us off. Was that the goal all along?"

"I don't know what you're talking about," Ryurikov spat. He hadn't meant to draw his bow, but damned if he was going to lower it now. "Put the flute down."

Valka lowered it, twirled it in her hand, then sheathed it at her hip opposite the sword. In turn, Ryurikov swung the bow onto his back and the arrow back into the quiver. He held up his hands in surrender.

"Hand to hand, then," said Valka.

Behind him, Awimak snorted his displeasure.

"And keep that oversized imp out of this."

"Hey!" Ryurikov wiped a hot trickle of blood from his cheek. "That imp has a name, and it's Awimak. I'm not fighting you. And neither will he, isn't that right?"

His demon snarled. Ryurikov took that as a reluctant agreement.

"Too bad," said Valka, then ran at him.

They had sparred often as children. Combat knowledge was required for both of them, armed and unarmed, but even back then, Valka had always been bigger, stronger. Ryurikov was lithe, faster on his feet. It took little to out-manoeuvre her, to side-step her forward lunge, or to evade—an elbow connected with his shoulder blade, sending him crashing to the ground. The next blow was delivered to his head, and to his gut, and his ribs.

Ryurikov gasped, blinking rapidly to clear the black spots from his vision. Valka had always hit hard, but *this* was on another level, each blow fuelled by unbridled rage, her furious scream contorted by hatred. A hard kick to his shoulder forced him on his back. She straddled his throbbing ribcage, each blow that connected with Ryurikov's face brutal. Until the skin broke, until the bone in his cheek cracked.

Until it all stopped, and Ryurikov coughed hard enough to bring blood up. It splattered back down onto his face. He couldn't see, vision blurry and obstructed by red, but based on the grunts of outrage and struggle nearby, he guessed Awimak had intervened.

He swore, spat out more blood, and nudged one of his front teeth with his tongue, certain it was loose. Although it was hard to tell when his face blazed with pain.

"You fucking *bastard*!" Valka shouted. "You killed them all!" Her voice quaked and broke. "Our cousins, all our friends!"

Ryurikov struggled to sit upright. When he managed it, he slouched forward. Awimak had Valka in a firm hold while she fought to free herself. Like a proper tree however, his demon didn't move.

"And you dare show your face to me?"

"They're not all dead," Ryurikov said, wiping the spittle clinging to his split lip.

They weren't all dead. How could they be? He'd survived, Vasili too. Others would have survived.

"No one's left alive, except for *you*," Valka snarled, her words acidic enough to melt his skin off.

"Horseshit." He glanced at Awimak for confirmation, but got nothing. "How–How could they all be?"

"Because you sent them all to hell!"

Ryurikov shook his head. "No."

Valka had ceased her struggling, now only stood with her neck trapped in Awimak's arms, braided hair a mess. "Anya, Milo, Zoya, Mom and Dad—*everyone*!"

His mind stopped turning, his heart wasn't working properly, either. Resolutely, Ryurikov shook his head. He looked back up at Awimak.

"No." This time, it sounded more like a question, and this time, Awimak answered him.

YES.

Nineteen

Multifarious faces stared down at Ryurikov, massive and crowding the entirety of the hag's disconsolate underkeep. He glared right back at their sinister features. Ancestors of some sort, he presumed, since they resembled skulls more, but he never cared enough to ask.

"Hurry up," he said, snapping his fingers at the old woman shuffling to fetch the item he'd requested.

Radmila or *Beldam*, as Ryurikov preferred to call her, scowled, unsightly face barely visible under the long, grey hair hanging in limp mats. An oversized and stained frock hid her scrawny frame. She was of such short stature she needed a stool to reach the cupboards. Her hands always trembled, from old age Ryurikov assumed, but there was a particularly strong tremor to them now. Bony fingers wrapped around a leather pouch. She nearly toppled off the stool.

"Are you dying?" Ryurikov asked. "If you are, tell the King. We'll need to replace you."

Radmila grumbled something, he didn't especially care what. She had been in their employ for generations, well before he was born, according to Vasili. It didn't seem likely that the crone would croak today.

"I better not get in trouble for this." Radmila slapped the pouch into his outstretched palm. She returned to the tome she'd been pouring over before his intrusion, large and in some foreign text, bearing sketches of peculiar bird-like skulls.

Ryurikov grinned. "If you do, will it be my problem?"

She looked up at him, orange eyes alight with anger and contempt. She fucking hated him, and it filled him with glee.

"No, I don't reckon *that* will be your problem," she said.

"Exactly." He winked, then pivoted to head out the door. The giant, glaring masks always became a touch too unnerving after a while. Vasili never wanted to enter the witch's dungeon because of it.

His Keeper stood at the top of the dark and winding staircase, waiting for him, as always. He was a few years older than Ryurikov and had an impressive set of shoulders, but even in his thick, fire-yellow surcoat and armour, he looked like a padded flagpole.

Ryurikov puffed out a tired breath once ascending the last of the stone steps and slammed a hand down on Vasili's shoulder for support. "Fuck, I don't know why we have to keep her so far down."

"Too old to make the climb up," Vasili replied, stiffly. "The alternative is to keep her in chains."

"Like in the good old days. Well, I got what I needed." Ryurikov led the way down a long, cold hallway with his Keeper in tow. "How's your back?"

"It's fine."

Abruptly, he stopped and faced Vasili, all mirth slipping away as he looked into those umber eyes. "I've already told you, but I'm telling you a second time. If you ever pull that shit again, I'll whip you myself."

"I would do it again in a heartbeat."

"*Don't*, you fucking block. I can handle a bit of drowning, but I don't ever want to see anyone flayed like that again."

Vasili's thin lips mustered a ghost of a smile. "Your concern for me is touching, your Highness."

Ryurikov made a face, turning in a whirl of his fur-lined, fire-yellow cape to saunter on.

"Should I ask what's in the pouch?" Vasili looked nervous when

Coil of Boughs

Ryurikov cast him a cheeky smile and tossed the pouch up, catching it again.

"Ask."

"What's in the pouch?"

"You'll find out."

"I would prefer not to."

Through large archways, they strode into a courtyard, overly spacious like everything else in the Maksim castle. The echo of splashing water bounced against grey stone, the behemoth of a fountain at the very centre, where Valka sat clad in a knee-length tunic and breeches of the same cobalt blue as Ryurikov's own, keeping their cousins company.

"Don't hold it out of the water too long," Valka said to Anya, who had one of the fountain's fish in her hands, lambent and shimmering like sapphire.

"Young Lady Zoya," Ryurikov sang upon approach.

Zoya pulled away from the fountain's edge to look up at him. He knew little about her, less still about children in general and could only guess at her age. Thirteen, possibly. He *did* know she'd lost her father in the war against demons up North only a month ago, and that she hadn't been the same since. Her once plump face now sallow, green eyes listless and skin without colour, making her look like a ghost with auburn hair.

Ryurikov bowed to present the leather pouch in an open palm. "A gift, for the prettiest lady in all the Thuidal kingdom and beyond."

Zoya took it, cautiously. "What is it?"

"Trust nothing my brother gives you," Valka teased, perching on the edge of the fountain to keep the youngest from throwing himself into the water, fingers curled into the back of his tunic.

"I'm offended," Ryurikov drawled. "This will cheer you up, Zoya, but don't unleash it until the feast tonight, you hear?"

"What am I supposed to do with it?"

His smile broadened. "Empty the contents into this ugly fountain." He sneered up at the statue of his father, standing with exaggerated poise, both hands on a great sword. Ryurikov was well familiar with that sword. His father often used it to remind him he would never be great enough to wield it. "I promise you, it'll be worth the wait."

Valka hauled Milo away from the fountain again. Clicking his tongue with impatience, Ryurikov grabbed the rambunctious five-year-old by the underarms and with a great swing, tossed him into the hedges lining the paths. He then motioned for Valka to follow him.

"I've something to tell you."

"You okay, Milo?" she called out to the lad struggling only with a fit of giggles.

Ryurikov took Valka as far as one of the elaborate archways, away from any guards, aside from Vasili, who was obligated to stay within six feet of him at all times.

"Listen," Ryurikov began, pulling his sister closer. "This person you keep meeting in the forest—"

"Ruri, I'm not telling you—"

"I don't need to know, but you said they can take you places, away from here? You're certain?"

Valka sighed in exasperation. The surly grey skies dulled the gold embroidery of her tunic as she moved to clasp his face in both hands. She lightly shook his head. "Let it go. It's too late. Prince Gerung arrived hours ago—"

"Yes, I was there to greet the ponce." He clutched Valka's hands, squeezing them. "You deserve to marry someone who isn't named *Gerung*, don't you think?"

She made a loud, unattractive noise, pulling away. "And you deserve to marry someone more sane than Princess Mauvella. But here we are, both betrothed for the betterment of our kingdom."

Ryurikov cast a look about for any potential eavesdroppers, then pulled Valka further behind the stone arch, ignoring the way Vasili shifted closer, still. "I've got it sorted."

Well, he continued to refine the details as he went along.

"What have you got sorted?" she asked with a suspicious arch of her brow.

Ryurikov debated telling her what he'd witnessed of Gerung's father while welcoming their arrival, but he had yet to confirm his suspicions and wasn't about to get Valka involved—*at all*. She didn't need to know the visiting king was, in all likelihood, possessed by the very demons their armies had been losing against for the last year.

A sudden splash, and they both peered around the pillar to see Milo flailing in the water. Valka moved away, but Ryurikov held her back.

"He's fine, children are buoyant," he said in a rush. "During the feast, I need you to meet me in the meadow. Will you do that?"

She made an impatient noise and yanked her arm free of his grasp. "Assuming you can even get out."

"Assume that I will."

"Fine, if it'll make you happy."

"So happy!" Ryurikov called as she darted away and hoisted a spluttering Milo out of the fountain, reprimanding Zoya and Anya for not helping.

He smirked at Zoya's defiant, "But he has to learn how to swim, sometime." Maybe kids weren't that bad, after all.

"What have you sorted?"

Vasili came up behind him, so close the man's warm breath brushed across his neck. He kept doing that, invading his personal space when there was no risk to his life. Sometimes, Ryurikov was tempted to give in, just to let his Keeper get it out of his system, but the idea sat about as well as a cap sewn out of someone's buttocks.

Ryurikov moved away. "Don't worry about it."

The look on his Keeper's face clearly stated Vasili did worry about it. Too bad for him.

The feast was as any before it. Tables brimmed with food and drink, and the criminals they had lined up in the centre of the wide room pleaded for mercy as they wept, barely dressed and on their knees.

Ryurikov fingered the brim of his silver goblet, already drained of wine, looking on with distaste at the elderly man begging for his life. The whole line-up was unimpressive. They were no more than peasants, their crimes unworthy of such cruelty.

Alas, his mother had developed a taste for it, and his father was a perpetual enabler. Ryurikov's gaze lifted off the quietly sobbing elder who had stolen only a loaf of bread, and settled on King Munderic at the adjacent table. A truculent bear of a man who looked like he had indulged in some heavy opiates, twitchy as he was. Of course, Ryurikov suspected it was something else entirely, but how to obtain proof?

Pissing him off would be one way, from what he'd heard.

The prince with the unfortunate name, Gerung, sat beside the king, the polar-opposite of his father. Young, elegant. Skin like ebony and clad in rose-gold and white. Long flaxen hair pulled in a graceful bun, braids festooning the sides of his head.

Unsurprisingly, his eyes were trained on Ryurikov rather than Valka. The shine Gerung had taken to him had been immediate, not that he blamed him. For the hell of it, Ryurikov winked at the prince, just as he caught Valka's wary glance. She leaned into Gerung, who politely inclined his head, and murmured something into his ear.

Being the well-bred man he was, Gerung immediately rose when Valka did, bowing with a hand across his chest. He did not watch her leave. Instead, his eyes flicked back to Ryurikov. There was a suggestion in that amber gaze, and Ryurikov's cock stirred at the thought of it.

Alas.

A servant drifted past to refill his goblet, and he downed it in a few gulps before rising, the harsh scoot of his chair drowned out by laughter. Queen Maksim had decided not to forgive the ageing man.

Ryurikov sneered. He did not share his parents' taste in what they considered entertainment, unfortunately for the five peasants who had yet to plead their case, he had learned the hard way not to interject.

Slipping away was easy enough. Everyone was distracted and, if Zoya did her job, would soon be too busy to realise he was gone. He hurried down a cavernous hallway, Vasili once again his shadow.

"Prince Leonid."

Ryurikov stopped in his tracks. When he turned, Gerung glided up to him, all smiles and white teeth and dazzling hair, shimmering in azure flames of the torches lining cold stone walls. Fucking hell, he was pretty. No wonder Valka wasn't overly opposed to marrying him.

"Ryurikov, if you please. Leonid is the King."

Gerung's smile wavered. "Ah, of course." He came to a graceful stop just a foot away. "I understand, although you should count your blessings."

"Oh?"

"At least your name isn't *Gerung*."

Ryurikov laughed, he couldn't help it. "Fuck. My apologies, I didn't mean—"

"That's quite alright." Gerung's smile was genuine and, honestly, exquisite. "Wherever you're headed, would you care for some company?" Those bright amber eyes flicked to Vasili, but a few feet away from them, fingers tight around the hilt of his short sword. "Assuming your Keeper doesn't mind."

Ryurikov wrenched his gaze away from those full lips. "I'm sorry, I have a matter to attend to." Gerung's expression dropped, and he didn't like that. Swiftly, he added, "I'll find you after, if that's agreeable?"

"After?" That smile returned. "Then, I'll be waiting."

Ryurikov had half a mind to forget about everything and drag Gerung into a spare bedroom to fuck him senseless that same moment.

"Alas," he murmured, once again on his way.

"Your Highness, *please*," Vasili uttered, darting after him. "Don't do it."

"Don't do what?"

"Him!"

Ryurikov rolled his eyes, shouldering open a door leading down a long and narrow staircase. "It's none of your business."

"It is my business if you're putting the entire kingdom on the line! If King Munderic finds out his precious son has been deflowered, he'll have our heads or worse, declare war on us."

"Lower your voice," Ryurikov snapped, bounding down, down, *down*. It would only be a matter of time before others questioned his whereabouts, he didn't need his whimpering Keeper to speed things along. "I'll fuck him discreetly. Besides, does he strike you as a virgin?"

He reached the bottom of the stairwell at last and made his way along a dark corridor, crowded with rats and cages holding prisoners long since dead. Skeletal arms with but a thin sheet of leathery skin extended past the bars, fingers still set in clawed desperation.

A hand clamped down on his shoulder and forced him 'round. Ryurikov glared at Vasili. In the scattered torches, he could scarcely make out the taut features of that annoying face.

"Don't, Ruri."

Vasili only ever used that name when he was being possessive, and by fuck, he was possessive as all hell, having gotten it into his head that he and Ryurikov were meant to be. He had realised this insane notion the day his parents betrothed him to Princess Mauvella, and had been fending off Vasili's advances ever since. Much like now, when that hand slid up his neck to cup his face.

"Just, don't," Vasili pleaded. "Don't break my heart."

Ryurikov smacked his hand away. "You're forgetting your place, *Knight*."

"I am more than that! I'm your Keeper—"

Ryurikov stalked off. "I don't have time for this right now."

A lengthy dash through the dungeons eventually led him to a heavy door that, with enough kicks, opened into the grounds outside the castle. Overgrown ivy and brush snagged his clothes. It was a pain to shut again, so he signalled for Vasili to do it for him.

"Does this have anything to do with your scheming the past few days?" Vasili demanded in a whisper.

Ryurikov shushed him, crouching by the wall, out of sight of guards standing at the parapet above, and waited for the sky to light up.

Come on, Zoya.

Dark grounds stretched ahead of him, remittent moonlight a whisper of silver across grass. He sat to rest his back against the wall, wondering if Valka had already made it to the meadow. It was easier for her to get around, not being chained to the castle like he was, just because he was the eldest and therefore a target.

His Keeper knelt beside him. By the look of strain on Vasili's face, his flayed back continued to give him trouble. Ryurikov knew he ought to feel...*something* about that, about the way Vasili tried to help him while his father lost control teaching Ryurikov not to give into torture. Aside from the gut churning disgust at seeing skin whipped off bone, however, he didn't feel strongly about it.

"Please, tell me what it is you're planning."

He sighed and skirted a glance over Vasili's worried expression. "I'm sending Valka off to adventure like she wants to."

"But—"

"She can't get married, for fuck's sake. Living life as a ruling monarch would kill her spirit."

"Ruri, we *need* to combine our kingdoms if we have any hope of defeating—"

"It's fine. Gerung being so taken with me will have its advantages. No one is going home in a huff, alright? We'll still be able to join efforts."

Vasili looked unconvinced. "And Princess Mauvella? I'm certain she will have something to say about you being with Prince Gerung instead."

Ryurikov shrugged. "I'm kind of hoping the rumour of her disappearance is true. Then she won't be a problem, and Queen Garnetha will feel bad enough to join forces, anyway."

"And if the rumour is just that, a rumour?"

"Rumours always hold a seed of truth." Ryurikov craned his neck.

Voices from atop the wall floated down. The guards were changing shifts already. He licked his lower lip. Maybe Zoya wasn't curious enough to find out what was in the pouch. Fuck. He pushed to his feet, hand splayed against the wall behind him. He readied to run during their moment of marginal distraction just as an explosion illuminated the night sky, turning it into an expanse of shimmering sapphire.

Ryurikov bolted forward, Vasili's stumblings and clinking chainmail behind him. Another flash, and glimmers sprinkled down like fat snowflakes—fish scales.

"Oh, fuck."

"The royal fish!" Vasili gasped.

That wasn't supposed to happen. Fucking Radmila.

Past the first line of trees and into the old forest, Ryurikov didn't stop running until they were under the full cover of umbrageous canopies. Glowing insects flitted by as he strode over underbrush, providing just enough light for him to see his way to the meadow, tucked deep within. Once upon a time, when his father didn't rule him with an iron fist, he and Valka often met in the meadow to get away from things.

She was there, ethereal in the moonlight as she gadded about, boots crushing violet irises.

Ryurikov hid behind a tree and pulled Vasili to him. It was too dark to see his face, but he heard the sharp intake of breath, his gloved hands flying up to grasp Ryurikov's forearms. The sheer need radiating off his Keeper was pathetic. His own hands found the man's shoulders and squeezed.

"I need you to do me a favour," he whispered.

"Anything," Vasili choked out.

"Stay here and don't listen in."

"Ruri, I have to—"

"You said *anything*." It was cruel to take advantage of Vasili like this, when he'd disarmed him so easily, but times were desperate.

His Keeper remained silent, so Ryurikov patted his shoulders before easing out of the tight grasp. Valka's attention snapped to him when he emerged from the trees. More light bloomed across the sky, and yet more fish scales flickered down.

"What the hell is happening?" Valka asked.

"Zoya having fun, hopefully," he said, although spared a moment to consider the possibility that Zoya might currently be looking at exploded fish. Whoops. "Now's your chance."

Ryurikov closed the gap between them and clasped Valka's neck in both his hands to pull her forward. She didn't resist the embrace he caught her in.

She readily returned the hold, squeezing him tight. "Chance for what? Tell me."

He leaned back and smiled, peering into her shadowed hazel eyes. "To run. Get away from this. I've got it all figured out. You don't have to worry. You can go be free."

Valka's brows furrowed with doubt. "Come on, be serious."

"I am." He gave her a slight shake for emphasis, hands now tight around her face. "Go, adventure. Be better than *this*, than our parents."

Her hands came to his shoulders and for a moment, clawed at the fur lining of his cape. "Don't toy with me."

"I'm not."

"I can't."

"Yes, you can." He pulled her down a fraction to rest his forehead against hers. "Please, I'm begging you, get the fuck out of here."

Away from the food hoarding, the greed, the eternal torment their subjects suffered, starving to death in the castle's cells, in their very own streets. Away from the ruthless, mangled mess that had become their rule.

Valka's eyes closed, turmoil contorting her face. "Ruri, I'm not leaving you to Dad's mercy."

"I told you," Ryurikov murmured, "he never lays a hand on me. It's all just yipping."

When she opened her eyes again, they glistened with unshed tears. "And I can just go on adventures?"

"Like you've always wanted. I've put a lot into this." Ruefully, he smiled. "If you don't go now, I'll have pissed Radmila off and die of the liquid shits for nothing."

Valka chuckled. "Swear to me that everything will be okay. That you won't get into trouble, and our kingdom will join with Florewen and Noxnynth?"

For a fraction of a second, Ryurikov hesitated. Then, "I swear it."

He was going to burn for his lies, but Valka would be well away from this place before that ever happened. By the time she discovered he'd lied… Well, it would be too late. Their Kingdom would likely have succumbed to the army of demons drawing nearer each day.

"You have to go *now*, while they're too distracted to notice anything."

"Ruri. I—"

"*Go*." Hands on her shoulders, he pushed her. "Go with whoever you meet. I *know* they're basically at your beck and call." He grinned at her abashed expression.

She took the first step away from him, and Ryurikov's heart clenched tight.

"Eat your greens, Ruri," she said with another step. "You want to be as big as your little sister sometime, right?"

Yet another step, and he thought his heart might shatter at the sight of her back. Before her form could disappear into the shadows entirely, a sudden panic tightened its hold on him.

"I love you, Valka!"

She turned. Another blast of cerulean light mantled the sky, its hues brushing her pale face. Her lips held a smile. It was sad. "And I you."

And then she was gone, the crunch of leaves and twigs masked by more fireworks.

She hadn't told him where she was going, where she *wanted* to go. Almost as if she knew he was a liar, that he couldn't know where she would go because their father would wring it out of him. Ryurikov simmered on that possibility during his return to a fretting Keeper.

"Calm down," he muttered distractedly.

"Where is she going?"

He didn't answer. By the time they crossed the grounds back to the castle, the last of the explosions had died down. All had become quiet, eerily so, the scrape of the heavy door dreadfully loud. He rubbed his thumb across the length of his pointer finger, heart thudding with certain fear. Only a matter of time before the King and Queen questioned where he'd gone to, before they asked about Valka's whereabouts.

The courtyard was empty, carcasses of fish much larger than they ought to be littering hedges and pathways. Their scattered scales a lustre of sapphire, livening up an otherwise grim scene. Poor Zoya, he had to find her and apologise. Assuming she hadn't been traumatised further. Fuck.

Rather than brave the main hall where the feast would likely have resumed, Ryurikov veered off into the west section of the castle, where he could await Gerung in the guest chambers.

"Where are we going?"

Of course, Vasili would have already realised what he was going to do, trailing behind him, as always.

"I don't have a choice," he muttered.

"*Ruri.*"

"Just, shut up. I'm trying to think."

Get Valka away from all this, *done*. Sleep with the Prince of the Noxnynth Kingdom, *could do*. Get him to fall in love and propose, *easy*. Bank on Princess Mauvella's disappearance, also easy.

He was at the door before he knew it, looking at ornate carvings of fish and floral swirls. Before his knuckles connected with the dark wood, the door swung open. Ryurikov quirked an eyebrow at Gerung's startled look, his curvaceous frame outlined by flickering orange hues of the hearth's fire inside.

"Decided to ditch the feast, then," said Ryurikov.

Relief flooded Gerung's face. "Yes, of course. My father has, as well. He's in his assigned chambers. Is everything alright?"

"Why wouldn't it be?"

Gerung tilted his head, sending rivulets of flaxen hair to slip over his shoulder. "The explosions."

"Oh, that." Ryurikov waved a dismissive hand. "Just a kid playing a prank."

Gerung smiled. "Shall we head back to the feast? It'd be a shame to miss out on such splendid food."

Food taken right out the mouths of their subjects.

Ryurikov stepped closer. From the corner of his eye, Vasili's whole body took on the rigidity of a tombstone. He could practically hear his Keeper screaming on the inside when he entered Gerung's chambers, when the door shut, and when lips crashed against Ryurikov's in a heated kiss. Gerung pulled away shortly after, embarrassed and covering his mouth with a few fingers.

"I'm—I'm sorry. I've been *aching* to do that since meeting you."

In fluid movements, Ryurikov undid the clasp of his cape to let it drop to the floor. His fingers found Gerung's chin and he guided him close. Their lips met again, with a little more finesse this time. Finesse he practised throughout. While easing the prince to his elaborate bed, while undressing him.

While fucking him with slow deliberation, relishing in the wanton moans and lust-laced pleadings for more, more, *more*.

Ryurikov kissed him, deeply, guiding him to the pinnacle of pleasure, and he kissed Gerung again once they collapsed to gather their breath, skin glistening with sweat. Their lock of lips came undone, and Gerung's half-lidded eyes held Ryurikov's for the longest time as he reached out to stroke a palm over the man's soft sides.

"I hate to do this," Ryurikov murmured, stealing another kiss before he sat upright to swing his legs off the bed. "But I need to go, for now."

"You'll return?"

Gerung was splayed out for him again, nothing but dark skin and radiant beauty. Unable to resist, he leaned over to capture those full lips in another kiss, languid and tender.

"I'll return."

He fumbled with the clasp of his cape after shutting the door behind him. It was still quiet, aside from the snuffling to his right. Ryurikov started at the sight of Vasili, slumped on the floor, shoulders shaking with uncontrolled sobbing.

Something akin to guilt slithered up his spine. He didn't know what to do with it.

"Vasili..."

"Fuck—" Vasili violently inhaled a large clump of snot, furiously wiping his face. "*You*!"

"Hey, now—"

His Keeper stumbled to his feet, face red and damp with tears, distorted with a rage Ryurikov had never seen before. It shocked him into silence.

"I fucking *hate* you."

The venom behind those words sparked Ryurikov's own anger. "Too bad for you, then."

Vasili gaped with hurt and disbelief, then shook his head and stalked forward. For a moment, Ryurikov thought he might attack. Instead, Vasili shoved him out of the way, his angry stomps echoing through the chilly, glum hall as he walked away from him.

He'd never done that before, either.

Ryurikov rubbed his shoulder, glanced out the arched window closest to him, then walked in the opposite direction.

His wandering became mindless. Mostly, he was trying to avoid facing anyone, Vasili's weeping still haunting the forefront of his mind. He didn't see the wide man emerging from his chambers until he practically ran into him. Ryurikov grunted and moved back, his gaze meeting King Munderic's.

Even in the dim blue light of the torches, the man's eyes were unfocused, muscles in his face spasming in a way that was truly un-fucking-settling. He looked wider and taller than Ryurikov remembered.

"How was he?"

The voice sent frost into Ryurikov's very bones, worse than any of Radmila's muttered revenge-spells. That was not the voice of the king, he'd not even opened his mouth to speak. Ryurikov jostled back, heart thudding harshly. Munderic's head cocked to the side, as if blind and listening for sounds.

Ryurikov did not speak, he held his breath.

The King faced him in full. His neck looked oddly distended, limbs even more so, as if something were stretching him from the inside.

"Was it worth it, Prince Ryurikov? Was he a good fuck?"

Ryurikov laughed. He didn't know what else to do. The King somehow knew he'd just undone the carefully woven tapestry of planning between the distended man in front of him and King and Queen Maksim.

Oh well, he supposed he might as well burn everything down while Valka could no longer get hurt. His father was going to kill him for this anyway, or at best, torture him. And this kingdom—*his* kingdom—deserved to fall, weak and cruel as it was.

So Ryurikov laughed again. "He was an excellent fuck. What's the matter, would you like me to take you for a ride too? I bet you're a little harder to tame than your well-travelled son."

Munderic's head cocked again. His mouth opened, releasing one of the most awful sounds Ryurikov had ever heard a man make. His mouth, now gaping, widened still. Until it tore at the corners and kept tearing, a large, bone-like protrusion emerging from it, like a beak. Arms and limbs extended, cracked, and tore to reveal scythe-like legs. Blood splattered across the stone, somehow catching fire.

Ryurikov pivoted to run. Something hard clobbered him in the back. He crashed to the floor with a strained grunt. Raised himself back up. Heat singed his back. It took him far too long to realise his cape was on fire. He rounded a corner, fighting to undo the cape. It dropped to the ground, but the fire had latched onto him, crawling up his side, scorching fabric into his skin.

He cried out in agony, trying to rid himself of his clothes entirely, thinking only of the fountain where he could douse himself. Shouts of shock and terror echoed around the castle, chased by the frenzied noise of bone clacking against stone.

Ryurikov dropped to the floor, screaming, engulfed in flames.

TWENTY

The downpour of rainbow-touched water fell mutely. Ryurikov's ears pounded with the rush of blood, the ache in his face nothing compared to the throttlehold anguish had on him. His mouth was dry, it had been hanging open for too long, trying to form a response. In a limbo of wanting to wail and shout with anger, Ryurikov didn't move while Awimak's significant form lowered by him.

Fiery eyes looked at him. His breath hiked, a sob threatening to spill free. Ryurikov's fist clenched around the haft of his dagger without command. He staggered upright and glanced around, overwhelmed. Helpless. His free hand closed around the other dagger.

He needed to kill something.

Skin Crawlers were only a few jumps down. Ryurikov made to move, but thick arms swiftly encased him.

"Release me."

He'd be more careful this time, probably. Now knowing what to expect, he could kill them all. He had to kill them all. It wouldn't bring anyone back, but—Ryurikov shook his head, he tried to move again. Awimak held him tight, and he pushed back against the embrace.

"Let me *go!*" His voice broke. *Fuck*.

NOT THIS TIME, RYURIKOV.

"Awimak!"

At some point, he'd dropped the daggers to slam his fists against the massive chest, fighting to get free, to get away before, *before*—

A sharp burn grasped his lungs, pressed up into his throat. His eyes stung, his vision became nebulous. Awimak's hold on him didn't relent, only tightened, the ululating cry that wrenched itself free at last twisted Ryurikov's whole body.

He wanted to scream that he hadn't known, but he couldn't say that.

Because he *had* known.

Waking up in a foreign bed in a modest hut, in hellish pain and covered by dressing, he'd panicked and escaped. He'd seen it then, from a distance. The fires consuming what was once an unyielding castle, turning grey stone into bright orange. Few could have survived that. An understanding he pushed into the back of his mind, locking it away. Allowing himself to forget with each rapid step he'd taken to flee the lands.

But he'd never truly forgotten. The terrible knowledge that he'd doomed everyone had always been there, lurking in his subconscious, telling Awimak what Ryurikov refused to face.

There was no choice but to face it now, and it cracked his chest all the way open. It tore out his heart, his lungs. He couldn't *breathe*. His face throbbed, pressed against a cool chest as large hands stroked over his back. *Comforting* him. Ryurikov clung on, his fingers digging into chilled skin, a feeble attempt to control the onslaught of sorrow threatening to break him entirely.

Gelid stone connected with his backside. Ryurikov's quivering inhale echoed, and he blinked, furiously, to try and clear his vision. He'd ended up inside a cave, brightly lit by sunlight pouring in from above. A brook weaved through rock nearby, eroded over the years. Awimak bent low over it, cupping crystalline fluid into a hand.

Ryurikov flinched, water splashing onto his cheek, but didn't fight it, too tired to do much else than sit there and let Awimak wash him. His fingers found the fabric around his knees, torn and stained by blood. His weeping had fatigued him, wiped away any upset he might have otherwise felt at the state of his clothes.

More water rinsed away blood. His throat flexed around the need to say he could do this himself, but he ended up croaking, "I don't deserve it."

Awimak turned to him from where he knelt by the brook, sun-like eyes desaturated in the light. GUILT WILL ERODE IF YOU ALLOW IT TO MOVE FREELY.

Ryurikov jerked his head, unsure of the meaning.

GUILT DOES NOT SERVE A PURPOSE. IT CORRUPTS THE MIND AND SPIRIT.

"I'm still not sure what you mean." Fuck, his head hurt on top of everything else.

His demon moved near again, cupping yet more water, holding it up to his face. DRINK.

Ryurikov did as told, setting his lips to the claw and sipping. So crisp, it hurt his parched throat. He struggled to swallow.

ONCE YOU ALLOW GUILT TO CONSUME ONE PART OF YOU, IT WILL TRICKLE INTO ALL OTHER PARTS. Awimak ran a dampened palm over his back, sitting beside him. THEN, IT WILL LEAD YOU TO BELIEVE THINGS THAT ARE NO LONGER TRUE.

"Meaning?"

YOU ARE AS GUILTY OF WHAT HAPPENED AS THE STONE WE SIT UPON.

Ryurikov snorted and instantly regretted it. He settled his throbbing head in his hands and didn't resist when Awimak's arm came around his shoulders to pull him close. His side was brisk, allowing Ryurikov to root himself.

"You're forgetting that every trickle has a source, and that source is as surely water as the brooks that branch off it."

MEANING?

"I'm guilty of one thing, everything else that follows is also my fault."

I DID NOT REALISE YOU WERE ALL-POWERFUL. HAVE I MET MY MATCH AT LAST?

Ryurikov glanced up, brows furrowing with the beginnings of vexation.

THE SKIN CRAWLERS WOULD HAVE EMERGED SOONER OR LATER, RYURIKOV, AND WOULD HAVE DONE SO WITHIN YOUR KINGDOM REGARDLESS.

"Doesn't change that I should have…" Warned others. Tried to get his cousins out instead of only Valka. The thought worked to undo him again. He clutched at the torn surcoat, wishing he could up the ache inside him to toss it away.

YOU OVERESTIMATE YOUR ABILITY.

"Fuck, Awimak," he ground out. "Not now. My head hurts too much for this."

IF YOU HAD BEEN ABLE TO WARN OTHERS WHILE IGNITED, THAT WOULD HAVE INDEED MADE YOU ALL POWERFUL.

"Fuck you."

THAT IS BETTER.

A massive claw came to rest atop his head, and Ryurikov relished in its coolness. "Didn't you say their entire presence is my fault?"

Balefully, he glanced up from under long fingers, but Awimak did not provide him with an answer because it was obvious. Awimak had only been reflecting his own thoughts, locked away in his subconscious.

He sighed and succeeded in not melting under the thumb stroking across his hair. He hated feeling…whatever the fuck made him want to weep and cling to Awimak until things were better. It was awful. He longed to get rid of it. Would Awimak let him kill things yet?

"Now what?" he asked in a mutter.

"You get the hell off my mountain."

Tension snagged his shoulders and pulled him upright. He faced Valka, her anger still past boiling point, fingers clenched around that flute. Ryurikov would have answered, but shadowy shapes flitting across her jerkin, the pattern of its fabric looking an *awful lot* like a stained glass window, caught his focus. At the sight of three birds vanishing into the distance of a blue patch, he reeled.

The fucking doves in Jezibaba's window.

"How long?" Ryurikov asked hoarsely.

Valka wrenched her gaze off Awimak and to him. "What?"

"*How long—*" He'd raised his voice without meaning to, paused, and tried again. "How long have you and that fucking hag been communicating?"

She looked at him, hazel eyes cold. "I owe you no answers."

DESPITE WHAT YOU HAVE TOLD YOURSELF, YOU OWE YOUR BROTHER MORE THAN YOU ARE WILLING TO UNDERSTAND, Awimak said, a fierce anger haunting his snarl. The kind of anger that was protective, and hell, it was unnerving.

Ryurikov couldn't remember the last time anyone was angry on his behalf.

Valka visibly bristled. Her mouth moved and twitched the way it always did while she mulled her choices. He didn't think she would give him an answer, yet she said, "A little before the second time she killed you."

The doves had flown off the moment he'd set foot into the room with the mirror, Ryurikov remembered. Had they gone to tell Valka of his presence?

"And just what were you two talking about?" he asked, then realised he knew the answer to that.

Valka harrumphed and turned to one of the yellow drakes tugging at her breeches with thick claws, Ryurikov muttered, "The contest was your idea." It fit, when that hadn't seemed like Jezibaba's style. "You and the hag planned to get me captured and boiled."

He couldn't quite keep the heartbreak out of his voice, and longed to curse loud enough to bring the cave crumbling down on them. Feelings were the fucking worst. He needed to leave. Needed to work on putting all those shitty emotions away, deep where they couldn't resurface again.

"I really thought Vasili would be better than he turned out to be." Valka glanced at the piece of parchment the drake handed her. "But, you've always been a slippery dick."

Ryurikov worked his jaw, fighting to suppress the awful stinging in his heart. He wasn't the best at thinking things through, he'd not set any expectations for when he finally found Valka, but being this complete mess of hurt had not been part of his half-assed plan.

He mustered the coldest look he could, then walked past Awimak, his footsteps inaudible over the brook and purling cascades.

The drakes had resumed their studies, lost among the flowers but for their metallic scales glinting sharply in the sunlight. He wondered from where they got their claws on parchment and ink, while he looked out across the horizon. The pall of smoke below kept him from seeing anything but. At the sound of hooves, he turned to witness Awimak's eyes blazing.

"I don't know what I was expecting," Ryurikov admitted.

COMPASSION, PERHAPS, FROM SOMEONE WHOM YOU TRIED TO SHIELD ALL HER LIFE.

It wasn't even a question. When he said nothing in response, only frowned, Awimak positioned himself beside him. Together, they overlooked the scenery, or lack thereof.

WHAT WILL YOU DO NOW?

"Get some new clothes, I suppose." Ryurikov picked at loose threads on his sleeve, chest twisting with loss.

FOR WHAT IT COUNTS, I PREFER YOU IN GREEN.

A weak laugh whisked past Ryurikov's lips, and Awimak gathered his hand in a claw, so massive compared to his own. His gloves too were ruined, blood streaking brown leather, still wet and glistening. Awimak glanced down at him, likely expecting him to pull his hand free. Out of habit, Ryurikov wanted to. He'd become too accustomed to shying away from anything resembling affection, and holding anyone's hand was new to him entirely.

He didn't hate it.

The way down was decidedly easier than up. After finding his daggers for him, Awimak insisted he sit on his shoulders. Ryurikov wasn't opposed. The day had caught up to him, he was exhausted. Idly, he

Coil of Boughs

played with the roughened texture of the horns, squinting against the smoke drifting around the mountain's side. They had descended another way to avoid the wasteland, edging its outskirts once reaching the bottom. He held on tight when Awimak nearly toppled over loose stone before they reached level ground.

"Steady on," he murmured, patting the skull.

YOU DO NOT NEED TO WORRY, MY DRURY. I WON'T EVER DROP YOU.

Ryurikov hummed. Low flames inched across fresh grass, leaving nothing but scorched earth in its wake. Like flattened waves, the spread wasn't linear, making its way to a town that didn't seem to have suffered fire damage. Steeply pitched gable roofs and half-timbering homes were only faintly visible behind a thin wall of briar and, more peculiarly, a barrier of what appeared to be rain. Only, it moved from the ground up to disappear into the smoke shrouding the sky, barely allowing sunlight to filter through. It cast all in a disconcerting amber hue.

Soldiers clad in black and ebony chain-mail occupied the line behind the barrier, casting him wary looks. Ryurikov had descended Awimak, unsure if he'd appear to be floating otherwise, and reached out to touch the barrier by the entrance of the town.

"Don't touch it!"

He *really* wanted to touch it now. "How am I supposed to get through?"

A soldier came to him, her glare blurred behind ascending droplets. "State your business!"

Ryurikov sneered. "Trading."

"It's you!" A man scampered to stand beside the soldier, clad in a black robe featuring embroidery of some intricate image on his chest.

IT IS THE MIATHOS MONK.

Oh. He'd not even recognised him, despite the bald head.

"Good afternoon." Ryurikov glanced up. "I think."

"Let him through, let him through!"

A wave of the accosting guard was all it took for the rain to part like curtains, upside down droplets splashing into others, forming wobbly globules. Ryurikov lingered long enough for Awimak to go first before following. He had to suppress a smile at the sight of his demon towering imposingly above the soldier and the monk. Those idiots had no idea.

The monk scurried to Ryurikov's side, grabbing his arm without permission. He tried to yank it free, but the hold was surprisingly firm, held against the shorter man's chest as he guided him along the path and across an arched bridge that had seen better days. A wall of briar surrounded the other side of the stream, the water below restless with minktoads, their glowing eyes peering out from beneath mushroom caps, furry bellies extending with each shrill chirp.

"We have plenty of food and drink, and perhaps a bath?" the monk said, dragging him along.

Ryurikov cast a look at Awimak on the other side and silently formed the words, "Kill him." His demon chuckled, but did not murder. Damn him.

"That sounds fine," he said at length.

The town itself was mostly unscathed and despite the suffocating smoke, busy with traders and open shops. There was a tavern Ryurikov wanted to dive into, but that monk still had an intense hold on him.

"Release my arm or lose both of yours, monk," he snapped.

The monk immediately let go, looking flustered. "My apologies! I mean well. Come this way."

Ryurikov stopped by the tavern, its front covered by thick branches, blossoms cascading in white obscuring the sign. Although he thought he saw the word "Ancient" peer through.

"A fine tavern yes, but I offer the best!"

"You just want more coin." Ryurikov glared in warning when the monk tried to touch his arm again.

"Well, yes! You did seem to have plenty to spare."

At least he was honest.

"Alright, then."

"What brings you to Briarmour, my kind sir?"

Ryurikov sighed. "I just want something to eat. I'd like to bathe, and then sleep. No talking."

"Of course, of course!"

Briarmour was only a modest town, yet had too many homeless

subjects hiding within its alleyways. The sight of their starved faces strangled Ryurikov's heart. He needed to look away, to pretend he saw nothing.

It took a while to reach what appeared to be the Jarl's palace. As far as palaces went, it was humble, but unmistakable in its opulence. That fucking figured. Ryurikov clenched his teeth, rage bubbling to the surface, barely subdued by Awimak settling a claw across his shoulder and squeezing.

"Why did you bring me here, monk?" he demanded, ascending wide steps to large doors.

The balding man turned to him, cheeks rosy and mouth stretched in a grin. "Yavor Hospod, sir. Because you are officially a special guest!"

Ryurikov spun on his heel and stalked off. "Not today, fuck-rag."

His face still throbbed. Every bite he'd endured stung like wounds suffused in salt. He wasn't in the mood for whatever nasty surprises lurked inside. He had enough of those to last him a lifetime.

"Wait, please!" Yavor called. "I promise comfort and great food!"

I CANNOT SENSE A THREAT, IF THAT WILL PUT YOU AT EASE, said Awimak behind him.

Ryurikov stopped in his tracks, turning to face the edifice again, looking at the trailing ivy as though it would tell him Awimak was right. Just because he couldn't sense anything didn't mean there was no risk. On the other hand, it would accommodate his demon better than any tavern and, truthfully, Ryurikov longed to have Awimak with him.

With a sigh, he strode back to Yavor, who broke out into another grin and scampered up the steps.

The door was heavy, groaning low on its hinges. Smoke had permeated every inch of the town, the air stuffy even inside. Silver carpets and inky wood lavished the interior. Corners featured tall bears the Jarl must have hunted, and walls held the heads of deer and boars.

Awimak released an unhappy snarl beside him. *KILLING ANIMALS TO FEATURE THEIR MANGLED REMAINS IS NOTHING MORE THAN A PORTRAYAL OF CRUELTY.*

Ryurikov considered this, but didn't respond. The Maksim castle had been full of those things, he'd gotten used to them.

"The Jarl will be most pleased to greet you!"

"Why have your robes changed?" asked Ryurikov, idly.

"Oh, I no longer worship Miathos." Yavor halted in a generous hallway to beam up at him. "Goreldion, now and forever!"

"The god of black stone?" Ryurikov's brows drew together, his gaze lowering to the monk's chest. The silver embroidery featured a stylised hooded figure juggling six stones. "Why?"

Yavor gestured at the floor. "We return to the earth, transformed into the very stone the foundation Vale is made of. Whyever *wouldn't* I worship Goreldion?"

DOES HE NOT REALISE GORELDION REPRESENTS PLAGUE AND DEATH?

Ryurikov snorted in amusement.

"Not a man of faith, I gather?"

"Only when it suits me."

An open space greeted them, with a large firepit at its centre and a throne in the back. A servant clad in black sat turning a swine on the spit, its fat dripping down into flames and sizzling. It smelled fucking fantastic. Ryurikov's stomach took that opportunity to rumble with hunger.

Although he was more than ready to sink his teeth into the pig, Yavor led him around the firepit and to the throne. A long-bearded man occupied it, legs spread so wide his ballsack should have split. He too wore black, as did the young women flanking him on either side. His daughters, presumably. Six in total, each on their own ornate throne.

"Who do you bring to me, Hospod?"

"The very man who has made me see reason and join you, lord Blann!"

No sooner had the words begun to echo than Ryurikov groaned. Fucking *damn it*, he'd walked into a sect of some sort.

"Last time I take *your* word for it," he grumbled to Awimak under his breath.

"Well then, I welcome you, sir...?"

Ryurikov cleared his throat, casting for a name. "Dracus."

The Jarl's dark brows lifted. "Sir Dracus. A friend of Hospod is a friend of mine. Please, make yourself at home."

He would have responded with, "No, thanks," but Yavor beckoned him to sit by the firepit. Okay, fine. Fuck. He was hungry. He'd fill his stomach and go. With a tired exhale, he lowered himself onto a bench and watched the monk pry off a sizeable chunk of pig to slap onto a silver plate. Awimak sat beside him, the wood creaking with complaint. Ryurikov wondered what would happen should someone choose to sit in that exact spot.

"You look like you've seen better days."

Ryurikov stiffened. The Jarl had come up behind him, moving to straddle the bench on the other side, steely grey eyes boring into the side of his face.

"It hasn't been the best, today."

The Jarl tutted. "How do you like my barrier?"

"Barrier?"

For some reason, his ignorance amused the Jarl.

"The one surrounding Briarmour!" said Yavor, handing him a plate laden with meat. "A miracle, truly."

Ryurikov glanced sideways. "A miracle, or the work of crones?"

"Six crones. Alas, we're down to four now. We lost two to drowning. The barrier was not easy to craft, and more difficult still to uphold."

So this man, this Jarl, could afford to keep six witches, while his subjects were without home and food on the streets.

"Is it worth it?" Ryurikov asked, making no effort to keep the disdain out of his tone.

"It's keeping the ever-consuming fire at bay, so yes."

That brought him to actually look at the Jarl, even while he bit into the meat, too hot to chew. He sucked in several breaths, trying to speak. The Jarl chuckled, eyes crinkling.

"It has kept this town from burning down for five months now." He toyed with his thick, long beard, fingers adorned in rings holding sparkling black stones. "We've even tried pushing forward and reclaimed some land, but being short on witches, we weren't able to push for long."

Ryurikov considered this, astounding information as it was. In mostly a whisper, he said, "We can fight back."

"That we can."

He gazed up at Awimak, his heart giving a thud of hope. "We can fight back."

Awimak was smiling at him, he could feel it. *PERHAPS WE CAN.*

Twenty-One

He'd been plied with food and drink, shown to the guest chambers, had taken a bath, and now roamed the bedroom in contemplative circles, wearing only a fresh black tunic. The hearth's fire kept him warm, but the persistent stink of smoke irked. Ryurikov's head throbbed, the copious amount of wine he'd consumed had done nothing to ease it. Rubbing his forehead, he hissed at the sharp flare of pain.

SIT AND REST.

Awimak looked out of place, perched on the edge of an enormous bed, overshadowed by all the dark wood, black bedding, and silver canopy. Ryurikov walked to him, dropping into bed to lie on his back, legs hanging off the side. He heaved a heavy sigh, staring up at immaculate fabric overhead.

"We need to harness that magic, Awi."

STEAL THE WITCHES?

"Doubt I can, when every crone knows my face. They'll melt it off before I can threaten them."

PERHAPS IF YOU ASK NICELY, INSTEAD?

"Politeness doesn't work on hags."

THIS IS WHAT YOU KNOW.

Ryurikov glanced at the back of his demon's head. "Yes."

DIFFERENT TO WHAT IS TRUE.

"Is it?" He sat up, meeting sun-like eyes. "Even if being polite works, removing them would doom the townspeople." He had done that to Eastcairn, he wasn't about to repeat such a mistake. "Maybe Jezibaba can do it." Ryurikov flopped back down with a sound of disgust. "That means I have to go back to the hut."

IT WOULD BE RUDE TO LEAVE PERMANENTLY WITH HER BROOM.

"Maybe I'll get lucky and she'll drown trying to work water magic."

Awimak made a noise of amusement. It didn't sound entirely sincere, more like he was humouring him. With a tired grunt, Ryurikov crawled further on the bed and under the sheets. He didn't expect to feel Awimak shift, then wrap him in an embrace to pull him against that firm, chilly torso. He peered at the demon over his shoulder. His giant horn flattened the pillow, torrid breath dragging over Ryurikov's neck and shoulders. At least some part of him would remain warm.

"How often do you need to feed?" he asked, settling himself against Awimak.

I WILL NOT BE SIPPING FROM YOUR MIND TONIGHT.

It wasn't easy to find a comfortable position for his face, or to drift to sleep. A tempest of thoughts consumed him. When eventually slumber found him, Ryurikov was plunged into restless dreams.

Fire and smoke choked him wherever he turned. Skin Crawlers screeched, from a distance. Close by. The rapid *clack, clack, clack* of their scythe-legs chasing him down hallways of grey stone, lined with blue-flamed torches. He heard Valka shout before he saw her, visage flickering and blurred like the surrounding fumes. She radiated with fury and hatred, all directed toward him.

He'd sworn to her. He'd lied, allowing his friends and cousins to perish in a blaze now at his feet, gnawing its way up his leg. His skin bubbled and hardened to charcoal, wrenching horrified screams from him.

Ryurikov cried out. He flailed hard, his limbs connecting with toned muscles and bark. He sat up, his rapid exhales catching in his throat when the first thing his bleary gaze set on was the hearth's fire, now but embers. Smouldering, hot, the stink of smoke twisting up his nose, clawing at his brain.

"Fuck, Awimak!" he snarled the second he managed to form words.

Awimak was still beside him, now leaning against the headboard. His eyes blazed, and Ryurikov's anger contorted. He lashed out, but his hands didn't connect, caught in massive claws that pulled him roughly against the chest he'd been trying to beat.

IT WASN'T I WHO CAUSED IT.

He struggled against the hold, briefly, then all fight left him in one breath. Ryurikov slumped against Awimak in a shuddering pile. His lips sought the demon's mouth, bone sharply pressing into his injured cheek. It wasn't easy kissing Awimak, he wasn't even sure if he found his mouth. He was within its vicinity and it would have to do.

Great claws held him tight, his frantic breathing transferred into heated pants once the pointed tongue snaked out to delve into his mouth. He clawed at Awimak's shoulders as he moved to straddle robust hips, stiffening cock pressing into a hard abdomen. He ignored the stinging bite marks while roughened palms roamed up his torso, pushing the tunic up, helping him out of it. The article went flying, and Ryurikov leaned down to press his lips back under Awimak's skull just as clawless fingers left, slathered up.

Slickened fingers found the cleft of his ass, dipped between, and pressed in without hesitancy. Ryurikov gasped, shakily, raking his own digits through silken hair, diving under the horns to seek out the ears and give them a gentle few strokes. Awimak purred under the touch. It sounded as raspy as anything else. So terrifying before, now the only comfort he had. A second finger pushed in, curling into Ryurikov in a way that had him gasping, arching his back, stroking his own cock. He rocked his hips with urgency, desperate to free himself of the persistent ache in his chest.

Awimak complied, shoving a third finger in while simultaneously flipping Ryurikov onto his back. His head spun. Everything still hurt, but he groaned with pleasure, fingers stroking deep and deliberate. He wanted to reach out and touch Awimak's cock, but his demon didn't seem concerned with that, staying just out of reach while stretching him.

And then Ryurikov was on his stomach, flipped with such swift force he was left reeling. Powerful hands around his thighs hoisted his hips off the bed and a tongue lashed at his hole, saliva hot and slick. He turned his face so as not to rest on the injured side, reaching behind him to grab hold of a bark-covered forearm, his own breath raspy with desperation.

Other than releasing one thigh, Awimak didn't warn him before pressing the tip of his long, thick cock against the centre of his body. A firm pressure, and Ryurikov's pained grunt jounced the chambers as the head of Awimak's cock pushed in. Filling him in such a way he no longer had to think about anything but pain in his ass, intermixed with spikes of pleasure.

A fierce rhythm built up, the wet slap of rocking hips and harsh groans filling the room. A hand came down onto his shoulder, pinning him down. Ryurikov fisted the sheets, bit into the pillow to muffle his cries.

Awimak was merciless, now clutching both his shoulders to pull him down hard onto his cock. Over and over again, driving up to the hilt each time and still he pushed in further, as though trying to fuse them both together. Between trying not to make too much noise and keeping his face off the bed, Ryurikov struggled to breathe. He shoved his hand between himself and the bedding to fist his erection, soft cotton fabric adding to the friction.

His gasping became frantic. He clenched down around Awimak pounding into him with hard, controlled thrusts. Ryurikov spilled, the moan he'd been biting down on escaping. A hot deluge filled him shortly after, Awimak's snarls and flaring breath bringing his already feverish skin to a boil.

The last wave of his climax faded, and Ryurikov collapsed in a heap, covered in sweat and panting, unable to summon the strength to move off the injured side of his face. Awimak eased out of him, his sweltering come slipping between Ryurikov's thighs to stain the sheets. A swift breeze brushed over his rapidly cooling skin, then something fluttered across his body. Awimak had covered him with his side of the sheets.

REST NOW, MY DRURY.

He slept better after that, but didn't feel especially refreshed.

Ryurikov sat up, his head throbbing worse than after a night of drinking and fucking his brains out. One of which he'd done sufficiently.

He groaned in misery, blearily staring at nothing in particular. Every single part of him hurt. Cold sweat clinging to his skin made him shiver, and his ass cheeks were stuck together.

The smoke outside kept light from entering the room, but still he squinted as he glanced at Awimak, seemingly fast asleep. The hollows of his skull were empty. Did that mean his eyes were closed?

Ryurikov struggled to get out of bed, his entire body aflame with discomfort. He went to the silver ewer and basin situated on a clunky dresser by the window to wash his face and the mess Awimak had made of him. After which, he reclaimed the black tunic and slipped into the equally abyssal breeches he'd been provided with the night prior.

GOOD MORNING, DRURY.

He got ready to greet Awimak the usual manner, but when he turned, the "fuck you" fell away. His demon lay on his side. An absolute giant, hooves touching the foot of the bed, and one arm under the side of his head to support it while the massive horn would likely have permanently flattened the pillow. The burning spheres were inside the sockets again.

"Good morning." He winced at the sound of his voice, no better than the s.

YOU SOUND TERRIBLE.

Ryurikov cleared his throat. That didn't help, it only hurt. "It's the smoke."

Gathering his boots, he stiffly walked back to Awimak, now sitting upright. He hesitated, then leaned forward. He hesitated again. His demon was motionless, as if waiting, the beautiful details on his skull once more lighting up and gleaming with a rising sun they couldn't see.

Ryurikov pressed his lips to just above the skull's nostrils, but did not linger, moving away fast enough to make his head spin. A raspy hum of satisfaction was his reward all the same.

Clearing his throat again, he slipped into the boots, gathered his equipment, and wrapped himself in the cloak. Ruined though it was, he wasn't about to walk around exposed.

"Come on," he croaked.

Awimak rose, his horns a leaf's width away from scraping along the ceiling. *WHAT ARE YOU PLANNING?*

"Locate me some witches."

Finding the way back to the presence chamber was easy enough when Yavor hunted him down just so he could lead him there again. He babbled about noises in the night, but Ryurikov paid him no mind, unable to focus on anything other than how fucking awful he felt.

Not until Awimak said, *YOU WERE RATHER LOUD*, did he realise what the monk was on about.

"I understand of course, his daughters are all lovely! Charming, truly, despite their quirks," Yavor continued. "Although I'm not sure how the Jarl will take—"

"I didn't touch any of his daughters, for fuck's sake."

The monk peered at him, eyes wide. "No? Then..."

Ryurikov whirled. "Do you enjoy playing with your gunny sack? Roll it around your palms, maybe give it a little twist?"

Yavor's cheeks flushed. "That's none of your—"

"Fucking business. Exactly."

PERHAPS YOU NEED SOME FOOD.

"Stop infantilizing me," Ryurikov snapped, then immediately regretted it.

"I—I wasn't," Yavor stammered, with more to say, no doubt, but Ryurikov stalked away from him to plonk down on the bench by the firepit.

The servant turned the spit with goose, this time. He ate the bread and goose provided, ignoring the way the Jarl's daughters tittered when they bustled past him to sit on their thrones. Their father was nowhere to be seen.

"Am I permitted to visit the crones?" Ryurikov asked the monk, who perched himself on the bench beside him. Awimak had moved much further away and wasn't looking at him. *Fuck.*

"I–I doubt it."

He wrenched his attention back to the monk. More laughter echoed down to him. Had *they* heard him get fucked? "Where is the Frue?"

"Ah," Yavor leaned in, whispering, "the corruption opened the door."

"Skin Crawler?" Ryurikov asked. Yavor nodded.

So it was true. The morally corrupt were the first to be burrowed into, used as a host. Fed on until the Skin Crawler was strong enough to emerge and spread more fire. Ryurikov thought about his parents. How, as far as he knew, they hadn't been burrowed into. Maybe they would have been, sooner or later, and doomed the kingdom either way.

It left a bitter taste in his mouth. He'd chewed the bread for too long, swallowing with difficulty.

He set the plate on the bench, let the knife clatter down to it, and rose to make his way to Awimak dawdling by the leaded windows. Standing beside him, he looked out onto streets muddy with smoke and beggars. His demon wasn't acknowledging him, only looked out the window, and it made Ryurikov's chest hurt more.

"I'm..." he jerked his head to the side, "*sorry.*"

Awimak still did not regard him. *WHAT ARE YOU SORRY FOR?*

Ryurikov grunted in frustration. "For being a cock. I..." He cast his gaze back out the window, his words clipped, "I just—Awimak you are —I—"

Finally, Awimak turned to him. *I THOUGHT YOU WANTED TO BE BY YOURSELF.*

His brows furrowed. An unfamiliar ache dominated the cavern in Ryurikov's chest. He wasn't sure what to do about it, let alone how to handle the sudden need to hold his demon close.

"I don't want to be by myself," he said, surprised to find he meant it. "I..."

Although it took courage he didn't truly possess, Ryurikov reached out. He waited, stomach twisting, until Awimak took it in a great claw. The breath Ryurikov released was annoyingly shaky.

YOU ARE FORGIVEN, said Awimak in as soft a tone as he was likely capable of. Then, more sharply, *DO NOT SPEAK TO ME LIKE THAT AGAIN, OR ELSE.*

There was promise in that threat, filling Ryurikov with a peculiar blend of dread and excitement. Was it wrong to smile right at that moment? Probably. But fuck it, he couldn't help the twitch of his lips.

"Ready to find those witches? Yavor told me I won't be allowed to see them."

Awimak's exhale rattled with interest. *WE ARE DUE FOR SOME ENTERTAINMENT.*

It *had* been a while since they last caused chaos.

"That we are."

Ryurikov turned, remembering then that others couldn't see Awimak, which explained why Yavor and the Jarl—who must have snuck in—were gawking at him. Yavor more so, while the Jarl stroked his beard with a look of intrigue.

"To whom do you speak, Sir Dracus?"

"A dead loved one," replied Ryurikov without missing a beat. "In times of hardship, I see their ghost."

"I saw a ghost once," said the Jarl, drawing near. "Of course, it turned out to be a touch more than that." Grey eyes flicked to his hand, and Ryurikov swiftly squirmed it out of Awimak's hold. "My beloved succumbed to the Skin Crawler. I saw it before it emerged, and I put her down."

Ryurikov narrowed his eyes. "Are you threatening me?"

The Jarl laughed. It did not sound sincere, yet he waved a hand as if to dismiss the concern. "Of course not. You are my guest!"

"In that case, let me meet the crones."

"Why would you want to?" the Jarl asked with affectation.

"You said they've mastered water magic, and not just *any*, but the kind that can fight against the Skin Crawlers," said Ryurikov. "If I can transport such magic effectively, I can take the fight to them."

More laughter met his words, and Ryurikov glared.

"My apologies, don't think me rude," said the Jarl. "But what do you hope to accomplish? There is no fighting a fully fledged Skin Crawler. I would know," he pulled aside the collar of his black tunic, revealing a pronounced collar bone mottled with scarring. "I have tried."

"As you can see, I've met them too," said Ryurikov. "On more than one occasion, and I've lived."

BARELY, said Awimak.

Ryurikov ignored him.

"I'm afraid the witches are indisposed. It wouldn't do to distract them from a task that requires their full attention."

"Then, pray tell, how do you allow them to shit, or eat?"

It was the first time Ryurikov ever felt any sort of indignation toward the treatment of crones. He couldn't say he *enjoyed* feeling sympathetic, mostly because they were all ornery, but not even his own parents had treated Radmila quite *that* poorly.

The Jarl only smiled, his sharp profile lined by the glow of the fire when he turned to make his way to his daughters. They had been watching the exchange with keen interest, grey eyes trained on Ryurikov in particular. It was honestly unsettling.

SOMETHING IS REMISS.

Ryurikov withheld a sigh. Of course it fucking was.

Yavor approached him with a smile that looked nervous. "If you're done eating, perhaps I will show you around?"

Although he kept his gaze fixed on the Jarl, Ryurikov shrugged. "I suppose."

"I know you said you believe in a higher power only when it suits you," said the monk as he led the way down a stuffy hallway lined with yet more dead animals on display. "However, perhaps you'll reconsider once I've told you more about Goreldion!"

"No, thanks." Ryurikov smirked at Awimak's amused snort behind him.

"Oh, please, do humour me," said Yavor, cheeks growing red. "I promise you won't regret it!"

"Yeah, right." Ryurikov clamped the monk's shoulder and forced him to a stop. "Listen, vacillating *monk*, I don't care about your deities, but I care about that water magic. Lead me to the crones, and I will pay you handsomely for it."

Yavor squirmed out of his hold, anger now splotching his face. "I certainly will not be bribed!"

Ryurikov rolled his shoulders, then whipped out his long dagger from his belt, holding its tip against Yavor's throat in one swift, practised move. "I asked politely, now I'm not."

The monk squeaked, a trickle of blood gliding down the blade. That squeak promptly turned into blabbering terror.

"Get a hold of yourself," snapped Ryurikov. "Point the way."

With a violently shaking hand, Yavor pointed down the hallway. "D-Do-Door t-to the–le-le-le—"

"Good grief." He brought his fist down on the monk's temple, sending him sideways into a stuffed deer. Ryurikov peered at Yavor's limp body, ensuring he was out cold before moving on.

"This is what happens when I try to be polite."

AT LEAST YOU TRIED.

Ryurikov gave Awimak a wary look. "You sound like the Quinary."

Something his demon seemed to think was hilarious.

There were many doors to the left, all of which he needed to check before opening one leading down a steep stairwell into darkness.

"That'll be the one," he guessed.

The stairs wound deep, torch flames flailing in a draft, the surrounding stone damp and freezing cold to the touch. After what seemed like forever, Ryurikov reached the bottom, along with a set of heavily bolted double doors. He wiped sweat off his forehead and muttered a swear, sliding the bolt open before shouldering his way into what was, unsurprisingly, a dungeon.

And yet, Ryurikov froze at the sight before him.

In the centre stood a large stone well. Bright, crystal clear water swirled within it like a waterspout. Evenly spread around it, six large cabinets. He didn't need to look twice to know those were iron maidens. Open, the crones trapped inside, their arms tied up, palms facing the vortex.

The wretched stink of death and shit lay heavy, he wanted to gag, but walked further in to round the iron maidens for a closer look. Contraptions of rope and wire ensnared the crones' arms. Should they lower them, the fronts would shut and kill them.

With each witch he inspected, their orange eyes would only briefly flick down to him. Their whimpering and strained, close-mouthed cries sent a chill down Ryurikov's spine.

As the Jarl had said, only four of the six crones were alive, but the two dead hadn't been removed, their cabinets still shut, pools of blood long since dried at the bases.

Twenty-Two

The waterspout was no louder than a brook. It trailed off into the well, dividing into rivulets to disappear in every direction underground, from what Ryurikov could see. This had to be connected to the stream surrounding the town. Its celeste glow drowned out the torch lights, but the sound did nothing for the pained whimpers echoing through the circular dungeon. Rivulets of red trickled down scrawny legs, collecting at bare feet, each witch dressed in mere rags stained brown by old blood.

Ryurikov rubbed his thumb along the index finger in thought. He could leave right now, say his goodbyes, forget he saw anything. Go galavanting with Awimak, rob many a fool, find better attire. They could fuck each other silly. His demon didn't blame him for the Skin Crawlers, that was all he needed.

Alternatively, he could *attempt* to free the hags, likely fail, need to kill everyone siding with the Jarl, and thereby doom this entire town and its unfortunate inhabitants.

He regarded Awimak, standing near one of the devices, and readied himself to say they should leave. Sun-like eyes met his gaze, and something *awful* stirred in his chest.

"Fuck," Ryurikov muttered in resignation. "I don't even know where to begin with this."

Scouring the nearest witch, he refused to let her terror get to him. He took hold of his serrated dagger, stepped up into the iron maiden, and reached to cut free an arm. He froze when the hag croaked something, incomprehensible with panic.

"It'll be fine, probably," he said. Then, without looking at her, added, "If I kill you, understand it was an accident."

Awimak came to him, curling his claws over the top of the device's door. With a nod from him, Ryurikov cut through rope and wire, catching on the blade's teeth before relenting under their sharpness.

A faint creak as the door fought against Awimak's hold. Ryurikov's free hand shot out, his fingers curling into the fabric of the witch's rags the moment her arm dropped and she swayed toward the spikes behind her. She clutched his arm for support with a weakened cry, her body already sagging, chest heaving with air she barely managed to take in. Ryurikov struggled to keep her upright, awkwardly twisting 'round to work on the other arm.

"We'll have to be quick," he murmured, unable to keep from gagging at the stink wafting up his nose, so foul he tasted it in the back of his throat. "First thing we'll do is throw you into that well for a bath, beldam."

His hand trembled, fingers sweaty around the hilt of the dagger, clothes beginning to stick to him from perspiration running cold. Ryurikov momentarily squeezed his eyes shut against the blurring of his vision, the hammering of his heart.

DRURY, uttered Awimak, his deep, wraith-like snarl concerned.

"I'm fine. Just bracing myself."

He tugged the blade down, sawing through wire, and yanked the hag forward the same moment the door creaked. Her bony knees collided with stone flooring, the clangour of the iron maiden's doors slamming shut echoing. Ryurikov stepped away, grunting when something jerked him back.

"For fuck's sake." He tore the cloak free of the device's snag, tattered fabric turning an already sour mood mordant.

The hag remained where he'd tossed her, lacking the strength to do much else than lay on the ground, curled up like a woodlouse, as Awimak released the other door, letting it slam.

They only needed to do it thrice more, something that wasn't a huge problem until hurried footsteps and the clank of armour echoed in through the heavy door. Ryurikov swore, stepping away from the second hag. He switched to his long dagger and drifted to the wall by the entrance. Awimak stayed as he was, holding the front to the iron maiden open, the hag struggling to steady herself, one arm still trapped. She trembled, pitifully, peering at the demon as though she could see him. If she could, she said nothing.

The door opened with slamming force, bouncing against the wall and wobbling. A soldier stormed in, and Ryurikov knew they weren't looking to talk things out. In one swift move, he slid the dagger into the side of their neck, cutting through black fabric and flesh. A rope of blood chased his withdrawing blade. A *thud* of the body collapsing and clatter of their sword followed.

Ryurikov swung his right arm up, blocking the lunge of a shortsword through the doorway. Sparks sprinted off metal, he staggered under the force to his dagger. He stepped away, ducking around another forward lunge, sweat beading on his forehead, dripping past his brow and into his eye.

He blinked against its burn, feeling unsteady and worn. The next thrust he barely dodged, the blade catching his side, cutting through fabric. He threw his left fist up, aiming for the soldier's jaw, caught instead by a gloved hand. A knee collided with his stomach, slamming the air out of him.

Ryurikov collapsed to his knees, winded, the clatter of his blade a distant noise as his hand flicked to the hunters knife he kept in his boot. He hedged under the swinging shortsword, rammed the knife up into the soldier's belly. Staggered to his feet, pulled the blade out, then knived the man again. And again, and again. Until his stomach opened and disgorged a melange of blood and organs.

Dizzy, Ryurikov flung the door shut, belatedly realising it couldn't be bolted from the inside. He swore at the thunder of more footfalls down the stairwell. Too many. He couldn't take them on his own.

He hastened back to Awimak and worked to undo the hag's other arm, scarcely managing to pull her out in time, her rags catching on spikes as the front slammed shut. Awimak released the other shortly after.

The two hags now huddled by the well, and Ryurikov moved to the back of the empty torture device to push it over. He tried to roll it, then tried to scoot it, pushing with all his might, but hardly got it to move. Fortunately, his demon didn't need asking, and lifted the thing up like it weighed nothing, throwing it against the door to block entry.

Ryurikov panted, "Thank you."

YOU DO NOT LOOK WELL.

"I'm fine."

He had no choice but to be. They were in this mess now, and they were trapped. The least he could do was spare the witches an awful death. Although, perhaps they would all die here. Ryurikov tried not to think about that, resuming his task of freeing the third. He'd only cut the first arm loose when soldiers barraged the door. The iron maiden blocking it slightly shifted, more still with each thud against the timber until a crack along the planks appeared.

A sharp whistle preceded an equally sharp pain and Ryurikov flinched away on instinct. The tooth of his serrated blade cut through the wire. Awimak warned of something. Ryurikov stumbled back, an arrow firmly lodged in his arm. The iron maiden's front door slammed shut on a piercing cry.

A pool of fresh blood gathered at the bottom of it. He watched in horror as it dripped past the metal lip and onto the stone floor. The two freed witches wailed, while Awimak released the front he'd been holding rather tastelessly, Ryurikov thought. The crunch and squelch that followed seared itself into his memory.

DO NOT DWELL ON IT.

He glanced up, both in disbelief and admiration of Awimak's unflinching deportment. His demon was right, of course, there was no point in dwelling. Instead, he took hold of the arrow wedged deep in his bicep, and yanked.

Fucking *ouch*.

Then there was the persistence of the soldiers, and the last remaining hag, still struggling to keep herself upright.

Sibilating a swear, Ryurikov ducked to evade another arrow whistling past his head. He made to dispatch the soldier peering through the crack of the door with a crossbow, but Awimak beat him to it. Hooves clomped across stone, bough-like horns ramming into and through the door. Wood splintered, soldiers cried out, and crossbows and cudgels dropped. Claws tore into flesh. Blood splatters plumed. Gurgling screams lost in echoes.

Wiping more sweat from his brow with the back of his hand, Ryurikov darted to the last witch, waiting for Awimak to return before he set to freeing her. His fingers gripped her frail wrist and he swung her forward to join her sisters. They embraced each other, a smelly pile of old women Ryurikov would have thrown straight down the well for a wash, had he any strength left. Just as well, he supposed, as the waterspout began to dwindle.

The breath he released quivered, and he rested his back against the closed iron maiden. Awimak's eyes were on him. He didn't need to open his own to know, and chuckled, faintly.

"I may...not be well."

INDEED.

"Some rest, perhaps, after all this is dealt with." Ryurikov mustered a smile. "In the bed again, if you care to join me."

Awimak faced him, blood dripping off his claws. And by gods, Ryurikov had never seen anything sexier than this great demon before him.

THAT SOUNDS FINE.

First, they had to get out of here.

With a grunt, he approached the hags. They stared up at him with their orange eyes. Scared, confused, maybe a little angry.

"I'm sure you know who I am," he said, swallowing against the hoarseness in his voice. "But seeing as I just saved you, perhaps we can overlook the fact that we're mortal enemies. At least for now. I will gladly oblige your attempts to kill me at a later time."

"We've heard stories about you," said one, her hair a short, messy nest.

Ryurikov waved a dismissive hand, his gaze darting to Awimak. "Yeah, I'm sure you have."

Fucking Radmila. He hoped the witches wouldn't divulge just what kind of stories they were. He didn't want Awimak to know all he'd done to her. Then again, maybe Awimak already knew. He seemed to know everything else.

"None of them ever spoke of you saving our kind," said the same one. She struggled to rise. It was embarrassing to watch, honestly. "My name is Darinka." She gestured at the one with the longest hair, mostly a matted braid. "Branka, and Una."

"That's because I've never done it before and make no mistake," he continued, snidely, "I'm not about to make this a habit. Now come on."

"We can't leave," said Una, wobbly on her legs, thin as sticks. "We refuse to doom this town. The people deserve better."

Ryurikov squinted at them in disbelief. "They were happy enough to let you die like strung up rats."

"Nobody knew we were down here, aside from the Jarl and his soldiers!" said Darinka, helping Branka up.

"Suit yourselves." He walked away. Passing Awimak, he swirled his finger in the air, then pointed at the door.

"Thank you, Prince Leonid," one of the hags called out. He wasn't sure which, they all sounded as though their vocal cords were mummified.

"Ryurikov," he snapped without turning.

"You should get treatment!"

"Fuck you."

Mangled bodies blocked the bottom of the steps, fingers still twitching as Ryurikov stepped over them. He swayed, catching himself on the cold iron of a wall torch before a large claw came up on his back.

"I'm not sure what I've done to deserve you," Ryurikov murmured, "but I'm glad you're here."

The open palm on his back pushed, encouraging him to climb the stairs. *LIKEWISE, MY HUMAN. I WOULD PREFER IT IF YOU DID NOT DIE SO SOON.*

Ryurikov huffed. "Right back at you."

PERHAPS YOU SHOULD ALLOW ME TO TAKE CARE OF THE REST. Awimak's massive arms came 'round to trap Ryurikov in an embrace from behind.

He allowed it, for now.

"And let you be entertained all by yourself? It's only a fever, I'll walk it off."

A pat on one bark-covered forearm prompted Awimak to release him.

The moment's peace didn't last for long. They reached the door at the very top and clanking announced more soldiers. Good grief, how many of these well-fed assholes did the Jarl have under his boot?

Ryurikov sighed, grabbing hold of his long dagger again, but a hand squeezed his shoulder, then eased him against the wall—out of the way. Deciding it was a touch too risky to be fighting now anyway, he permitted Awimak to take charge.

Watching his demon tear through several men and women like they were no more than wet straw dolls was *satisfying*. Were Ryurikov not feeling so ghastly, he would have pounced Awimak right after he tore someone's arms off. His gigantic, enchanting demon looked at him, eyes like a forest fire.

Ryurikov staggered across butchered bodies, tutting at the blood staining his boots. The monk was nowhere in sight, likely the one to rat him out. Walking alongside Awimak through the hall, Ryurikov cleared his aching throat, scouring their surroundings. He slipped his hand into Awimak's hold, quietly relishing in the way it squeezed him. The sudden heat blooming across his face was most certainly due to his fever.

The presence chamber was not empty. Ryurikov had almost hoped it would be, but wasn't surprised when more soldiers stormed them, swords raised, bravery affixed to their stupid faces. Until Awimak showed himself to them, and their courage shrivelled like an earthworm out in the sun. Those who didn't run were rooted by terror as a great hulking beast bore down on them with claws larger than their helmeted heads.

Casually strolling past the massacre and dodging a string of blood lashing toward him, Ryurikov beelined for the throne, where the Jarl sat with his six daughters, watching.

"Jarl," Ryurikov said, damning himself for sounding so hoarse.

"Sir Dracus." The Jarl stroked his silver dusted beard, unfazed. Unlike his daughters, who were twitchy in their seats, the thick velvet of their black dresses rustling with each nervous movement. "Don't suppose you've seen Hospod?"

Ryurikov mustered a smug look. "I'll give him your regards once I find him."

He flung his dagger at the man's head, smoky light reflecting off blood-stained steel as it speared the throne's backrest. Strands of dark hair streaked with silver clung to it, the Jarl looking no more bothered than he had a moment ago. He rose, his black boots scuffing murky stone, and strode forward.

The last few paces he lunged for Ryurikov, who swung himself to the side. The glint of the Jarl's narrow blade could have easily been mistaken for the many rings on his hand. It was short, sharp, no more insidious than a tapestry needle.

"How deep are your coffers, *Jarl*?" Ryurikov surprised himself with the venom behind his words, the utter resentment. "How much do you hoard, while your people starve to death outside, in this smoke-plagued shithole?"

Now that wasn't entirely fair. Briarmour was a lovely town, were it not at the doorstep of Skin Crawlers and burnt wastelands.

"Coming from one who consorts with demons," the Jarl countered, jerking his head to where Awimak watched, the echo of dripping blood audible in the sudden silence sweeping the chamber.

The fever had clearly taken a hold, for the next thing Ryurikov knew, his chest rumbled with satisfied laughter. "That's not all I do with him."

A sneer was his only warning before the Jarl hurtled toward him again, astoundingly quick. His shoulder connected with Ryurikov's chest, slamming him against the window. Lead and glass cracked under his back. Ryurikov brought his knee up. Rammed it into the man's stomach. Used the leverage to push him away. Then brought his elbow down on the Jarl's head, dropping him to the floor.

"And after this is done, you and I are going to fuck," Ryurikov panted, swaying when he spun to face Awimak.

READY WHEN YOU ARE. Awimak motioned at him. *FOR NOW, INSPECT THAT WOUND.*

Ryurikov glanced down at his stomach, a pain making itself known. He clicked his tongue, pulling the fabric of his tunic away, sticky with blood.

"It's fine. Only a pinprick."

Having taken an arrow to the arm, Valka's fists to his face—never mind the drake bites—was decidedly worse. Unless, of course, the Jarl had dipped the prick in poison. Ryurikov felt the colour drain from his face.

"Is—Is it poison?" he asked.

Awimak shook his head. *I CANNOT DETECT POISONS.*

"Wait a fucking minute," Ryurikov snapped. "You told me nothing in Jezibaba's garden was poisoned!"

I WAS BASING THAT ON DEDUCTIVE REASONING. WHY WOULD SHE SPREAD POISON THROUGH HER OWN GARDEN?

He stared at his asshole demon in disbelief. "You've got to be fucking kidding—"

The shoulder colliding with his stomach robbed him of his breath. Glass shattered, his world rapidly flitting past until his back slammed into the earth.

Ryurikov wheezed out an agonised cry, vision too blurry to see much else other than Awimak's shape filling the window he'd fallen from. A strained shout preceded wet snaps and crunching. Something fell to the ground directly beside Ryurikov, a splatter of hot metallic fluid pelting his cheek.

He grunted in disgust, wiping his face as he sat up. Only once his vision cleared did he realise the Jarl had joined him outside. Well, his head had. The rest of him was probably still by Awimak.

"I like the way you murder," he said, affectionately.

ONLY FOR YOU, MY DRURY.

"I'm sure you say that to everyone you court." All the same, he couldn't help the smile.

Ryurikov dusted himself off. People had gathered already, the sickly and homeless coming in for a better look at their dead Jarl. Ignoring them, he limped back to the window and reached up to let Awimak grab his forearms and pull him back through. Just as he'd suspected, the Jarl's body was beyond it, bony under his feet. The daughters had disappeared, Ryurikov didn't especially care where to.

"Come on, let's look—"

Awimak's claws had found the hem of his shirt, lifting it. Ryurikov glanced down again.

ARE YOU WELL?

He shrugged, trying not to shudder under the tender touch, fingers brushing around the tiny wound. "I don't think it was poisoned." Then again, if it was, his fever was certainly impeding his ability to tell. "I better find the Quinary as soon as we get the coffers."

WE TAKE AND GIVE, said Awimak, sounding rather cheerful while following him.

"Indeed."

Finding the Jarl's treasure didn't take long, the coffers as large and ornate as all else in the main bedroom. Ryurikov eyed the bed with longing. He wanted to fuck, but more so, he wanted to sleep this damn sickness off, wherever the hell it might've come from.

Exhaustion, maybe, although spending one more day in the smoke-beaten town was the last thing he wanted to do. Strangely, he longed for the warm breeze in Jezibaba's garden, the soothing rustle of leaves and clucking of chickens.

Awimak helped him drag the ornate coffers outside, where Ryurikov kicked them open, spilling a nimiety of crones and ores across the street. Even jewellery slid across the gold and silver avalanche, landing at the feet of startled and confused peasants.

"All yours," he said, then looked up at Awimak. "Maybe you should show yourself to them?"

WHAT FOR?

Ryurikov shrugged, wincing at the pain in his arm. "Might be nice for people not to be terrified of you."

I DO NOT CARE WHAT THEY THINK.

He huffed, bemused. "You really don't, do you?"

Regardless of how shaky he was and how exhausted he felt, Ryurikov reached out to hold Awimak's claw again. Because he could, because Awimak didn't mind. Because it was *nice*. Looking up at his demon, there were a great many things Ryurikov longed for. His entire body strummed with that peculiar feeling again, strong and warm, consuming him with a nigh painful need.

It had been so long since he'd experienced anything of the sort. The last time he felt an inclination only vaguely similar to this, his eyes were altered without his consent.

"Awimak," he began, and those sun-like eyes set upon him again. Fiery and full of passion, of a feeling so similar to what Ryurikov held in the deepest cavity of the abyss that was his soul.

The excited babble of the wretched scrambling for coins became a distant sound, despite being directly at his feet. His heart gave a fierce thud of fright, and thrill. He wet his lips, unsure of what to say, but longing to say it.

"I—"

The sharp whistles blowing past him didn't register. The many arrows that pierced Awimak's chest a strange sight Ryurikov wasn't sure how to make sense of just then. His demon grunted, claw sliding out of his hand, hooves scraping across stone. More arrows winged past. Into Awimak's shoulders and back, pincushioning him. He buckled to his knees.

Ryurikov's breath wedged itself somewhere in his chest. He moved forward, a cry spilling past his lips, terror disembowelling his heart. Awimak's name plummeted from his mouth, repeatedly, his hands hovering over one of the many arrows piercing the demon's heart. Blood vivid and hot like lava sluiced across his dark grey chest, scorching arrow shafts.

DO NOT FRET, Awimak ground out, rising to his full, stately height. He held out his arms on either side, and the ground beneath them quivered and shook. *IT WILL TAKE MORE THAN THAT TO KILL ME.*

Every tree within the vicinity came to life, roots pulling up like legs out of dirt, swinging, and tree-crowns rustled as trunks shifted, lashing through the air, whip-like. Flowered branches snagged soldiers off rooftops, slamming them down onto the streets below. Bows and arrows rained down around them as bodies broke against cobblestone.

Totteringly, Ryurikov inspected the damage to his demon while his vision swam and his heart beat so harshly it hurt. The townsfolk who hadn't immediately run for cover whimpered behind him. He ignored them, gritting his teeth against a calamitous fear threatening to strike him down. Awimak might have told him not to worry, but the amount of blood now cascading over him was alarming. It dripped to the ground, blackening as it grew cold.

"Fuck," Ryurikov breathed. "We–What the fuck do we do, just pull the arrows out?" They would definitely need to go back to Jezibaba now. She'd likely know what to do.

Although Awimak didn't seem too worried, only chuckled, and anger rose like a wildfire within Ryurikov. How dare he trivialise his worry? He took an angry step forward. A blue necklace crunched under his boot.

The clamouring behind Ryurikov had yet to die down. Someone bumped into him, and it followed a pressure. He grunted and glanced down. Something had slid into him. Swift, sharp. The tip of a blade peered out from the bloodied fabric by his stomach. It pulled away. Reemerged a second later through his chest.

Ryurikov wanted to swear, but spluttered blood instead.

Twenty-Three

A flutter of black velvet was all Ryurikov saw before he collapsed into Awimak's arms. He grasped the claw pressing down on his chest, opening his mouth to say something. What, he wasn't sure, but Awimak silenced him with a hiss. A shush.

Ryurikov coughed, launching bolts of agony through him. Blood splattered back onto his face. His body jostled, now resting against Awimak's chest, and a hot, searing pain against his side and arm had him whimpering.

I'M SORRY, DRURY.

Awimak's blood scorched even him, then. Good thing he'd never poked his wounds. The thought made him want to laugh. He succeeded only in coughing again, bringing up more blood.

It occurred to him they must be moving. That he must be dying. Did it even matter? Surely the Quinary would help again. He'd done their bidding, he would continue to do so. He would owe them thrice, but that was fine, if it meant being with Awimak just a little longer.

That they were nowhere near a forest also occurred to him, moments later.

With every rattling breath Ryurikov tried to draw, more blood flooded his chest. Panic gurgled into the back of his throat, metallic, overpowering. Hot as it trickled past his lips and down his jawline. He reached out, trembling fingers curling under Awimak's chin. A weak attempt to pull his demon down for a kiss. Just one more.

Awimak's roar rumbled his chest, yet was inaudible over the thundering around them. All Ryurikov could see were blurred shadows, tinged yellow. Ryurikov arched his back, throat clenching as he fought to breathe.

"What do you think you're doing with him, anyway? You can't meddle with humans to such a degree!"

THAT IS A CONCERN FOR ME, AND ME ALONE.

"Not when you bring this to my doorstep!"

Ryurikov groaned in absolute misery. That croaky, grating voice bored into his skull. He wanted it to stop.

BE SILENT, ENCHANTRESS, AND TEND TO HIM. OR I WILL BRING FAR MORE TO YOUR DOORSTEP THAN YOU WILL EVER BE PREPARED FOR.

"Don't you threaten me!"

I DO NOT THREATEN.

"I can and *will* talk to your mother about this!"

"Please, Radojka, just keep helping him."

There was a pause, then a relenting sigh. Something cool slid across his chest. Ryurikov would have slapped the bony hands away, touching his bare skin like that, but they alleviated some of the hellish pain.

He groaned again.

DRURY?

He sounded so worried. Ryurikov forced his eyes open, and regretted it instantly. *Fuck* it was bright. He reached out instead, and the familiar chill of Awimak's claw enveloped his hand.

"How am I supposed to—"

"Shut up," Ryurikov croaked. He squinted against sunlight pouring in through the rippled window. It took a while for the blurry shapes to coalesce. Though he could scarcely make out the details, he knew he was looking at Jezibaba at the end of the bed. "Your voice is worse than a pig being roasted alive."

"I'll gladly kick you back down, you ungrateful weed."

He ignored her, focusing on Awimak. They were inside the witch's hut, that much was obvious, and his demon clutched him tight enough to hurt, kneeling by the bed. One of many beds.

Ugh, they were in the children's room.

"How'd you manage to get up here?" As he recalled, the staircase wasn't exactly wide.

IT TOOK SOME SQUIRMING.

Ryurikov smiled, then sagged further into coarse bedding. Good grief, he was tired. Hoarsely, "The Quinary?"

HELPED.

He hummed. The first time they'd resurrected him, he'd only been a little stiff. The second time, it took longer to recover. It made sense that the third resurrection would take more. He better stop dying. The fourth death would undoubtedly be ghoulish.

"Aren't I lucky," he said around the lingering taste of blood.

"You are."

Ryurikov's eyes flew back open. He bolted upright, and instantly regretted it, the pain shooting through his chest worse than the lightheadedness. Ignoring it, he fought the sheets to get out of bed.

YOU AREN'T READY—

He fell face first to the ground with a startled cry. Twisting around, he caught sight of his legs, ensnared by the blankets, while the rest of him dangled off the bed, his shoulder and neck at an awkward angle against the floor.

"I can't move my legs," said Ryurikov flatly, as Awimak gathered him back up and propped him against the headboard, fussing with the sheets around his naked hips.

"Valka?" He tried to peer past Awimak's big horns, reaching up to feebly push them out of the way.

His sister, still wearing that blasted stained-glass tunic, moved from the window to stand beside Jezibaba. Flute at her hip, sabre on the other side. At least she didn't look ready to use either, only fiddled with the leather belt, her hazel eyes trained on him until he tried meeting them. She looked away.

"Can you please *wait*?" Ryurikov ground out. "I just recovered from dying."

"Recovering," Valka corrected, unhelpfully. "And this is the last time, Ruri."

"You'll make sure of that, will you?"

Valka sighed, vexed, arms dropping at her sides. "That's not what I meant."

SHE MEANS THAT THREE RESURRECTIONS ARE ALL THE QUINARY CAN MANAGE.

"Oh, fuck." No more dying for him, then. At least not any time soon.

"Lucky," continued Valka, "since the drake's bites are poisonous."

Ryurikov pursed his lips. So *that* was what the cold sweat had been about. And if he hadn't gotten stabbed, then by the time he'd realised what was happening, it would've been far too late to reach the Quinary.

Lucky, indeed.

He shook his head, furious Valka had so readily attacked him, to *kill*, when all he'd wanted was to talk. "Why are you here?"

Valka's expression became uncertain. She crossed her arms, uncrossed them. Crossed them again. "I..."

WAS IT SOMETHING I SAID?

Ryurikov side-eyed Awimak. He sounded so damn smug.

"Fine, alright," snapped Valka. "Yes, you were right. And I'm sorry, okay?"

"What did you say?" asked Ryurikov.

When Awimak slowly turned his head to regard him, Ryurikov was sure his demon was smiling. Fucker. He wasn't going to tell him. It didn't matter, he supposed. Valka had come back, and she wasn't trying to kill him again. They were off to an excellent second start.

"I spent years hating you," she said.

Maybe not that great of a start. "I've no doubt."

She moved to sit on the edge of the bed by his feet, twisting 'round to look him in the eyes. Ryurikov did his best, but his vision was still so blurry. He hoped that wasn't permanent.

"I left with Radojka and didn't hear about what happened until months later. I tried to find out what had happened, but all anyone ever told me was that you were responsible. I'm sorry. I should've known better than to believe the rumours."

Ryurikov freed his hand from Awimak's grasp long enough to comb fingers through his hair. He winced when that too made his chest hurt. Finally, he looked down, and grimaced at the remnants of several wounds littered across his abdomen, slathered in some glimmering indigo salve. They weren't open, exactly, but they looked raw and like they'd come from different blades. At least most of the bite marks had faded. Strangely, the burns he'd gained from Awimak's blood had scarred over, quilting across his existing scars.

"Who's Radojka?" he asked, unsure of what else to say. His sister had chosen to believe rumours over thinking for herself, that was an injury he wouldn't recover from any time soon.

Valka jerked her head at Jezibaba, now sitting on a bed in the far end of the room, scowling.

"Wh–Oh, right." Jezibaba was the name given to all crones who abandoned their posts. There weren't many, most of them simply *couldn't*. Briarmour was an extreme example of why. "That reminds me, there are hags who have developed magic that can fight against Skin Crawler fire."

Both Valka and Jezibaba leaned in at that.

"How?" asked the crone.

"How the fuck am I supposed to know?" Ryurikov snarled. "Go talk to them, I'm sure they'd be *delighted* to meet another one. Or use your damned window-doves to communicate with your fellows." He cast an ugly glare at his sister, who had the decency to shrink under it. It caused his anger to flare, regardless. "Why are you *here*? Don't your stupid lizards need you for something?"

Valka shrugged, rubbing her hands across her thighs. "They can get by without me for a while."

YOU'VE DONE WELL WITH THEM, said Awimak, and Ryurikov

shot him a look of betrayal.

"Don't compliment her!"

"He's right, you know, I *did* do well with them," Valka said. "We went from just a rocky mountain to paradise."

"That was all you?" Despite his anger, pride stirred, and it only served to annoy Ryurikov further.

Valka managed a strained smile. "I've taught them how to cultivate and stop ruining things with their poison and...butts. I've been trying to teach them how to write too, but I don't think they're capable of it."

Ryurikov frowned, vaguely recalling something Apatura had told him. "They are." It was likely just in a language Valka couldn't read. "And they must have been sending messages, for word to get around that you were captured by a dragon."

Valka hummed in interest. "Yeah, funny story."

For some reason, that soured Ryurikov's mood to a state worse than curdled come. "I don't want to hear it." He laid back down, failing to suppress the sharp groan of pain when he rolled onto his side. "Leave me alone."

He resolutely didn't look at anyone even as he heard Jezibaba shuffling out, then the creak of the bed, a weight lifting off it. Only once certain they were gone did he reach out again, to the gigantic mass sitting on the floor right by him. Awimak took hold of his hand A slick tongue dragged across, lavishing his knuckles.

"Thanks," he mumbled, peering up from the lumpy, reed-stuffed pillow. "You're alright?"

I AM. I DID NOT THINK I WOULD REACH THE FOREST IN TIME.

"Well, you did."

He didn't resent Awimak for saving him, yet again. Of course he didn't. He was glad to be alive... Again. Ryurikov wasn't even sure why he felt as curmudgeonly as he did, but it worsened as Awimak stroked him across his back.

"I'd like to rest."

OF COURSE, MY DRURY.

Awimak didn't leave.

"Preferably on my own."

He ensured he wasn't looking at the demon. The guilt pinching his gut was bad enough, he didn't need to see Awimak's hurt. After a long pause, hooves and horns scraped across wood, shoulders had likely met a doorframe, and a struggle echoed down the staircase.

When all became quiet, Ryurikov strained onto his back to stare at the ceiling. Thick, knobbly branches, some sprouting delicate leaves shimmering like shards of glass. The chimes of snails and pinecones moved in the faint breeze pulling in from the window, set ajar.

Under the ugly knitted blanket, he rubbed his thumb over the length of his pointer finger, mind stumbling back to the moment just before the first blade greeted his chest. The fear he'd endured, thinking Awimak harmed, came back to clobber his insides. His heart stuttered at the very idea of losing Awimak, of his demon dying.

How had this happened? When had he begun to *care*? Why could he only think of holding Awimak?

It was loathsome, feeling so vulnerable. Having a *weakness*.

Thinking.

Ryurikov needed every last driblet of strength to sit up. He tried moving his legs and failed. Swearing, he glanced around for something to help. All he saw was a tankard of water, set on a makeshift bedside table—a thick log. Its mere presence was offensive and he scoffed.

He hurtled himself out of the bed shortly after.

The fall was uncomfortable. Painful, really. He leaned up on an elbow to glare at his legs, still refusing to move.

"Fucking *work*!" He smacked the uncooperative limbs.

Since that did absolutely nothing, Ryurikov dragged himself across the floor, naked and all. The sound of something massive struggling its way back up the stairwell made him panic, and he didn't even know *why*. He just wanted to get the fuck away from this place, from Awimak.

DRURY, said the demon, twisting and turning through the doorway, holding a bowl of carrot soup. Ryurikov could tell because it all sloshed down to the wood flooring. *WHERE DO YOU INTEND TO GO?*

"Away from here," he said, anger causing spittle to cling to his lips.

He wiped his mouth while Awimak freed himself and moved to crouch by him.

IT WOULD BE BETTER IF YOU REST FIRST, THEN WE CAN—

"No, Awimak. I'm going away, *alone*."

The demon became eerily still, like a tree in the dead of night.

I UNDERSTAND.

Ryurikov let his shoulders sag in relief. "Alright, then... I'll be on my way." He would have liked to leave, but his legs still weren't working. He hoped that wasn't permanent, either.

WHY?

"What do you mean? You just said you understand."

Awimak's breath plumed a misty white, and his eyes roared. *I UNDERSTAND, RYURIKOV, BUT I WOULD LIKE FOR YOU TO SAY IT OUT LOUD.*

"Say what?"

THAT YOU CHOOSE TO BE A COWARD.

Ryurikov scowled, in particular at Awimak's tone of indifference. "I am *not*—"

YOU ARE RETREATING BECAUSE YOU ARE AFRAID.

"I can't do it, Awi!" The shouted confession rolled through the dusty room, as ineffective as his limbs. Ryurikov raked trembling fingers through his hair and tossed an angry look out the window. "I can't deal with–with—"

WITH WHAT?

"With you! And me. And–And *this*." Helplessly, he flapped his hand between them. "You disarm me, Awimak, and I don't know how to handle it! Maybe I am a coward, but at least I won't get hurt if I run!"

Another bout of silence, stretching until Ryurikov forced himself to look at the demon. Still holding the bowl, thumb right inside it.

"And anyway, this is no good for you, either."

WHY? This time, Awimak sounded offended.

"You said you're much older than I am! What are human years compared to yours? I'll die of old age and only a year would have passed for you."

SEASONS PASS FOR ME MUCH LIKE THEY DO FOR YOU.

Ryurikov grunted in annoyance. "You know what I mean!"

I DO, Awimak said. *MY DRURY, HEAR ME WHEN I TELL YOU THAT I WILL UPROOT ANCIENT TREES AND MOVE ENTIRE FORESTS FOR YOU. AND WHEN YOU DIE, I WILL LIE DOWN AND BECOME PART OF THE EARTH ALONGSIDE YOU.*

Finally, Ryurikov met Awimak's gaze. His eyes surged more than the rising sun, tailing orange with every subtle shift of his head. And his words, they seared themselves inside Ryurikov's chest, as poignant and reverberating as a church bell.

LET ME LOVE YOU, RYURIKOV, IN THE WAY YOU NEVER THOUGHT YOU DESERVED.

Ryurikov's eyes burned. He gasped, realising what was happening, and swiftly raised a hand to cover his face. Massive arms encircled him, he couldn't summon the desire nor the strength to fight it. He grit his teeth, silently commanding the tears to cease, but succeeded only in giving himself a headache from the strain. Awimak gently squeezed, as if prompting him to do something other than fight himself.

He opened his mouth, and absolutely loathed the hiccup that rattled his entire body. "F-Fuck. If–If you *must*, Awimak."

I MUST, AND I DO. Awimak lifted Ryurikov off the ground, his legs sliding uselessly across old planks until he was settled in a silken-haired lap. *I CANNOT HELP BUT GROW. PERHAPS ONE DAY, YOU WILL BE ABLE TO ADMIT THE SAME.*

That prompted Ryurikov to snort. "Just don't fucking die on me."

LITTLE CONCERN THERE.

"Yeah?" Deciding Awimak knew enough about him already not to be dissuaded by ugly tears, Ryurikov looked up, *balefully*. "Is that more deductive reasoning on your part?"

Awimak shrugged. *THE WORST THAT WILL HAPPEN IS I DO WHAT EVERYONE ELSE DOES. SOMETHING YOU HAVE DONE THRICE ALREADY. ONCE IN MY ARMS.*

He understood the meaning, of course. If Awimak was still here after he'd died in his arms, then Ryurikov had no right to be scared about something that was far less likely to happen to his demon. His shoulders sagged in defeat. The last remnants of fight left him completely, and he let himself rest in those massive arms.

After a while, he muttered, "Why the hell can't I move my legs?"

Awimak squeezed him tighter. *I BELIEVE YOUR SPINE WAS SEVERED.*

"Ah."

IT WILL TAKE SOME TIME TO FULLY RECOVER.

"Fuck."

ONCE YOU'VE RECOVERED, WE SHALL.

"I'll hold you to that." He wrapped his arms around Awimak's neck as his demon shuffled on his knees to the bed, returning Ryurikov to its itchy blankets. "I'd be much happier in the garden, you know."

Awimak hummed in agreement, reaching behind him to grab the bowl of soup abandoned on the floor. *PERHAPS I WILL BUILD YOU A NEST OUTSIDE, THEN.*

He held the bowl out, but it was nearly empty, a few pieces of herbs clinging to the side.

"Ah... Thank you."

Twenty-Four

Sunlight spilled past bright green leaves, dappling across Ryurikov and the bed Awimak had made for him under the apple tree. Well, less of a bed, and more like a den of blankets, roots and branches. A bird twittered above him, a spherical shadow underneath the light. Ryurikov glared.

"This bower is mine," he said to it. A robin, he thought. "And don't shit on me."

He wiggled his toes, grinning in triumph. The fierce pinpricks in his legs had yet to subside, but he was comfortable enough, clad in a white linen tunic with his legs raised over the brim of the nest, head resting on the fluffiest of moss. He almost preferred it over a feather stuffed pillow.

"You can move your toes!"

His heart burst straight out of his chest at Valka's sudden appearance. She'd been the one to carry him down to the garden while Awimak worked his magic, and he still resented her for it. Ryurikov glowered at the tankard she held out for him. Ale, he realised, once he finally took it.

"Just a little while longer, and I can kick your toned ass all the way up that fucking mountain."

Valka sighed. "Well, I'd deserve it, that's for sure." She sat in the grass beside him, reaching over the short wall of his den to rub sword-calloused hands across his shins. "I was kind of hoping you'd forgive me."

"You set Vasili on me!" he snarled so viciously, Valka flinched away.

"He's the reeve, why *wouldn't* I? Besides, he's the only one who ever managed to persuade you to put your scheming out of your mind, at the very least delay them." When Ryurikov said nothing, she shrugged, adding, "I was surprised he was even alive. I...didn't think anyone had survived, other than you."

He scoffed. "Makes you wonder how any of these rumours about me even spread."

Words dropping from his lips with ease, yet had Ryurikov realising he'd just made an excellent point. He stared at Valka, and she gaped back.

"I–I have no idea," she uttered. "Vasili?"

"Based on what he said while he tried to force himself on me, I don't think it was him." Ryurikov snapped his mouth shut so hard his teeth clicked, swiftly looking away from Valka's stunned expression.

"He did what now?"

"Where's Awimak? He said he'd be right back."

"Ruri, what did you just say?" Valka's leather glove creaked, her fingers clenching around the hilt of her blade.

He looked everywhere other than at his sister. "You *know* he's always been obsessed with me."

"Well, sure but—" Valka's expression became explosive, freckles disappearing under the crimson flooding her cheeks. She stood in one swift move.

"Awimak already took care of him," Ryurikov said before she could take a step away.

Her eyes met his, burning with anger. He wasn't sure how to feel about that. Good to know she hadn't *intentionally* set Vasili on him, at least not in that way. Likely, she would have been fine with him being roasted for his crimes, though. Fucking *asshole*.

Loud twittering jerked his anger upward. That bird, too, was an asshole.

"He's a good one, isn't he?" Valka said loud enough to be heard over the noisy chirping.

"My demon?" Ryurikov snapped off a protruding twig near his head and hurtled it up at the bird, though it was too light. It fell immediately, landing in his drink. "He's a fucking tree who insists on being nice to me."

"Gods, I know it's been a few years, but you were never *this*..." She swayed her hands in lieu of an adequate description.

"This much of a cockhead? I've always been one. You might've noticed if you hadn't been too busy running off with a jezibaba."

With another sigh, Valka seated herself beside his nest again, leaning an elbow across its brim, the neatly folded branches bending slightly under the weight. "I deserve that."

He picked the twig out of his ale, flicking it aside, before guzzling the drink in its entirety without a single breath in between.

"You always left me," he panted, flinging the tankard into the bushes. His complaint sounded whiny even to him, and he grimaced. "I mean, it would've been nice if..."

If every once in a while, she'd been there to comfort him after beatings from their father, who had claimed it was to work on his resistance, should he ever be abducted. Of course, Ryurikov had never been honest to Valka about it, stayed away while he recovered, never once mentioning what the king did to him. Could he really be upset with his sister for not being there?

"I'm sorry."

He flicked away crumbs of lichen scattered on his chest, shrugging. "I don't blame you for wanting to leave. I never have. And I don't blame you for taking me at my word and actually leaving, either."

Valka reached over to clasp his shins again, a storm of pinpricks bursting up under the touch. "I appreciate that. I shouldn't have left, though. I'm sorry."

Ryurikov shook his head. "Had you stayed, you might not be alive now, and then where would I be?"

Not having died for the third time, for a start. He flattened his lips.

"Let me get you something to eat?"

Coil of Boughs

She seemed to take his shrug for a yes, her fine black boots pressing marks into the grass as she rose and hurried away. Behind him, she made a noise of surprise, said something Ryurikov didn't catch, before the sound of heavy hooves pricked his ears. He eagerly flopped 'round, holding out his hand for Awimak to take.

"I was beginning to think you might pull the same stunt I tried to, earlier," he teased, then frowned. "What's wrong?"

His demon released a snort, sounding tired. Awimak ducked into the bower, large enough to comfortably accommodate both of them, and wrapped Ryurikov in several blankets before pulling him firmly against his chest. Those incredible arms held him tight, as if Awimak was in need of comfort, blankets blocking out the earthy cold pressed into his back.

WILL YOU TELL ME OF A FOND MEMORY YOU HAVE?

Cheek resting against soft, cool moss, Ryurikov flicked his tongue over his lower lip. "Ah–Sure. Horses."

RIVETING.

"Fuck off," Ryurikov grumbled. "I haven't even started. So–Horses. Yes. I ah–I loved riding, one of the few joys that I didn't get bea—I had this mare. Wild as anything, worse than any stallion. She was a beauty, the most unusual combination of browns and greys I'd ever seen. A bit like you, actually."

A glance over his shoulder. Awimak's sweltering breath grazed his temple. His eyes must have been closed, Ryurikov couldn't see their fire.

GO ON.

"I tried breaking her in. She was difficult, but I was confident I could out-stubborn her." He settled back down, closing his own eyes. "When she'd thrown me off for what must have been the hundredth time and had me under her hooves, I realised maybe not." Awimak released a faint huff of amusement, which pleased Ryurikov a great deal. "There was a moment, just before she got ready to trample me to death, where we locked eyes. I was terrified, but we just stared at each other. For *ages*, it felt like. Until she backed off. I then realised I'd been apologising to her, over and over."

YOU DID NOT DIE, HENCE IT IS A FOND MEMORY?

"You're witty today," Ryurikov drawled. "It's a fond memory because it was the first time in my life I was made to respect someone and it felt *deserved*."

DID THIS MARE PERMIT YOU TO MOUNT AFTER?

"No. I released her. Too stubborn even for me. Watching her run free though..."

It had given him the idea to let Valka run free, too.

THANK YOU.

He shifted within the firm grasp as best he could, useless legs making it a struggle. "You'll tell me what troubles you now?"

I WAS HUNGRY.

Fuck. "Awi—"

I NEEDED ANOTHER SOURCE. THERE ARE FEW WITH PLEASANT DREAMS AS YOURS WERE. Awimak's skull nudged his forehead, shifting from side to side. He was being nuzzled. NIGHTMARES LEAVE A BITTER TASTE.

Sounded like they were unsatisfying, too. "Do they satiate your hunger?"

NOT LIKE YOURS DO.

A chill coiled down his spine, and it wasn't a bad one. "You should take the next good dream I have."

I WOULD NOT.

"Nonsense."

Since Awimak's eyes were nothing but hollows of black, Ryurikov pressed a quick, silent kiss to the side of his elongated jaw. The flames flickered to life within the skull. His heart jumped with inexplicable panic, and he swallowed against it.

"You take care of me, I will take care of you."

Awimak made a most pleased sound, massive claw trailing down his arm, fingers grazing the back of his hand. Ryurikov lifted it, bringing both hand and claw in for a better look. He splayed his fingers, pressing palm against open palm, his hand but a fraction of Awimak's. His demon could crush every bone in his body and it would take less than an inhale to do so. He remained an enigma, Ryurikov longed to know more, but he knew Awimak would never intentionally hurt him, and that was more than he'd known about anyone else.

Gazing into those enchanting eyes, he pressed his lips to the tips of those long digits, giving each a gentle kiss worthy of Awimak's kindness. The skull's flames burned like a falling star, as intense as the tempest of emotion inside Ryurikov's chest.

"Aw."

He started, then glared over his shoulder at Valka. She grinned, holding out a bowl.

"I've never seen you like this with anyone. It brings a tear to my eye."

"You trying to murder me several different ways brings a few tears to mine."

Hazel eyes rolled at him. "Take your bowl. Once you gather your strength, we're going to Briarmour. Radojka wants to meet with the other witches to learn about this magic you mentioned."

"Why do I have to come along?" Despite his harsh tone, he was *famished* and sat up. Ryurikov groaned, scowling into the bowl. More broth, and it was unlikely to be of the bone variety.

"To act as a mediator, maybe?" Valka shrugged. "Radojka isn't on good terms with the others. Since you saved them, they might listen to you."

Ryurikov made a face, ignoring the way Awimak knocked into him upon sitting up, spilling some broth on his tunic. "Hard pass."

Valka crossed her arms. She lingered, tapping her foot with impatience while Ryurikov *drank*—broth was not food, and whatever this was barely passed for vegetable tea. When it became clear he was adamant on ignoring her, she stalked off, sword and flute swinging at her hips.

I DO NOT BLAME YOU FOR NOT WANTING TO RETURN.

"Thank you. I'm glad someone understands."

YOU WERE MURDERED THERE. NATURALLY, YOU WOULD BE AFRAID TO GO BACK.

"I beg your pardon?" Ryurikov glared up, sensing something akin to mirth. "I'm not *scared*, I just—you know what, fine. I'll go if it's *that* important."

I WILL REMAIN BY YOUR SIDE, MY EYEWORTHY.

Fucking hell, why did that make warmth creep across his face? He buried his face into the bowl to polish off his tea.

Valka's eyes kept darting his way, a smile tugging at the corners of her mouth every time, and Ryurikov tried very hard to ignore it. His hold on Awimak's arm tightened, his legs unsteady, dirty boots shuffling through leaf-wilt.

I COULD CARRY YOU, Awimak said for the third time that evening.

Ryurikov grunted with effort. "I know you could."

"I can carry you too," said Valka.

"I *know* you could."

"I'm not carrying you," muttered Jezibaba, several paces ahead, her shuffling no better than Ryurikov's.

"Nobody asked you, dead wood."

"Ruri!"

He snickered. "What?"

"You don't have to be so mean."

"Ah, but I do. Unlike you, she *actually* killed me. Twice. It really hurt the second time, too."

Jezibaba clicked her tongue, carefully shuffling past a circle of delicately glowing mushrooms. "Serves you right, for being so witless."

Ryurikov bared his teeth. Would have stomped the mushrooms out of spite had Awimak not gently guided him away. "Fuck you, child-eater."

Valka gasped. She swung 'round to stop him in his tracks and instinctively, Ryurikov tightened his hold on Awimak's forearm. His legs were not strong enough to kick her away.

"*Don't* say that," Valka hissed. She glanced over her shoulder, but Jezibaba quietly carried on. "I'm sorry I tried to kill you and everything else, and I'll do what I can to make it up to you, but you cannot ever call her that."

Her tone and dour expression made Ryurikov consider his retort—briefly. "I'll call her what I like, especially if it's true."

"But it's *not* true, Ruri!"

"Leave the boy to his beliefs," Jezibaba called. "What difference does it make?"

Valka faltered, clearly torn between getting him to change his mind and listening to the crone. In the end, she hastened after Jezibaba, speaking to her in a murmur too quiet for Ryurikov to hear.

"You'll tell me if they plot to kill me again?" he said to Awimak, now out of breath.

I WILL LAY WASTE TO THEM MYSELF.

Ryurikov's eyes flicked up to Awimak, sun-like spheres once again ablaze. "Alright, but don't kill Valka completely." He wobbled, legs threatening to give out entirely.

AS YOU WISH, DRURY.

Apparently having had enough of his stumbling, Awimak gathered Ryurikov into his arms. He grunted, but didn't argue. Being off his legs was a relief, honestly, but he'd never admit it.

Cradle carried against a solid chest, he nestled his head along the crook of Awimak's shoulders, lazily scouring the forest they threaded.

They walked its edge, not close enough for the Clutchers to spot them, but enough to find their way back to Briarmour. Smoke of the wasteland curled past the trees, tinged burgundy in the setting sun. Fern and tiny white flowers dotted the ground, dampened by ash that had broken past the barrier of leaves above. It would only be a matter of time before this too was all devoured, yet more of Awimak's earth ruined.

"Do I recall something being said about your mother?" Ryurikov asked and took note of the tension drawing into Awimak's long jaw. "Awi?"

PERHAPS.

"Don't be evasive," he grumbled. "I don't suppose you'll ever introduce us?"

YOU HAVE ALREADY MET.

Ryurikov raised his brows. "Unless she's an oak somewhere in the Unbroken Wilds, I'm *fairly* certain I've not met her."

Awimak grunted in amusement. *SHE IS NOT AN OAK. SHE IS THE EARTH.*

He tilted his head back understanding. "Forged from the earth."

YES.

"Alright. But by *whom*?"

MEN.

"Humans?"

YES. BLACKSMITHS OF THE ARCANE FORGED ME FROM FLESH AND BONE, TO EXIST AS HUMAN. AND METAL AND SOIL, TO LIVE WITH TERRENE TENACIOUSNESS.

Ryurikov mused on that. "So, somebody somewhere fucked something earthly. A horse?"

The sound that left Awimak was one of dismay. Ryurikov's stomach clenched with a laugh. "Why the long face?" He wheezed, hands tightening around the sturdy neck for fear of being dropped. "I lo–*ah*, you're brilliant as you are. Long face, horse legs, and all. Wouldn't change a thing."

Fortunately, Awimak did not drop him.

"Where's the town?" Valka was, once again, refusing to be discreet with her glances and smiles.

"Hard to miss," Ryurikov said with a sigh. "It's a fucking town surrounded by—"

IT MAY HAVE CHANGED SINCE OUR DEPARTURE.

Once they emerged from the forest, another large boscage greeted them, surrounded by a regressive barrier of rain. The trees looked different to those of the forest. More gnarly and ancient, contorted around familiar stonework and half-timbered structures. So large, they blocked the foot of the mountain where the town lay. Ryurikov gaped.

I SAID I WOULD MOVE FORESTS FOR YOU.

He didn't need to explain it. Ryurikov understood his demon had tried to summon the Quinary to him by creating an *entire fucking forest*, town be damned. It left him speechless. Moved so deeply, he felt dizzy.

"Well," he breathed once done reeling, "it looks much improved."

Jezibaba spent some time standing before the barrier, muttering to herself, bony fingers tapping her shrivelled mouth in thought. It took a ridiculous amount of time, considering all the hag needed to do in the

Coil of Boughs

end was slap her hands together, then part them again. Like a translucent veil, the rain moved aside, while Ryurikov's feet reconnected with the ground as Awimak gently set him down.

A lingering touch, and a lingering look. Ryurikov wasn't particularly fond of *not* touching Awimak just then. His hand slid around the toned side just above the woven fabric attached to his hips, thunder grey skin silky smooth under his gloveless touch. Heat stirred his groin at Awimak's low hum of pleasure, at the way his large claw came to cup his face, stroked his lips with a thumb.

"Oh, thank *fuck*," Ryurikov murmured.

WHAT?

He gestured at his own crotch. "It's back."

Awimak's eyes blazed. *I SHALL LIONISE YOUR COCK WHEN WE GET A MOMENT.*

Valka's snicker pulled Ryurikov out of his lusty haze. "You two are adorably nasty. Ready?"

"Just because *you* haven't gotten laid in a while," Ryurikov quipped.

"It has been a while." She sighed with rue, adjusting her hold on his equipment and glancing up at giant trees overcasting the entire town. "Maybe I can find myself a demon-lady."

Shadows darkened the stream. The minktoads continued to trill away, and the arched bridge was far more lopsided. Colossal roots pushed up its slats, lurching under Ryurikov's feet. Trees more massive than he'd ever seen ensnared homes and shops alike, their dark green leaves keeping most of the smoke out.

What should have been an unsettling return to a place where he'd been murdered less than four days ago became strangely calming. Awimak was by his side and held his hand, soothing any stray nerves abrading the edges of his mind.

Ryurikov caught sight of the same inn the monk insisted he not go into, and his stomach grumbled. "I could do with a proper meal."

He would have gladly ditched the hag and Valka, but a sudden commotion further down the shaded street had him sighing with exhaustion. Several of the townsfolk remained, appearing unbothered by the forest that now occupied their town, more concerned by his presence.

Or rather, *excited*. They looked *happy* to see him. Men and women, even some children running to him, their voices overlapping to the point he couldn't make out what they were saying. "Jarl" and, "new leader" were, unfortunately, unmistakable and impossible to ignore.

"No, thanks." Ryurikov hastened past the gathering crowd. Panicked, when they followed. "Valka!"

His sister slowed her gait. The hag too turned at his perfectly normal, not-at-all flustered tone.

Valka's eyebrows rose. "You're popular."

"You want to make things up to me?" Ryurikov panted, his hold on Awimak's hand still firm. "Get rid of them. Where are the other crones?"

"In the palace," muttered Jezibaba.

Ryurikov followed the hag up the crooked cobblestone path, but stopped in his tracks when he heard the melody of a flute.

He whirled, eyes widening at the way those in the crowd shifted and struggled, fighting internal manipulation. The youngest moved away without resistance. Only the adults were capable of an attempt at fighting it. Until their shoulders drooped and bodies slumped, and they moved away as though puppeteered.

"What the fuck, Valka!"

She looked at him, startled. "What? You asked me to—"

"Not to fucking manipulate them!"

"What's wrong with that?"

A question that made Ryurikov's vision spin with fury, crippling his ability to say anything at all. Had it not been for Awimak steadying him by the shoulders, he thought he might have collapsed.

Leaning against his demon's body, he clutched at the bark-armoured forearm and glared at the thing that called herself his sister. "Why don't you also liberate them of their organs?"

Her expression darkened. "I'm not a Clutcher. This is dragon magic!"

"I don't give a flying *fuck* what kind of bullshit it is. You're robbing people of their autonomy—"

"Don't judge, Ruri." Valka faced him, securing the flute at her hip. "I've helped so many people with this."

"Hurry up, you fools," Jezibaba snapped. "I want to go back to my hut before morning."

With a last look of disgust at Valka, Ryurikov spun on his heel and stalked after the witch, Awimak in tow. He didn't blink once at the strung up bodies of the headless jarl and several of his daughters, dangling from the lowest branches of ancient trees. Two of them were missing. He wondered if they'd been the ones to knife him.

The presence chamber was as they'd left it, the window still shattered, what little light filtered through refracting on shards littering the floor. There was no animal being roasted. Rather, two of the crones he'd rescued sat on opposite sides by the fire. They still looked frail, but clean with a change of clothes. Black velvet dresses looked blood orange in the fire's warmth, once again reminding Ryurikov that he was hungry.

"Brave of you to come here, Radojka."

"We said we'd spell you into oblivion if we ever saw you."

Ryurikov had discarded their names soon after leaving the crones, and did not care enough to ask. He was more focused on their hostility toward Jezibaba, grinning when the old buzzard turned to him with a glare, silently suggesting he ought to help. He didn't step in, at least not until Awimak gently nudged him forward.

His legs felt stronger now, confidence returning to his stride as he approached the other witches. "I'm sure you recall I saved your lives."

"That was four days ago, of course we remember," said the hag with the short, nest-like hair.

"Then perhaps you'd be willing to do me the courtesy of explaining to that creature," Ryurikov motioned at Jezibaba, "how your magic works?"

The one with the long, messy braid bristled. "Why, so she can give it to her sister to mangle?"

Ryurikov's eyebrows shot up. "Pardon?"

The short-haired crone side-eyed him. "You did not realise Radmila is her sister."

"We thought it strange," continued the other, "you keeping the company of the very one whose sister you tormented."

His mouth went dry, realisation crawling up his spine to hook its claws into the back of his skull.

Not only did that explain Jezibaba's absolute hatred for him, but it solidified what everyone keeping witches in their employ suspected. All hags had some kind of connection. They shared things with each other, they would have known about the childish cruelty he'd subjected Radmila to. Things even he felt a little guilty about now.

Short-Haired added, "Especially as it was Radmila who summoned the Skin Crawlers."

Wood scraped across stone flooring. Ryurikov barely realised he'd collapsed to the bench, his legs gone weak. Awimak rushed to his side, reaching out to squeeze his shoulders, but Ryurikov was back on his feet again, rage spurring him forward. Spittle flew from his mouth with snarled swears. He lunged for Jezibaba, shock replacing her scowl. His fist connected squarely with her face.

There was no satisfaction to be had, despite Jezibaba's tiny form flying backward and crumpling to the floor. Valka's outcry echoed, she swooped down to the hag, her hands trembling, breathing pitched with panic.

"All this fucking time!" Ryurikov bellowed.

The long dagger was in his hand before he could think. His foot connected with Valka's arm, her attempt to block no match for his wrath. His fingers twisted into the maroon fabric of Jezibaba's long tunic, yanking her upright, blade pressing firmly into that wrinkled throat, drawing blood.

"All this time," he snarled, "I thought it was *me* who had evoked them. And you let me believe it!"

"Awimak, please, stop him!" Valka's plea was no more than a pathetic whimper.

Jezibaba's orange eyes looked glazed, her nose clearly broken, no doubt seeping blood into the back of her throat. It cascaded over her jaw, dripped onto his fingers in green. She groaned, slowly recovering from a wallop that would have killed a lesser hag.

"It–It *was* your fault," she said, voice muddy.

Ryurikov pressed the blade harder into her neck, longing to draw out her death, to make it as painful as he could.

"As mu–much as it is mine," she added, to which he scoffed in disgust. "As much as it is Radmila's."

"No," Ryurikov managed, applying yet more pressure to the blade. A little more, and she would die choking on her own blood. "It *wasn't* my fault."

"You terrorised my sister!"

"I was a child! A stupid, arrogant, fuckhead of a child. And so what, she condemns everyone just to punish me? Gets my sister to *hate* me?"

"She didn't know what she was doing!" Jezibaba's bony hand came up over his, but didn't push the blade away. "You and your entire family pushed her into it. She was too far gone with hatred to know any better."

Ryurikov's mind hurtled back to that day again. The way Radmila had trembled, more than usual. The hatred in her eyes when he came in and she'd looked up from her tome, glowing a faint blue. He faltered. Awimak had said the Skin Crawlers weren't his fault. He was not a liar. There had to be more to it.

"Awi," he said, shakily. "You–You said this wasn't my fault."

IT IS NOT. His demon had come up behind him, doing nothing to stop or encourage him.

"I believed you!" he cried, cursing the crack in his voice.

IT IS NOT YOUR FAULT, RYURIKOV. Awimak gently stroked him across the back. *I CANNOT SPEAK FOR THE ENCHANTRESS, I HAVE NOT SEEN HER MIND. MY DRURY, IT WOULD HAVE REQUIRED IMPOSSIBLE KNOWLEDGE TO SUMMON CREATURES SUCH AS THE SKIN CRAWLERS.*

Twenty-Five

Crackling fire and the repeated tapping of his foot interrupted an otherwise silent presence chamber. Ryurikov's gaze remained fixated on Jezibaba, tended to by Valka. Her nose had stopped bleeding, but it was displaced. It was an improvement.

"How do you communicate with each other?"

His voice rang clear, commanding, shattering the silence in full.

"When we're awakened to our magic, we develop a link to all other witches," said the short-haired hag. "A link which *cannot* be severed, even if one of us forsakes another to take her place."

Ryurikov's lips thinned into a stern line. "Forsakes?"

"Do you think it's a joy to be mistreated?" snapped the one with the matted braid. "That we enjoy working for the entitled and their spawn?"

"Why do you do it, then?" He sighed, realising his mistake shortly after, and leaned back to rest against Awimak's muscular thigh behind him. A claw came 'round his neck, cupping it. The chill sent a tiny shiver through him.

"Were you taught nothing?" Short-Haired rasped. "We were—"

"Hunted and flung into the Vermilion Vertex, if not outright burned. Yes, yes." Ryurikov waved it aside. "Who took Jezibaba's place, then?" The two hags gave him a look, like the answer was obvious. He sighed a second time. "Radmila. And here I thought I was a shitty sibling."

"We all do selfish things, Ruri," Valka murmured, unable to look at him properly.

SOME MORE THAN OTHERS, said Awimak, his harsh rasp echoing through the chamber.

Ryurikov smirked before sobering up again. "Can you teach others this water magic? Are you able to make it portable?"

"You need a steady source," said Short-Haired.

"Like the well," mused Ryurikov, thoughts flicking to the tree-well at the hut.

"What do you plan on doing, if we give it to you?" asked Braided.

"Take the fight to the Skin Crawlers," he said. "Protecting this town is all good and well, but how long will you fare, just among the three of you? I assume the other one is still alive, keeping the barrier up."

"Branka is," said Braided. "She's down there with the remaining two of the Jarl's daughters." When he raised his brows in askance, she continued, "They showed a proclivity for magic."

"I didn't realise young witches existed," said Ryurikov.

"They don't, because unleashing magic before you're sixty kills you."

Well, he supposed he couldn't blame them. A thumb had taken to stroking his cheek. He leaned into it, pressing an open-mouthed kiss to the tip.

"You'll teach the Jezibaba, then?" he asked, distracted. His cock became restless, need stirring his stomach.

"It'll take some time," replied Short-Haired.

"Great." Ryurikov refrained from giving the thumb a long suck, *barely*. He rose instead, to stretch with a loud groan. "I'm taking the Jarl's room." With a glower at Jezibaba, he added, "Stay and learn, Beldam. Or my dagger will find your rimpled neck again."

Grandiose, filled with luxurious pelts, and gloomy, but the Jarl's chambers were spacious, at least. Awimak didn't have to crouch much, only to avoid the dark beams running across the ceiling. The heavy door shut behind Ryurikov and he leaned against it with a shaking exhale.

TIRED, MY LOVE?

Abruptly, he forgot how to inhale, eyes snapping to Awimak standing but a few feet from him. If he were to take a moment to reflect, Ryurikov would realise he envied the ease in which his demon expressed himself. And maybe, before this, he would have avoided thinking about it entirely. Now though, he had to wonder. Worse still, he had to wonder out loud.

"What do you see in me?"

It echoed Jezibaba's accusation, one that had occupied the recess of his mind ever since, her hoarse words endlessly stoking his anger.

ASIDE FROM YOUR UNWAVERING DETERMINATION TO EXIST?

"That's debatable, but yes." His hands flattened against the door, growing damp with sweat.

THERE IS A KINDNESS IN YOU THAT NO FIRE CAN BURN AWAY. YOU CARRY THE HEAVIEST OF GUILT, AND STILL YOU STAND. Awimak closed the distance between them, ducking once under a beam, then again to level their gazes. He reached out, cupping Ryurikov's cheek in a gentle claw. *YOU ARE UNYIELDING IN YOUR TRUTH, AND MORE GENEROUS THAN YOU REALISE.*

Ryurikov huffed, his heart disfluent with nervousness. "And those are desirable traits, are they?"

THEY ARE TO ME. Awimak dipped low.

His elongated jaw moved to reveal that grey pointed tongue, snaking out, gently sliding across Ryurikov's lips. He opened his mouth to greet it, and as their tongues met, a reigning heat reawakened, deep in his belly. Reaching up, Ryurikov hooked his fingers into the nostrils of the skull to pull him down further. He sought Awimak's mouth again, grunting in frustration when there were no lips to claim.

So he pressed a firm kiss to the side, against sharp, canine-like teeth, then eased out from between demon and door. "Come on, sit on the bed."

Awimak gave a curious rasp, but did as prompted. Ryurikov strode to the gilded dresser, dark like charcoal, and gathered a comb, its bone-white aglow in the low light of the dying fire. Ornately carved, hooded figures stared up at him from the comb. He brought it over, sliding behind his demon, now perched on the edge of the massive bed.

"You'll tell me more about yourself?" Kneeling, he ran his fingers through abyssal hair, smooth but with the occasional knot and stray lichen he carefully picked out.

WHAT WOULD YOU LIKE TO KNOW?

"If you're meant to devour nightmares, why are the Unbroken Wilds your home?" He ran the comb through fine tresses, taking his time. "Wouldn't it make more sense to live nearer people?"

IT WOULD.

"And anyway," he continued, "if you're supposed to eat nightmares, why are so many afraid of you? I've heard the stories."

Awimak's head shifted, his mane cascading further down his back.

WHAT STORIES WOULD THOSE BE?

Ryurikov stopped short of snorting. Like Awimak didn't know. "Just the usual ones circulating demons. That you eat human flesh, wear their entrails as jewellery."

I DO NOT MUCH CARE FOR THE TASTE, NOR THE STENCH OF WEARING THEIR INNARDS.

His eyebrows shot up and movements stilled, for a spell. Then, when he was almost certain his demon's words were a jest, Ryurikov chuckled. "Is it alright if I braid your hair?"

DO WHAT YOU LIKE.

"I'm exposing your ears."

IF YOU MUST.

"Oh," Ryurikov snickered, "I must."

He gathered the silken hair in his hand, exposing a flawless neck, and couldn't resist but drop a kiss to the nape. Then another, once he was sure the slight movement under his lips had been a shiver.

Most of the arrow-induced injuries were gone, with only the deepest lingering as feathery marks of light grey, stippling the muscular back. Ryurikov's gaze journeyed down the spine, to where dupion fabric hid what had to be shapely buttocks. Did Awimak have a tail, he wondered. Better yet...

"Can I fuck you?" Awimak's back visibly tensed, and Ryurikov regretted blurting the question. He swiftly set to braiding the hair, hoping that was enough to keep his demon with him. "It's fine if not. I was just wondering."

IT IS...POSSIBLE. Awimak sounded uncharacteristically hesitant. *YOU WOULD BE THE FIRST.*

Ryurikov froze. Did that mean what he thought it meant? Not only was Awimak a virgin in that regard, but had he just said yes? "I'll need clearer consent than that, Awi."

YES, RYURIKOV. YOU MAY MAKE LOVE TO ME.

He didn't know whether to reel with honour or feel disgusted at the phrasing. He chose to continue braiding. Awimak's glossy hair was wavy, and slippery. The braid wasn't as great as the ones he used to do for Valka, and he had nothing to tie it with, but it exposed those adorable goat-like ears.

Ryurikov dusted his fingers over them, stroking the soft fur. Dark with an umber whisper, like the fur on his legs. Awimak relaxed under the touch, so much his shoulders slumped and head tipped forward.

With a faint chuckle, Ryurikov deposited a kiss to a shoulder blade, then patted Awimak's side. "Lie down."

Awimak did as told, laying on his stomach.

"As much as I appreciate the quiet enthusiasm," Ryurikov said, amused, "Not tonight. Lie on your side."

If he was going to *make love* to him, he wanted to do it right and give Awimak the pleasure he deserved. For now, his demon would have to deal with being held. Ryurikov toed off his boots, then flopped down on the bed. He slid right up behind Awimak and wrapped a leg and arm over his side to hold him close.

Awimak shifted slightly, massive horn keeping his head off the pillow. *YOU'LL BECOME TOO COLD LIKE THIS.*

"It's fine. I highly doubt I'll get much sleep, anyway."

YOU ARE WORRIED?

"I'm surrounded by hags who are less than fond of me," Ryurikov muttered into the back of Awimak's nape. "Even if I saved them from a miserable existence, there's no guarantee they won't come to skin me alive."

He made a sound of disgust with a sudden realisation.

WHAT IS IT?

"I saved a bunch of hags." How absolutely revolting.

AND THIS IS A PROBLEM?

"No, I just—I never liked—" He cut himself short when his head rattled with yet more understanding. He didn't like hags much, but his experience with them had only ever been restricted to Radmila. And Jezibaba, more recently. Beyond those two though, he didn't *know* any of them. There was no way for him to know if they were all horrendous. "I'm...not sure where my distaste for them came from."

Awimak moved out from his hold, turning to pull Ryurikov against his chest instead. While he would have been happy enough to hold his demon, listening to the deep pulse of Awimak's heart was equally satisfying. Something wet slithered across his temple, slicking his hair. A kiss.

REST, DRURY, KNOWING I WILL KEEP YOU SAFE.

"Fine. But if I have a good dream, you take it."

Darkness laid like a pall when Ryurikov's eyes fluttered open. The bedding, the canopy, the shade of the colossal trees outside—it all made for a very glum room. It was jarring, having grown accustomed to sunlit forests. He palmed his eyes and sat up, groggily glancing across at a blurry figure. Too short and slight to be Awimak, even though the spot beside him was empty.

"Who the fuck are you?" He reached for the dagger at his belt before his vision could even focus.

A startled whimper. "My deepest apologies, sir! I was only tending to the fire."

An elderly man, dressed in all black, his greying hair lambent with orange from a fire that had, indeed, been resurrected.

"You're a servant?" Ryurikov untangled himself from the sheets and swung his legs off the bed to put his boots back on. "You realise the Jarl is dead? You no longer have to serve."

"Yes, sir." The man bowed so far, Ryurikov thought he might never again straighten back up. "And you're here to take his place."

Said with such confidence, Ryurikov would've believed him if he were anyone other than the man who most definitely wasn't taking the Jarl's place.

"What gave you that idea?" He glanced around for Awimak, but his demon was nowhere. Not outside when he looked out the window, and not through the doorway leading to a bathing tub and chamberpot.

The servant straightened up, thankfully, his expression most sombre. "You returned to us from the dead, with your family and another witch, after freeing this town of Jarl Blann's crushing grip. You have blessed us with treasures and enchanted trees that keep the eternal smoke out. You are also in the Jarl's chambers. I am simply putting things together."

Ryurikov narrowed his eyes. "All just a coincidence, I assure you."

"Indeed, sir. Shall I prepare you a bath?"

"Sounds fine." Ryurikov flattened his lips. "You're under no obligation, you're free to leave."

"Wouldn't dream of it, sir."

"I can't pay you," Ryurikov said, headed for the door.

"Very well, sir."

He groaned, turning back to the old man. "What will it take to get rid of you?"

"My home is here. I was never paid, but provided with room."

"Fine, stay. I don't give a shit. I won't be here long, anyway."

He found Awimak in the presence chamber. Along with Valka and Jezibaba, both looking worse for wear, and two of the other hags. Short-Haired was nowhere in sight. Awimak was bent over the fire and Ryurikov ran a hand along the small of his back, allowing his fingers to tease the edges of the fabric keeping his demon modest, just above the curve of his buttocks. Awimak's eyes burned hot when he handed him a deep metal bowl.

I INTENDED TO BRING THIS TO YOU.

Peering into it, Ryurikov kept his grimace to himself. Although the roasted vegetables didn't look bad, there were no traces of meat. "I'm going to have to start eating those around me."

"That's what Blann and his sort did."

Ryurikov pivoted to the witches. He would have liked to curse them for spelling the joy out of his jest, but frankly, that was far too unsettling information. Not surprising, of course. Those who worshipped Goreldion were known for their peculiar...*tastes*.

"Rest assured, hideous hags, I am an excellent hunter."

"You'll have to make do, Ruri," said Valka, coming to stand by the firepit. "Not a lot of animals around here to hunt, considering our neighbours."

Ryurikov took the bowl, muttering his thanks, before facing Valka. "Why is everyone talking as if we're staying here?"

"Was that not your intention when you killed the Jarl?" asked the one with severely matted hair.

"*No*. I killed him because he attacked me. Any luck in learning this water magic?" He regarded Jezibaba, continuing before she could open her mouth, "I'm not accepting 'no' for an answer."

"I learned it, *weedling*," Jezibaba snapped. Had her nose returned to its original position? "If you're going to wield it, give it the respect it deserves by using the correct name."

Ryurikov popped a chunk of squash into his mouth. "Water magic?"

"No, you blithering—"

"What happened to you, anyway?" he asked Valka, sitting beside Awimak on the bench furthest from the witches.

Valka tiredly rubbed her eyes. "Just nightmares."

Ryurikov cast Awimak a sideways glance, certain his demon was smiling. With a quiet snort, he pressed a kiss to Awimak's massive bicep. "We'll head out and kill us some Skin Crawlers shortly, assuming the salamander has enough of a grasp on the *water magic*."

"We?" Valka plopped down beside him, bench scooting and nearly sending him off it with her eagerness. "You'll have me at your side?"

He shrugged. "I could use your blade. Anyway, people here will need sunlight, eventually. Are you able to move the trees if we can get the smoke to clear?"

There was a brief pause while Awimak regarded him. *I CAN, MY LOVE.*

An awful noise left Valka. A cross between a squeal and fuckness-knew-what. "*My love?*"

He ignored her.

As Ryurikov emerged from the palace, the townspeople were less insistent on crowding him this time. Perhaps being manipulated had taught them a lesson, not that he was willing to forgive Valka for the transgression. If he didn't think that damned flute would come in handy at some point, he would have already snapped it in half.

Only a few ran up to him, bearing gifts and praise, none of which he accepted, swift to duck away from them. Ryurikov resisted the urge to use Awimak as a shield, figuring he must once again be invisible to everyone else. He missed his cloak. Missed hiding in the forest, away from prying gazes, he missed—

Ryurikov stopped in front of a boutique, a lantern inside permitting him to see what it offered past lattice windows. Tilting sideways, he peered in through the open door to better see, eyes locking onto one of the most stunning dark teal cloaks.

From where he stood, he couldn't discern what type of fabric, but he pointed at it, and lovingly whispered, "I'm coming back for you."

There was little point in a change of attire now, when they were headed out to face the Skin Crawlers.

"Are you able to enchant my arrows with water?" he asked the hag hobbling after him.

"I don't know," she grumbled. "They've taught me the art of Dowthera, but enchanting items with it is an entirely different pouch of seeds. I'll need to figure it out. I might not even be able to do it."

To which Ryurikov said, "Not an option."

The hut was where they had left it, safely tucked away deeper in the forest, away from the smoke and fiery wastelands. As the trees parted and he walked up to the front door, Ryurikov felt strangely at ease. Like he had a purpose.

His demon moved around the hut's side, and he followed. Valka and Jezibaba too, until they reached the tree-well. The chickens lingered nearby, clucking audible over the gurgling water.

An aged hand unfurled bony fingers. Jezibaba glared at Ryurikov. He scoffed, then grabbed an arrow from his quiver and handed it over. Crossing his arms, he leaned backward against Awimak, ignoring the prod of the quiver into his back in favour of focusing on the *other* thing pressing into his upper back. Ryurikov craned his neck to meet Awimak's gaze and quirked an eyebrow. Fiery eyes rallied with vigour, bark-armoured arms snaked 'round his shoulders to hold him closer.

Ryurikov groaned at the exact moment Jezibaba had spelled water from the well to encircle the arrowhead. It held for as long as it took for a bird nearby to take a shit, then fell with a similar splat into the grass.

"Your resounding failure hurts me, Beldam."

Jezibaba croaked gibberish, then screeched, "Get out of my hair! Leave me to focus, you oversexed beasts!"

"My pleasure." Ryurikov snorted. "And I'm still the least of your problems, *hag*, what with all the beetles in your hair!"

DO YOU THINK YOU AND THE ENCHANTRESS WILL EVER SEE EYE TO EYE? Awimak asked, settling down in their den. Ryurikov was swift to join him, although inwardly chided himself for how eagerly he'd flopped into the demon's open arms.

"Not if I have anything to say about it."

Awimak hummed, just as Valka came to a standstill near a vegetable patch. She adjusted her jerkin, patted away some imaginary dirt, fussed with her hair. Looked at Ryurikov, then away. Her shoulders dropped slightly, then she wandered up the back porch and into the hut.

WHAT ABOUT YOUR SISTER?

Ryurikov made himself comfortable in Awimak's lap. Despite his cock knocking against the inside of his trousers, demanding to be let out, they couldn't very well fuck with the hag just around the corner. He didn't exactly trust Valka not to spy on him out of boredom, either.

A nap was in order, and maybe he could satiate Awimak with a dream or two.

"What about her?" he muttered at length. When his demon said nothing, he peered out of one eye. "You're trying to get me to talk to her, *now*?"

Awimak appeared to smile. *YOU KNOW ME WELL.*

"I know your heart." He groaned. "Very well. If it'll please you."

After a firm lick across his forehead that slicked his hair, Ryurikov pushed out of Awimak's lap with a grunt and stumbled out of the den into the hut. She wasn't in the kitchen, or the area beyond it. She wasn't anywhere on the second floor, either.

He found her in the children's room, and couldn't help grimacing at the sight of all the toys. Valka sat on the ledge by the window, a leg drawn up to her chest, flute and sabre resting on the floor by her foot.

Ryurikov sauntered inside and dropped into a different bed to the one he had awoken in. "Don't suppose you know what this room is about?" The look Valka gave him was so wretched, Ryurikov needed to do a double take. "Are you crying?"

"*No*," snapped Valka, her features hardening. "Of course I know what this room is. I helped build it! And the toys, and the beds."

He cocked his head to the side, scouring what was, apparently, Valka's work. "I didn't realise you were that good with your hands. Hang on—"

"Radojka doesn't eat children."

"You read my mind." Ryurikov grinned, but Valka's look turned so miserable again, he sobered up. "Tell me."

"I don't know where those rumours even came from. I'm the one who took them."

"Valka, you better explain yourself."

"Not on purpose, not at first. I was just trying out the flute my then-girlfriend gave to me." She lowered her leg to reach for the instrument, tracing its delicate engravings with a fingertip. "Didn't know what it could do, and it ended up luring kids to me."

"There are less dubious ways to obtain children," Ryurikov said, trying *very* hard to keep his scorn to himself, and failing. "I hear birthing them can be effective."

Valka gave him a look. "I didn't *want* any of the children, but they... They weren't well."

Ryurikov slowly raised a hand to tap his forehead, questioningly.

"No! They were *ill* and left abandoned. I thought I could help them. That *we* could help them. Make them happy and give them a home."

Darkness settled in the pit of Ryurikov's stomach, gnawing his insides. He looked around the room again, devoid of young life. "Fuck."

A loud sob. Valka hid her face in gloved hands, contorting Ryurikov's heart to the point it hurt. Before he could stop himself, he was beside her on the window's ledge, an arm around her solid shoulders and pulling her head against his chest to run his fingers over braided hair.

"I couldn't take it anymore," she said between the spill of tears. "Radojka said we were giving them better lives, but none of them ever survived! How is that better?"

Ryurikov kicked aside his instinct to insult the witch, instead took a moment to ponder what Awimak would say. Fuck, he wished Awimak was here, he'd know exactly what to say. Should he offer Valka go embrace his demon? His earthy chill always made Ryurikov feel better.

"I'm sorry." He grimaced. "I..." Had no idea? That was fucking obvious. He propped his chin atop Valka's head while she blubbered into his chest. "You did your best?"

Valka sniffed, then pushed away with a limp-wristed smack against his chest. "You're terrible at this."

"I know." He chased after Valka with a hand, brushing freckled cheeks dry.

Another loud sniff, then she gathered her composure. "Anyway, you don't have to comfort me. I should be the one to—"

"I forgive you."

Hazel eyes brightened with surprise. "Ruri, you know you're not obligated to."

"I know."

"But I killed you."

"No," he held up a finger to forestall her arguing, "blades did that before the poison could. So I forgive you for *trying*."

If Valka had anything else to argue with, it fell away with a creak of the door. Ryurikov grimaced again at the sight of the rotund toad waddling in, rubbing its belly. "Fucking thing. I don't know how it keeps finding me."

Valka laughed, thickly. "Radojka named it Mauvella."

A snort, and he got up to approach the toad. It eagerly croaked when he picked it up, slapping splotchy feet around his fingers.

"You are one fat fuck of a toad," Ryurikov muttered, holding it up at eye level. "This thing's a giant, look at it." Easily the size of Awimak's ballsack.

Valka's smile was slight, but sweet, and it egged him on, as it always had. So he pressed his lips to the toad's, needing to see her cheer in full.

The next thing he knew, he squinched up at the ceiling, head throbbing from where he must have hit it on the floor. His ears rang. Vaguely, he recalled some kind of explosion of orange dust.

He groaned, pushed to his feet and caught sight of a woman lunging for him. She screeched, brown hair a mess, and her scrawny frame entirely nude.

TWENTY-SIX

Ryurikov hadn't known pinecones could be threatening. Yet there he was, staring down the pointy end of one, a whisper away from his eyeball. Blue eyes stared at him, empty but for the madness turning them to steel.

"Fuck–ing–*hell*!"

He brought his knee up into a bare stomach, sending the skeletal thing flying off and across the room. The door banged open again to his side, and a panting Jezibaba hobbled in, her rasped swears incoherent.

"Can't I leave you alone for five minutes?" she cried, coming to stand over the thin woman's quivering frame. Nothing but skin and bones and—

Ryurikov yowled in dismay, raising both arms to shield his eyes as the woman flailed to get back on her feet. "Someone give her something to wear!"

The woman released a mongrel of a noise, a window-shattering shriek and manic laughter. Having seen *far too much*, Ryurikov scrambled to his feet but didn't turn around, trusting Valka to have his back. A tussle behind him, a grunt, followed by a thump, and caterwauls of unwillingness.

"Calm down!" Valka shouted.

An abrupt silence followed. Then, "Who are you?"

Ryurikov dared a peek, relaxing at the sight of a frumpy umber blanket covering the scrawny form. She clutched it to her chest, now sitting on the floor, eyes wide and pinned on him. He had only seen her once, long ago, but thought he recognised what remained of Princess Mauvella. As fat as she had been in toad form, her face was now gaunt, the ripple of ribs visible along her side with every slight shift. Jezibaba grumbled under her breath, unintelligibly, but her annoyance was luculent.

"You're Princess Mauvella, aren't you?" asked Valka. She addressed Jezibaba, rather than the woman who had, apparently, been held captive for years by the witch.

"I had a reason," said Jezibaba.

Ryurikov tensed his jaw, whirling on the crone, ready to tear her insides out. Then he took pause, gaze snagged by the blocks stacked on a shelf, crudely fashioned out of oak. And the blankets, ugly and clumsily knit, but made to keep little bodies warm on a winter's night. His lips thinned into a line.

"Explain, then," he said, moving to lean out of the doorway. "Everything's fine, Awi." Just in case his demon was listening in.

"I was asked to take her," said Jezibaba while Valka helped Mauvella sit on a bed nearest the window. "She is mentally damaged and her mother told me to help. I...couldn't. I'm sorry, child."

Mauvella released a whimper, it bordered on manic. "It's fine! It's fine. I liked the flies. The flies were good."

"Why the fuck turn her into a toad?" Ryurikov demanded.

"I grew tired of her attacking me." Jezibaba met his gaze and held it.

He sighed. "Fair enough."

The hag's surprise was clear in a rise of silver brows. Aside from that, she gave nothing else in response, turning to rummage through a chest in the far corner. A bounty of clothing spilled free, mostly child-sized, and he hated spotting the mossy-looking thing he'd seen Jezibaba knit before. She brought over a shapeless frock, along with an orange sash. Ryurikov gave them some privacy, turning back only once he was sure it was safe to look.

"Are you hungry?" asked Valka.

Mauvella jumped up. "More flies? Yes!"

"No, no flies—"

A piercing cry.

Ryurikov's only warning before Mauvella pounced, tearing down another wind chime on her way. Her weapon of choice this time was an acorn, and he was ill prepared to find it shoved up his nose. He swore, slammed his hands down on frail shoulders, and shoved her to her ass with minimal effort.

Removing the acorn proved more challenging.

"Turn her back!" Ryurikov shouted, flicking the oval nut away.

"*I can't*, you nitwit, or I would've done it already!" Jezibaba stood to the side, glaring as Valka rushed to help Mauvella back up. "I take it *you're* the idiot who decided to kiss a toad?"

"And it would have been amusing too, had this," Ryurikov flapped his hand at the Princess, "not been..." He got his other hand involved. It seemed like a two-hand situation. "*This*."

Sea-like eyes snapped up to him again, and it caused his hair to stand on end. He made a quick escape down the staircase, unwilling to find out where Mauvella would try to stuff the next object she found.

Awimak lurked by the steps below the raspberry bush, holding an arrow in a great claw. Ryurikov reached up for it to admire the fletching —vibrant green leaves. And the shaft, more like a branch, its wood similar to the trees now occupying Briarmour. Crystalline water swirled around the point, sparkling like fine jewellery in the sunlight.

"So, the hag's done it."

IT REQUIRED MY WOOD TO DO IT.

Ryurikov bit down an amused snort. "That's not all your wood is good for." A claw settled atop his head, and stayed there for a moment. "Now to test this out. Will one arrow be enough?"

UNLIKELY. Awimak gathered a wooden sword from the den. *WE HAVE CREATED THIS FOR VALKA.*

Similar to her sabre, with burls and streaks of bark, it too had a swirl of glimmering water encasing the blade.

"You've been busy."

A crash sounded behind him. Ryurikov scampered to hide behind Awimak. He spun back around, prepared for another ambush. When none came, he asked, "Did you know the toad was a princess?"

I DID NOT. NEITHER DID I KNOW YOU ENJOY KISSING AMPHIBIANS.

Ryurikov gave pause. "Awi."

His demon turned to him. *MY APOLOGIES. I WAS NOT SPYING. I WAS—*

"Making sure I was safe. I appreciate it. Hang on," Ryurikov closed the distance between them, craning his neck to look up at his demon. "You're not worried, are you?"

YOU WERE BETROTHED TO HER.

He laughed, unable to help it. "*Were* is right. For what it's worth, I'd much rather be betrothed to you."

The words cascaded with such ease from his lips, yet unspooled his mind so quickly it left Ryurikov feeling lightheaded. Awimak faced him in full, claws coming to cradle his head, to brush thumbs across his fire-hot cheeks. Thankfully, Awimak said nothing, silent in his acknowledgement.

They weren't permitted to linger on it, anyway. Crunching behind his large demon jerked Ryurikov out of the touch.

"Big boy," said Mauvella, shoving the core of an apple into her mouth. Her throat flexed around a gag.

"Sorry!" Valka hopped down the porch onto the wide stepping stones, boots kicking up a veil of dust. She smacked Mauvella across the back to help dislodge the core. It spilled from her mouth into the grass, chased by a string of saliva.

Ryurikov warily eyed the apple stem still pinched between Mauvella's fingers. Anything could be a weapon in those hands.

Crunch.

Ryurikov's sideways glance stopped on Mauvella, eating what had to be her fourth apple.

"Any more and you'll get the shits."

"*Oooh*! Wonder if I remember how to?"

He snorted, shifting his focus back to the burning lands ahead, his beautiful demon-crafted arrow already nocked. The scenery hadn't changed, an endless stretch of blackened wastelands. With a last look over his shoulder at Awimak, whom he had expressly told to stay put, he and Valka moved forward. Mauvella tried to scuttle after them, her borrowed boots a touch too large, but Awimak's claw shot out and grasped her hand.

"We'll be back soon, Mauvie!" Valka called.

Ryurikov's expression fell into a flat look. "Mauvie?"

Even under the gloom of thick smoke, Valka's face darkened with a tinge of rose red. "I like her."

"You've known her for the count of four apples!"

"She's nicer than Nebujin!"

He stopped dead in his tracks, fire-thinned bones breaking under his boot. "Valka," he said, acerbically. "You aren't referring to the sky dragon?"

Valka's eyes flicked past his shoulder. She signalled for him to duck. Swiftly, he moved behind molten stone that might have been a home once, dodging a stray flame feasting on crispened fur. Rabbit, perhaps.

"Valka," Ryurikov said again.

"Where do you think I got the flute?"

He glanced at the damned thing on her hip, scrutinised its tooth-yellow tinge. "For fuck's sake. Your girlfriend was a *dragon*?"

"Like you're one to talk!"

"I'm not judging on *what* you decide to fuck—you know what, yes I am. Awimak's not a dragon, for a start. How does that even *work*?"

Valka shrugged. "There were some logistics we had to figure out. Oh don't look at me like that!"

"Sorry." Ryurikov faltered. "It's just—*Nebujin*!"

"Yeah?"

"She's the size of an island!"

His sister clicked her tongue. "An exaggeration. More like a cay."

She peered over the congealed wall, the crunch and crack of several puppets audible beyond it, and her hand tightened on the hilt of Awimak's sword.

"Don't waste it," said Ryurikov. "Wait for them to pass."

There were far too many. Only once the noise of dry bones breaking no longer reached them did he move away from the wall, skirting through thick layers of ash with Valka in tow. The screech of a Skin Crawler serrated the air, from a distance. Another screech followed as if in answer from elsewhere.

"I can't tell where it's coming from," Valka said, hushed.

The hills were too wide and too open, with little to hide behind other than more molten stone. They would just need to figure it out, and Ryurikov said as much.

"I thought you might have a better plan than just running into this."

"I died three times. Do I seem like someone who plans?"

"That reminds me." Valka straightened from her crouch, causing him to squirm with the need to tug her back down. Although, other than hazy orange horizons and skies as murky as vegetable tea, there was little else to see. "Radojka told me about the stew. Why the hell would you eat something a witch gave you?"

Ryurikov settled a knee into ash as pliant as fresh snow. He met her gaze, but found he couldn't hold it. There was little he could think to respond with. Admitting that deep down in the darkest, shittiest parts of himself he had a death wish seemed too upfront a response. One Valka was unlikely to understand. Calling himself a fool would not have been entirely accurate. Telling her that he thought it'd be safe would have been an outright lie.

"It smelled nice and I was hungry."

The silence that followed suggested Valka didn't believe him. Thankfully, she didn't push the subject, only groaned in frustration. "Where are those things?"

Ryurikov shrugged. "They found me easily enough in another town, like they sensed I was there." He jerked at a sudden holler, eyes widening in disbelief. "Valka! What the *fuck*?"

She lowered her hands from her face, her call still echoing. "What?

I'm bored."

A screech responded. It was swiftly followed by dull *clack-clack-clacks*.

Ryurikov swore, pivoting to ready his bow, unsure where the noise came from. Until he saw a dense cloud of ash in the wake of a Skin Crawler, barrelling forward. Fully fledged—*older*. Twice the size of those in Eastcairn. Valka's feet appeared to have grown roots beside him while Ryurikov aimed for the demon's thin chest. He cast the arrow, muscle memory taking over even as his heart threatened to beat itself out of his ribcage.

He didn't wait to find out if he hit it, grabbing Valka by the scruff and yanking her out of the way of a flailing scythe. Her bulky frame hit the ground. Right behind them, the muffled thud of a scythe connecting with the earth had Valka kicking through ash to get away from it. Ryurikov nocked a second dousing arrow, aimed, then loudly cursed.

The magic had gone from its tip.

"Run, Valka!"

She didn't need telling, already tripping over her own feet to flee. Ryurikov spun to grasp the enchanted sword from her hip, its wooden blade sliding from the leather harness with ease. He whirled again, the demon now above him, so tall its underside brushed the top of his head. The arrow stuck dead-centre from its bony chest, otiose. With an upward swing, Ryurikov thrust the blade into its belly, surprised to feel the flesh give with such ease, sending blood spilling.

It ignited across his forearm. He yanked the blade free and fled out from under the demon, its shrill caw echoing as it staggered. Ryurikov tore the once-white tunic off him, flinging it aside, but the flames had sunk their teeth into his skin. Panicking, he ran the flat of the sword over his arm. Crystalline water trickled off the blade to swirl around his limb, dousing the flames before evaporating with a hiss.

"Ruri!"

A second Skin Crawler scuttled up the incline, whirling cinders and smoke in its wake. This one had to be young, freshly hatched from someone's corpse, skin and shattered bone stretched over its limbs like ill-fitted clothing, bleeding fire.

Valka's feet had set anchor again. Ryurikov darted forward, snagging her by the jerkin. She cried something about where they were headed, but he could barely catch his breath from the searing pain in his arm, let alone respond. The two Skin Crawlers followed so close behind, charcoal flicked his back.

A scythe arced high above his shoulder. He shoved Valka out of the way. They both stumbled sideways, struggling to find their feet in pliant debris.

Through the smouldering miasma, the ancient trees of Briarmour fell into view. Ryurikov pushed against Valka's back, urging her to run faster. She was heavy on her feet, too slow—something caught him in the back, digging into his bare skin. He cried out, flailed, unable to free himself from the hook the eldest Skin Crawler had on him. Ryurikov fell to his knees, ash shrouding his vision, drawing into his mouth with each sharp intake of breath.

"Go!" he rasped through clenched teeth, reaching behind him to grip the scythe scraping across bone.

"Fuck that!"

Valka unsheathed her sword, stomping toward him. Lacklustre light snaked along the blade as it swept over Ryurikov's head, the steel axing into bone. With a grunt, she planted her foot against the limb, dislodging it from his back. Her gloved hand came 'round his underarm, effortlessly hoisting him up. He stumbled forward, feeling the hot cascade of blood across his skin. His own hand came around the inside of Valka's elbow, but she moved out of his grip, steadying her blade as the Skin Crawler snapped its skull-beak at her.

"Princess Valka," it gasped.

"No," said Valka, surer than he had ever heard her speak. "Not anymore." She took her stance, holding the blade low. "It's Piper of the Drakes."

The demon chirmed, canting its head, empty orbits focused on her. The younger one advanced, trailing fire, clicking its skin-coated beak with famished eagerness. Ryurikov took hold of both his daggers, Awimak's sword now lost.

"We can't take these on," he hissed. "Can't you use the flute?"

"Nope," said Valka calmly, so unlike the sister he'd known. "It doesn't work on demons. It's fine, Ruri. You get away. I've got this."

"Fuck that."

If they were going to die, they would do so together.

Then his thoughts flickered to Awimak, gutting him with the realisation that he *couldn't* allow himself, or his sister, to die. Unfortunately, they were too far away from the town, there was nowhere to hide, and the persistent trickle of blood down his back had yet to cease.

"But if you don't mind," Ryurikov continued in a strain, "fuck dying, too."

Valka glanced at him. "I wasn't planning on it."

She launched forward. Ryurikov drifted to the side, both dodging the rapid swipes of a bone-scythe. They flanked the eldest. Valka brought her blade down against a forelimb, it stumbled forward. Ryurikov drove his long dagger into a hindleg. Used it for leverage to hoist himself atop it, momentarily sliding against gossamer-thin skin flaking away under his grip. The Skin Crawler bucked, and he rammed the serrated dagger into its spine, twisting it.

The youngling scampered up the side and flailed to reach him. It missed his leg by a leaf, so did the flames flaring up from where he had his dagger in the spine. He jerked his hand away, sliding off the Skin Crawler's back and landing on his feet. Pivoting, he jammed the long dagger into a hindquarter, repeatedly, until its bony wound bled, and he needed to move on. Valka had adopted a similar tactic, dodging every gush and spurt of fire-blood as they worked on the large demon, avoiding the youngling scattering flames fieldwide.

"We need to move!" Ryurikov called when his foot nearly caught a line of flames left in the youngling's wake. "Run, I'm right behind you!"

He darted back to the larger demon, scaling its crumpling form again after Valka yanked her blade out of its throat. With a few hard tugs, he retrieved his serrated dagger, slid forward and jumped, nailing the blade directly into the nape on his way down. Ryurikov ran after Valka, vaulting over ruins, soon catching up.

A glimpse behind him—the demon struggled to chase, youngling ambling by its side. Giant trees drew nearer with each frantic fall of their feet. Ryurikov reached out for his sister's hand as they ran. She took it, clenching tight. He stumbled, his vision blurring.

"No, you don't!"

Valka slowed to curl her arms under him and scooped him up, cradling Ryurikov against her chest. Were it not for the fierce draw in her brows, he would have been convinced he weighed nothing at all. Her biceps shifted into his back, painfully, but he wrapped his arm around her neck, keeping his eyes glued to the Skin Crawlers slowly fading into the haze.

They hadn't yet reached Briarmour, and Valka lost steam, soon forced to lower him back down. He wobbled, clamping a hand around her shoulder to support her as much as himself while they tried to catch their breath. She coughed against the inhale of ash and smoke, her hazel eyes meeting his. He failed to smile, could only grimace. They were closer to Briarmour now, but his strength drained from him faster than he could count.

DRURY!

Enormous claws lifted Ryurikov by the hips, raising him against a solid chest. He wrapped his left arm around Awimak's neck and uttered a swear against grey skin, which he shortly kissed, vision bouncing while Awimak walked.

"Red, red! Was it me? Did I do that?"

Ryurikov peeled an eye open to glance at Mauvella over Awimak's shoulder, shuffling through charred grass beside a sweaty, panting Valka.

"I'm afraid not," he muttered. "Maybe next time."

TOUCH HIM AND I WILL UPROOT YOUR VERY EXISTENCE, MAUVELLA.

Did Awimak sound angry? Ryurikov would have commented, but he was exhausted.

Curtains of rain parted. Planks of wood groaned under Awimak's weight. Ryurikov leaned his head against the broad chest, breathing in the scent of forest and soil, and tried not to grimace at the clamour springing up around him. He was more exposed than he cared to be, in a state he didn't appreciate.

He must have faded, since the next thing Ryurikov knew, he was on his stomach in a bed. Voices carried over him, a pair of warm hands working something into his wounds, easing the pain in his arm and back. Awimak crouched low by his side, fiery eyes flickering. He was angry, still.

"What is it, Awi?" Ryurikov slurred. He reached out to brush his fingertips through soft hair trailing over pronounced clavicles. Awimak snorted, breath flaring before him, scalding enough that Ryurikov needed to withdraw his hand.

I SHOULD NOT HAVE LET YOU GO ALONE.

"Hey, do I count for nothing?" Valka grumbled from somewhere.

Ryurikov pushed air past his lips. "You *couldn't* have gone. I prefer you uncooked."

WE WILL DISCUSS THIS, Awimak said. *AFTER YOU REST.*

He'd gotten so used to Awimak's wraith-like voice, it no longer perturbed him, but there was a sharpness to it he hadn't heard before. He would have responded, were it not for someone jostling him.

"Fucking *ouch*," Ryurikov snapped, yet his tone was nothing to the snarl of fury erupting from Awimak. Long nails dug into the bedding, as if he had to restrain himself from lashing out. Fuck, they were going to need to have a conversation.

"I'm so sorry," whimpered a feminine voice Ryurikov didn't recognise. "I–I haven't practised in so long!"

"Move over, child."

He groaned at Jezibaba's croak, dead-cold fingers grazing his feverish skin, applying dressing to his back. Murmured instructions accompanied by Awimak's hot breath across his face lulled him into a sleep he tried to fight.

A battle lost.

Twenty-Seven

Ryurikov stirred awake to darkness. Although that being the natural state of the room, he didn't know if it was night. A hot slather trailed up his good arm, the long tongue ending with a flick across his already drenched cheek. Wrapped up in blankets, he lay nestled in Awimak's hold. A good way to wake up.

"What time is it?"

THE SUN HAS SET PAST THE TALLEST TREE.

He shifted in Awimak's hold to peer up into fiery eyes. "You seem calmer."

I BURN HOTTER WITH ANGER THAN VALE'S CORE, RYURIKOV.

With a confused look, Ryurikov laboured upright. Most of the pain had subsided, but *fuck* he was sore, in particular his right arm. Even in the low light of the yielding fire, it looked raw. "I didn't die, and more importantly, neither did you."

Awimak followed, sitting up, his horns catching on the silver canopy. YOUR PLAN WAS FLAWED IN THAT IT WAS NO PLAN. Cutting words contrasted by the gentle touch to his knee. I SHOULD HAVE COME WITH YOU.

"You need a forest to work your magic, and I don't know if you realise this, but forests in particular are flammable. And it was a fine plan, *if* the dousing magic had worked."

NEXT TIME, I WILL REMAIN BY YOUR SIDE.

Ryurikov shook his head. "I can't have you with me."

Ignoring the frustrated snort, he struggled free of the blankets, sliding off the other side of the bed. He'd been robbed of his boots and breeches, entirely nude aside from the dressing covering his back and chest. Hooves thudded across the floor behind him.

WE HAVE TRIED IT YOUR WAY.

"I *can't* have you with me," he said again, more strained, the nascent of fear tightening his chest. He walked to the window, gazing through soot-dirty glass, down at streets now lit by lanterns. A group of townspeople had gathered outside.

I WILL NOT STOP YOU FROM DOING WHAT YOU FEEL YOU MUST, BUT NEITHER WILL I ALLOW YOU TO GO WITHOUT ME AGAIN. Firm words, once again softened by gentle claws sliding around his sides to stroke across Ryurikov's stomach. Heated breath raked down his nape, and bone nuzzled the side of his face.

FROM NOW ON, I REMAIN BY YOUR SIDE.

Ryurikov scoffed, softly, turning in the embrace. "Allow?"

He craned his neck, unresisting when Awimak eased him closer to the window, until his back bumped into cool glass. Those same claws came around his ass, raising him off the floor with ease. Like he weighed no more than a broken twig. He sought horns for support, rough under his touch, his legs slinging over powerful arms as his head dropped backward to rest against the ceiling's wood beam.

Awimak's tongue slid across the inside of Ryurikov's thigh, curling around his balls and vining the shaft of his stiffening cock. He groaned low, tightening his hold on the horns as Awimak's mouth enveloped him in full, the heat of it nigh scalding. Nasal bones dug into the skin of his pelvis before Awimak sucked back up to the tip. Pointed tongue dipped into the slit, teasing until Ryurikov helplessly bucked his hips.

Awimak's claws dug into his rear, eliciting another groan. The long mouth swallowed him again, and though sore, Ryurikov released his hold with his right arm to let his fingertips search for an elongated jaw, hoping to feel his cock slide inside that mouth. He couldn't, only felt the motion of muscle under the chin, a quick rhythm building. Wet slurps accompanied his groans, Awimak's low, hungry growls.

The wood was rough against the back of his head, catching Ryurikov's hair with every movement. Up there, the heat of the room lingered, intensifying the dizziness brought on by pleasure. Arching forward, he squeezed his eyes shut, pressing an open-mouthed kiss to Awimak's forehead. A gasp against bone, heavy with need, laced with surprise, and he spilled himself. Under his aching fingertips, Awimak's throat bobbed with a thick swallow.

They shifted back to the bed and ever so gently, Awimak eased him down. Sat on the edge and facing tenting cloth, Ryurikov reached up. He trailed his fingers over the muscular abdomen, to a stomach barely featuring a navel. More like a scar.

"I wouldn't mind returning the favour." He leaned forward to mouth the bulge, leaving the fabric damp. "To taste you."

A colossal claw cupped his face, thumb brushing his chin, prompting him to look up.

I WANT ONLY TO MAKE YOU HAPPY.

The words echoed in the room, in his mind. Pinging his heart with the understanding that Awimak *did* make him happy, more than he could ever confess to. Ryurikov licked his lips, slowly easing the fabric out of the way, stopping when a stem, like that of overgrowing ivy, snapped where fabric met skin. He sucked in a breath, flicking his gaze up in question.

IT HAS BEEN A LONG TIME, Awimak murmured.

Ryurikov didn't know why that broke his heart, just a little. How long had Awimak been on his own before they stumbled across one another?

He tried not to wince every time something broke or snapped as he pulled the fabric away. Woodsy dupion rustled to the floor, revealing a thicket of dark silken hair cloistering a girthy erection leaking with excitement. It radiated heat and smelled strongly of earth, each inhale like drawing in the steam of a hot drink. Ryurikov set his hands on powerful thighs, where the beginnings of fur blanketed skin, and brought his mouth

mouth to the mauve tip. He swirled his tongue around, lapping up the taste of nature.

It was Awimak's turn to groan, blunted fingers dragging across his scalp. Ryurikov slithered his tongue along the underside, relishing in the heavy, velvety texture. Awimak must have taken it for teasing, grunting with restlessness.

Or maybe Ryurikov had misread and he'd upset him, since Awimak moved away and lowered to his haunches between Ryurikov's widely spread legs.

I WISH TO ENJOY YOU FURTHER.

Through half-lidded eyes, he watched his demon, trailing his fingertips over the long jaw. "Whatever makes you happy."

Awimak placed an open claw against his chest, so large the base of his palm pressed into his stomach, encouraging him to lie back. Ryurikov ignored the sharp pain in his shoulder blade, focused on the way Awimak grabbed the underside of his knees, hoisted his backside up, and exposed him to the fullest. His eyes rolled into the back of his head when that devilish tongue trailed from thigh to thigh, then to his centre, slathering up his hole. A wraith-like growl of satisfaction, and the slick muscle pressed into him.

Ryurikov could feel it swirling inside, curling upward into his prostate, repeatedly. He released a series of curses in an attempt not to squirm too much, hoping to spare himself the agony of reopening his wound.

Fingers enclosed his cock, pumped, and with a startled, loud moan, he came again. Still, Awimak's tongue pushed up against the sensitive cluster of nerves, until he'd spilled all he could, and Awimak lapped up his pleasure as though he were starved.

Panting, Ryurikov let his hands flop down on either side of his head, too tired to flinch away from that slick tongue vining his cock again. Fingers pushed into his asshole then, and he careened onto his side, too sensitive and exhausted to fight it much more than that. He moaned instead, loudly, almost miserably.

A raspy rumble of a laugh. *I AM NOT DONE WITH YOU YET.*

"I can't come again."

And yet his cock was hard once more, and those fingers opened him up, twisting and prodding and delving deep. The bed dipped under Awimak's weight while Ryurikov buried his face into the many blankets. The tip of a thick cock replaced fingers, eased inside, so slowly he was convinced his demon's intent was to torment. Awimak straddled one leg, lifting the other far enough to strain thigh muscles, and pushed further into him.

"Oh, *fuck*!" Ryurikov helplessly bit into a blanket, wool itching his tongue. Awimak was deeper than ever before, the slide of balls hot across his thigh when he shifted back out.

Ryurikov braced himself for the inevitable, yelped regardless with the hard thrust into him. Merciless. He twisted to lie on his stomach, giving his demon access to push and pull his hips as he pleased. To fuck him so soundly, all Ryurikov could do was grunt and shudder while Awimak pistoned him with relentless mastery. A massive fist gathered his cock and he whimpered, utterly helpless.

The third orgasm neared, and at that point he wasn't even sure he wanted it. Awimak slipped all the way out of him, long enough for Ryurikov to catch his breath, to feel a sense of loss.

YOU ARE BLEEDING, MY DRURY.

"It's–It's fine," he gasped. "I don't care." He couldn't even feel it.

He *could* feel that tongue sliding up from the cleft of his ass, tracing the line of his spine to end on his shoulder blade. His cock hadn't yet been released, and the thought that Awimak was stealing a taste of his blood while simultaneously thrusting deep into him horse-kicked Ryurikov over the edge.

With a cry he came, so violently his body convulsed, thighs quaking and limbs too weakened to keep himself upright. Not that it mattered, since Awimak lifted his limp body and manoeuvred him onto his back, unmindful of the blood staining the sheets. He wasn't done yet, and Ryurikov could only lie there while his demon held him by the thighs and hammered into him. Awimak doubled over, tongue now lapping across his sweaty chest, up to his throat, into his open mouth. He met it with his own, tangled with the taste of earth and metal, before it pulled back.

LET ME CALL YOU MINE.

Ryurikov forced open his eyes. Blood smeared the lower half of Awimak's skull, orbits blazing like a forest fire.

What could he do but nod?

Awimak thrust into him hard, jerking free another a strained shout. It was a demand for a verbal response.

"Y-Yes," Ryurikov managed.

Another forceful drive of demon hips, sweat-slick fur peeling away from the underside of his legs as Awimak pulled out to the tip again.

LET ME PROTECT YOU.

Awimak drove back into him. The bed trundled, creaking in complaint. Fulgent breath raked Ryurikov's already feverish body, teasing sweat from him in places he didn't even know could sweat. He fisted the blankets, bit down on his lower lip to keep from crying out, his frustrated, "*Fine!*" spinning into persistent swears as Awimak's rhythm turned frantic.

His demon arched back, bright orange flames erupted. Ryurikov was far too enwrapped to worry about the bed's canopy catching fire or the claws that had regrown their nails, now digging into his skin. Drawing blood.

One last, harsh plunge and a *roar*. So loud it trembled the surrounding wood, the glass of the windows, his *skull*. Awimak's cock inside him pulsated with the thrum of a thunderstorm. A sweltering deluge followed. Ryurikov's legs twitched involuntarily while Awimak pushed more and more of his seed into him, until he thought he might burst.

At long last, his demon released a great exhale, then slid free, leaving Ryurikov shivering and gasping for breath. He groaned weakly at the hot fluid spilling from between his legs, too tired to do anything about it.

A panting Awimak settled beside him, wasting no time in gathering him into musclebound arms to hold him close. The chill of his skin seemed less so, now reminding Ryurikov more of a pleasant spring evening.

Slickness trailed across his sweaty neck, to his equally sweat-damp face.

In a satisfied murmur, Awimak said, *MINE TO PROTECT.*

Twenty-Eight

Looks of fright and awe followed Ryurikov while he held Awimak's claw, his stride steady along herringbone cobblestone roads despite the previous nights' endeavours. He'd found nothing to wear but the late Jarl's black clothes and, not wishing to be mistaken for anything, covered the embroidered image of Goreldion with a studded leather vest he'd taken off a soldier's corpse. It even had a hood attached, and he'd immediately pulled it over his head, gleeful in the security its finely woven fabric provided.

White wisteria cascading the tavern's front remained bright even in the gloom cast by colossal trees. Ryurikov ducked through the door, holding it open for Awimak while his demon figured out how to get his horns past the frame. Did they seem larger?

Gasps behind him had Ryurikov smiling, slyly. Because he'd requested his demon show himself. None of the townsfolk ran for their lives. Although after being oppressed by a cultish Jarl who demanded suffering as part of taxes, he supposed a tall demon wasn't much of a concern.

It helped that the townsfolk saw Ryurikov as some kind of saviour. The thought still made him want to curl in on himself. He wouldn't have gone out, but he was *hungry*. There was plenty of food at the palace, of course, prepared for him not only by servants, but the townspeople coming to pay their respects. Unfortunately, *none* of it contained meat. Not to mention he'd learned the servants hadn't been fed in a while.

Hence, he needed to fend for himself now, more or less. Guiding Awimak through the door, he claimed a seat at the bar, pleased to see how well kept everything in the tavern was. Dark wood dominated, the stools were polished and clean, much like the bar itself. Even the flagstone floor was spotless.

Awimak carefully lowered onto a stool beside him. It creaked, threateningly. Lips twitching up into another smile, Ryurikov reached out to toy with Awimak's claws. A wingbeat of nervousness awakened as their fingers touched, explored, then laced.

Thumping pulled his attention to the barkeep hobbling toward him, crutch in one hand, two tankards in the other. His gaze flicked from Ryurikov's face up to Awimak. The intricacies of the deer's skull were illuminated with a rising sun no one could see. There was a split second of fear, but the barkeep masked it quickly, and well.

Coming to stand before them, he set the tankards down. "My Jarl."

"No, no. *No.*" Ryurikov ignored Awimak's amused chuckle and released his hand. "I am not your Jarl, or your *anything*."

"Not Prince Leonid Maksim either, who beshrew all land, here to steal what belongs to Monarch Mulgar?"

His expression must have darkened several shades to murder, since the barkeep immediately held up both hands. "Word travels, your highness. I meant nothing by it."

"Not *that*, either," Ryurikov snapped. "I just want something to eat that once frolicked on four legs! Is that too much to ask?"

What few patrons occupied the tavern fell silent, yet the barkeep's look softened. "I'll fetch you something."

Ryurikov shook his head, watching the man retreat. "The sooner we get rid of those things outside the sooner we can get the fuck out of here."

I WOULD BE INTERESTED TO KNOW WHO SPREAD THIS INFORMATION.

A baleful look at Awimak, who leaned in closer to nuzzle his temple.

Blood encrusted his skull still, he hadn't wanted to clean it off even after Ryurikov offered to do it for him.

"You mean you don't know?"

I DO KNOW.

With a groan, Ryurikov rubbed his stiff neck. "The hags."

Awimak's face nudged him, ever so affectionate with the way he rubbed against his cheek, his neck. His shoulder. *I BELIEVE THEIR AIM WAS TO INSTIL HOPE.*

"What am I supposed to do with that?" Ryurikov muttered, petulantly. "It's not my fault Mulgar is a piece of shit."

GOLD DUSTED ORDURE, COMPARED TO YOUR PARENTS.

He tutted. "Witty."

YOU CAN DO BETTER THAN THEM, MY LOVE.

Ryurikov groaned. "Not you, too."

The door to the kitchens squeaked open and the barkeep emerged with a plate, which meant he could avoid further discussion of taking responsibility for something he didn't want. The plate slid across highly polished wood toward him, and Ryurikov raised his eyebrows.

"Minktoad," he said, flatly.

"Four legs and frolics. Or used to, that one." The barkeep grinned. It was annoyingly jovial. "They're fine to eat. We have to make do."

"Well, if it's good enough for you." He picked up a leg to give it a careful nibble. It wasn't all that bad. Mild like chicken, and well seasoned.

"I'm afraid I don't know what your companion prefers," said the barkeep, regarding Awimak again.

DREAMS. I WILL COME FOR YOURS WHEN THEY ARE HAPPY.

Ryurikov snorted with laughter. The barkeep looked rightfully worried, and hastened away—as much as he could, being one leg down.

YOUR SISTER IS LOOKING FOR YOU, said Awimak then, and Ryurikov hurried to clear his plate before she could find him and steal what little meat there was.

Not two mouthfuls later and she burst through the door, completely winded. "There you are! I've been looking everywhere for you."

"I said I was going out."

Lantern light transformed her hair into a fiery mess as she darted to him. "We figured out why the magic didn't work—ooh, what did you have to eat?"

"Vegetables."

Valka shrugged. "I told you, they don't have livestock here aside from a few pigs."

"Pigs?" Ryurikov slammed his feet down on the ground in a hurry to leave. "Where? I'll gut one myself."

"Focus!"

"Right, right. Jezibaba's magic is limp-dicked."

"Not impotent, just not combined with the right material. We need *silver*."

He rubbed his face with both hands, already tired. He hadn't stopped *being* tired. "Should I ask why?"

"Like you care." Valka walked back to the door, signalling for him to follow with a jerk of her head. He really didn't want to.

"You're right, I don't. Get me something that works and I'll use it. Until then, I'd like to be left alone."

"We need to find a blacksmith who can work with the right kind of silver." Valka crossed her brawny arms. "Apparently, not everyone can."

"I have a silver bow. That'll do the trick, I'd wager?"

"I know. It's exactly what we need. And I'd like a blade of the same silver. You need silver arrows too, I think."

"No." Ryurikov pivoted, walking past Awimak to look for a back door. Regrettably, no matter how hard he slapped the wall's dark panels, no door appeared.

"Ruri!"

"I know what that means and I'm *not* going back there." He faced Valka, who ran to block his path to the only exit. In a hiss, he added, "I killed way too many people there. And I'm pretty sure I gave the owner of the silver bow a bit of head trauma."

"Gods. Yes, I know, Ruri. Rumours of the shitfest you left behind has already reached the drakes." Valka's lips thinned into a line, and fuck, she reminded him too much of himself just then. "You won't have to go, I will."

He narrowed his eyes. "You want to go after Vasili."

"That'd just be a bonus. You're still recovering, *especially* after you made it worse."

If the heat that rose to his face was visible, Valka didn't acknowledge it.

I DO NOT THINK EITHER OF YOU WILL NEED TO LEAVE FOR THAT.

They both looked at Awimak, whose attention was pinned to a wall. Tension claimed those glorious shoulders, his claws digging into the counter, notching pristine wood.

HE IS HERE, WAITING BEYOND THE BARRIER WITH ENFORCERS.

"Fuck," Ryurikov breathed, while Valka said, "Good. I'm going to cut his head off."

Ryurikov rolled his shoulders against the strain in them and wincing when it aggravated his injury. He was too fucking tired for this. All the same, he marched out of the tavern, waited for Awimak to free himself from its doorway, then motioned at the palace.

"Go inform the hags," he said to Valka. "Then gather what people can fight in case we need to defend this place. *Don't* argue."

She gave him a petulant look, but spun on her heel and stomped away. He supposed it was a good thing they hadn't yet gotten rid of all Blann's dead soldiers. Their gear would arm the townsfolk sufficiently.

Awimak grasped his hand, holding it tight as they made their way to the bridge. The ancient trees rustled in a wind that didn't reach them below, as if in agitation. Past the stream on the other side of the bridge, the blurred crimson and yellow images of enforcers loomed. And based on Awimak's low growl, Ryurikov guessed Vasili was at the forefront on horseback.

"What happens if anyone touches the barrier?" he asked in a whisper. "Does it prevent people from entering?"

NO. IT WILL ONLY DISTURB THE FLOW OF MAGIC AND THE SKIN CRAWLERS WILL SEE IT AS AN INVITATION.

"Let's hope Vasili doesn't know that." Stopping just shy of the unstable bridge, Ryurikov squirmed free of Awimak's grasp to clench

Coil of Boughs

his fingers around the hafts his daggers at the belt. "What the fuck do you want, *Vasili*?" He spat the name like a malediction.

"You've claimed land you have no right to, Prince of the fallen Thuidal Kingdom!" Vasili's horse snorted, restlessly pawing the ground. A beautiful roan with white socks and a dark mane.

"I claimed fuck all." Ryurikov stepped forward, his demon following so closely, Awimak's chill encapsulated his back.

"Then you'll have no issues leaving this town."

"A town the Monarch left to the Skin Crawlers," Ryurikov said. "You're only here because it wasn't destroyed and you want what stopped it. Mulgar left these people to die."

Vasili laughed. An ugly, bitter sound. "A bit like you did your people?"

Ryurikov gnashed his teeth. The words cut him worse than a blade to the stomach, and he hated it. He would have liked to counter with insults, but the ancient trees shifted and swayed. Those nearest bowed, branches fluid in their sway, disturbing the barrier of rain as they whipped out, narrowly missing Vasili and the enforcers.

"Don't threaten me, demon," the bastard shouted, nudging his horse forward. "You do not belong here, either. Get back to the woods you were banished to!"

A frown tugged at Ryurikov's brows, but the claw coming to rest on his shoulder settled it. "Talk to him like that again and I'll wreak meticulous havoc on every inch of your body."

"Part the barrier," Vasili edged closer to the bridge still, "or I will run it through and leave this town to the Skin Crawlers."

Panic snaked its hold around Ryurikov's heart and squeezed. He didn't want to leave these people to the mercy of either Mulgar or Skin Crawlers, especially not when he still needed the hags and their magic. They would likely be the only ones who knew how to fight against the Crawlers.

He slid out from Awimak's touch, crossed the bridge halfway to stop by the barrier. Vasili took it as an invitation, for he dismounted his horse and approached. His face remained blurry, mostly, but looking at him again, a deep seated anger roiled Ryurikov's stomach. His hand clenched more tightly around the long dagger, itching to draw it.

"We can stop them," he ground out. "I know how to kill the Skin Crawlers, but I can't do that without this place, without the hags tied to it. I'm taking responsibility, Vasili."

"That'd be a first."

The urge to slam his fist into Vasili's nose was overwhelmingly powerful.

"But I can see your use, now," said Vasili, and Ryurikov stayed his hand. For now. "Let me through and we'll discuss this. I might even be able to convince Monarch Mulgar not to let you hang."

"Last I heard, Mulgar was more an appreciator of the Brazen Bull."

Vasili chuckled, the sound void of humour. "They are. So what will it be? Cooperate, or doom this town and face a slow, burning death? It'd be a fitting end for you."

Ryurikov released his dagger long enough to run his thumb along his index finger. He couldn't permit the barrier to be compromised, but what hell would he invite into Briarmour by allowing Mulgar's enforcers inside?

"Some conditions," he said at length.

"I'm not sure you're in a position to make any demands."

"I'll gut you before you can step away. Do you value your life, the lives of those under your command? I've heard you already lost a few of them."

"Fuck you, *Ruri*."

"Fuck you too, *Keeper*."

They glared at each other. Ryurikov flexed his fingers around his daggers again, his hair standing on end, body tight with tension. A hot trickle ran down his back, the injury throbbing.

Then, finally, "What are your conditions?"

"Your clots of dung stay outside. Only you enter. We'll discuss the means of defeating the Skin Crawlers, and when that's accomplished, you leave this town to me."

"You realise I can't make any promises."

Ryurikov scoffed. "I'm sure you've sucked your way up to Mulgar's favour." Was Vasili narrowing his eyes in anger? He smirked. "You said the Skin Crawlers might be the end of Vale. We have the possibility of doing something about it and increase the chances of success by joining forces with Mulgar's hags. What's there to lose, a bit of land? Mulgar was happy enough to abandon it. It can't be that valuable."

Vasili crossed his arms over his chest and shrugged. "I forgot how sharp you could be. All those years of scheming have served you well."

"Is that a yes?"

"Yes, Ruri. I will pass on whatever we come up to the Monarch."

He tried not to squirm at the softened familiarity, how Vasili now spoke to him like they were friends. He hesitated, then waved at the barrier. Even though Ryurikov didn't know *how* it worked, the receding raindrops parted.

It gave him a clear view of the man who had been responsible for keeping his life safe since birth, who had betrayed his trust only yesterday, for what it felt like.

Vasili ducked inside, stepped too close, and Ryurikov staggered away in sudden panic. He hadn't *meant* to, neither had he meant for Awimak to see, who was by his side that instant. Vasili's umber eyes widened at the sight of the tree-tall demon. Bark scraped Ryurikov's leather vest, Awimak's arm wrapping around his shoulders and across his chest, pulling him out of reach and against his powerful front.

MINE.

A dangerous snarl, loud enough to hurt his ears, to make Vasili question his decision to enter alone. His startled gaze flicked from Awimak to Ryurikov's face, then back up. Sudden disdainful realisation replaced his expression of shock.

"Did you *blood-swear* yourself to this thing?" Another laugh at Ryurikov's look of confusion, hollow and cruel. "I nearly believed you when you said you're not into power imbalances."

Indignation boiled his insides, both at the accusation and the increasing sense Awimak wasn't telling him something—*several things*. He twisted out of the hold, jumped over thick roots, heading for the palace while his head whirled.

Blood-swear. He'd done no such thing. Had Awimak? He froze mid-step, his foot hovering over displaced cobblestone.

The refusal to wipe the blood from his skull.

I AM ABLE TO EXPLAIN.

He jumped. Awimak's sudden appearance beside him had Ryurikov glowering. "You better, Awi. But not now."

PLEASE, LET ME EXPLAIN.

Said with such aching desperation, Ryurikov paused, forcing himself to relax the angry expression that pulled his face tight. "It's okay." He exhaled, slowly. Vasili was only a few feet away. It made his skin crawl. "I know you'd never do anything against my will."

NEVER.

He had to ignore Vasili's jeering laugh. It was either ignore it or eviscerate him. "You'll tell me more later." His tone was soft, but it wasn't a request. Awimak seemed to understand, for he nodded.

Only Short-Haired and Jezibaba were inside the presence chamber, both looking lethally acrimonious, like he'd just interrupted an argument. He strained a smirk, refusing to give into the fretting his mind wanted to indulge. Valka was thankfully nowhere in sight, but Mauvella *was* and much like she'd done that morning, instantly lunged for him.

Ryurikov sidestepped her, waving Awimak down when his demon caught her by the wrist and looked ready to fling her across the chamber.

"I'm sorry, I'm sorry!" She cackled, kicking her ineffectual feet against muscular legs until Awimak set her down. "I found something."

"Can it wait?"

Mauvella furiously shook her head. She dove a hand into the pocket of her frock, pulled it back out, knuckles pronounced as she held out her fist. "You said you wanted meat!"

Ryurikov eyed her, then the naked tail protruding from between her thin fingers. "Ah. No, thank you."

"Princess Mauvella? It can't be!" Vasili gave Awimak a wide berth, making the grave mistake of approaching her.

Ryurikov could practically see Mauvella throw her hackles up. She hunched her shoulders, flashed her teeth and hissed, spittle flying from her mouth to pelt Vasili's cheek. He backed up even as she scuttled away, mouse still in hand. She jumped out through the broken window, her footfalls soon retreating. Ryurikov wondered if he ought to give chase.

"Anyway," he said, hovering near an empty bench by the firepit to take a moment and gather himself, to calm the flurry of thoughts. He eased down, and Awimak immediately positioned himself behind, close enough that the dupion tickled his back.

"The knowledge of dousing magic can be passed onto other witches. So unlike healing, it's not an inherent trait." Ryurikov inclined his head at Vasili across from him, who clearly had a hag capable of healing, either working for him or the Monarch. Awimak had broken several of his bones in Enlumine's Wish, without a doubt. "Just think of what we can accomplish if we combine all crones across the land."

Jezibaba cast Ryurikov a look of surprise, but said nothing.

"We might very well stop the Skin Crawlers entirely." Vasili traced an idle finger along his lips, toying with the edges of his moustache. "They've been edging closer to Midwood Marsh."

Closer to the Monarch, then. No wonder Vasili was willing to entertain him. Ryurikov stopped himself from scoffing. "Then you and Mulgar have everything to gain by this."

"And what of you?" Vasili kicked out a leg and leaned back, watching him. "You set the Skin Crawlers on this world, you should be held—"

"It wasn't me, you toad fucker," Ryurikov snarled. "It was Radmila."

Vasili's watchful gaze turned into a cold stare. Something worked in his mind, Ryurikov could see the shit-coated waterwheel turn. Then he stood, brushed himself off, visibly keeping his composure. "I need to get back to my enforcers."

"Hang on." Ryurikov quickly moved to stand in front of Vasili, keeping a wide distance but blocking his path. "What is it?"

"Nothing that concerns you."

"Twenty-two years I've known you, I *know* when something has your balls in a twist. Out with it."

Vasili's look turned uglier than it already was. "Radmila is currently under the employ of Monarch Mulgar."

Ryurikov had to actively force himself not to splutter. He turned on Jezibaba. "I thought she was dead!"

"Nobody said she was," said the hag.

Then, he turned to Short-Haired, who shrugged like it meant nothing. Ryurikov swore, under his breath, then loudly enough to draw Awimak up to his full height in alarm. "Fuck off and take care of it then, *Vasili*. Come back with whatever other hags you can."

"No." The asshole's gloved fist creaked when it tightened around the hilt of his sword. "*You're* coming to us."

"We need the water well that's here, *specifically*, or it won't work." Ryurikov hoped to fuck Vasili was still shit at reading his bluff. "Besides, I won't doom this town—*my fucking town*. It's mine and Awimak's now, do you hear me? If Mulgar wants it, they can come and take it back themselves."

Vasili narrowed his eyes, his body stiff, a foot sliding back across the stone floor.

Ryurikov watched his past Keeper ready to attack him on behalf of Mulgar, someone they once deemed their enemy. Fury and loathing seared his chest, he barely remembered how to breathe.

He launched at Vasili, bringing one hand around his throat, the other fisting the collar of his fancy crimson surcoat. Their faces so close, he could spit down Vasili's throat and hit the inside of his asshole.

"Don't fucking test me," he snarled. "*I will kill you*. I will kill all your soldiers while you bleed out and watch. I will lure every fucking Skin Crawler to Mulgar and slit their throat before they can so much as shake a breast or cock at me."

With a growl, Vasili grabbed him around the biceps, his jaw jutting forward in defiance. Ryurikov squeezed his throat harder, until pale skin turned red, veins bulged, and the resistance in those umber eyes relented. Once that hold on his arms slackened, he shoved Vasili away to look at him with everlasting, incurable contempt.

"Fuck. Off. *Now*."

Vasili's receding footsteps no longer echoed through the presence chamber, and only then did Ryurikov dare to breathe again. And when he inhaled, it was with difficulty. When he exhaled, his breath shook. He raised his hand to tuck into his hair. He stared at the tremble in it.

A hoof scraped across stone. He knew Awimak would try to comfort him.

"Not now." Ryurikov didn't think he could take it. "Please, just make sure that fucker leaves."

AS YOU WISH, DRURY.

Twenty-Nine

He found the pigs.

It took some wandering but eventually, Ryurikov located a quaint, half-timber house three stories high, near the north end of Briarmour. Lopsided, courtesy of colossal roots pushing it upward.

He strode through long grass to a fence. Beyond it, a mud patch where the pigs indulged in caking themselves. Their snorts and the stream's lullaby were oddly comforting. Ryurikov rested his forearms across the well-maintained fence to watch the drove, just as the back door to the wonky house banged open. A lad in simple attire and old boots, carrying a bucket, nearly stumbled down stone steps leading into the garden, his feet catching on stray roots.

Hidden under the cover of shadows, Ryurikov went unnoticed. Until he didn't. The lad dropped the bucket with a yelp, spilling slop the pigs instantly darted to with delight.

"Sir!"

The boy seemed young, hair tousled and eyes keen, reminding Ryurikov a little of Andrew. A strange pang resonated deep within his chest, but since he didn't know what it meant, he kicked it aside.

"I don't mean to intrude."

"My Jarl, you could never—"

"*I'm not your fucking Jarl!*" Ryurikov pinched the bridge of his nose between his fingers. He hadn't meant to break loose. "Sorry."

"It's okay," said the boy, his smile uncertain. "I don't like being called Pascal, but it's my name."

"That's not—" Ryurikov pressed his lips together. "What do you want to be called?"

"Dracus!"

He tilted his head back. "Is that right?"

"I know that's your name. Not your *real* name, but I like it. What do you want to be called?"

With some hesitation, "Ruri is fine."

A pig's ass swung into the lad's legs, nearly sending him down to the ground. He grunted, and walked a little closer to the fence. "They say you're a prince."

"People say a lot of things."

"A rogue prince."

Ryurikov huffed. "Tend to your pigs, Dracus, before I grab one and cook it."

He patted the fence before pushing away from it. His feet carried him along the stream lined by thick briar on the other side. It was peaceful, birds had found their way to the trees, mere flecks of bright violet from where he stood below. Only a day since Vasili had left. It would be another two weeks before he'd return with whatever decision Mulgar made.

Ryurikov hadn't spoken to Awimak for that entire day, or even seen him, occupying himself by wandering through town. He'd gotten to know some of its people, and slept in a tree. It felt wrong. He missed Awimak, but he didn't know how to confront him now that he knew his demon hadn't been honest with him.

What if the truth was something horrific?

What if this blood-swear bound them together, in a way he wasn't yet prepared for? How did it affect what he and Awimak had?

Ryurikov swivelled on his heel with a sudden determination to ask. Stopped mid-pivot, when he caught sight of his demon, standing some distance from the drove of pigs. Blood remained streaked across his skull, blazing eyes intense. Tightening Ryurikov's chest in a way that made him want to run to him.

He didn't run, but walked.

Until the last few steps, during which he lost all sense of himself and darted into Awimak's open arms. Ryurikov grasped enormous horns and pressed his forehead against the skull while lifted off the ground. He kissed the bone, eyes fluttering shut. His lips parted to greet the tongue gliding into his mouth.

Claws on his thighs kept him secure as Awimak carried him off to sit behind an ample trunk by the stream. Ryurikov straddled his demon's hips. He ran his hands over the rough horns, down to flirt with the silken tresses, curling them around his fingers. The pointed tongue retreated, and briefly, he chased after it to lick along the slippery muscle. A low, satisfied growl, the claws on him clenching around his waist, pushing their groins together.

I'VE MISSED YOU.

"I can tell." Ryurikov moved forward, the sway of hips fluid, bringing their clothed erections to collide. He leaned in again, dipped his head to the side, and pressed an open-mouthed kiss to Awimak's elongated jaw. "Same. To you."

Another lap at his cheek, leaving the skin sticky. *YOU CAN SAY IT.*

He littered kisses down Awimak's neck, inhaling as much as his lungs would allow, starved for that earthy scent. Then, Ryurikov moved back to gaze into sun-like eyes. Still stroking the dark hair, he shook his head.

"I can't."

YOU CAN. Awimak gently brushed his knuckles across the scars on Ryuirkov's face. *I WILL NOT PUNISH YOU FOR SOMETHING YOU HOLD DEAR.*

He jerked his head to the side, panic fastening its iron grip around his chest. Thanks to his traitorous subconscious, Awimak knew a great deal about him. Including his father's treatment of him. About the way he relentlessly beat anything Ryurikov dared to enjoy out of him, calling it a waste of time. A weakness.

He'd not expected Awimak to be so up front about it, the urge to run off and occupy himself by killing things quickly became overwhelming.

"I'm not worried you'll punish me," he managed, throat tight. He moved to get away, but Awimak secured his hold, keeping his hips pinned. "*Don't.*"

SAY IT, MY LOVE.

He shook his head again, his ability to breathe at risk of escaping.

If he didn't say he missed Awimak, or that he loved him, then it wasn't real. When the inevitable happened and he was once again robbed of that shred of happiness he'd found, Ryurikov could shrug it off, say it didn't matter. It hadn't been real anyway.

I LOST CONTROL, said Awimak then, momentarily easing Ryurikov out of his struggle. *BUT PERHAPS I DID INTEND TO BLOOD-SWEAR. I DO NOT REGRET IT.*

"What does it mean?"

Awimak had yet to ease his hold on his hips. *IT MEANS THAT SHOULD I FAIL TO PROTECT YOU, I WILL SUFFER THE SAME FATE AS YOU.*

"So if I die...?"

Without needing to lean in, Awimak lapped at Ryurikov's throat, slowly, as if to savour the salt clinging to his skin. *WHEN YOU ARE SADDENED, I WILL SUFFER MELANCHOLY ALONGSIDE YOU. WHEN YOU BLEED, I BLEED. AND YES, WHEN YOU DIE, SO TOO WILL I.*

Ryurikov's touch drifted to broad shoulders and clenched. Loosened. Clenched again. How was he meant to respond to something so intense?

MY LOVE FOR YOU EXTENDS PAST THE DEEPEST OCEANS. IT REACHES FURTHER THAN THE SKY. I WOULD NOT HAVE IT ANY OTHER WAY.

Awimak pulled him against his chest and held firm, both bringing home his words and preventing escape. Ryurikov could only inhale, sharply. Grasp at him more tightly. Bury his face into the crook of his neck. Feel the steady thrum of his heart against his own.

DO NOT WORRY. Awimak nuzzled the side of Ryurikov's head. *I*

WILL WAIT FOR WHEN YOU ARE READY.

"What if I'm never?"

THEN I WILL WAIT FOR THE REST OF OUR LIVES. BUT I WILL WAIT.

All he could do was cling to Awimak, struggling to think of something to respond with. Even after being released and allowed to relax, sitting with his back resting against Awimak's abdomen, words continued to evade Ryurikov. All he managed was to stay, stroking his fingertips across the claw that in turn, stroked him across the stomach.

A trickle of sunlight found its way past smoke and the dark green canopy, turning the stream into bright, blinding lustre. As far as settling anywhere went, this wasn't the worst place to do it. Now that he'd claimed this town for himself out of spite, he supposed he had no choice but to keep it.

"Is staying here agreeable to you?" For some reason, his voice was hoarse, like he'd been screaming in agony for years. Before Awimak could respond, he added, "Since apparently, you were banished to the Unbroken Wilds?"

AH.

"You'll tell me?"

I WILL KEEP NO SECRETS FROM YOU.

And yet it took a good while for Awimak to speak again.

I WAS NOT ALWAYS AS I AM NOW. WHEN I WAS YOUNGER—Ryurikov bit down on the need to jest about Awimak being a sapling—I ONCE LOVED ANOTHER. HIS MALEFICENCE HAD AN UNINTENDED EFFECT ON ME. I DID THINGS ON HIS BEHALF THAT WERE QUESTIONABLE.

Ryurikov raised an eyebrow. "More questionable than murdering humans and Candescent on my behalf?"

THAT WAS DIFFERENT.

Amusement laced his exhale. Ryurikov wasn't so sure he believed that. "I'm not going to ask you for the details unless you want to divulge."

I HELPED HIM REAWAKEN THE DEAD. I PUT HIM IN A POSITION OF POWER.

Craning his neck, Ryurikov trailed his gaze over Awimak's jaw, up to the narrow sphere of fire within the skull's orbit. His eye was trained on him, likely to gauge his reaction.

"I regularly put mouse droppings in Radmila's dinners."

Awimak canted his head. *WICKED, BUT NOT THE SAME.*

"We all do stupid shit as kids, Awi." He gave the bark-armoured arm a firm squeeze. It didn't yield the slightest, only shedded some lichen. "Who banished you, and what does that mean for you now that you're here?"

MY MOTHER. SHE TOLD ME I WAS FREE TO LEAVE THE WOODS WHEN READY. IT WASN'T BANISHMENT, BUT PAYING PENANCE.

Ryurikov hummed. "Lucky I found you at the right time, then."

YES. A firm, brief squeeze to his stomach.

They fell into a silence heavy with reflection, but companionable. Eventually, Ryurikov sighed, patted Awimak's arm, and got up. He held his hand out.

"Will you stay here with me, Awimak?"

I WILL STAY HERE WITH YOU, MY LOVE. Awimak grasped his hand, clearly playing along while Ryurikov helped him up, then stooped low to slather his face with saliva.

"Come on then, my radiant imp," he said, leaving his skin retted, "we'll see what we can do for this stupid town."

As Awimak turned away, Ryurikov was certain he'd caught amusement. His own faded when he saw a large, crooked gash along Awimak's shoulder blade. It was open, and looked as painful as his own. He had no idea how he'd missed this. Awimak hadn't sported the injury that following morning, he was sure of it. It must have developed over the past day.

His mouth thinned into a line, teeth clenched so hard his jaw quaked. Awimak faced him again, a question in his burning eyes.

"I love you." Choked words, they'd come out angry. Defiantly. Leaving a strange but not unpleasant taste in his mouth and an even greater impression in his heart.

Ryurikov stood there, utterly terrified. Not of Awimak's reaction, but of what he'd just carved into stone, and who might come to bring it down. Smash it apart, kick it to dust. He'd made it veridical, *breakable*.

There was no going back now.

ARE YOU GOING TO LOSE CONSCIOUSNESS?

Ryurikov started. Through gritted teeth, he barked, "No!"

YOU LOOK PALE.

"I'm a red-head, that's a given!"

PERHAPS A TO THE TAVERN FIRST. YOU NEED SUSTENANCE.

"Awi!"

His asshole of a demon closed the distance to gather him in gigantic arms. Angry and confused, Ryurikov didn't *want* to be embraced, but seemed that Awimak didn't care about that just then, squeezing so hard, he thought he might shit himself.

"You better make sure I don't regret this," Ryurikov ground out and nosed Awimak's hair until he uncovered a furry ear. He clamped his teeth around it, just hard enough to get a scalding snort rolling down his back.

The day didn't pass terribly. In fact, though he was hesitant to call it that, Ryurikov thought his trip around the whole town with Awimak was...*pleasant*. Its people seemed to have learned that he preferred space, and didn't approach or stare at Awimak unless he spoke to them directly.

Most of them, Ryurikov had no business with and so didn't address. Those he spotted on the streets in rags he approached with pursed lips and great reluctance. Awimak's eyes burned holes into his back as he bent low and hoisted a gaunt-faced man to his unsteady feet.

"Bring yourself to the palace," Ryurikov told him in a pointlessly quiet mutter. "Eat what you can and rest. Stay as long as you want."

Bewildered stammering was the response, and he gave the old man a mild shove to get him moving.

BETTER THAN THEM. YOU ALWAYS WERE.

He rubbed his palms across the length of his thighs. "And bathe, you old splotch! You're disgusting."

STILL BETTER THAN THEM.

Ryurikov ignored him, muttering to himself, "That's the fifth vagrant I've peeled off the streets."

Why, when late Jarl's coffers had been filled to the point of eruption? Of course, they both knew the answer to a question he needn't give voice to. There were hoarders, and it didn't take long to hunt them down, either. All it took was asking around.

The sole of his leather boot collided with a tired door to a dwelling just as fatigued. It creaked open, and his hand hovered over the hilt of his dagger. A pale face peered at him. Only a teenager.

"Your parents?" Ryurikov demanded.

"My Prince," she quavered, bowing low as she opened the door wide to allow him entry.

He stepped inside an overtly modest home, floors bare but for one sheepskin. The beds too were plain, only boards with straw. That didn't exactly surprise him. He glowered at the two parents seated by a shoddy round table all the same, laden with food, a display of their greed. No meat, though.

"Whispers speak of your name, Borg." Ryurikov addressed who he presumed was the father. "They tell me you've been avaricious."

Shock upon his arrival morphed into terror. It flickered to life within grey eyes, then overtook the man's body in fierce tremors. The father stammered, incomprehensibly, while his wife opened and closed her mouth around strangled words.

"I'm not here to hurt you," Ryurikov said, folding his arms over his chest. "I'm not going to rule you through fear of pain, or being eaten, or whatever the fuck else that wank-hose came up with. No, you're my charge and you'll be well fed and looked after. You'll have everything you've ever hoped for." He swept closer to the table, glaring down his nose at them. "Your nights, however, will be haunted by your worst fears. You'll endure nightmare after nightmare until you fight the need to sleep. Until you begin to see things that aren't there. Anything good in your life will lose all meaning with relentless exhaustion—unless you relinquish anything you took beyond your fair share. Do that, and you'll live a happy life."

That was all it took, and Ryurikov left the ramshackle dwelling with surplus riches.

A HUMAN'S RELUCTANCE TO FACE THEIR INNER TURMOIL WILL NEVER CEASE TO PERPLEX.

Ryurikov regarded his demon with a faint tilt of his head. "Would've thought you'd gotten used to that by now, drinking from my subconscious."

Awimak's gaze flickered with mirth. *SUCH SELF AWARENESS, MY LOVE.*

He narrowed his eyes, then promptly turned on his heel and walked off—slowly, unwilling to let Awimak think he was angry.

Valka returned to his side on the way to the palace with news of having found a handful of townsfolk capable of combat. Ryurikov suggested she train them, and offered them the title of Defender to entice, stationing the handful of men and women at the town's entrances. It would have to do until they found more people willing to help.

"What of the silver weapons we need?" Valka asked.

Ryurikov rubbed his thumb and pointer fingers together. "I don't want to leave Briarmour until I've dealt with what I need to. Can't risk Vasili showing up while I'm gone. I know he wants those hags."

"I can go, then. Let me?"

He gave his sister an odd look. "Since when do you need my permission for anything?"

A shrug. "You're in charge now, and I'm good at following orders." For some reason, that statement was followed by a wink.

"Get the fuck out of here. Do what you want," Ryurikov snapped. "But bring... I don't know, drakes with you? I'd rather you didn't go alone."

"Aww." Valka swerved into him, her shoulder bumping his with a force that shouldn't have surprised him as much as it did. He staggered, but at least she didn't knock him over. "Can I take Mauvie with me?"

"Absolutely not."

"You said I can do what I want."

"Within reason! Mauvella is—"

They reached the wide stoop leading up to the palace. A bush along their path emitted a screech. Mauvella burst out, broken twigs and leaves fluttering in her wake as she launched herself at Ryurikov.

A large claw caught her by the face with ease, her body dangling like a poppet. She flailed, bony fists slamming into bark-armoured forearms, her screeches muffled. The moment her feet reconnected with the ground, she settled down.

Awimak snorted angrily. *ONE DAY, MAUVELLA.*

"But not today," said Ryurikov dryly.

Mauvella eagerly held out both fists. In each, a worm-like tail dangled between her fingers. "Found more!"

"You'll put the cats out of a job," he said, then glanced at Valka. "You deal with this, I'm exhausted."

Exhausted *and* starved, but as they entered the palace, the cacophony of chatter and laughter assailed his head. Ryurikov groaned, then quickly shifted to the side as several children darted through the gap between him and Awimak. *Ugh.*

"None of them better sneak into our room."

Which, once he finally reached it after ducking away from admirers and those wishing to express their gratitude, or servants trying too hard, appeared to have changed somewhat.

Ryurikov's eyebrows raised at what had essentially become a large bower. Thick, ancient branches ensnared the room, blocking out the hideous dark walls and ceiling with rich, moss-covered wood and verdure. Lanterns dotted the place, and the window had become a large gap to better welcome more light. The dresser below was caged in, the fireplace now beautifully framed, while the bed had become much like what Awimak built in Jezibaba's back garden.

Nightingales perched by what now served as the window, singing a late evening song. A sweet lullaby to settle the tension in Ryurikov's neck. Stepping further inside, he admired the abundance of furs covering the den, the faint citrine glow of whatever magical insects these trees attracted, and the plush moss blanketing the bower. In the very centre, a stash of fresh fruit and a rundlet.

He turned to gaze upon his demon, who hesitated by the doorway.
I NEST WHEN ANXIOUS.
Ryurikov smiled.

He guided Awimak into their nest. Removed the cloth around his hips. Feathered kisses across every inch of dark grey skin. He drew Awimak's cock into his mouth, slid his finger past the ballsack, and explored. What he found was that Awimak had one more secret to share with him.

Upon shepherding him to bend over the thick edge of the den, Ryurikov showed Awimak just how pleased he was to see a tail, soft and furry. Not unlike a deer's. He trailed kisses and nips down the toned ass, stopping on the inside of muscular thighs just where skin met fur. Awimak was sensitive there, ticklish even. More responsive still as he slipped slick fingers inside him, taking his time.

He sunk into Awimak's clenching heat with a loud groan, a backward roll of his eyes. Stroked his demon up and down his spine, all the way to the tip of the tail, and back. Kissed anything he could reach. Awimak seemed to like that.

Seemed to like other things, too. Ryurikov was under no illusion that he could somehow reach the deeper parts of his demon, but he thought Awimak enjoyed himself. Ryurikov's climax resulted in whispered confessions of love to spill from his lips with startling ease.

For a long while after, they simply laid with each other, arms twined to hold one another close, languid kisses peppered throughout a serene silence Ryurikov hadn't known before.

Thirty

Days passed in a hazy blur and suddenly, two weeks had gone by. Valka had left for Enlumine's Wish to hunt Shitty Theo down for information, leaving Ryurikov to deal with a string of newcomers who'd heard of what Briamour had become.

A haven for the unwanted. Or so the whispers claimed.

He stood in the deepest shade near a shop, Awimak at his side. Ryurikov watched a throng of newcomers nervously walking across the crooked bridge, pleased to see the two newly appointed guards on either side were paying attention.

His gaze flicked to a familiar form then, dressed in maroon and deep purple robes, trying to hide behind a hood. Unfortunately for Yavor, there was no hiding that round face, or the haircut that looked like someone had taken wet strips of hide and sewn them onto his head. Ryurikov cast Awimak a sly look. His demon's amusement radiated like summer's heat, roots springing from between cobblestone, festooning Yavor's legs and trapping him. The man's face paled as Ryurikov sauntered toward him.

"Bold of you to come here, monk." He flicked his attention to the robes. "I recognise those colours." Briefly, he cast for the name, then snapped his fingers before pointing at the monk. "Lakunna."

"Ye–Yes!" Yavor squeaked. "G–Goddess of the Void!"

AT LEAST HIS CAPRICIOUSNESS IS CONSISTENT.

Ryurikov bit the inside of his cheek to keep from laughing. "Ready to join Blann and his ilk by hanging from a hook through your neck?"

An idle threat, more or less, when their bodies had finally been removed and used as kindling. Including what was left of the two witch-prone daughters.

Yavor stammered, fruitlessly tugging at the ensnaring roots. "I had nothing to do with Jarl Blann's orders to have you killed!"

Ryurikov crossed his arms, glad for the swift mending of his back's injury. The hag's balm had worked wonders and in turn, Awimak's mirrored wound had healed, too. "I'm supposed to believe you didn't squeal?"

"I swear it on the Void we all walk after death!" Yavor mopped sweat off his brow with a wide sleeve, dampening the deep purple. "Be-Besides, I was seeing stars—*reason*, perhaps—for most of it! You–You did hit me aw–*awfully* hard."

Tilting his head from side to side, Ryurikov pursed his lips. "True."

He would have enjoyed tormenting the monk further, but a commotion near the barrier drew his attention. Newcomers scattered away from the bridge, its planks slanting dangerously with each careless step of boot and sandal-clad feet. And at the parted curtain of rain stood Vasili.

Alone, with merely one hag in his clutches.

Unlike most hags, this one was plumper, younger, her silver hair a shimmer of dusk in the smoky skies above. One of the Monarch's witches, no doubt, although she didn't look particularly pleased, her frail wrist clutched with bruising force. Ryurikov could see that even from where he now approached.

"What the fuck," he snarled. "You bring us only *one*?"

Vasili's lip curled. "That's all I could get Monarch Mulgar to agree to."

"I see self-preservation isn't at the top of their list." Frustration burdened Ryurikov's exhale. "Fucking moron. Fine. Bring her in, we'll get her acquainted." Vasili dragged the witch along, so roughly it had

Ryurikov's mouth twitching with a sneer. "She's capable of walking on her own, you limp pike."

Umber eyes darted to him, brows with dashes of grey quirking in askance. "Since when do you care about hags?" All the same, Vasili swung her forward and let go, nearly sending her to the ground.

"Why are you alone?" Ryurikov asked, falling in step with the staggering witch. He caught sight of her shoes, the leather scorched. Had they made her walk through the wasteland? He leaned sideways, and ever so quietly whispered, "You'll be among friends here."

Her bright orange eyes skipped to him in surprise, but she said nothing.

"I know all too well what those flames can do," said Vasili. "I'm not risking my soldiers. I don't care what the Monarch says."

"Disobeying commands with such ease," Ryurikov drawled, mockingly. "Never thought I'd see the day."

A smile tugged at Vasili's lip. It made Ryurikov's skin crawl, and the urge to hit him right in the mouth nearly won out. Not a chance that foul brute was on his own, though. Where had he stashed those under his command, Ryurikov wondered. His focus slid to Awimak, and they exchanged a knowing look.

This was a trap of some kind.

"We're not ready yet, so you'll need to wait," said Ryurikov as they approached the palace. "And we're taking out the neighbouring Skin Crawlers first. *Then* we'll see about doing your Monarch any favours." He pointedly glared at Vasili. "Maybe we'll kill just one Skin Crawler, for the one hag they've provided. Reciprocation, and all that."

"You haven't changed one bit, Ruri."

Said so fondly, it made Ryurikov's blood boil.

"Neither have you." He spat the words with all the hatred he had in his soul for the man, having congealed to a lethal venom ever since he dared lay a hand on him. "And I mean that in the worst possible way." Just in case there was any confusion.

Vasili harrumphed in response, although said nothing else.

Permitting him to enter the palace felt like a violation. Each step Vasili took over roots pushing through the floor, every time he carelessly stomped through the beginnings of verdure peering out from the stone flooring, had Ryurikov tighten his hold on the long dagger. His grip on the haft turned sweaty, and the gritting of his teeth became painful.

MY DRURY.

He started and came to a stop just before the presence chamber, which Vasili had already invaded, the hag in reluctant tow. Awimak held his massive claw out for him. Ryurikov didn't hesitate taking it, letting his own gloved fingers slide across the palm, its size forever a surprise.

Without warning, his surroundings shifted, yellow-hued light sweeping through blurred shadows. Ryurikov glanced around, taking note of the indistinct forms within the presence chamber and the two guards he'd stationed just outside of it.

"What is it?"

LISTEN.

Ryurikov cocked his head and strained his ears.

"We'll need to find another source to tap into soon if that rogue prince can't find more of us." One of the hags. The braided one, he thought, her voice as loud as though she shouted right into his ear.

"When's supper, Dad? I'm hungry." Ryurikov had no idea who that was. A child, based on the prepubescent squeak.

An audible smack to the back of someone's hand. "This isn't for you. It's for our prince."

"I think one of the pigs is sick." That was Dracus, he thought.

"Sit down with the other hags, or I'll cut your feet out from under you." And the toad-fucker.

"I hear everything," said Ryurikov, his own voice an odd, drawn-out echo.

INDEED, MY LOVE. WHAT DON'T YOU HEAR? Awimak paused, waiting for a response he must have realised wouldn't come. *HIS ENFORCERS AREN'T PRESENT.*

Ryurikov's brows knotted with concern. "Not a chance he didn't squirrel them away somewhere. The other forest, maybe?"

I WOULD NEED TO DRAW CLOSER TO FIND OUT.

He shook his head. "Don't...leave my side. We'll deal with them when the time comes."

Coil of Boughs

"Come on, Mauvie! Stop touching Theo's head."

"So pretty! Tap, tap, tap. I want that little flame. Can I have it?"

"That would kill me," buzzed Shitty Theo dryly.

"Valka's back," Ryurikov said. "Would you mind detouring her? She'll lose her shit if she sees that asshole. Oh, and free Yavor, if you please."

Awimak squeezed his hand. Their surroundings shifted from blurry, shadowy shapes back to dark stone and people in focus. A lingering, languid lick across his wrist, a section of it exposed between glove and black sleeve, and Ryurikov was tempted to drag his demon off into a private chamber. Shame they had things to deal with. Reluctantly, he released Awimak and watched him gallop away before turning back to the issue at hand.

Vasili. That limp-dicked dilberry.

Invading *his* space, his town. His fucking region, if Ryurikov were but a fraction more ambitious.

Maybe he ought to be.

Chin up, he strode into the presence chamber like he owned the place. He nudged a wayward youngster over, claiming a seat on the bench across from Vasili.

"Why are there so many people here?" Vasili asked.

"They are my people, and they are welcome wherever they wish to be."

Ryurikov tried his damndest to ignore that same youngster now climbing onto his back, her sticky hands finding his throat for support. Unfortunately, he couldn't stop the glottal noise that tore free when she all but strangled him in her attempt to scale his shoulders. Mercifully, her mother noticed, simple grey frock swishing in her rush to gather the child into her arms and away from him.

"I beg you, please, forgive us," she gasped, dark eyes stricken with a panic that didn't entirely surprise Ryurikov.

"It's fine," he murmured. It wasn't fine, he now had to resist the urge to bathe, just to get the weird mix of sand and tackiness off his skin, but held his tongue on the matter. "In any case—"

As he regarded Vasili again, the man's eyes held an awful gleam.

Awful in the sense that it was *admiring*, mixed with longing. Ryurikov sneered.

"What are your policies then, in regards to accepting newcomers?" asked Vasili.

"You aren't welcome here."

The man tutted. "Shame. I'd like it here. Now tell me about this dousing magic, if you please, *your highness*."

It didn't take long to explain when it boiled down to throwing water onto a fire.

"And you need a consistent source?" Vasili helped himself to wine from a pitcher someone had abandoned on the table behind him. Ryurikov hoped it was laced with poison.

"Only answer I could come up with, when there's a time limit to how long the magic exists without a source."

"If the well here can't be moved, then what is your plan?"

Ryurikov glanced at Jezibaba and her wrinkled mouth pursed. They would have no choice but to bring her hut out into the wasteland, something he hadn't yet discussed with her. He opened his mouth to do just that, but then she gave him the subtlest of nods.

"...I have that part already figured out," Ryurikov said instead, ignoring yet another toddler crawling its way toward him. "The only thing *you* need to worry about is staying the fuck out of my way."

"You understand, I'm coming with you to fight them."

Instinct urged him to tell Vasili to get fucked. His head, however, suggested that maybe it wasn't the worst idea. At best, he would have another hand to kill the Crawlers. And at best, again, Vasili would die in the process.

"If you insist," Ryurikov said, then rose as smoothly as possible while he had a child latched onto his shins. He shook the thing off, unbothered by the look of distraught. "Stay here while I deal with things."

He found Valka in the tavern, impatiently tapping her fingers across the bar while Mauvella hovered around the Candescent at a table, adorned in a dress of pale green silk. Their head turned in his direction when he entered, squeaking lightly.

"Shitty Theo," Ryurikov said in greeting. "Why have you brought me this one, when we need a blacksmith?"

"You're looking at 'em." Valka heaved a great sigh. "I would've been back a lot sooner, but it took some convincing before Theo told us what we wanted to know." His gaze lowered to the flute still at Valka's hips. "I had to use it, I'm sorry Ruri. I know you don't approve."

Ryurikov shook his head in an attempt to dismiss the surge of discomfort. "Where's Awi?"

"You're obsessed." Valka smiled. "He said to tell you he's tending to a pig. I didn't question it."

"Fair enough. And I'm not obsessed."

Just in love. The memory of those blurted words made him want to shrivel up. Too late to take them back now. Besides, he wasn't so sure he wanted to take them back.

"Right," he continued, "Frida is Briamour's blacksmith and an absolute delight." She wasn't. An old woman more crotchety than Jezibaba and all her kind combined. "I'm sure she'll be more than happy to accommodate your needs."

"You tried to kill me," Theo buzzed, three thick metal fingers clanking atop the table. A seam of silver glinted in the overhead light, where the arrow had been lodged in the top of the lantern. "You stole my bow. I won't be doing you any favours."

"It's not a favour to me," Ryurikov said. "You'd be doing everyone on Vale a service. With silver weapons we can fight and most likely kill the Skin Crawlers."

Theo's pale flame flickered, the white dots of their eyes shifting between him and Valka. "You did not tell me this."

"Oh, I guess that would've been...helpful." Valka ducked under Ryurikov's glare. "Sorry!"

"So, you'll help?" Ryurikov asked, already knowing the answer.

"Provide me with the tools and material, and I am."

"Great." He strode back to the door. Before leaving, over his shoulder he tossed a casual, "I'm keeping the bow."

Thirty-One

Four fucking weeks, known to some as a month, before Theo managed to produce a sword adequately inlaid with silver. And for the whole gods-be-damned month, Ryurikov had put up with Vasili, the hags, children, Mauvella, *the entire fucking town*—

The nightingales that had made his window ledge their home perked up with the setting sun. Their songs echoed down to the cobblestone streets below, chipper and loud.

"Shut the fuck up!" he bellowed, but remained unsatisfied as they fluttered away, leaving one lonely feather to drift downward in their wake.

YOU'RE STILL AGITATED, MY LOVE.

Ryurikov's feet stilled in their pacing. Awimak lay in their bower, baring all, a fine layer of sweat glistening in the low light of the lanterns, turning stormy skin fulvous. With a sigh, Ryurikov ran a hand through his hair.

"Fuck, Awi, there's so much that can go wrong."

AND SO MUCH THAT COULD GO RIGHT.

The corners of his mouth curled into a sardonic smile. "Based on past experiences, I can tell you that things are far more likely to go wrong."

YOU WILL DO EVERYTHING IN YOUR POWER TO ENSURE THINGS DON'T END IN DISASTER. AFTER THAT, IT IS OUT OF YOUR HANDS.

Ryurikov glowered. "This would be a fuck load easier if you and Valka didn't insist on coming along."

A one-shouldered shrug. *ALAS.*

Darkness emerged and moonlight stretched into their chamber before Ryurikov could stop his fretting long enough to rejoin Awimak. He burrowed into the furs and slept with his face pressed against his demon's chest, listening to the rhythmic thunder of his heart until he drifted off.

Even then, his sleep was fitful, disturbed by nightmares that come morning, he knew weren't Awimak's doing.

Far sooner than he was ready for, Ryurikov stood under an ashen-yellow sky, at the edge of the wasteland. Valka and Awimak were on either side of him, Vasili a pace ahead.

Bold of that fucker to turn his back to him.

Not that he'd done anything to so much as raise an eyebrow the past few weeks. He'd even treated the servants with surprising respect. Ryurikov didn't buy into it. The feeling Vasili was up to something hadn't yet gone.

He cast his gaze to the other forest, its line barely visible beyond the turbid haze. Jezibaba had said she would meet them halfway.

A bright flash flicked across his eyes and he winced.

"Sorry." Valka stopped fidgeting with the silver blade, gleaming too bright. She shrugged her shoulders against visible discomfort. It had nothing to do with the stained-glass jerkin she still wore.

Ryurikov could only hope the blade would last long enough, his grip around the silver bow tightening with frustration.

"So, it's just us?" Vasili asked without turning. "I thought you might get your peasants to assist, seeing as you've armed them."

"You won't risk yours, I won't risk mine," Ryurikov growled. And yet, Valka and Awimak were right there with him, imperilling themselves. Obstinate fucks. "Let's get the fuck going."

A pool of fanned out indigo flames was all the evidence that remained of their fight a month ago. Ryurikov had been under no illusion he and Valka permanently downed the elder Skin Crawler, but the lack of a carcass amid the fire was disappointing all the same.

They skirted the wasteland's edge through layers of ash pliant underfoot, muffling their footsteps. As the forest drew into clearer view, flames licked up the trees, gnawing through the greenery.

Ryurikov sprinted at the sight of three large trees moving, roots kicking up plumes of ash as Jezibaba's hut spilled forward, out of the safety of the forest and into desolation.

He pivoted toward Awimak, grabbed hold of a horn and swung up, then jumped for the tree-legs. A ledge, newly formed of branches, greeted Ryurikov at the top, the garden's fringe now clear of fruit trees. Bark scraped under his gloved hands as he pulled himself up. There, a hag awaited him. Scraggly, thin as sticks—*Una*. She'd reminded him of her name only two days ago.

"Ugh, Ruri!" Valka struggled to catch the ledge and he bent low to grab her by the forearms.

With a strained grunt, he hoisted all that bulk up. Valka muttered her thanks, then ascended the short wall of the garden's edge, and positioned herself on the ledge at the other side of it.

Vasili was next to arise, his body lurching high up into the air, limbs flailing wildly. He landed none too gently at Ryurikov's feet, nearly rolling back down. His indignant screech had Ryurikov belting out a laugh.

He nocked an enchanted arrow, needing to shrug off a sudden onset of arousal. He would have to thank Awimak for bodily throwing Vasili around.

"That fucking demon!" Vasili snarled, ungainly in his attempt to rise as the hut lurched with each step.

"I will be fucking him, later."

Discordant shrieks raked the ashen wasteland, rolling a shiver down Ryurikov's spine. He positioned himself beside Vasili and resisted the urge to kick the bastard down.

"Something occurs to me," said Vasili, drawing his sword, "if your concern for that demon was that he'd burn, what of the hut's legs?"

Ryurikov had given Vasili only slivers of information, unwilling to divulge too much lest he attempted anything stupid, although even Ryurikov wasn't sure what would become of the hut.

A downward glance revealed the roots already ablaze, and Awimak bounding alongside them, creaking branches protruding from his arms and twining the midriffs of Darinka and the younger witch, Jadrana, as he oscillated both. Up, back down. Silver hair fluttered in the wind as the two wove dousing magic from its source and around the trees, conquering blue flames wherever they erupted.

An upwreath of soot jerked Ryurikov's focus forward. The eldest of the Skin Crawlers barreled toward them, the youngling behind it, no less unnerving. He righted his aim as crystalline water twirled around the arrowtip, manipulated there by Una, and waited, needing to close the distance just another step.

"I'm taking the nestling out first," Ryurikov shouted, then let his arrow fly, water sparkling gold in the smoky murk.

A direct hit, water and silver-dipped arrow wedged into its skull. The youngling jerked away with a screech, shook itself off like a dog, and freed itself of the arrow. It dashed to catch up with the elder as the hut tilted in a sidestep.

Ryurikov dug his heels in, leaning against the sway, and glanced down. Anxiousness battered his heart as Awimak flung the two witches up a branch and dodged a whip of fire. He circled the elder Crawler and bulled into its ribs, sending it crashing to the ground. Ryurikov loosed his next arrow, hitting the Crawler's exposed abdomen. Gossamer-thin skin bled blue flames, magic-encased arrow sizzling before it vaporised.

The hut staggered, throwing Vasili into Ryurikov, who caught himself on a wayward branch. He bellowed a swear into Vasili's ear and shoved him off.

"Ruri!" Valka cried from the hut's far side, past his line of sight. "I need to get down there!"

"No!" Ryurikov fired arrow after arrow, some without dousing magic as Una struggled to keep up. He refused to let the Crawler get back on its feet while Awimak had vanished from sight.

Valka shouted again, "They're flanking the hut!"

He swore. Snarled at Vasili, "Get down there and help," and hoped Darinka and Jadrana were strong enough to ascend the trees on their own.

"How far does this magic reach?" Ryurikov asked Una. She stood atop the wall of soil leading into the garden. Vasili's boots churned through it in his climb, and shot past her.

"Would I be here if it extended as far as you're hoping?"

"Gods fucking damn it!"

DRURY.

Ryurikov whirled to see Awimak scaling the ledge, large chest heaving. Torrid eyes told of trouble.

MY TREES ARE HURTING. I FEAR—

"That conniving piece of shit. I'm going to skin him alive!"

There'd be no time for that just yet. The town was under attack, and now it was a choice between its people and Jezibaba's hut.

"Go. Keep them safe. We've got this here."

A nod. *KEEP WELL, MY LOVE.*

"And you."

No time to watch Awimak leave, to feel the dread squeezing his insides. The elder Skin Crawler writhed, shaking loose the last of his arrows as it rose back up.

"Why the fuck isn't this working?" Ryurikov snarled.

Una didn't respond, too busy transferring dousing magic between her, Jezibaba, and the stump. With a restless growl, Ryurikov held up his dagger. He barely waited for her to encase it, descending the ledge. The hag shouted after him—something about not being able to reach that far, her scratchy voice drowned out by the thump of his boots, the clicking of a beak.

Beaks.

At the edge of the incline in the distance, smoke dragged past demonic silhouettes. Thinly masking the flailing, scythe-like legs and the haunting screeches.

Ryurikov counted five before he ducked under the elder Crawler's swipe. Cloak fabric tore behind him as he drove his dagger between its ribs. Hoping, *praying*, it had a heart. That he'd hit it.

The Crawler reared, its death-cry a deafening rattle. Ryurikov flicked fire off his blade, glowing red hot, and swung away from the demon's final thrashing as it collapsed. Its blood pooled outward, devouring the hut's tree-legs. Behind their staggered tromping, Valka and Vasili ran to keep up. In their wake, a very dead Skin Crawler.

"There's more!" Ryurikov shouted, frantically gesturing at the hilltop.

"Obviously, we've seen them!" shouted Vasili, rattled already.

At the crest of the hill, the hut's legs kicked out, roots lashing, scattering the demons into motion. Ryurikov lunged for the nearest, swinging his dagger into a hindleg. Realising too late the magic had gone.

"Una!"

She would not be able to hear him. Darinka and Jadrana were too preoccupied holding on for their lives beneath the hut's foundation. Ryurikov swivelled away from the Crawler's knifelike limbs. Ignoring the churning of his stomach at the sight of the deboned face flapping from its beak, he scaled a trunk, narrowly avoiding the hungry licks of blue fire.

A bony hand helped him over the ledge, and a swirl of water hovered just by Una's shoulder. She swung it onto his dagger, the swish of cold air a short-lived reprieve. Ryurikov descended again, branches creaking with the promise of an early demise—although the trees were lower to the ground, truncated by flames.

He jumped. Plunged his dagger into a Crawler's elongated neck. It bucked with a screech, its pronounced spine digging into his stomach. Ryurikov struggled to keep hold, tore the dagger free and straddled the creature's ribcage. He brought the blade down into its side. Repeatedly. Until he hit its heart.

Bleeding fire latched on to his wrist, singeing fabric into the skin. He grit his teeth against the agony, flying forward as the Crawler buckled with a final caterwaul. Smoke and ash whirled into his mouth, down his throat. He choked on a cry, flinging his arm across the ground, panic blurring any coherency as the fire crept along his forearm.

The relief he felt upon water entwining his limb was only shallow.

Coil of Boughs

Ryurikov collapsed onto his back, rasping for breath he couldn't catch, spittle coating his lips with each strained cough. Through dusty clouds, Una stood up to her ankles in ash, fright etched into the abundance of wrinkles.

"Get up, bantling!" she quavered.

He did, casting a wayward glance at his scorched arm, the magic gone and skin still sizzling like pork roast. Fucking *ouch*. Clenching his jaw, Ryurikov switched to his left hand, the dagger still aglow and useless. Una gaped at him, just as useless.

"Climb back up!" he barked, dashing to shove her out of another Crawler's way.

Flames had gnawed the trees past their second joint, boughs supporting the hut's foundation ready to give. Beyond, a swaying scythe knocked Valka to the ground, her sword missing.

She fought to crawl away from blue fire as Vasili swung his sword in an arc at the Crawler. Only for it to do absolutely shit-all, its dulled blade bouncing off. The other demon caught his leg, wrenching an echoing, agonised howl from him as bone-limb tore through his shin.

Above, Jezibaba's hut had begun to wail, ear splittingly.

Ryurikov wrapped an arm around Una's waist, yanking her out of the way of another attack, staggering as he dragged her scrawny form past limping trees and a shrilling hut toward his sister. He released the hag, using newfound momentum to clamber up the Crawler's hindquarters and slammed his blade into it.

The dagger bent, down to the hilt, and shattered.

He bellowed a swear, dove for the serrated dagger at his belt, and rammed it into a protruding spine before he was bodily flung back. Ryurikov haphazardly rolled through cinders and the staggered tromps of ruined trees. He pushed himself to his feet and strained to breathe as the hut stumbled away.

At the garden's edge stood Jezibaba, manipulating dousing magic toward Darinka, dangling in the air by a series of ugly knitted garments, knotted together. She strained to pass the shimmering water on to Una, who struggled to catch it, to keep up and out of the way of the three Crawlers descending upon her.

To his right, Valka scrambled to escape, dodging one strike and weaving past another on unsteady legs.

Ryurikov leapt after the hut, a glint catching his eye. He swept low without stopping, gloved fingers wrapping around a hilt unfamiliar to his hand.

His sister's terrified scream chased him. It tore straight through his heart.

"Here!" He swung Valka's sabre high, caught the swirl of water, and flung himself over Una in an attempt to shield her.

With the last motes of strength, he pivoted, swinging the sword at the surrounding Crawlers. He sliced their limbs. Surged the sabre skyward. Brought it back down, once again encased in a whirl of shimmering magic.

He dipped around a spray of scorching blue and plunged the blade straight into a thorax. Quickly pulled it free again. A fierce thresh of limbs nearly impelled him to his knees. He shoved Una out of the way, darted backward, and chanted a prayer to every god that might be listening.

Bleeding scorching heat, the demons staggered toward him. The clacks of their beaks snapping, the wind of their swinging extremities pursued his every duck and sidestep. Ryurikov pointed the sabre at ominous clouds above, eyes widening as the crystalline glimmer of water pulled toward it the unmistakable crackle and thrum of thunder.

A vivid flash of light. A soul-clenching crash. Lightning struck the blade's tip—and the last thing he knew was sheer agony.

Thirty-Two

Echoing roars of thunder. Demonic death rattles. All of it muffled by the thumping inside his head, stuffed with cotton. And there was dust, so much dust. In his mouth, up his nose.

Ryurikov spluttered, flailing to get up off his back. The cry spilling between aching teeth vibrated his throat, though barely penetrated his ears. He saw little more than blurry smears among the hazy smoke. His knees collided with the pliant ground, ungodly pain working him over worse than a blacksmith's hammer.

He swore, still muffled. Something curled around his hand and he startled upright, swaying in his attempt to flee. Only to realise someone was holding onto him. Haggish hair glinted silver, the woman's stature so little, Ryurikov needed to look down.

"Fuck, it's you," he slurred, squinting at Jezibaba.

"Be quiet, hatchling, I'm trying to help."

Whatever the blazes she was doing, it *was* helping. Ryurikov's vision cleared and so did his scrambled head. He looked around to gather his bearings.

The three Skin Crawlers had been reduced to smouldering carcasses, collapsed in a pool of dying blue flames and blackened ash. Beyond them, a burning mass. Jezibaba's hut.

"Did I do that?"

"No," Jezibaba croaked. "They did, but you summoning the lightning certainly sped things along."

"Shit." He almost felt bad.

Fuck. He *actually* felt bad. Might have ruminated on it a little longer too, were it not for the realisation that he was still holding the hag's hand. Ryurikov jerked away and turned his focus to the quavering voices behind him.

And that was when it hit him, like being rammed in the stomach by Awimak.

Valka. He'd abandoned her. Left her to die.

Swallowing against the dryness in his throat, Ryurikov shakily approached Una, Darinka, and Jadrana standing near his sister's body, who lay half buried in the ash, face covered in strings of dusty hair. Vasili hovered nearby, his leg coated in bloodied fabric, but Ryurikov ignored him.

The choice he'd made stung his eyes, but he refused to close them. He would confront the consequences of his decision, even if it killed him.

Ryurikov dropped to his knees, the pain pulsating through his whole body dulled by the squeezing numbness laying waste to the hollow of his chest. Hollow, for surely someone with a heart would not have made the same choice.

His sister's name tumbled past his dry lips, followed by a broken, "I'm sorry."

"For what, Ruri?"

Valka rolled onto her back, a smug smile visible beneath burnt debris and ash. Ryurikov swore, but clapped his hand into hers and helped Valka up to her feet. It strained his aching muscles and he grunted in pain. Every breath he took hurt his *teeth*.

"I forgive you," said Valka before he could speak up.

The burn in his throat spread into his chest. Ryurikov squeezed his eyes shut against the stinging smoke, the shake in his hands.

"I didn't want—I had to," he stammered.

"I get it."

"It was–it was either you or—"

"I get it, Ruri."

"Fuck, Valka, I–I *had* to."

"Ruri!"

Ryurikov started, forcing himself to look at his sister.

"You couldn't let the hags and the whole town die just to save me. *I get it*. I'm fine, see?"

Ryurikov's gaze scoured Valka's scorched clothes, partially burned into her skin. She'd be scarred for life, much like himself. His breath swooped out in a tremor.

"Unfortunately," Valka continued, kicking at burnt waste. "Vasili saved me."

"You don't have to sound so annoyed about it," said Vasili with a scoff.

Valka turned on him. "I'm not annoyed, I'm *pissed*! You—"

"Thank you, Vasili," Ryurikov ground out. The bastard's expression shifted from surprise to *smug*, and he grit his aching teeth. "Let's get back to Briarmour. Share the good news with everyone."

He jerked his head at the hags, who had been waiting for some kind of command. Fucking hell, he hoped he wouldn't have to keep doing that.

"You though, stay." Ryurikov pointed at Vasili. "We've things to discuss."

"What, here?" Vasili looked irritated as he inspected his calf. "I'd rather tend to my leg."

"Stay. The rest of you, go. Make sure Awi and the townspeople are alright."

His order was followed with only the merest hint of protest. He ignored Valka's lingering, questioning look and watched the four catch up with Jezibaba. She hobbled more than usual while holding Valka's hand for support, likely exhausted.

"That was good work, Ruri," said Vasili.

Ryurikov shifted from one foot to the other, then moved, slowly and stiffly, to circle the man. "I have my moments."

Vasili turned to face him. "How did you summon the lightning?"

Ryurikov shrugged. "I have a few tricks up my sleeve."

He might have no choice but to believe in a deity or two now, certain his prayers had been answered, however painfully.

"Whatever's left of it." Vasili motioned at the state of his arms and moved with him, clever enough not to turn his back on him. "I saved Valka."

"So you've said." Ryurikov's anger boiled. "You also had your soldiers attack *my* town."

Thick, dark eyebrows rose in mock surprise. "That wasn't on my command."

He snorted, feet crunching over charred bones. "Oh, come on. You didn't exactly travel back here on your own."

"Obviously."

"So where'd you stash them?"

"I left them to camp in the other forest. Stop moving!"

He bared his teeth. "You think I'm going to let this slide? I told you this town is mine, and by fuck I'm going to make sure it stays that way!"

The bastard closed the gap between them and had the gall to place his hands on either side of Ryurikov's shoulders.

"I saved your sister. You *owe* me."

Red snapped into his vision. Bright and blinding, bringing with it the taste of metal. Ryurikov held Vasili in one arm, plunging the hunting knife deeper into flesh. Twisted it clockwise. A guttural groan into his ear had spittle coating the shell, and Vasili dropped out of his hold.

Cinder crunched under his collapsed body and ash feathered. The blade's hilt protruding from his gut gleamed in slivers of emerging sunlight. Umber eyes, glassy with pain, stared up at him. Strangely, not with disbelief or shock, but knowingly. Serene, almost.

"You say that like she couldn't have helped herself." Ryurikov shook blood off his hand, mostly devoid of a glove, its leather devoured by lightning. He lowered to a knee, glancing at the blade, and gave the hilt a flick before yanking it out.

"I-I di-didn't know," Vasili wheezed. "I swear."

"I almost believe you."

Blood pooled along Vasili's leather jerkin, streaming down his side to mingle with the wasteland. He jostled with moribund breaths. "Mulgar kn-knows I have a–a soft spot for you. Knows I—"

More pained gasps interrupted whatever else he had to say and Ryurikov scowled. Fuck, he was probably telling the truth.

"Oh well." Ryurikov slipped his knife back into the cuff of his boot and stood, ready to walk away.

"Y-You planned this."

He regarded the struggling man at his feet. "I did."

There was a reason he hadn't told Vasili about needing a silver weapon, after all.

Ryurikov left no room for his Keeper to ask him why, or for him to fall into the trap of illustrating all the reasons keeping the bastard alive was a shit idea. There were other things to focus on now, not least of which was Monarch Mulgar, who would come down on Briamour with the wrath of a goliath suffering haemorrhoids.

The trunks of ancient trees barricading Briarmour had shifted, more warped than before. It was one of only two signs a battle had taken place. The second, mangled corpses of Mulgar's soldiers littering the ground.

Two halves of a body hung like banners from nearby boughs as Ryurikov crossed the crooked bridge. Large green eyes peered from beneath the hoods of mushroom heads. The minktoads had resumed their hopping and shrill chirping by the stream, while townspeople already worked to clean the viscera. Heavy scrapes of scrubbing brushes across cobblestone followed him while he searched for his demon, dreading what state he might find Awimak in.

At the pathway leading to the palace stood Awimak, along with Valka and the hags. Relief and yearning unfurled within Ryurikov at the sight of his demon, but regret soon overwhelmed as he scoured the great form.

Those wide shoulders were hunched, dark grey skin covered in swathes of burns and cuts, volcanic blood crusting into scoria. His beautiful hair had been singed, sections of it shorter than others. No doubt mirroring each and every injury Ryurikov had sustained. He sped up his strained limp to reach Awimak's side.

His demon turned to him, concern clear in his rasped, *MY DRURY.*

"I knew you'd defend this place with the effort of squashing a glowant." Ryurikov mustered a smile and reached for a claw. At least Awimak's grip was as strong as ever, though careful in the way he held his hand.

On the stoop, Jezibaba sat with the dolour of losing all she had. It was certainly something he could relate to, and the ache in his chest tightened.

"Where's that pot of piss?" asked Valka, gently stroking Jezibaba's back.

"Dead." Ryurikov continued before she could ask more, "This isn't the end of it."

IT IS NOT. Awimak reached for Ryurikov's face, the pad of his thumb firm in stroking away grime.

"You think Mulgar's going to keep coming after us?" asked Valka.

"No, they're going to keep coming after this town. Me being here is just an added bonus for them."

A DISADVANTAGE, YOU MEAN.

Ryurikov smiled, allowing himself to lean into the large, cupped hand first before moving out of the touch.

"Why?"

He rolled his throbbing shoulders, regarding his sister. "Because they're a mixture of disease-riddled genitalia and...they might still be pissed that I kept hunting game on their land."

That, or Mulgar still had their braies in a twist that he'd wanted nothing to do with them, even after a most rousing proposal Ryrikov would've been tempted by, had he been in a better state of mind to appreciate it at the time.

"Then there's the issue of Radmila." He glanced at the hags, whose lizard-like gazes flicked up to him.

The tense silence that followed became a clear indicator that things weren't about to resolve themselves so easily, that this was further from done than Ryurikov would have preferred to believe. He sighed.

"A problem for future us," he said, to the visible relief of those around him. "Let's focus on recuperating. I'm in desperate need of a bath, for a start."

"Me too." Valka gave Jezibaba's frail shoulder tender pats. "You should get some rest."

The hag didn't respond, and for some gods forsaken reason, Ryurikov chose to wait until the others had gone. All aside from Awimak. He lowered beside her with a tired groan, the stone chilly under his rear, and stared at the shady bushes lining the path ahead.

"Any chance you can regrow your hut?"

Jezibaba croaked an empty laugh. "Not unless you can find three ambulating saplings."

"Where might we find some of those?"

Orange eyes, brimming with unshed tears, briefly glanced at him. "The Underforest."

"That's easy, then. Awi?" Ryurikov looked at his beautiful demon. So stately despite mirroring all his injuries.

THERE IS MORE TO IT, MY LOVE.

"In the Underforest deep, where earth's embrace does secrets keep. Amidst Vale's black stone she sits, the birth mother of magic, fixed in meditative sleep."

"You missed your calling as a bard." He kicked out both legs and leant back. "What's that got to do with walking trees?"

"The mother is who granted us *our* magic," said Jezibaba tersely. "I was once her favourite, but due to Radmila's actions and my *inactions*, I've fallen out of favour."

"Alright, and?"

The hag sighed in exasperation, as if Ryurikov was somehow challenging her patience.

"She's the one who gifted me the trees."

Well, too bad for Jezibaba, then. "You did...alright today. Thanks, you know. For the–for the help."

She did not reply.

Ryurikov strained upright, glad to have Awimak's help in doing so. A clamour of townsfolk awaited him inside the palace. He cast one look at the many eager faces peering out of the presence chamber, and beelined for the stairs that would lead him to his chambers.

"Any deaths?" he asked, weary.

SOME. I DID WHAT I COULD.

"I know."

It couldn't have been easy, trying to defend the town while also suffering any and all injuries acquired during the scuffle with the Skin Crawlers.

"Thanks, Awi."

His demon guided him to the bower, his silence filled with concern as Ryurikov's breath hissed past his teeth while lowering onto the edge to sit. Now that the rush of imminent death had dwindled to a promenade, his body was keen to remind him of every cut, burn, and thump he'd earned.

Awimak's clawless fingers glided over his injuries without touching, as if itching to help unstick burnt fabric from raw skin, the likelihood of hurting him all that stayed the urge.

I WILL LOCATE THE DOCTOR.

"It's fine. I'll just have a soak. Besides, you don't look much better off."

IT MAY HAVE ESCAPED YOUR NOTICE, BUT I AM NO ORDINARY HUMAN.

Ryurikov weakly huffed. "That you are not."

Awimak shifted to leave. Ryurikov's hand shot out, fingers clenching around roughened forearms. He didn't want to be alone, needing to ask his demon stay and hold him. Swallowing hurt his raw throat, and the request hooked itself behind his teeth.

Thankfully, Awimak understood, lowering to sit beside him and wrap a great arm around his aching shoulders. Ryurikov flopped sideways into the hold, his eyes drifting shut. Sleep, it was all he wanted to do now.

"Did you get hurt at all?" he mumbled, then feebly flapped his hand. "Besides what I did to you, I mean."

YOU DID NOT DO THIS TO ME, MY LOVE, I DID.

Blearily, he forced his eyes open to look at the underside of Awimak's jaw. "Doesn't seem fair."

WHAT DOESN'T?

"It should be both ways. The blood-swear, I mean."

Rather than respond, Awimak rose to his hooves and took Ryurikov with him, careful in the way he cradled him in those large arms. The doorway to the bathing chamber had been pushed apart to accommodate his horns, without a doubt larger after the blood-swear, Ryurikov was sure of it now. He ran his sore fingers over them, admiringly, as he was lowered into an empty tub.

"Ordinarily, one requires water to bathe," he lightly teased, then chuckled at Awimak's deliberating pause.

I AM AWARE.

Ryurikov was happy enough to let his limbs dangle over the tub's sides, watching while his demon carefully liberated him of his boots and peeled his breeches off. Removing the rest of his clothes proved a bigger challenge. By the time he'd been freed of his tunic, agony blurred his vision.

I'M SORRY, DRURY. I WILL GET THE DOCTOR NOW.

"Just slap some of that salve on," Ryurikov strained.

Fiery eyes shifted around the sockets in search of the cauldron, left in the corner of the chamber. It had to be nearly empty by now, but Awimak duly slid his fingers through it, scooping up what was left and gently spreading it across Ryurikov's chest.

The relief was immediate. Although tempted to slump back and let Awimak soothe his wounds, Ryurikov ran the tips of his fingers through the salve on his pecs and brought it up to a wide shoulder. Skin once grey was now blackened and rumpled, the pink of injured flesh peering through.

"I got hit by lightning," he murmured, conversationally.

I THOUGHT I FELT A TICKLE.

He shook his head. "You'll recover?"

Awimak leaned in and ran his tongue across Ryurikov's cheek, swiping away grime. *I WILL RECOVER. AND SO SHALL YOU.*

Thirty-Three

A brook had notched a path through the foyer, tiny white flowers and fresh grass peering through cracks within the dark stone surrounding it. A week after its first trickle, and still Ryurikov forgot about the rivulet, splashing into it anytime he hopped down that last step of the lopsided staircase.

He grunted, shaking off his boot-clad foot and grimaced at the stiffness in his leg. Dodged several children darting past him, too, and sidestepped more roots that had grown to push up walls and flooring.

The presence chamber smelled of freshly baked bread and ale, brimming with newcomers and residents alike. Ryurikov wove past tables and chairs and make-shift beds of fur and hay alike. There was not a day, or night, that the chamber wasn't full. Ryurikov couldn't say he hated it. Not that he'd ever admit it out loud.

Valka sat on a bench by the firepit, her shoulders sagged with fatigue, but her gaze lit up once she caught sight of him.

"I knew that colour would suit you." She nodded at the dark teal cloak she had fetched him. Paired with the fire-yellow tunic, reinforced leather jerkin, and deep brown breeches, Ryurikov whole-heartedly agreed. "Nice to see you up."

"Where's Awi?"

Valka rolled her eyes. "Why is that the first thing out of your mouth every time you see me? I've been killing Clutchers with Mauvie all morning, I don't know where your lover is."

With a tired groan, Ryurikov dropped to the bench beside his sister. "When are you going to get rid of that fucking jerkin? It no longer works, does it?"

"So?" Valka patted away ash from its fabric, mended into a pattern even more pied. "It looks good. Besides, the drakes won't tolerate anything less. Speaking of, they've agreed to help rejuvenate the surrounding land."

"Perfect." Ryurikov had already lost interest, scanning past the many heads for any sign of his demon outside the window, now without glass entirely. Awimak's trees were gradually taking over the entire place.

"Still no sign of Vasili's body."

"Ah. Some Skin Crawler probably just tried him on for size."

"I don't know, Ruri, something feels wrong about it."

He waved it aside. "I'm going to look for Awi."

"Are you going to be alright walking around?" Valka chased after him.

Ryurikov ignored her question because it was a ridiculous one. Of course he could walk. It was just with a different gait, a stiffness in his body that had yet to wane.

Outside, thick moss encroached the stoops and pathways, soft underfoot as he veered off to the left along the stream. The ancient trees whispered in a cool breeze and he inhaled, trapping fresh air in his lungs as long as he could.

The smoke had cleared days after defeating the Skin Crawlers. It had taken less time for rumours to fly, and even less for people to continue pouring into Briarmour. Housing was quickly becoming a problem. The sooner they restored the surrounding lands, the sooner they could expand the town.

Then Mulgar would certainly have something to weep about.

"It's really nice here," Valka murmured beside him, her hazel eyes flicking from one bit of greenery to the next. "Too shady for the drakes, but... You really fit in here."

Ryurikov hummed in agreement, unsure of what to say. Briarmour was all he had come to love. The forest, the sunlight, the quiet early summer breeze laced with birdsongs. Everything the Maksim castle hadn't been.

"It feels like I belong here," he admitted, quietly. "It can be your home too, you know."

A smile graced Valka's lips. She wrapped her arm around his shoulders and pulled him against herself as they continued their stride. "I'll hang around for as long as you need me. What are we going to do once Mulgar decides to send more soldiers?"

Ryurikov shrugged in her clasp. "We'll burn *that* bridge when we get to it."

He stopped in his tracks at the sound of whispers, carried along the zephyr, irritatingly familiar. He shifted out of Valka's hold, slammed the side of his palm down into his uncooperative knee to unlock it, and rounded a particularly massive tree.

"Hey!" he bellowed at five snowy silhouettes, fencing in a young woman who must have taken a spill in the grass, a basket of fruits scattered nearby. "Stop that right now!"

The Quinary turned to him, eyes glinting with recognition.

"Owes us," they hissed in unison.

Ryurikov stopped a foot away from them to glower down. "Nobody owes you anything, you little shits."

"You no longer do," whispered one, pointing a long finger at him. The remaining four shifted to encircle him. They bowed their heads. *"The deal is done."*

"Well fuck you very much," he groused. "I didn't give you permission to trick my people into doing *your* bidding."

That same spindly digit shifted to the bewildered looking woman, leaning up on an elbow. *"Owes us, anyway."*

"I only twisted my ankle!" she cried.

Ryurikov glanced at her, his lips twitching with mirth. "You have my congratulations on being so dissolute that these assholes decided to intervene. Nothing I need to worry about?"

"No, my Prince, I swear it!"

The Quinary whispered in frustration, and Ryurikov sighed. "I'll pay whatever penance you think she owes you. Agreed?"

Shadowy faces exchanged looks. Then, *"Agreed."*

Despite the niggling suspicion that this wasn't the last time he'd need to deal with them, he left.

"What's up with them?" Valka asked, to which Ryurikov shrugged.

"I fell to my death and they decided they wanted to redeem me. Don't suppose *you* happen to know why?"

"No. All I know of is their whimsicality. I don't know who they answer to, if anyone."

It didn't matter. Awimak was still nowhere to be found, and it worried him. During his recovery, Awimak had left his side exactly once, to scold the witches into creating more of the indigo salve to treat his haggard body with.

Ryurikov continued to follow the stream, grinding his thumb over his pointer finger in thought, until he reached a modest half-timbre house in the furthest reaches of town. A tree had set its roots around it, caging it in moss-laden bark and shade. At its front in the only sunlight afforded to her, Radojka worked on what appeared to be a vegetable patch.

"Where's Awi?"

"Hatchling," she croaked in greeting, working her hands through soil while kneeling. At least for Valka, she mustered a half-smile. "I haven't seen him."

Ryurikov allowed himself to lean against a nearby root to rest. Still he cast his gaze about in search of his demon, the notion that Awimak might have left him quick to work its way into his heart.

"He hasn't abandoned you," Radojka said.

"How do you know?"

Beside him, Valka made a horrible cooing noise. "I didn't know you were so insecure!"

"Shut up."

"It's physically impossible for the damn fool," said Radojka.

The blood-swear. Ryurikov flattened his lips into a line. He'd asked Awimak about it several times during his recovery. Hinted quite strongly he longed to reciprocate the act. It seemed better than the alternative, which was to ask—

He shook his head. Unfortunately, his demon had evaded giving him an answer, and now he was nowhere to be seen. Had he grown weary of him?

Ryurikov swallowed against the lump forming in his throat. "You're staying here, then?" he asked to distract himself, adding, "I don't mind if you do."

A brief glare upward, though whatever snide remark Radojka might have conjured remained tucked away. Instead, she grumbled, "Thank you. This...is as good a place as any."

Mirth laced Ryurikov's huff. "Mulgar's inevitable attacks notwithstanding." He hoped by that time, they would have the numbers to help fight them off, and with yet more hags among them.

A faint rumble in the earth below his feet had Ryurikov sidestepping a root that emerged to serpentine through dewy grass in a spiral, before diving back into the soil. He met Valka's worried look.

"How long until this entire place is just roots?" she asked.

Ryurikov wouldn't have answered even if he wanted to. At the appearance of a stately figure walking toward him, his mouth dried up.

Thunder grey skin teemed with dappling sunlight, and burly arms were wrapped around the bodies of several children, many more in tow. Ryurikov recognised them, but couldn't take his eyes off his demon. His horns weren't all that had grown. Awimak himself was at least a foot taller and wider, more muscular than a creature had any right to be.

And by fuck, Ryurikov was hard just thinking about impaling himself on that cock of his.

"Ruri, sir!"

Like being clobbered in the head by a giant slab of ice.

Ryurikov startled, straightening up and hoping to hell nothing gave him or his depravity away. He grunted, his neck cinched tight by an embrace, the scratch of stubble against his scars a discomfort. He raised his arms as if readying to fly away, refusing to enable Andrew's invasion. A helpless look directed at Awimak only prompted amusement as his demon lowered that great, beautiful body to release the urchins he'd been carrying.

"Aw, did you adopt these?" Valka took the youngest out of Awimak's hold to cradle against herself. A dirty thing with auburn curls like the rest of them.

"What the fuck? No!" Ryurikov spluttered, pressing both hands against Andrew's forehead and pushing. He wasn't ready to be a father —*ever*. "I agreed to no such thing!"

THEY WERE ALREADY ON THEIR WAY HERE. I MERELY HELPED THEM CROSS THE WASTELAND.

"Oh." He paused. Then, "Why the fuck *are* you here?"

Andrew stepped away, pale cheeks rosy and honey-coloured eyes filled with that same, awful admiration. "We heard about the Rogue Prince who saved an entire town from Skin Crawlers and Monarch Mulgar's conquest. I knew it had to be you."

"That was some gamble you took," Ryurikov admonished.

He would have liked to scold Andrew further, in particular for risking his siblings, but bit down the urge. They had come all this way, even after he'd given Andrew more coin than the lad had ever seen before. Something must have been remiss.

"We're tight on housing right now," he said instead, an idea occurring to him while watching Radojka garden. "You can stay in this house. It's not ideal, but better than what you had."

Orange eyes flicked back up to him, and a wrinkled mouth parted around a rebuttal. Wordlessly, Ryurikov dared her to oppose.

"What am I supposed to do with,"—Radojka's gaze flicked from toddler to teenager to young adult—"*twelve* of them?"

"That's a problem for you to sort," he said, then walked away, grateful when the sound of thick hooves followed.

"And where have you been?" Ryurikov asked at once, the nervous lurch of his stomach clipping his voice.

I WENT TO FETCH THESE. Awimak held out a great claw. Within, a bounty of seeds. Seeds of what, Ryurikov didn't have a clue.

"Hang on!" He tilted backward to peer at Awimak's sculpted ass, covered by the woodsy dupion. "Where did you keep those?"

NOT THERE, Awimak rasped with humour.

"Well, I know of something else that can—" Ryurikov's knee buckled as he came to an abrupt standstill. He was grateful for the powerful fingers curling around his biceps, keeping him upright, his mind steeplechasing with a sudden realisation.

WHAT IS IT?

He looked up at Awimak, brows pulled in a frown. "Apatura."

THE LYKE YOU MET IN THE GUILD TOWN.

"She's the one!"

Awimak silently regarded him.

"She had a tome in front of her when we met. Slammed it shut the second I came close enough to read it. I remember thinking she needn't have bothered since I couldn't make sense of the unusual script. I've seen it before in Radmila's dungeon on the day the Crawlers came into the castle."

THAT VERY SAME TOME?

Ryurikov glanced out across the expanse of grass to the lopsided houses beyond, thinking. "Maybe. You said it would have required impossible knowledge to summon demons like them. It had to have been Apatura who helped her. Fuck, is that why she was rotting from the inside out, why her magic rejected her? Because she's the one who brought Skin Crawlers into Vale?"

Only once Ryurikov regained control over his leg did Awimak release him, gently guiding him to rest by a tree. Yet he remained silent, sitting beside him, until Ryurikov nudged his side with an impatient forearm.

I WAS NOT MEANT TO MEDDLE.

"What are you on about?" he asked, yet feared the answer. "Awi, you said you wouldn't keep secrets from me."

Sun-like eyes lowered, setting on him. *THERE IS KNOWLEDGE I POSSESS. KNOWLEDGE I CANNOT REVEAL. NOT EVEN TO YOU, MY LOVE. IF I DO,* Awimak continued, silencing Ryurikov's flaring sense of betrayal, *I WILL BE PUNISHED. I HAD SAID TOO MUCH THEN, AND I CANNOT SAY TOO MUCH NOW.*

His anger deflated. He ran his fingers through his hair, distracting himself with how short it had been cut. It barely reached the tips of his ears now.

I'M SORRY.

"No, don't be." Good grief, Awimak must have known the connection all along. Unable to say anything, fretting he might be punished for saying too much. And not once had he been able to talk to him about it. "Do you...have possession of certain knowledge because you're a demon?"

YES.

"So then," Ryurikov glanced upward, "if we connected through say —oh I don't know, just off the top of my head—a mutual blood-swear, would that make me privy to such knowledge?"

Awimak cradled the back of his head, encouraging him forward. Although he would have preferred to sit there and wait until he got an answer, he'd ached for his demon ever since waking up that morning. Ryurikov stiffly crawled to straddle large thighs. He ran his palms over smooth skin, already healed, up to a strong neck to toy with a mane that too had been trimmed. Giving him better access to the ears he stroked between his fingers.

"Come on, Awi, don't make me beg. Answer me."

YOU USE MY WEAKNESS AGAINST ME, Awimak said, purring under the touch, eyes but fiery notches. His tongue darted out and lavished Ryurikov's cheek and forehead with attention.

He let himself be guided down into the grass on his back, claws on either side of his shoulders gentle, shifting to undo his cloak and the straps of his jerkin. Soon pushing the tunic up, exposing Ryurikov's stomach to the air chilled by Awimak hovering over him.

"And you use mine against me." Ryurikov arched into the open palm gliding across his abdomen, up to his chest. Fingers splayed out and grazed his nipples.

Awimak leaned low, nasal bones of his skull dragging over scarred skin, cooling further under the slick of his tongue. *DO YOU RECALL WHEN I ATTEMPTED TO SUMMON THE QUINARY TO ME?*

"Sure," Ryurikov said, distracted, running his palm over his own aching cock, longing to release it. "Why?"

YOU WERE DYING. I HELD YOU WHILE I WAS WOUNDED.

He stilled, cracking his eyes open to peer up into Awimak's. That tongue whipped out across his lips, parted around a breathy acknowledgement. "Right, I remember."

Awimak hesitated. *I DID NOT TELL YOU FOR IT WAS UNINTENTIONAL. I HAD NO WISH TO BURDEN YOU, OR FRIGHTEN YOU ANY MORE THAN YOU ALREADY WERE.*

It was hard to focus when his goliath of a demon kept nudging his legs up, until his ass was nestled against Awimak's groin. "Wait, what?"

MY EYEWORTHY, WHOM I'VE MARKED ALREADY. MARKED TO BE MINE.

Ryurikov stared, blankly, and Awimak chuffed.

I BURNED YOU WITH MY BLOOD. YOU ARE ALREADY SWORN TO ME.

Still he stared, all he could do while his brain worked hard to piece things together. He'd been on the edge of death, barely remembered being burned. But the scars were there to prove it, running down his arm and ribcage like the tracks of a snake.

His brows furrowed, and Awimak leaned away to give him room. At length, Ryurikov muttered, "I don't feel any different."

DOES THE HUMAN TRADITION OF MARRIAGE MAKE YOU FEEL DIFFERENT? OTHER THAN, PERHAPS, ENRICHEN THE LOVE ONE HAS FOR THE OTHER?

"Wait," Ryurikov strained to sit up, "we're married?"

After some deliberating, *IF YOU'D LIKE.*

Delight burgeoned as a smile across Ryurikov's lips, surprising him so much, it left him speechless.

Well, almost speechless.

"Fuck yes, I would like."

The End

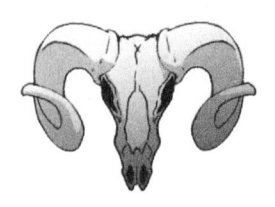

Thank you for reading Coil of Boughs, the first in the Underforest Duology!

The chaotic power couple will return in **Thorns of Vale**.

I hope you had as much fun reading this book as I had writing it. If you'd like to rate and review this story, it would go a long way to helping others find it too!

About the Author
penny-moss.com

I'm Moss and I'm awkward. So awkward, in fact, that I refuse to talk about myself in 3rd person even though that's standard.
I reside in soggy UK, lament their terrible food daily, and am old enough to have used a rotary phone as a kid. I grew up with religious and strict parents, so naturally, I'm a bisexual wreck who has forever had a love for monsters.

Sign up to the newsletter and be the first to get cover art and blurb reveals, sneak peeks into chapter art, quotes, and upcoming ARC opportunities.

Penny Moss Novels
mossy_rebellion
mossy_rebellion
pennymoss

Acknowledgements

Thank you to every one of my beta readers for taking the time to read and give me feedback. And thank you to all the Letterheads members for your unwavering support and encouragement.

Blaine Maisey, honestly, where would I be without you and your endless patience? Your genuine desire to see me flourish and your ability to push me to be a better writer makes you like none other. I'm gonna hold on to you with my sweaty, grubby fists until I die. I hope you know this. :')

TJ Rose, thanks for being so supportive, and laughing at my terrible jokes. <3

And thank you to my street team, who have tirelessly flogged this book. Your efforts and time are so appreciated!

On Instagram:

Kaila @duffettereads
Steph @bookfan_2022
Thera Tiffany @thera_loves_to_read
Michelle @shelleylovestoread
Miriam @book_reader_addict
Sazzle @MM_booksta_sazzle
Tanya @tdl2188

Printed in Great Britain
by Amazon